Pillow Talk

The sheets rustled and the mattress bounced again as Sammi flipped over. Chase opened his lids to find her gazing at him.

"I bet you wish you'd never met me. Then you wouldn't have a concussion, and your wallet wouldn't be all chewed up, and . . ."

Aw, hell. He couldn't let her think he was rejecting her because of a few klutzy moves. Convincing her she wasn't bad luck was the whole reason he was coaching her. He rolled onto his side and touched her hand. "If none of that had happened, you wouldn't be here."

Her palm turned up and she took his fingers in hers. Since when had holding hands become so intensely erotic?

He should have looked away, but his gaze seemed Super Glued to hers. Electricity hovered between them like thunderclouds, hot and heavy and highly charged. Then his mouth was on hers and lightning was striking all over the place.

Oh, God, her lips were soft—soft and plump and hot. She moaned against his mouth . . .

Praise for *Between the Sheets*

"Has Southern heat, secondary characters who will steal your heart, and a hero and heroine who deserve their happy ending."

—CHRISTIE RIDGWAY,
USA Today bestselling author

more . . .

ALSO BY ROBIN WELLS

Between the Sheets

HOW TO SCORE

ROBIN WELLS

FOREVER

NEW YORK   BOSTON

Cover design by Claire Brown
Book design by Giorgetta Bell McRee

Forever
Hachette Book Group
237 Park Avenue
New York, NY 10017
Visit our Web site at www.HachetteBookGroup.com

Forever is an imprint of Grand Central Publishing.
The Forever name and logo is a trademark of Hachette Book Group, Inc.

Printed in the United States of America

First Printing: June 2009

10 9 8 7 6 5 4 3 2 1

To Ken, the love of my life; to Taylor and Arden,
two mobile pieces of my heart; and to
my terrific parents, Charlie Lou and Roscoe Rouse.

Acknowledgments

With special thanks to Dick for being the best cowboy lawyer ever, and to Taylor, Jeff, and Matt for the tour of Tulsa.

Chapter One

"I only stayed out until nine, but Mother was in a tizzy when I got home," Horace whined. "She said she'd carried me for nine months and suffered through sixteen hours of labor, and I was a terrible son because I didn't want to stay home and keep her company."

Chase Jones rubbed the bridge of his nose as he listened to Horace's nasal whine through his brother's cell phone, wondering, for the umpteenth time, how Luke managed to listen to losers like this all day long without going bonkers. More to the point, how was *he* going to listen to them for the next six weeks? He must have been out of his mind, telling Luke he'd fill in for him as a life coach.

"I tried to explain to Mother that I needed some time to myself, just like you said, but she wouldn't listen." Horace's voice trembled.

Shaking his head in disgust, Chase gazed down at the open file sprawled on the dining table of his Tulsa apartment. According to Luke's notes, Horace was forty-four years old, lived with his mother, and never made a move without her approval.

"I just don't know what to do, Coach," Horace whined.

How about growing a pair? Unfortunately, the words weren't on the list of conversational prompts his brother had left for him to use. Instead, the page was filled with namby-pamby, touchy-feely phrases such as *"How did that make you feel?"*

Chase stifled a groan. Feelings made people act irrationally; he'd seen plenty of proof of that growing up, and as an FBI agent now, he saw more proof every day. In his opinion, the world would be a better place if everyone kept a lid on the primal stuff and just stuck to logic. His brother's let's-talk-things-out, tell-me-how-you-feel approach only made things worse.

This right here was a prime example. Horace had spent more than four decades wallowing in his feelings, and it had gotten him nowhere. The poor sap needed his butt kicked off the pity pot and into action. A few weeks of Quantico-style basic training and Horace would be a new man.

Chase was itching to tackle the project, but he'd promised to follow his brother's instructions. With a sigh, he swallowed his distaste and forced out the lame-assed question "How did your mother's reaction make you feel?"

"Frustrated," Horace said woefully. "And upset. Like I don't have a life of my own."

That's because you don't, Chase thought dourly. He glanced back at his brother's notes. *Follow up with an empathetic statement, such as "Those are understandable emotions."* Hell. Much more of this and he was going to gag.

"So, Coach, what should I *do?*" Horace whimpered.

Chase had a few suggestions, but none of them would have met with his brother's approval. He scanned the conversational prompts. *When he asks you a question, turn it around and make him answer it himself.* "Well, Horace, what do you want to do?"

"I'm not sure. That's why I hired you to be my life coach."

Actually, Horace, old buddy, you didn't hire me; you hired my younger brother, Luke. I'm an FBI agent, not a sports psychologist turned life coach, and I don't buy into this nursemaid crap. I'm filling in for Luke for a few weeks because thanks to me, he witnessed a mob hit and is temporarily in the Witness Protection Program. But I can't tell you that, Horace, my man, because you're such a quivering mass of jelly-bellied insecurities that you'd never believe it, and you'd think Luke was giving you the brush-off, and if you thought that your life coach was rejecting you, you'd feel even more inadequate than you already do, and you'd probably never seek help again. Which is why I'm sitting here like an idiot, wasting a perfectly good Thursday evening, impersonating my brother on the phone.

"So what do you think I should do?" Horace whimpered.

Besides grow some gonads? Chase blew out a sigh and forced his gaze back to the list. *Ask him to visualize his ideal life.* "Let's talk about what you'd like your life to be like."

"You mean—if I were a superhero or something?"

Chase rubbed his forehead. "Why would you be a superhero?"

"Because I love comics, remember?"

"Oh. Yeah." This was the first Chase had heard of it.

"Superheroes can do anything, and they're never afraid."

Chase wasn't sure just how sick this dude really was, and he damn sure didn't want to encourage him to see if he could fly or something. "For the purposes of this exercise, Horace, you don't have any superpowers, but you're the kind of guy you want to be, and everything in your life is just like you want it. I want you to describe it to me."

"Oh, golly—I don't even know where to start."

How about with dropping the word golly *from your vocabulary?* Man, this guy was pathetic. "Let's start with your mother. If everything in your life was ideal, would you still live with her?"

"Oh, no," Horace said emphatically. "I'd have my own place."

"Well, what would it look like?"

"Gee . . . I don't know. It'd just be a little apartment, I guess."

Press for details, the notes said. *Engage his senses.* "Can you visualize it?"

"Not really."

"Come on, Horace—work with me here. What color would you want the walls to be? White? Gray? Beige?"

"Red." Horace's voice perked up. "A bright, shiny red—Corvette red. Mother *hates* red. And I'd have a black leather couch, and black satin sheets on my bed, and a huge TV, and I'd have the remote all to myself. And there would be no knickknacks or dolls or doilies anywhere in the place."

Now they were getting somewhere. Chase leaned back

in his chair and stretched his long jeans-clad legs out in front of him. "Good," he told Horace. "What else?"

"I'd have Cheetos in my pantry, and beer in my refrigerator."

Nothing like dreaming big.

"And I'd have pictures of cars hung all over the walls, and maybe a bearskin rug on the floor." Enthusiasm fueled Horace's thin voice. "It would be a real bachelor pad."

Chase looked around the large room that comprised the dining, living, and kitchen areas of his apartment. His place was a real bachelor pad, but it damn sure didn't look anything like what Horace was describing. His walls were plain vanilla and completely devoid of pictures. His floor was covered with ordinary tan carpet, and his furniture was some basic, sturdy stuff that he'd picked out during a twenty-minute visit to a furniture store seven or eight years ago. His gaze rested on his giant plasma TV against the central wall. The TV was the only thing in the place he'd recently purchased, and he wished he hadn't done that, because it was indirectly the reason his brother was in hiding and he was here on the phone with Horace.

"If I lived by myself, I'd drink milk straight from the carton," Horace continued. "And I'd put my feet on the couch whenever I felt like it, and I'd stay in the shower until all the hot water was gone."

Wow. Let's not get carried away, Horace, my man. "Anything else?"

"Yeah. I'd play my accordion whenever I wanted, and I'd play the kind of music *I* like to play."

Chase's eyebrows rose. "You play the accordion?"

"Yep. But Mother only wants me to play organ-grinder music."

"What do you like to play?"

"Rap."

Chase stifled a laugh. "Accordion rap?"

"Yes. I've written some lyrics, but they're really awful."

"Well, lay some on me."

"Oh, I can't."

"Sure you can."

"Well . . ." Horace drew a deep breath, then lowered his voice into a bad imitation of Snoop Dogg:

I went to the store to get some Cheese Whiz,
and I ran into a pretty girl named Liz.
She said, 'Hey, Horace, you're lookin' real fine.
Would you like to shoot your cheese on these crackers of
mine?'

Chase let out a loud snort.

"I told you it was awful," Horace said mournfully.

"Hey, I think it rocks."

"Really?"

"Yeah. It's hilarious."

"But it wasn't meant to be funny." Horace's voice grew small and wounded.

Uh-oh. *Whatever you do, don't hurt his feelings*, Luke's notes said. "Well, funny is good."

"Really?"

"Sure. Everyone likes a laugh. And women love a guy with a sense of humor."

A sigh floated wistfully through the phone line. "That's what I'd really want in my apartment—a woman."

You and me both, buddy. It had been nearly a year since Chase had broken up with Sara. Like all the women Chase had ever dated, Sara had wanted to move things to the next level. Not that he had anything against commitment—in fact, marriage was part of his Life Master Plan, and according to his LMP timetable, he should be in the marriage-execution phase right now—but Sara just hadn't had all the attributes he was looking for.

He had yet to meet a woman who did. He had very specific criteria. He called the search Operation SCABHOG, because he wanted someone who was smart, competent, active, beautiful, honest, organized, and goal-oriented.

"Lots of girls have those qualities," Luke had told him when he'd complained about it over a beer at their favorite watering hole a couple of weeks ago.

"Not as I define them."

Luke's dark eyebrows, a mirror image of Chase's, had quirked up. "That's because when you say 'smart,' you really mean 'rocket scientist.'"

"No," Chase had said defensively. "Just sharp. Quick on the uptake. Perceptive. Level-headed. Knowledgeable. Able to think on her feet and come up with creative solutions."

"Uh-huh." Luke had taken a pull on his bottle of Coors. "In other words, brilliant. And what's your definition of 'competent'?"

"A woman who has her act together and has the track record to prove it. Someone efficient and stable and capable and reliable, who always follows through and doesn't come with a lot of baggage. Someone who won't disrupt my life."

Luke had rolled his eyes. "Like that's gonna happen."

Chase had bristled. "Hey, there's no reason I can't find a woman who doesn't turn my life upside down."

"There's a very good reason. She doesn't exist." Luke

had taken another sip. "I'm not even going to ask about your definition of 'beautiful.' "

"Well, I've got to find her attractive, don't I? I mean, there's got to be some sizzle."

"Which means she needs to look like a supermodel."

"No. Supermodels are way too skinny."

Luke had shaken his head. "Want to know why you can't find the right girl? You're setting the bar too high."

"I refuse to settle."

"Which really means you refuse to settle *down*," Luke had said in that annoying I-know-it-all-because-I'm-the-psychologist tone of his.

Horace's whiny voice interrupted Chase's thoughts. "For some reason, women just don't seem attracted to me."

Golly gee—I wonder why not?

"I bet you don't have that problem," Horace said.

As a matter of fact, Chase didn't. His problem was keeping non-SCABHOG women from trying to drag him down the aisle.

"Can I tell you a secret?" Horace asked.

Chase closed his eyes. He hoped to God Horace wasn't about to disclose details about his master-of-his-domain status.

"I've never even kissed a girl," Horace blurted.

Wow. Chase was talking to a real-life forty-four-year-old virgin. He scanned the list of comments in the file, searching for something appropriate to say. *Use lots of sports analogies,* Luke had told him. *My clients love it.* Chase sincerely doubted it, but his brother was a sports psychologist and his speech was peppered with sports terminology. If Chase were going to pull off this impersonation, he'd better step up to the plate.

Chase reached for the list of sports comments on top of the stack of files and rapidly scanned the page. "Well, you've got to shoot before you can expect to make a basket."

"Huh?"

"If you want to win at the game of life, you've got to know how to score."

"But I don't know how to score. I can't even get a date."

Chase searched the list for something more appropriate. "As you gain self-assurance in the outfield, you'll become a better batter."

"What?"

Apparently Horace wasn't a big sports fan. "If you get better in one area of your life, the other areas will improve, too."

"Oh. You think?" Horace said eagerly.

Not really. I think you're a hopeless mess. "Absolutely." Chase glanced at his Seiko chronograph wristwatch and blew out a sigh of relief. "Our time is nearly up, Horace. So here's what I want you to do before we talk again." He flipped to the page of assignments his brother had outlined for Horace. "I want you to read the classified ads and pick out three apartments that sound like places you might like to live."

"But-but—I can't!" Horace's voice squeaked with alarm.

"Why not?"

"Mother would have a conniption."

"Sounds like she has those on a regular basis anyway."

"But-but . . ."

Reassure him that he doesn't have to do anything he's not ready to do. "Whoa, there, Horace. Calm down. This is a practice session, not the actual game. No one's asking you to really move. You just have to read the classifieds."

"But Mother always watches me read the newspaper."

"So take it into your bedroom."

"She won't let me. She says everything has a place and there's a place for everything, and the newspaper is always read at the kitchen table and then put in a basket for exactly three days before it goes into the recycle bin. And she watches everything I do."

This guy wasn't just living with his mother; he was living with Big Brother. "Well, then, buy a newspaper of your own on your lunch hour."

"After I've already read ours at home? That would be wasteful."

"So splurge a little."

"Oh." Apparently the concept would never have occurred to him. "Okay."

"I'll talk to you on Tuesday. And Horace . . ."

"Yeah?"

"I'd love to hear some more rap lyrics then, okay?"

"You really liked them?" Horace sounded like an eight-year-old boy desperate for a parent's approval.

The neediness in his voice dredged up an old memory in Chase's mind.

He'd been eight years old, and he'd had the role of the lead elf in the school Christmas play. His dad never came to school events, but Chase had begged him to come to this one, and Chase's mom had made it happen.

Chase had practiced and practiced, and the night of the play, he'd acted his heart out. Behind the curtain, his teacher and the play director had raved about his performance, but it wasn't their praise he was after.

Chase had eagerly run up to his father. "What'd you think?"

His dad had swayed, the bottle of cheap booze sticking out of his coat pocket. His breath had reeked of whiskey. "You looked like a little fag up there."

"Richard!" Chase's mom had gasped. "You don't mean that."

"I sure as hell do. Can't believe you made me miss the game for that."

Yeah, Chase knew what it was like to yearn for approval.

"You were great," he told Horace now. "I'm looking forward to next time."

"Really? Golly, wow!"

Chase shook his head as he hung up the phone and pushed back his chair. Pitiful, just pitiful—and in Chase's opinion, his brother's approach to coaching the poor bastard was pretty pitiful, too. Horace had already wasted forty-four years of his life, and at the rate Luke was inching him along, it would be another forty-four before he ever moved out on his own. What Horace needed was a swift kick out of his comfort zone. If he were thrown into a sink-or-swim situation, he'd be forced to grow a backbone and earn some genuine self-confidence.

But Chase had agreed to handle things Luke's way, so he'd keep his mouth shut and follow his directions. After all, this whole situation was his own fault.

Chase rose from the table, put Horace's file on the short stack next to the mountain of files he was sorting through, and glanced at that damned wide-screen TV. It had all started when he'd bought it last spring and invited Luke over to watch the Yankees play the Red Sox. "I'll call in a pizza and you can pick it up on your way over," Chase had said. "I found this great little place that makes real Chicago-style ones."

As it turned out, pizza wasn't the only thing being ordered at Giuseppe's that night. The local mob had ordered a hit on a rival crime boss, and Luke had seen the whole thing—including the shooter, the getaway car, and the man in the passenger seat.

"Holy mother of Christ," Luke had said later, after the ambulance and police cars had cleared out and Luke was thumbing through a book of mug shots at Chase's desk at the Tulsa FBI office. "How the hell did you find that restaurant?"

"My partner and I were doing surveillance there a couple of weeks ago," Chase had admitted. "We had a tip it was a mob hangout, but we never saw any action, so we figured it was a false lead."

"Yeah, well, guess what?"

Chase had looked across his desk at his little brother— who at six-foot-one was just an inch shorter than Chase and not really all that little—and felt his chest tighten. He'd promised his mother that he'd look out for Luke, and he'd always done his best. He'd skipped high school sports to babysit him, gotten between him and the old man's fists, and worked two jobs to support him after their mother had died. The thought that he'd now put Luke's life in danger made him feel like he'd been kicked in the gut. "I can't tell you how sorry I am."

"Don't even try." Luke had raked a hand through his

hair, which was the same shade of dark brown as Chase's, but shaggier. "Just do me a favor."

"Name it."

"Next time you want pizza, just call Domino's."

That had been nearly four months ago. Luke had ID'd the shooter, as well as the man in the getaway car's passenger seat—who'd turned out to be Marco Lambino, the local kingpin Chase and his partner had been trying to nail for months, and Lambino's brother, Gianno. Both Lambinos were indicted and held for trial, and everything had been fine until last week—when the Tulsa district attorney had been forced by law to give the defense their witness list for the trial and, not coincidentally, when the Lambinos would have learned Luke's identity. The very next day, someone took a shot at Luke as he walked from his house to his car.

Which meant Luke was a marked man. Chase had damn near blown a gasket. He'd rushed his brother to the FBI field office in Oklahoma City and pulled every string available to get his brother into Witness Protection.

"You'll only need to stay in the program until after the trial," the craggy-faced regional commander had told Luke as they'd sat across from him at his mahogany desk. "We're sure the shooter was the Lambinos' nephew, Johnny, and we're confident the uncles will give him up in exchange for lighter sentences. Once that happens, you're home free."

"If you know who shot at me, why don't you just arrest him?" Luke had asked.

"We don't have any evidence," the commander said.

"So how do you know it was him?"

"Johnny is none too bright. If it were a real hit man, you'd be dead."

Luke had absorbed that silently for a moment. "What's to keep other members of the mob from coming after me?"

"This is the Calabrian Mafia, not the Cosa Nostra," Chase had explained. "It's made up of small family groups—usually just seven or eight operatives. Except for the nephew, we have the whole family in custody."

"What about the new family that's moving into town?"

"They have more reason to give you a medal than kill you," the commander said. "You've made it possible for them to take over."

"But what's to stop the Lambinos from hiring a hit man?"

"Money. We've confiscated all their loot."

"How do you know they don't have some hidden somewhere?"

"Because their first priority is keeping their asses out of jail, and they're so broke they're using public defenders. Once they're all convicted, you'll be in the clear."

Luke blew out a resigned sigh. "So where will I be while I'm in Witness Protection?"

"I don't know, and if I did, I couldn't tell you. You'll be out in the boonies—probably out west somewhere." The commander had leaned back in his chair and tapped his fingertips together. "You won't find out until you get there."

All in all, Luke had taken it pretty well—until the commander had left the room and Chase and his partner, Paul, had filled Luke in on the terms of the Witness Protection Program.

"What do you mean, I can't call my clients?" Luke had demanded.

"You're not allowed to have any contact with anyone you know," Chase had explained. "Not even me. And I won't have a clue where you are."

"Why?"

"Witness Protection policy," Paul had explained. The stocky man with salt-and-pepper hair had handed Luke a document outlining the rules. "You have to be untraceable. It's part of the deal."

"But I can't just bail on my clients!"

Chase had shrugged. "Tell them you're going on an extended vacation and refer them to someone else."

"It doesn't work like that." Luke's chin, so much like his own, had jutted out to a stubborn angle. "Some of these guys spent years working up the courage to reach out to someone. It's taken months for them to trust me, and they can't just transfer that trust to someone else. This could stop their progress dead in its tracks."

"How much progress do you think they'll make if *you're* stopped dead in your tracks?"

Luke had slumped low in his chair, his eyes filled with such utter defeat that Chase's heart had twisted. An idea had flashed through his mind—a bad idea, an idea so awful that it should have been immediately discarded. And yet, against his better judgment, he found it coming out of his mouth.

"Look—I'm responsible for getting you into this mess, so I'll stand in for you."

Luke's head had jerked up. "What?"

"I'll talk to your most desperate clients and pretend to be you."

"Oh, right," Luke had scoffed. "Like that'll ever work."

Paul had laughed. "Yeah. Not very likely."

Chase had felt vaguely offended. "Why not? Your sessions are conducted on the phone, and people always say they can't tell us apart on the phone. And I'm great at giving advice."

"They need *good* advice." Luke had looked at Paul, and both men had snickered.

"Have I ever steered you wrong?" Chase demanded.

"I can't believe you're even opening that door," Paul said dryly.

"Including or excluding your choice of pizzeria?" Luke asked.

Paul had roared.

"No offense, bro," Luke said, "but you don't exactly give off the sympathetic, supportive vibe my clients are looking for."

It was probably true. They looked alike and sounded alike, but that was where the similarity ended. Luke believed in talking things out, while Chase was all about action. Luke said they'd developed different coping tactics while growing up in a dysfunctional family. Since Luke had studied all that psychology crap, Chase would take his word on it.

"So I'll fake it." Hell, it couldn't be as hard as Luke was making it out to be. After all, Luke was doing it, wasn't he? And there were no licensing requirements for life coaches, so Chase wasn't technically unqualified.

"I just ran a new ad, and I'm booked solid," Luke had said. "It's a full-time job."

"So I'll refer the newbies to someone else and coach

your worst cases in the evening," Chase had said. "Write down what you want me to say. I'll follow your directions."

Luke had snorted. "That'll be a first."

Ultimately, though, Luke had agreed, because he didn't have a choice. Paul had retrieved Luke's files, and Luke had spent several hours at the Oklahoma City bureau office, writing detailed notes, lists of things to say, and instructions about his six neediest clients. He also jotted down a list of sports terms.

"Most of my clients call me Coach, and they expect a lot of sports talk," Luke had explained. "I use a lot of sports references, such as 'To win at the game of life, you have to learn how to score.'"

Chase had rolled his eyes. "Tell me you're kidding."

"No. I relate everything to plays and practice and strategy and skills."

When the transport team arrived, Luke had handed Chase an enormous cardboard box filled with files. "Promise you'll take good care of my clients."

Chase had taken the box and nodded, a hard lump in his throat. "Don't worry. I won't fumble the ball."

So far, so good, Chase thought as he gazed at the three stacks of files on his table—the tallest stack for the clients he'd referred to other coaches, the medium-sized stack for the clients he'd try to put on hold for six weeks, and the short stack for the clients he was actually coaching.

The next client was due to call in ten minutes. He strolled into the kitchen and grabbed a Coke from the fridge. So far tonight he'd coached a man who hadn't left his house in two years, an obnoxious braggart who couldn't understand why he had no friends, and Horace.

He'd bitten his tongue so many times it was a wonder it was still attached. It was excruciating, having to listen to these morons whine and moan, then respond with nothing more than pansy-assed, sports-laced suggestions. What these folks really needed—and probably really wanted—was a hard kick in the end zone. Left to his own devices, Chase would straighten out these gutless wonders in a few short weeks. Too bad he wasn't going to get a chance to prove it.

The apartment felt stuffy. Chase blew out a restless breath and strode toward his terrace, wanting to grab some fresh air before he got tied up with another pathetic loser. Popping the tab on his Coke, he opened the sliding door and stepped outside, leaving the door open so he could hear the phone.

It was September, but the night was hot. In Oklahoma, autumn didn't really kick in until mid-October. Still, Chase sensed a change in the air. The breeze carried the scent of rain, and the wind was brisker than usual.

Chase inhaled deeply, leaned against his terrace railing, and gazed out at the Tulsa skyline. Lightning zigzagged over the Williams Tower as a strong gust of wind plastered Chase's maroon OU T-shirt against his chest.

A noise like a small avalanche sounded behind him. Chase turned to see his brother's files crashing to the floor, the tall stack pushing the other stacks like dominoes, the papers tumbling out of the folders, the wind blowing pages and manila folders around the room like autumn leaves. With a muttered oath, Chase quickly stepped back inside and closed the door, but not before another gust scattered the papers like confetti.

The phone rang.

Great—the next client was calling, and Chase didn't have the file. Hell, he didn't even know the client's name. It took him two more phone rings to locate the appointment book from the heap of papers on the floor. He snatched up the receiver half a second before voice mail caught the call. "Hello?" he said gruffly.

"Luke?" purred a sultry female voice.

Out of habit, he almost said no, then caught himself. "Uh, yes."

"I took your advice about how to handle Joe, and it worked!"

"That's great, um . . ." Chase quickly flipped through the appointment book, looking for the name of his brother's 7:30 client. ". . . Samantha."

"It's Sammi—remember? Being called Samantha makes me want to twitch my nose and call for Darren."

Chase smiled. "Oh, yeah. Right." Where the heck was her file? He dropped to his knees and snatched up two manila folders. Neither was the right one. He crawled across the dining room floor, reaching for another.

"Are you okay? Your voice sounds kind of funny."

Hell. This girl was way too observant. He covered the mouthpiece, feigned a cough, and raised his voice to a slightly higher pitch. "I'm fine. I just, uh, have a little cold."

"Oh, you poor thing. You ought to take some vitamin C and zinc and eat some chicken soup."

"Yeah, good idea."

"You live in Tulsa, don't you?"

"Why do you ask?"

"Well, you advertised in the *Tulsa Tribune,* and you

have a local area code. So I was thinking I could bring you some homemade chicken soup."

The offer sounded oddly . . . nice. Too nice. Overly nice.

Crazy nice. "That's, um, very kind, but no, thanks. I've got some soup in my pantry." It was a lie; all he had was beef jerky, Doritos, and a box of stale Cheerios, but she didn't need to know that.

Where the *hell* was her file? Chase crept forward on his knees, grabbing at the scattered folders with one hand, holding the phone to his ear with the other. He'd encourage her to talk and just play along until he found her file or figured it out. "So—you and Joe are working things out?" he prompted.

"Oh, yes. Things are much better!" Her voice poured over him, silky and rich, with just a hint of a southern accent. It reminded him of a dessert he'd once had in New Orleans called Chocolate Sin. "You're a genius!"

He warmed under the praise, which was ridiculous, because she thought he was his brother. He didn't even know what topic, much less what brilliant advice, she was talking about. "Why don't you give me a play-by-play of how things went."

"Well, last night, Joe wanted to play with my shoes again."

Her shoes? Holy Moses, but his brother had some clients. He started to ask if Joe were her husband, but he was supposed to already know that. Moving across the floor on his hands and knees, Chase snatched up another folder, glanced at the name, and discarded it.

"I handled it just as you suggested," Sammi continued.

"Instead of just telling him no, I put on a pair of shoes that I didn't mind him drooling all over."

Drooling? Ye gads.

"They were spike-heeled sandals," she continued, "and he just went nuts."

Chase had to admit, this was a lot more interesting than anything he'd discussed with Horace. He grabbed and rejected another folder. "Oh, yeah?"

"Yeah. He started nibbling my toes and licking my instep."

Chase ran into some weirdos in his line of work, but they were usually just ordinary, run-of-the-mill serial-killer weirdos. This was a whole new world. "No kidding."

"Yeah. He particularly liked my toes."

Chase had nothing against feet—in fact, he'd been known to give a mean foot rub a time or two—but he couldn't understand why a man would focus on a woman's feet when she had so many other, more interesting body parts. All the same, there was something oddly erotic about Sammi's description.

It was probably her voice. With a voice like that, she could make skinning a snake sound sexy.

"He went crazy when I shook my foot in his face," she said.

"No kidding. How about you? Did you like it, too?"

"Well, not so much at first, but after a while, it was okay. I got a little worried when he started huffing and panting and breathing really hard."

Chase was breathing a little hard himself. Of course, he was on his belly, reaching for a folder at the back of his sofa, but still, her story probably had a lot to do with it. "How long did this go on?"

"Oh, ten minutes or so. I kinda lost track of time. And then he curled up beside me on the couch and fell asleep." She let out a blissful sigh. "That was the best part."

Chase frowned. He'd always thought women didn't like it when guys zonked out right after sex.

"And you were right," she continued. "Just a few minutes of playtime seemed to satisfy him."

I bet it did. But what about you?

"Ever since we started playing footsie," she continued, "he's left my other shoes alone. I'm so glad I no longer have to worry about stepping into a wet shoe in the morning."

Chase froze, his hand wrapped around a clutch of papers and dust bunnies. "Well, that's got to go in the plus column," he said carefully.

"Yeah. And I love it when he snuggles up and I get to stroke his pointy ears."

Chase sat up. "His ears are pointy?"

"Sure. He's a boxer."

Images of Mike Tyson and Evander Holyfield flitted through his mind. "I thought boxers had cauliflower ears."

She laughed as if he'd said something witty. "Good one."

Chase frowned. Something wasn't right here. Maybe this Joe was someone he was supposed to have heard of.

And then it hit. Joe the boxer. Joe boxer. Pointy ears.

She was talking about a *dog.*

Oh, man—he *had* to find that file.

He speed-crawled across the floor to the recliner

against the other wall. "So, um, how is the rest of your life going?"

She sighed. "No real change from the last time we talked. But I'm not dating anyone, so at least no one's gotten injured."

He was at an impasse. He was going to have to confess he had no idea what she was talking about. "Look—I, uh, apparently grabbed the wrong file, and I don't have my notes, so if you could just refresh my memory . . ."

"Oh, great." A despondent sigh hissed through the receiver. "My life is so boring that even my life coach can't remember it."

"No, no, it's not that. I don't think you're boring—not in the least. I just have a lot of clients, and I have trouble keeping people's stories straight, and . . ." Chase thought fast. How the hell was he going to explain such an incredible lapse of memory? "To tell you the truth, I'd just been to the dentist the last time we talked, and he gave me some kind of medication that messed with my memory. I'd really appreciate it if you'd give me a replay of your issues."

"I just have one issue."

Chase knelt down and peered under the chair. "Which is . . . ?"

"Murphy's law. *Everything* goes wrong for me."

"It can't be that bad." His belly on the floor, Chase stretched his arm under the chair and grabbed some papers against the wall.

"Yeah, well, it can, and it is. I moved to Tulsa six months ago because I was supposed to replace my boss at the Phelps Art Deco Museum and Mansion when she retired, but she just won't quit. I've adopted an oversized boxer with a leather fetish. The home I'm renting and hoped to buy needs a new roof, foundation leveling, electrical rewiring, and termite repairs before the bank will give me a mortgage, and my landlord won't fork out the money to fix it, so I can't buy it. And I can't seem to find a man who's not married, seriously weird, or a commitment-phobe—and if I *do* find a man with potential, I somehow end up injuring him."

"Injuring him . . . how?"

"Well, let's see—I cracked a date's rib, I broke a man's leg, and then I gave another guy a black eye with my elbow."

Yikes. "How long has this been going on?"

A soft sigh sounded through the receiver. "I've never been what you'd call lucky in love, but I didn't start injuring men until about a year and a half ago."

"What made you decide to seek help?" Chase's fingers curled around a folder.

"Well, two weekends ago, I went back to Dallas for a friend's wedding. I looked at everyone at the reception, and it hit me. They all have their lives together—well, except for my sister, and she's so weird she *thinks* she's together, even though she has blue hair and works as a tattoo artist. But everyone else has careers and husbands and houses and babies or prospects of babies—not to mention twenty-first-century wardrobes."

Twenty-first-century wardrobes? What the hell century did *she* wear?

Chase pulled out the folder and glanced at the label. Eureka—it said Samantha Matthews. He yanked it open and read his brother's notes scrawled on the inside of the folder.

Has had one free session. Explain I had to go out of town for a month, and suggest that she get another counselor.

"So here I am," she continued in that soft, sexy voice, "thirty-one years old and basically no further along than when I was just out of college. And I thought, there's *got* to be something that I'm doing wrong or not doing at all or just am not *getting*. At the very least, I've got to figure out a way to go on a date without sending the guy to the emergency room. So when I saw your ad in the *Tulsa Tribune* offering a free introductory session, I decided to give you a call." She paused. "Is any of this sounding familiar?"

"Uh, yes," Chase lied.

"Your ad said you help people score in the game of life, and I don't think I'm even on the right playing field. You really helped me with Joe—that dog-training book you suggested is working really well, and the shoe issue is under control—so I was wondering . . . can you help me with the rest of it? Especially the injuring-men-I-date part."

He didn't even have to lie. All he had to say was, "I'm sorry, I've got more clients than I can handle. You'd be better off with another life coach."

But this woman was offering him the perfect opportunity to prove to Luke that a little action beat years of talk. He was certain that if he put her through a modified form of basic training, he could turn her life around in a matter of weeks.

"Sure," Chase found himself saying. "If you're willing to follow my game plan and play by my rules, I'll teach you how to score."

Chapter Two

I can't believe you're actually going to get up at five-thirty and go jogging with your dog just because some bozo told you to." Sammi's sister, Chloe, reached into the clothes dryer stacked above the washer in the tiny pantry of Sammi's narrow galley-style kitchen and pulled out a pair of ripped jeans.

"He's not a bozo. He's my life coach." Sammi edged by Chloe to place a bag of Orville Redenbacher Butter Light in the microwave sitting atop the vintage turquoise-and-black-tiled countertop. "He says it'll help me develop self-discipline, which is the foundation of success."

"Why can't you develop self-discipline at a decent hour?"

The microwave beeped as Sammi punched the timer buttons. "Getting up early *is* the discipline."

"That's not discipline; that's punishment." Chloe folded the jeans. "Is it even safe to be out that early?"

Sammi nodded. "My coach said the path is lighted and heavily patrolled."

Chloe placed the jeans in the wicker clothes basket at

her feet. "Well, I don't know why you're paying someone for advice, anyway, when you've got me."

Sammi's gaze flicked over her sister's spiky blue hair, kohl-rimmed eyes, and black leather choker. "I hate to break it to you, but you're not exactly role-model material."

"I don't see why not. I'm perfectly happy with my life."

It was true. Chloe was completely content to live in a kitchenless garage apartment, cook on a hot plate, and work as a tattoo artist while trying to make it as a sculptor. It didn't bother her one whit that she was spending all her disposable income on art supplies, driving a wreck of a car, and coming to Sammi's house every other day to raid the fridge and do her laundry.

Sammi, however, craved a more settled lifestyle. She wanted a home, a husband, and a family—all of the old-fashioned, permanent, love-based stuff that her grand-parents had shared. Instead of moving in that direction, however, she seemed to be cruising toward a manslaughter conviction.

Chloe pulled a ridiculously short black skirt from the dryer. "So what's the story on this life coach? Is he an ex–drill sergeant or something?"

"No. He's a former sports psychologist."

"He's an ex-jock?"

"No. He helped jocks focus so they can play better."

Chloe's lips curved in a grin. "So he's an ex–jock supporter."

Sammi rolled her eyes. "He helped athletes think straight under pressure. He was known as the Choke Buster."

"The what?"

"When athletes choke—you know, freeze or mess up—it can start a cycle of being afraid they'll choke again, which makes it more likely to happen."

"Like you injuring men."

"Yeah. His ad said, 'Learn how to tackle your fears and score in the game of life.' And that's just what I need."

"Are you sure he's legit?"

"Yeah. I Googled him, and he checks out."

Sammi had Googled him again after their conversation half an hour ago, hoping to find a picture, but she'd had no luck. Which was disappointing; she hadn't noticed it the first time she'd talked to him, but tonight, his voice had sent shivers of attraction racing up her spine.

Chloe shook out the skirt. "Aside from self-discipline, what did he say you needed to work on?"

"Becoming more assertive."

Chloe made a snorting sound. "You're plenty assertive. In fact, you're downright bossy."

"Hey!"

"Well, you are. You just boss the wrong people."

"Meaning you."

"Yeah."

Sammi watched Chloe put the skirt in the clothes basket. It was similar to the six-inch skirt her sister currently wore—on top of black knee-length leggings and fishnets, along with three tank tops, a black mesh shirt, and a vest.

"You know, Chloe, if you didn't wear so many clothes at once, you wouldn't need to do laundry so often."

"See? There you go, bossing me again." Chloe reached

back into the dryer. "So how long are you planning to pay him to treat you like you treat me?"

Sammi peered into the microwave as the popcorn began rat-a-tat-tatting. "He thinks we can accomplish everything I want within four weeks."

Chloe snorted again. "That's not enough time to even tell him all your issues, much less get them solved."

Sammi put her hands on her hips. "First you don't want me to hire him, and now you think I should hire him for longer?"

"If he's going to have a prayer of helping you."

"I don't have that many issues."

"Yes, you do. You're a total mess."

This from a woman who dressed like a cartoon character and tattooed people's private body parts? "I'm not *that* bad," Sammi said indignantly.

Chloe pulled a red tank top out of the dryer. "Yes, you are. But I don't know why you're wasting your money, when I can tell you what your problems are for free."

Sammi opened a kitchen cabinet. "Which you're no doubt about to do, no matter how I try to stop you."

"You're too much of a softie."

Sammi pulled out a glass bowl. "I thought you just said I was bossy."

"You are. But the moment anyone has a problem, you immediately step in and try to solve it, without thinking about the consequences to yourself." She nodded her head toward the left. "That dog is exhibit A."

Sammi followed Chloe's gaze to the small breakfast area, where the enormously oversized brown-and-white boxer stood on his back legs, his front legs on the 1930s stainless-and-Formica table, his head straining toward Sammi's purse.

"Joe—no!" Sammi scurried toward him. "Down, boy!"

The dog jumped down and slunk away, his ears flattened, his eyes guilty.

Immediately contrite, Sammi knelt down beside him and held out her hand. "I'm sorry, boy. I didn't mean to scare you."

"See there? Like I said, exhibit A."

Joe crept toward Sammi's hand, his tail down, his head hung in shame. Sammi stroked his head. "He has an OCD thing about tanned leather. I shouldn't have put my purse where he'd be tempted."

Chloe placed the tank top in the burgeoning laundry basket. "His behavior isn't exhibit A. That's exhibit B. Exhibit A is the fact you have him at all."

Sammi rubbed the flat spot between the dog's two ears. "Oh, come on, Chloe. You know I had no choice." Sammi's close friend Yvette had promised her dying grandfather to take care of his dog—but two months after the funeral, Yvette's husband had been transferred to China.

Chloe shot her a get-real look. "You could have said no."

"And make Yvette choose between breaking her promise to her granddad or abandoning her husband?"

"She could have found the dog another home."

"She did. Twice. And each time, the new owner brought him back."

"Which would have warned a sane person that the dog is trouble."

"But Joe needed a home."

"Yes, but that was Yvette's problem. And then you stepped in and made it yours. You even drove all the way to Dallas and back to get him, and got your car upholstery chewed up in the process."

It might not have been the most logical course of action, but Sammi believed in following her heart, and her heart had never been able to refuse a stray. Until a severe allergy had forced her to find them other homes, she'd housed eight stray cats.

Chloe reached for one of Sammi's expensive wooden clothes hangers, the ones she'd bought to hang the 1930s-style dresses she wore for special programs at the museum. "You need to learn to say no."

Sammi gave Joe a final pat, then straightened. "Okay. No, you can't take my wooden clothes hanger. And the next time you want to do laundry here, the answer's no to that, too."

Chloe shook her head. "I'm serious."

"I am, too."

"You are not. You're too nice for your own good." The popcorn popped fast and furiously inside the microwave. "Not to change the subject, but can I borrow your car tomorrow? I need to put mine in the shop."

"Okay." Sammi moved to the sink and washed her hands. "What's wrong with it this time?"

"Ah-hah!" Chloe pointed the clothes hanger at her like a DA pointing out the criminal in a courtroom drama. "Gotcha!"

"What?"

"You didn't tell me no. How were you going to get to work if I had your car?"

"I—I guess I figured you'd give me a ride." Sammi dried her hands on a kitchen towel.

"What if I wouldn't?"

Narrowing her eyes, Sammi put her hands on her hips. "Why wouldn't you?"

"Maybe I had to go in the other direction."

"Well, then, I would have called a friend." Only she didn't yet really know anyone in Tulsa besides the people she worked with—and since she was the supervisor of everyone at the museum except Ms. Arnette, she wouldn't have felt right asking them to do her a personal favor. "Or I would have taken a cab. I would have managed."

"See there? You would have complicated your life because you didn't stop and think about the consequences to yourself before you said yes." Chloe shook her head. "You need to stop letting people take advantage of you."

"So you're admitting you take advantage of me?"

"I'm your sister. I'm supposed to." Chloe slid her jeans onto Sammi's good wooden hanger. "I'm talking about people like that old crone you work with."

"Ms. Arnette isn't a crone, and she isn't taking advantage of me, exactly."

Chloe blew out a derisive snort. "Let's review the situation, shall we?" She held out her hand and started ticking things off on her fingers. "She resents your very presence, she refuses to step down, and she treats you like a grunt instead of an equal. She tries to keep you from attending board meetings, she shoots down your ideas, she finds fault with everything you do, and she orders you around."

It was true. But Sammi sympathized with the older woman's plight. Ms. Arnette had suffered a heart attack six months before her planned retirement. Thinking that she wouldn't return, the museum's board of directors had hired Sammi to replace her. After she recovered, however, Ms. Arnette decided not to retire—so she and Sammi were both trying to do the same job. "It's a tough situation for her, as well."

"And then there's the matter of your landlord," Chloe continued.

Okay, Mr. Landry was a problem. Sammi had fallen in love with the little art deco house she was renting from him the moment she'd seen it. She'd researched the property and learned that it had been built by a famous architect in the 1930s—an architect that her great-grandfather had worked for, which meant that her great-grandfather had possibly done the masonry on this very house. She desperately wanted to buy it, but Mr. Landry refused to make the repairs the mortgage company required.

Sammi refused to give up hope. "I asked him to come over this evening," she told Chloe. "I've come up with an owner-financing agreement that might allow me to buy the place."

"Fat chance of getting him to agree to that." Chloe folded another T-shirt. "You can't even talk him into renewing your lease."

Unfortunately, Chloe was right. Sammi was living there as a month-to-month tenant, which meant her landlord had no obligation to fix anything that broke and could evict her with just thirty days' notice.

Sammi scowled as she pulled the bag of popcorn from the microwave. "Not that I'm ungrateful or anything, Chloe, but pointing out everything that's wrong with my life is not helpful."

"I'm not finished. I haven't even started on your other issue," Chloe continued.

"Which is?"

"Fear of intimacy, obviously."

"I do not fear intimacy!"

Chloe lifted her shoulders. "Physically injuring every man who gets close is a pretty effective way of keeping men at a distance, don't you think?"

"I'm not doing it on purpose! I *want* a relationship."

"You say you do, but actions speak louder than words." Chloe placed the shirt in the clothes basket. "Deep down, you're afraid of getting hurt like you did with Lance."

Even after a year and a half, the thought of her former boyfriend made her stomach tighten. Not because she felt any lingering affection—she was long over the cheesy cheating ratfink—but because the experience had rocked her trust in her own judgment.

"Thank you for that analysis, Dr. Freud." Sammi carefully pulled apart the corners on the bag of popcorn. Buttery-scented steam filled the air.

"Don't mention it. I'll send you my bill."

The doorbell rang, interrupting their conversation. Joe ran for the door, barking loudly.

"That must be Mr. Landry now."

"Good luck," Chloe said, taking the popcorn out of Sammi's hands and helping herself to a mouthful.

❧

The faint balsamic scent of sweetgum leaves wafted on the breeze as Walter Landry stood on the stoop of his rental house. He punched the doorbell again, then turned to look at the huge tree towering in the front yard. The sight made his chest tighten. Helen had planted that tree some thirty-odd years ago. He remembered chiding her for it at the time.

"Sweetgums drop those messy seedballs all over the place," he'd complained. "That tree will just litter up the lawn."

"Oh, Walter, it's worth a little fuss," Helen had said. "The leaves smell so sweet, and they're shaped like little stars. And they're such a deep shade of green that one tree feels like a whole forest."

Hadn't that been just like Helen, he thought with a bone-deep ache—always seeing the beauty in the world. And hadn't that been just like him—always pointing out the problems.

Loud barking inside the house made him turn back around. He heard Sammi's voice on the other side of the door, a noise that sounded like scuffling, then the click of the lock unsnapping. The door creaked open, and Sammi's apple-cheeked face appeared in the open doorway. Sammi's light brown—or was it dark blond?—hair fell in her face as she struggled to restrain an enormous dog by the collar. "Hello, Mr. Landry. Thanks for coming."

The dog lunged toward him, his pink tongue hanging out the side of his mouth. Alarmed, Walter pulled his hands from the pockets of his khakis and stepped back.

"Down, Joe." Sammi used both hands on the dog's collar to pull him back. "Sit."

The dog reluctantly obeyed.

Sammi looked up sheepishly. "Sorry. Sometimes his greetings are overly exuberant."

The dog's stump of a tail thumped on the floor. Walter relaxed a little. At least the monster looked friendly. "Got yourself a pet, I see."

"Oh—I hope you don't mind." Sammi's brow scrunched together over her hazel eyes. "I didn't think to ask about your pet policy." She talked fast, as if she were trying to chase away his objections. "He's completely house-trained, but I'll be happy to put up a deposit for him if you'd like."

Walter waved his hand. "No, no. Not necessary." He didn't allow pets on any of his other rental properties, but in this case, it didn't matter. The condition of the house was not likely to affect the property value of the place, because anyone who bought it was likely to tear it down.

"Well, come in, come in." Sammi stepped back, her hands still on the dog's collar.

Walter walked into the tiny foyer and paused. He hadn't been inside the house since she'd moved in. He'd given her carte blanche to do whatever she wanted to the place, and boy, had she been busy. The place looked like a million bucks when they'd first bought it in 1980.

He'd never thought much of the house—it was small, oddly shaped, and plain as a box—but Helen had thought it was adorable. Style moderne, she'd called it, pronouncing it the French way, with the first word sounding like "steel." For the longest time, he'd thought it must have a metal frame.

He and Helen had been living here when he'd bought the sprawling Georgian house in south Tulsa. To his shock, Helen had suggested forgoing the new place and staying here. Walter had scoffed. How would people know he was successful if he lived in a nine-hundred-square-foot shoe-box? He was proud of the way he'd managed to invest his earnings from his job at the power plant and turn a hand-some profit.

But Helen had loved the neighbors, the schools, and the location. She'd said they had all the space they re-ally needed. She'd thought the house was unique and charming.

Walter saw nothing charming about it. The place was squat and square, with a flat roof, stucco exterior, and oddly rounded front corner.

They'd had an argument over it—one of the worst in their forty years together. Walter had stormed out in anger. As usual, Helen had given in and Walter had got-ten his way.

God, how he regretted that now! He regretted ever telling Helen no about anything. If he'd had one iota of an inkling how much he'd miss her when she was gone, he'd have gone along with every one of her crazy ideas.

Which hadn't been all that crazy, in retrospect. She'd only wanted things like a family vacation, or Walter tak-ing a day off now and then, or the two of them signing up for ballroom dancing lessons—things that would have given them more time together. Good Lord, what he'd give for more time with her now.

"Why don't you have a seat?" Sammi pulled him back to the present by motioning to the sofa. Moss green, curved, and upholstered in a fan shape, it reminded him of something out of an old movie. The house smelled like popcorn.

His chest tightened. Popcorn and old movies were two of Helen's favorite things.

"What do you think of what I've done with the place?" Sammi asked.

"You've made it look real nice," Walter said, sitting down.

But it was like putting lipstick on a pig. New paint and tile didn't change the fact that the house was falling apart. It needed a new roof, new stucco, a new chimney, and extensive foundation work. He'd put in some new electrical wiring a few years ago and patched up the plumbing, but both systems needed complete overhauls.

The dog stood up and barked. Sammi tightened her grip on his collar. "I'll put Joe outside, and then I'll be right back. I have a proposal I want to run by you."

Oh, Lordy—not another one. Over the last few months, Sammi had hit him up with all kinds of propositions. First of all, she'd dug up a bunch of historical information about the place and pestered him to apply for a historical-property designation. Apparently the place had been designed by some hotshot art deco architect back in the 1930s. Walter had refused, of course; a historical designation would only limit his options.

Next she'd wanted him to sink thousands of dollars into the house so she could get a mortgage. When he'd refused to do that, she'd tried to negotiate a lease-purchase agreement, but he had no intention of getting locked into that. Lastly, she'd offered to use her own money to pay for repairs as she could afford them, but Walter had vetoed the idea because of liability concerns.

The bottom line was, it would cost more to fix up the house than it was worth. Nobody wanted a seventy-five- or eighty-year-old home with no master bath, no laundry room, and a kitchen so narrow that two people had to turn sideways to pass each other in it. The home's only value was its location. Wealthy yuppies or Gen-Xers or whatever the heck they were called nowadays were tearing down homes throughout the neighborhood and wedging oversized faux chateaux onto the small lots.

Sammi reentered the room and sank onto the edge of a low, overstuffed chair across from the sofa. She folded her hands on her lap. "I've researched owner financing, and I think it's a way we can both get what we want. In essence, you'd be my mortgage lender. That way I could fix the place up a little at a time as I could afford it, and when it's all the way up to code, I can refinance through traditional means and buy it from you free and clear."

Walter blew out a sigh. She was a sweet girl and he hated to disappoint her, but he really had no choice. He shook his head. "I don't want to get into the lending business."

Her brows pulled in an earnest frown. "It would only be for two or three years. And you wouldn't have any out-of-pocket expenses."

"You can't know that, Sammi. Once you get inside the walls, there's no telling what damage you might find. You're likely to run into something that you can't afford to fix, and I'd have to step in. Besides, any money spent to fix this place up is money just thrown away. This house is only depreciating."

"Not to people who love historical architecture."

Walter cleared his throat. "The fact of the matter is, Sammi, my real-estate broker thinks I can get forty thousand dollars more than your appraisal without any cash outlay."

Her face fell. "But that's all the bank said it would loan me. That's all I qualify for on my salary."

Oh, man. She looked like she was about to cry. Walter had never been any good at handling female waterworks. He shifted uncomfortably on the sofa. "Well, Sammi, you know the situation. The land is worth more than the homes in this neighborhood."

"It wouldn't be if you and the other homeowners had asked for a historic-neighborhood-preservation status years ago."

It wasn't the first time she'd brought this up. And hell, she might be right, but it was too late now. More than half of the lots in the neighborhood already held oversized McMansions, ruining what the historical-preservation people called "the integrity of the neighborhood."

"What's done is done, Sammi. There's no point in looking back."

"But it's *not* done. *This* house could still be preserved. It's a crime to let it just fall apart."

It wasn't going to fall apart. It was going to be demolished. That was the trend in the neighborhood, but she refused to see the writing on the wall.

"At least let me sign another lease," Sammi implored.

Walter shook his head. "I can't do that, not with the house in this condition. My attorney told me I shouldn't even be letting you live here as a month-to-month tenant, truth be known. In fact . . ." He hadn't planned to tell her yet, but while he was here, he might as well go ahead and break the news. "The truth is, I'm planning on moving to Arizona to live near my daughter and grandchildren, and I'm selling off all my holdings."

Her forehead pleated with worry. "You're going to sell this house?"

He nodded. "I'm selling it as-is."

She pressed her fingers together so tightly that the tendons on the back of her hands stood in bas-relief. "You won't sell it to someone who wants to tear it down, will you?"

No point in sugarcoating it. "I'm going to sell it for the most I can get for it."

"Which means to someone who'll tear it down." Her eyes blazed at him.

He stood with a sigh. "Sammi, I didn't tell you to argue about it. I told you so you could start looking for another place to live."

"But I don't want to live anywhere else!"

I know what you mean. He wasn't all that crazy about the prospect of moving, either, but there was really no reason for him to stay in Tulsa. No one here really cared if he lived or died. Helen had maintained all their social contacts, and since her death, he'd lost touch with all their friends. Oh, he'd received a few invitations to go out at first, but he couldn't bear to be around other couples without her, and after a while, the invitations quit coming.

Which was fine with him. Hell—he'd be lousy company, anyway. Helen's death had punctured a hole in his life. All of the joy had leaked out, and his world had shriveled like an old balloon.

Apparently he had shriveled, too. When his daughter had come to visit a few months back, she'd been appalled at the amount of weight he'd lost.

"Dad, you look like Howard Hughes!" Anne had gasped when she'd seen him at the airport. "Your clothes are just hanging on you. You must have lost twenty pounds!" Her blue eyes, so much like Helen's, had darkened with concern. "When was the last time you had a haircut, or went for a checkup?"

She'd redoubled her efforts to convince him to move to Arizona, and before he'd dropped her off at the airport for her return flight, he'd conceded. Why the hell not? There was nothing for him here.

Nothing to get up for in the morning, nothing to be grateful for at night. He had nothing but memories, and even those were overrated. The bad ones tormented him, and the good ones just made him miss Helen all the more.

He moved toward the door. "I'm sorry, Sammi, but it's a business decision. I need to get the most I can out of my investment."

A girl who looked like she was dressed for a Halloween party appeared in the hallway. She was wearing something that looked like a black ballet skirt over footless tights and hooker stockings. Her eyes were rimmed with black, and her black-and-blue hair was arranged in startlingly stiff-looking spikes. "I couldn't help overhearing your conversation," she said.

Who the heck was this? Mr. Landry inclined his head politely.

"This is my sister, Chloe," Sammi said, rising from her chair. "Chloe, this is Mr. Landry."

"So I gathered." Her somber expression, combined with her weird clothes and bizarre makeup, made her look like the angel of death. "You know, Mr. Landry, places have energy, and this house's energy is in perfect sync with Sammi's. If you disrupt that, you're going to create negative energy that will ruin your karma."

He was feeling a little negative energy brewing right now. He forced a smile. "Well, that's a very interesting theory, but I don't believe in karma." The truth was, he didn't believe in much of anything anymore.

He nodded to Sammi and made his way to the door. "I'll talk to you more about this later. Have a nice evening." He headed out the door and down the sidewalk toward his Coupe de Ville. The leaves of the sweetgum whispered dryly above him in the warm September breeze. The tree looked heat-battered and tired. The summer had sapped most of its color, and only the weary, about-to-give-up green of late summer remained.

The leaves looked like he felt, Walter thought as he opened his car door—used up and brittle, with nothing left to do but wither and die.

Chapter Three

The sky had lightened from night-black to gray, but the streetlights were still on as Chase stretched his quads in Riverside Park at 5:20 the next morning. He usually ran his daily five miles through his own downtown neighborhood, but this morning he'd decided to vary his routine to catch a glimpse of Sammi.

He braced his hands against the back of the park bench and stretched his left leg out behind him. He was pretty sure that spying on a client wasn't approved life-coach protocol, but Sammi's voice had intrigued the hell out of him, and he wanted to see the woman that went along with it. Besides, he might learn something that would help him coach her. Maybe she needed to join a gym or see a dermatologist or dentist or something.

Besides, what could it hurt? He didn't intend to actually talk to her; he just planned to take a quick look. She should be easy to recognize, because it wasn't likely that any other women with boxers would be jogging on this trail at this hour.

That is, if she even showed. Chase switched legs,

stretching his right one behind him and lunging forward on his left. Not everyone who said they wanted help was actually willing to do the work required to help themselves. A woman with a life as screwed up as Sammi's was likely to have some self-discipline issues.

Well, self-discipline was Chase's forte—or his Achilles' heel, depending on how you looked at it. More than one woman had accused him of being overly structured. And hell, maybe he was, but it sure beat the alternative. He'd promised himself he'd never be a lazy deadbeat like his father, and it was a promise he was determined to keep. He drove himself to excel at work, to stay physically fit, to keep his possessions and affairs in order, and, most importantly, to keep his emotions under control. That was the key. If a man didn't control his emotions, they'd end up controlling him. His father's out-of-control drunken rages had sure proved that.

Chase set off down the riverside trail, jogging slowly at first, then picking up speed as his muscles warmed. He breathed deeply, inhaling the earthy scent of the river, thinking about the day ahead. He and his partner were currently working with the Tulsa Police Department on a string of cold-case bank robberies, which meant that unless something new broke or they got a hot lead, he'd have regular hours for the next few days. That would make the phone coaching easier. His brother had told him to talk to his clients in a quiet environment, but with the FBI's twenty-four-hour availability policy, it was likely to be a problem at some point.

He wondered how his brother was faring. He couldn't help but worry about Luke—after a lifetime of being the protective big brother, it was second nature—but Luke was probably living it up in some scenic mountain setting, fishing and kayaking and having a high old time.

Chase saw a few cars on Riverside Drive, which ran parallel to the trail about fifty feet away, but the trail itself was practically deserted. In the first mile, Chase passed only one other jogger—a round-bellied, middle-aged man huffing and puffing like a locomotive. Two athletic college-aged young men raced by half a mile later, but other than that, the trail was deserted.

The trees between the path and the road thinned as he neared Forty-first Street, where he'd suggested that Sammi start her run. He glanced at his watch. It was ten until six, and there was still no sign of her. Looked like she was a no-show.

Disappointed, he was about to turn back when a giant brown-and-white dog charged around the bend, pulling a slender woman in a green T-shirt and black shorts behind him.

A jolt went through him. He didn't know what he'd expected, exactly, but it wasn't mile-long legs, a light brown ponytail, and pert breasts bouncing under a Texas University T-shirt. The dog looked like a boxer, but his gene pool had to contain some mastiff or Great Dane. The beast was enormous; his head came up to the woman's waist, and he looked like he weighed more than she did.

Chase didn't want to be caught staring. In normal jogger etiquette, Chase nodded an impersonal greeting and moved to the right side of the trail to let her pass.

She moved to the far side, as well, but the dog continued to chug straight down the middle of the trail, his nose twitching, his cropped ears tilted forward.

"Heel, Joe!" she ordered.

The dog did nothing of the kind. As their paths intersected, the beast locked his eyes on Chase, flattened his ears, and lunged toward him, yanking the leash out of the woman's hand.

"Heel!" she shouted.

The dog ignored her and surged toward Chase, his red leash flapping behind him. Chase put out his hands to fend him off, only to have the beast circle around and lock his jaws on the back of his jogging shorts.

"Hey!" The elastic waistband bit into Chase's stomach as the giant dog pulled down his shorts. Chase stopped and pivoted, trying to swat away the beast, but the animal refused to relinquish his mouthful of fabric. The dog held on as Chase lurched off the path and onto the grass, his shorts around his knees.

"Joe—stop it!" The woman ran forward, only to slip on the dew-soaked grass. Chase reached out to break her fall, but his shorts were now around his ankles, and he couldn't keep his balance. Down she went, pulling him with her. Chase's hands hit the ground as his body sprawled on top of her.

Chase gasped, not so much from the impact as from the flood of sensations washing over him—cool, wet grass on his hands and knees, warm, hard-breathing woman beneath his torso.

"Are you okay?" he asked.

Big hazel eyes stared up into his at disconcertingly close range. "Yeah." Her voice was soft and breathy. "You?"

"Yeah." Chase gazed down at her. She had a small nose, delicate eyebrows, and long eyelashes. Her breath smelled like toothpaste, and her hair smelled like fruit and flowers. Chase was pretty sure he hadn't hit his head, but gazing into her face, he felt distinctly dazed. His gaze shifted to her lips. Man, they were something—full and ripe and pillowy. So was the feel of her body beneath his.

"Okay, you two, break it up," ordered a gruff male voice.

Chase's gaze jerked upward. His first view was the underside of a navy-blue beer belly. The belly shifted, exposing a wide black belt holding a holstered service revolver.

Oh, great. A cop.

"Hell of a place to get romantic." The officer's weathered face frowned down over his massive belly. "You two drunk or somethin'?"

~

It took an effort, but Sammi pulled her eyes from the handsome face on top of her to the scowling mug of an overweight policeman hovering above them both. Her gaze immediately went to his holstered gun. The sight made her stomach tighten. Dear Lord, but she hated guns. "No," she managed. "I don't even know this man."

The cop's eyes narrowed. "He's attacking you?"

I wish. Her gaze went back to the man. He had a strong face, good-looking but not pretty, with high cheekbones, a broad jaw, and an angular chin. It was covered with a night's worth of dark stubble, as if he'd missed his morning shave. His nose wasn't straight, exactly—it looked like it might have been broken a time or two—but that somehow only added to his appeal.

"All right, you," the officer barked, resting his hand on his gun. "Get your hands where I can see them."

Belatedly, Sammi realized she hadn't answered the cop's question. "Oh, he's not attacking me. He tripped when my boxer got loose."

The crease between the cop's thick gray eyebrows deepened. "Looks like your pal here's the one with the loose boxers." He relinquished the handle of his pistol, pulled out his nightstick, and tapped the man's leg. "Pull up your pants, there, lover boy."

Chase rolled off Sammi and tugged up his shorts. "It's not what it looks like, Officer."

"It better not be, 'cause from where I'm standing, it looks like lewd and lascivious behavior, indecent exposure, and probably public intoxication."

"We're not drunk. And we don't even know each other." Sammi scrambled to her feet. "My dog got loose and grabbed this man's shorts, and we fell."

The policeman's squinty eyes darted from her face to the man's, then back again. "I don't see a dog."

Oh, no—where was Joe? She turned and frantically looked up and down the street.

The hunk touched her shoulder. "Over there." He pointed to a cluster of oaks near the river. Joe lay in the leaves under them, gnawing on something between his front paws.

Thank goodness! She'd never forgive herself if something happened to Yvette's dog the first month she had him. "Joe!" she called, starting toward him.

The cop stepped in front, body-blocking her. "Not so fast. Let's see some ID."

This guy was a real jerk. Probably because he had a gun, Sammi thought; something about packing heat turned even mild-mannered men into paranoid bullies. "I don't have any on me."

"Why not?"

"Because I don't usually jog with my purse."

Beside her, the hunk chuckled. The cop's eyes narrowed with displeasure. "What's your name and address?" he demanded.

"Samantha Matthews, 2100 Pendercross."

"Occupation?"

"Curator at the Phelps Museum. Why?"

"Because I just found you lying on the ground under a pantless man, and I'm trying to decide if you're a prostitute, a drunk, or a crazy." He turned to the man. "What about you?"

"Chase Jones, 2100 Court Place. And I'm none of the above, either."

The first bubble of a laugh made it out before Sammi could stifle it. The officer's face hardened. "I'll be the judge of that. Your occupation?"

"Special agent, FBI."

Oh, great—just her luck. The hunk was a gun toter himself.

But the policeman didn't seem to believe it. He squinted at Chase suspiciously. "They training you guys to drop trou in public these days?"

"No." Chase's tone was unamused, his lips tight. "Like the lady said, we fell."

"Humph." He clearly didn't believe them. "You got ID?"

"Yeah." Chase reached for his right hip. His hand froze, and his mouth flattened. "It's, uh, not there. I think the dog has it."

"Uh-huh," the cop said dryly. "I bet he ate your homework, too."

"Seriously. My whole pocket is gone." Chase turned around. Loose threads dangled from the seat of his shorts, and white cotton peeked out of a long rip.

Chagrin pulsed through Sammi. "I'm so sorry. Joe has a thing for tanned leather."

The creases between the cop's bushy brows furrowed. "You ever hear of leash laws, lady?"

"He's on a leash. He just got away. Can I go get him now?"

"Yeah. But come right back. And you . . ." He turned and pointed his nightstick at Chase. "You stay right here."

Sammi hurried toward the dog, slowing and holding out her hand as she drew near. "Here, Joe," she called.

The boxer picked up the wallet in his teeth and trotted off, only to plop down a few yards away and resume chewing.

"Come on, boy. Come here."

As she approached, the dog moved again.

Sammi decided to switch tactics. "Stay, Joe," she ordered, walking slowly toward him.

The dog stood, loped toward the river, then plunked down on the grass.

"Christ. We could be here all day," the cop grumbled.

Sammi opted for a different method. "Hey, Joe—want to play footsie?"

The dog stopped chewing and cocked his head to one side, the wallet hanging out of his mouth.

"Footsie, Joe?" She inched closer.

"Just how weird are you people?" the cop muttered.

She was now less than a yard away. The dog glanced at her sneaker-clad feet and decided to pass. As he rose to all fours, Sammi long-jumped onto his leash, trapping it beneath her white Nike. "Gotcha!" She bent and picked up the leash, then held her hand below the beast's mouth. "Give it to me," she ordered. The dog sheepishly dropped the wallet into her palm.

"Good boy." Sammi petted his head.

Joe wagged his tail, then trotted beside her as she jogged back to Chase and the policeman. She held out the wallet to Chase with an apologetic smile. "It's a little worse for wear."

She followed his dismayed glance down to the mangled wallet. It was now a slimy brown wad, pitted with teethmarks, covered with slobber, and missing a corner.

Sammi winced as he took it. "Okay, that's a bit of an understatement."

Chase gingerly pried it open. Half of a ten-dollar bill was missing and the wallet's fold was nearly torn in two, but from what Sammi could see, his credit cards and ID seemed intact.

She bit her lip. "I'm really sorry."

A muscle flexed in the man's jaw. He pulled out his driver's license and FBI ID and handed them to the police officer.

The cop looked at the cards, looked at Chase, then looked at the cards again. "Special Agent Jones, huh?"

"That's right."

The cop ran a hand across his mouth and sheepishly dropped his gaze. "I'm, uh, sorry. It didn't, uh, seem like a likely story." He handed the cards back to Chase and cleared his throat. "Okay, then. Everything seems to be in order here." He harrumphed again, then turned a stern look at Sammi. "Better keep that dog of yours under control."

And you better do the same with your paranoia. Sammi nodded.

The cop curtly dipped his head. "Okay, then. You two have a nice day." With that, he turned and plodded away.

Chase gingerly fit his cards back into the chewed-up wallet.

Sammi shifted the leash into her other hand. "I'm so sorry about your wallet. Why don't you give me your address, and I'll mail you a check to cover the cost?"

"Nah. I needed to get a new one anyway."

She was pretty sure he was lying. The fact he was being so nice about it deepened her sense of guilt. "Well, at least let me buy you a cup of coffee. There's a place about half a block up the trail."

"Oh, that's not necessary. Besides, you have the dog."

"They have outdoor seating, so Joe won't be a problem."

He hesitated.

"Please. It'll make me feel really bad if you don't let me do *something.*"

The corners of his eyes crinkled as his smiled. "Okay. But I'll buy since you don't have your wallet."

Her wallet. It was back at her place. Her face heated. "Well, then, why don't you come back to my house and I'll put on a pot?" she blurted, then wondered if the offer seemed weird. "Not that I'm in the habit of inviting strange men home." Okay, that definitely sounded weird. "But since you're FBI, I figure you're not going to attack me or anything."

Although part of her kind of wished he would. Good grief, but he was gorgeous. He had George Clooney's eyes, Brad Pitt's jawline, and, from what she'd glimpsed of his belly, Matthew McConaughey's abs.

"Of course, you're probably in a hurry. I'm sure you have to get to work, and you probably have a wife or girlfriend expecting you at home." She realized she was babbling—she always babbled when she got nervous—but she couldn't seem to stop. "I'm not married or anything myself, so . . ." Oh, dear Lord. She was just making this more awkward than it already was.

His grinned. "No one's waiting for me."

"Oh." His smile made it hard to think.

"And I don't have to be at work for a couple of hours. A cup of coffee sounds great."

She swallowed, suddenly nervous, and wondered what on earth had possessed her to issue the invitation. "Well . . . good. It's about a mile and a half away. Feel like jogging some more?"

~

As he followed Sammi and her dog onto a tree-shaded street fifteen minutes later, Chase was breathing hard—as much from watching Sammi as from the run. His initial theory that she was out of shape had been off base—way off base. The sight of her long legs, pert backside, and slender waist would have made him break a sweat even if he'd been sitting still.

She slowed in front of a small white stucco house. "Here it is."

"Cool place," Chase said, and meant it. The tiny, flat-roofed house had a curved corner built from square glass blocks, giving it a George Jetson kind of look.

He followed her and the dog up the stoop to the front door. She reached inside her T-shirt and fished a key off a chain around her neck. "It was designed by a famous art deco architect," she said, unlocking it. "He only built a few modest-sized homes, and this is the only one still standing."

And I shouldn't be here seeing it, Chase thought, but he'd been unable to resist the invitation. After all, the inside of a home gave real clues to the person who lived there.

She opened the door. "Come on in."

It was like stepping into a tiny time warp. A green-and-black tile fireplace with a gilt starburst mirror over the mantel dominated one wall. A kidney-shaped coffee table stood between a fan-backed green sofa and two low-slung black chairs with green and black geometric-patterned throw pillows. "Wow. This looks like the set of an old Bogey and Bacall movie."

She smiled broadly and flipped a light switch, lighting up an overhead fixture that looked like two swans holding a bowl. "Thanks. That's kind of the effect I was going for."

"You're an old movie buff?"

"I'm an art deco buff, but lots of movies from the thirties and forties featured the style."

He needed to play this as if he didn't know anything about her, other than what she'd told the police officer. "Oh, that's right. You work at the art deco museum." He looked around. "So this is art deco. I never really knew what it was."

"It has a lot of different interpretations, but it was basically the modern of its day."

"When was that?"

"Generally speaking, between the world wars. Tulsa has a ton of it because it was popular when most of the city was built."

"This place is in great condition for a house that old."

"Thanks. I've done a lot of work on the place. I've replastered, painted, retiled the fireplace, refinished the floors, and installed vintage light fixtures."

That was an awful lot of work and money to put into a rental. Only he wasn't supposed to know she was just renting. He wondered if she'd lie about it. "How long have you had this place?" He followed her into the kitchen, trying to keep his thoughts focused on the conversation and off her long legs.

"A little over six months, but I don't own it." The thought seemed to deflate her. "I'm trying to buy it, but it needs a lot of repairs, and I can't get a mortgage until they're fixed. Unfortunately, my landlord won't shell out the money to do them. And he informed me last night that he plans to sell it as-is, which most likely means he'll sell it to someone who wants to tear it down."

Chase leaned a hip against her turquoise-and-black tile counter. "He has to keep the place in good repair as long as you have a lease."

"That's another problem. I don't have one." She picked up the coffeepot and carried it to the tiny sink. "It ran out, and now I'm just a month-to-month tenant."

Not a very logical situation to be in—especially considering all she'd spent on the place. But from what he'd learned as her life coach, she wasn't a very practical person.

She turned on the faucet and filled the pot with water, then poured it into her Mr. Coffee. "I'm hoping that when the executive curator at the museum retires and I officially replace her, my salary will increase enough for me to qualify for a larger loan. Maybe then the bank will let me buy the place as-is."

"When's she going to retire?"

"Who knows? It was supposed to have happened months ago, but she changed her mind. I was hired as interim head curator with the understanding that my salary would go up when she stepped down, but I'm still waiting."

"So you're stuck as her understudy for as long as she wants?"

"Pretty much." Sammi opened an ancient turquoise refrigerator and pulled out a can of Cain's coffee. "She worked for Phelps Oil before the museum was even created, and all Phelps employees hired before 1970 have a guaranteed job for as long as they want one."

"Maybe she could be transferred to a different position."

"Oh, I don't want to push her out." She pried the yellow lid off the red can. The rich scent of coffee filled the air. "Her job has been her whole life, and I want her to leave on her own terms."

Sammi was too nice for her own good, lacking in drive, or missing the self-preservation instinct—and none of these possibilities boded well for her career prospects. "What if she decides to stay for several more years?"

"I refuse to think along those lines." She filled the coffee filter. "The head curator position is my dream job, and I have faith it will all work out when it's meant to."

Things worked out for people who made them work out, not for people who sat back and hoped for the best. In addition to being illogical, impractical, and irrational, Sammi was a Pollyanna. No wonder her life was a mess.

She punched the "on" button on the coffeepot and turned toward him. When her eyes met his, he felt as if she'd found his on button, as well. Since when did impractical Pollyannas have so much appeal?

The dog tipped up his snout and snuffled the countertop. Chase patted his enormous head.

"What about you?" Sammi asked. "Is the FBI your dream job?"

"I wouldn't exactly describe it as dreamy, but yeah, it's all I ever wanted to do."

She leaned a shapely hip against the counter. "What, exactly, does a special agent do?"

"Investigate federal crimes, search for fugitives, help out local law enforcement when they need it—whatever needs doing."

"Do you have a specialty?"

"I work a lot of organized-crime cases."

Her eyes widened. "You mean the Cosa Nostra?"

He shook his head. "Mainly the Russian mob or the Calabrian Mafia."

"I've never heard of the Calabrian thing."

"It's a group of much smaller, less organized crime families from another part of Italy."

Sammi's hazel eyes regarded him with rapt attention. "What sorts of things do they do?"

"Typical, everyday family activities—racketeering, heroin trafficking, murder."

Her eyes widened. "Yikes. My parents just took us to the park."

Chase grinned, then caught himself. What was he doing, running off at the mouth about his work? He was here to find out about her.

He looked around, and his gaze lit on a collection of photos on a narrow sideboard in the breakfast nook. He moved toward it and picked up a photo of a smiling couple. "Are these your parents?"

"Yes."

"Do they live around here?"

She shook her head. "My mom is traveling with a children's theater troupe, and my dad died about ten years ago."

"Sorry about your dad. Why was he in the wheelchair?"

"He was a policeman. He was shot in the line of duty."

"Oh, wow. That's rough."

"Yeah." A shadow passed over her eyes. "Another cop accidentally shot him during a scuffle with an armed-robbery suspect."

Chase winced. Injuring a fellow officer was every officer's worst nightmare.

"Did that happen in Tulsa?"

She shook her head. "We lived in Dallas. But I've always wanted to move to Tulsa. My grandparents lived here and we visited a lot." She picked up a photo of a smiling elderly couple on a porch swing and handed it to him. "Their house was my favorite place in the world."

"Oh, yeah?"

She nodded, her eyes taking on a soft fondness. "Just walking through their door made you feel good. Their house always smelled like baking bread or cookies or pot roast, and someone was always laughing. I think it was such a happy place because it was so filled with love." She blew out a wistful sigh. "They were married more than fifty years, and they still acted like newlyweds. They adored each other. In fact, my grandmother died six months after Gramps passed away. The doctor said she died of a broken heart."

Chase had heard of couples like that but had never seen one at close range.

He picked up the next photo, which showed a shorter, younger-looking brunette standing beside Sammi in a graduation gown. "Who's this?"

Sammi stepped beside him, so close he could smell the fruity scent of her hair. "My sister, Chloe. She lives across town. She looks a lot different now that her hair is dyed blue."

Chase's eyebrows rose. "What does she do?"

"She's a starving artist, complete with garret."

"I wasn't aware Tulsa had any garrets."

Sammi's mouth curved in a wry smile. "Leave it to Chloe to find one. But then, Chloe has special talents like that."

Sammi slid into one of the chairs at the small breakfast nook. "So tell me about your family."

He sank into the chair across the old table. Man, he hated questions about his family. "There's not much to tell. I have a younger brother, and that's it."

"What does he do?"

The last thing he wanted to talk to Sammi about was his brother. Better to just keep his background vague, avoid mentioning his name, and move this conversation to another subject, pronto. "He's, uh, into consulting." He shifted his weight and shifted the topic. "So—do you run every morning?"

"Usually every evening. I'm not much of a morning person. I was out this morning because my life coach suggested it."

She was up-front about things, he had to give her that. Unfortunately, he couldn't return the favor. He furrowed his brow and feigned confusion. "Your what?"

"Life coach. It's like a counselor or a therapist, only more hands-on."

His glance slid over her. *Man, I'd like to be more hands-on.* Annoyed at himself for the wayward thought, he forced himself to look away.

She tipped her head and regarded him. "You know, you sound kind of like him."

Uh-oh. She was way too observant. "Lots of people tell me I sound like someone they know. The FBI trains us to sound like Joe Average, and I guess it works." He'd have to remember to talk at a higher pitch next time he spoke to her on the phone. He leaned forward and clasped his hands together on the table. "How does this coach thing work?"

"He gives me assignments, kind of like a coach gives athletes exercises. He's trying to help me build skills to deal with my problem areas."

"Which are?"

"My job, my situation with my landlord, and my social life."

"What's up with your social life?"

"Nothing. That's the problem." She grinned and tucked a stray strand of hair behind her ear. "What about yours? What do you do when you're not chasing Mafia types or jogging?"

Other than impersonate my brother? "I love to be outdoors. I have a little piece of land in the Ouachita Mountains, and I go there whenever I can."

"Oh, I've heard that's beautiful." She rose and moved to the coffeepot as it gurgled out the last drops. "Isn't there some kind of scenic highway up there?"

"Yeah." He stood, as well, and moved back to the counter. "The Talimena Skyline Drive."

"Sounds terrific. The closest I ever get to nature is my backyard or Riverside Park. I'd love to try roughing it sometime."

I'd love to take you. The words were on the tip of his tongue. What the heck was he doing? He couldn't see her if he were coaching her. He shouldn't even be here now.

She pulled a sugar bowl out of the cabinet, then turned toward him. "Are you going up there this weekend?"

Why was she asking? Was she angling for an invitation? The idea had a dangerous amount of appeal. He shook his head. "Afraid not. I promised my partner I'd help out at his dad's booth at an auto swap meet. He and his dad are vintage car buffs, and they sell old parts."

"Oh." She glanced up, her eyes wide. "I didn't realize you have a . . . partner."

The odd way she said the word jolted him. Oh, hell— she thought he meant life partner! "My FBI partner," Chase said quickly. "I don't have the, uh, other kind."

"Oh." Her cheeks turned pink. She turned away and

pulled two spoons out of a drawer. "Not that I thought . . . I mean, not that you can always tell, but until you said that, I didn't think that you were . . . I mean, I don't want *you* to think that *I* thought that you were . . ." She turned back around. The pink was spreading down her neck. "Not that there's anything wrong with that. But you didn't strike me that way when you were lying on top of me." Her blush now reached the tips of her ears. "That didn't come out right, either. I mean, when we fell, I felt a certain chemistry . . ." Her face and neck were now completely crimson. "Not chemistry. That's the wrong word. More of a vibe. I mean, I just got the sense that you were . . . that you were very . . ."

Interested? Attracted? Aroused? "Straight?" he supplied.

She nodded.

"Good read." God, but the girl could blush. They should name a paint color after the shade of her face: Mortification Scarlet. He grinned at her. "I picked up the same vibe about you."

"Um . . . yeah." Her face was the color of a third-degree burn.

He grinned as she turned to the cabinet and stood on tiptoe, reaching toward a shelf of coffee mugs. Her shorts rode up, exposing the curve of two round cheeks. Oh, yeah. There was chemistry, all right. And it was making the room suddenly very warm.

She pulled down two mugs. One said, "Don't make me get the flying monkeys," and the other said, "Cowabunga, dude." She handed him the Cowabunga cup and poured coffee in it as the dog ambled past. She overfilled it, sloshing coffee on his fingers. He jerked back, only to find the dog behind him. The dog barked, and Chase lurched forward, causing more coffee to slosh out of the cup onto his wrist. Sammi reached out to take his mug and spilled still more hot coffee—this time straight from the pot—onto his shorts.

"Ow!"

"Oh, no!" Her free hand flew over her mouth. "Are you all right?"

His family jewels were parboiled, but aside from that, he was just peachy. Chase yanked the steaming shorts away from his skin. "I'm fine," he said through clenched teeth.

Sammi set down the coffeepot, grabbed a dish towel off the sink, and dropped to her knees. "I'm so, so sorry," she said, wiping at his crotch, her fingers working up the leg of his shorts as she mopped the wet fabric.

He looked down at her, kneeling in front of him, her hands on his groin, and felt a surge of heat unrelated to the spilled coffee. Apparently the scalding hadn't permanently wilted his spinach. Stifling a groan, he grabbed her hands, stilling them. "I'll take it from here."

"Oh." Her face was the color of a radish. "Sure. I, uh—" She rapidly thrust the towel at him and backed away on her knees. "I-I'm so, so sorry."

"It's okay."

"Do you need some ice?"

Yeah, but not for the coffee burn. What he needed was to get out of here, ASAP. "No. No, thanks. I'd better get going." He handed her back the towel. "Thanks for the coffee."

"But you haven't even had any!"

"That's all right. I didn't realize how late it's gotten. I'd better run."

Away. Fast. What the hell was he doing here, anyway? He'd intended to just get a glimpse of her in the park, not come to her house. This had been a bad idea—a very bad idea. One thing was for sure: she wasn't kidding about being a hazard to men.

"I'm mortified." Her eyes were twin hazel tortes of distress. "I just can't apologize enough."

"Don't worry about it. It's no problem." But it would be, if he didn't get the heck out of Dodge. He bobbed his head and backed toward the exit. "It was nice meeting you."

With that, he turned and hauled his burning crotch out the door.

Chapter Four

At precisely 8:15, Arlene Arnette parked her white Ford Taurus next to a yellow patrol car emblazoned "Guardian Security" in the staff parking lot behind the Phelps Mansion and Art Deco Museum. The night security officer inside the vehicle flashed a jack-o'-lantern smile and rolled down his window as she climbed out.

"Mornin', Miss Arlene."

"Good morning, Ernie," Arlene said, extracting the keys to the mansion from the side pocket of her black leather purse. "Did you have a quiet night?"

Ernie bobbed his lightbulb-shaped head. "Yes, ma'am. Downright boring."

"Well, I'm sure you're ready to get home and get some sleep." Although he'd probably gotten a good portion of his night's rest while he was on duty, Arlene thought wryly. She'd pulled up more than once to find him snoring in his front seat.

"Have a nice day," she said, giving him a little wave as she started toward the house.

"You, too, Miss Arlene."

Arlene pressed her lips together as she crossed the parking lot. It was hard to remember the last time she'd had a day that qualified as nice. Most days were simply to be gotten through, and others were full of problems. Ever since Sammi had arrived—and what kind of ridiculous name was that for a woman, anyway?—the problems had multiplied exponentially.

But she wasn't going to think about that now. Early mornings, when she had the mansion to herself, were her favorite time of day. She walked up the stone steps to the service entrance, inserted her key into three separate locks, and opened the door, then punched a code into the gray security box on the wall. She waved to Ernie— she'd instructed him to always wait until she made it safely inside before he left—then closed the door and locked it behind her.

The mansion greeted her with stony silence. She'd been the curator for twenty-seven years, but every time she entered the place, it felt cold and unwelcoming—just like the reception she'd received when she'd first come here for a Phelps Oil Christmas party forty-seven years ago.

Only now, Arlene thought with satisfaction, *she* was the woman who belonged here. She walked to the butler's pantry and proprietarily adjusted the thermostat on the wall. She did that every morning, and every morning she received an inordinate amount of pleasure from it. Her lips curving in satisfaction, she turned and headed down the hallway that led to the grand foyer.

She saw it every day, but it still dazzled her. Rumor had it that a famous Hollywood director had modeled the set of a Cary Grant movie after it, and although she couldn't confirm it, Arlene was convinced it was true. The floor was white marble, inset with a dramatic black marble starburst in the center. Above the inlay hung a monolithic starburst chandelier sparkling with fifteen hundred triangular crystals. Just beyond, two staircases gracefully curved upward. Black wrought-iron banisters that replicated the starburst pattern rimmed the marble stairs. The left staircase held portraits of the elder Chandler Phelps and his wife; the right side, Chandler Junior and Justine.

As always, Arlene veered to the right. The metal banister chilled her palm as her soft-soled Easy Spirit shoes squished on the marble steps. She deliberately avoided looking at the painting of Justine but paused in front of the portrait of Chandler Jr., as she did every morning. The painting didn't do him justice. Oh, it captured his physical form—his dark hair, his broad shoulders, his neatly trimmed mustache—but it didn't capture the sparkle in his eyes, or the sensuality of his mouth, the mouth that had fit so perfectly against her own. She closed her eyes for a moment and tried to recall it. She used to be able to almost taste him when she thought about it hard enough, but more and more, she couldn't really conjure it up. The memory was like a rail station fading in the distance as a train carried her farther and farther away.

At the top of the stairs, Arlene turned right and headed down the long hallway of the master wing. Most visitors to the mansion headed straight for Justine's suite at the end of the hall. It was the opulent room, the one that drew all the oohs and ahs. Filled with gilt furniture and covered in yellow floral chintz from the walls to the elaborate canopy bed, the room was dramatic, glamorous, and ultrafeminine.

But Arlene had no use for it. She marched straight to the bedroom next to it. Compared to Justine's room, it was stark and plain and almost severe. The furnishings were over-

sized style moderne—angular and unornamented rose-
wood, with clean lines and sharp corners. The bed was
draped in dark red wool, as were the floor-to-ceiling windows. Two club chairs upholstered in a red and blue cubist
print sat across from the simple marble fireplace.

Arlene took off her shoes, unhooked the burgundy velvet rope across the door that kept the tourists at bay, and
stepped into the bedroom. She closed her eyes for a moment and inhaled deeply; sometimes when she first stepped
in here, she thought she smelled the ghost of Chandler's
aftershave or caught the faintest hint of his cigar smoke.
Not today. She hadn't smelled either in quite some time.

With a sigh, she headed for the nightstand beside
his bed and picked up his chrome alarm clock, made in
France in 1925. It still kept perfect time. Winding the key,
she pulled out the alarm button.

And then, as she did every weekday morning, she
turned to the bed, pulled back the covers—and crawled
between the sheets.

～

Sammi's brow furrowed as she punched the buzzer at
the service entrance for the sixth time. This was weird. Ms.
Arnette's car was in the parking lot, so she must be inside,
and yet the door was locked and she wasn't answering.

Maybe she was down in the basement, sorting through
Justine Phelps's clothes. While Ms. Arnette was recovering from her heart attack, Sammi had discovered trunks
and trunks of Justine's designer clothing, and as far as
Sammi could tell, they hadn't been opened in nearly thirty
years. Almost all of the female visitors to the mansion
wanted to know more about Chandler Jr.'s beautiful wife,

so Sammi had gotten approval from the museum's board of directors to put together a collection of her gowns.

When Ms. Arnette had returned to work and learned about it, she'd thrown a hissy fit. She'd ordered Sammi to stay away from the trunks and then gone to the board and protested the project. "We don't have the time or the space for a display."

"We could put it in the basement," Sammi had argued. "And I'll handle all the work. I would love to go through the trunks and catalogue the contents."

"That's a task I would need to perform myself," Ms. Arnette had said in a prickly remember-your-place tone. "I know what's valuable and what isn't." *And you won't.* Ms. Arnette clearly viewed her as incompetent, even though Sammi held a bachelor's degree in history and a master's in museology. Ms. Arnette's credentials consisted solely of having worked as Chandler Phelps's personal assistant for twenty years, but in her mind, that trumped formal education.

Sammi brushed a strand of hair from her eyes and pulled her cell phone out of her purse. Ms. Arnette might not be able to hear the doorbell from the basement, but the basement had a phone extension.

Through the door, she could hear the phone ring, unanswered.

Sammi's chest tightened. Ms. Arnette was sixty-eight—older than Sammi's father had been when he'd died of a heart attack—and she'd already had one massive coronary. What if she'd suffered another?

Sammi closed her phone and pulled her keychain out of her purse. The board had given her a key to the museum when she'd first been hired, but when Ms. Arnette had returned to work, she'd requested it back. "The more people who mess with the locks and the alarm, the greater the margin of error," the woman had said.

Sammi had politely refused to return it. "I won't use it unless I have to, but the board wants me to have it in case of an emergency," she'd said.

For all Sammi knew, this was an emergency now. She inserted the key and unlocked the first deadbolt, then saw Mrs. Arnette on the other side of the window, scurrying around the corner. The older woman unfastened the remaining locks and opened the door, her face pruned into a scowl. "Sammi! What are you doing here at this hour?"

The scowl was nothing new, but she seemed out of breath, and her usually carefully coiffed white hair had a strand sticking out on the left side. Sammi looked at her curiously. "I'm just twenty minutes early."

Ms. Arnette looked at her wristwatch. "Twenty-five minutes. That's almost half an hour. And why are you using a key? I've told you not to."

What was the deal? Most bosses would be glad to have their employees show up early—and Ms. Arnette definitely considered Sammi an employee. "I wanted to put up the new exhibit descriptions in the kitchen before our first tour arrives."

"Hmmph." Her lips pursed in displeasure, the older woman put her hand on her chest and drew a deep breath.

Sammi leaned forward, concerned. "Are you feeling okay?"

"Of course. I'm perfectly healthy." Ms. Arnette's hand fingered the top button of her blouse. "It's just that you startled me, that's all. Practically scared me to death. And I don't like our security compromised."

Using a key hardly constituted a breach of security, but

apparently it had startled the older woman. "I tried to call when you didn't answer the door."

"Yes, well, I was down in the basement."

"Do you need any help down there?"

"No, thank you. I'm perfectly capable of handling it myself."

Sammi wasn't so sure. She'd checked the clothing Ms. Arnette was discarding on the very first day and discovered that the older woman was throwing away some very valuable pieces. Sammi had subsequently directed the janitor to quietly bring all the clothing in Ms. Arnette's discard pile to her office.

Sammi nodded. "Okay. Sorry to have disturbed you."

Mrs. Arnette turned and clumped down the hall. She'd always been aloof, but she was getting more standoffish, Sammi thought as she headed to the kitchen to put new exhibit descriptions on the displays in the glass shelves.

～

Five minutes later, a faint ringing sound pulled Sammi's attention from the green glass collection. She cocked her head and listened. It seemed to be coming from upstairs. That was odd; she knew for a fact that the alarm system sounded throughout the building, not just upstairs. Maybe the janitor had left his cell phone.

But the janitor hadn't been scheduled to come last night—and Ms. Arnette insisted on cleaning the two master bedrooms herself every Wednesday. Frowning, Sammi headed up the servants' stairs, the wooden steps creaking underfoot. Sure enough, the ringing grew louder as she reached the second floor. She followed it to the master wing and into Mr. Phelps's bedroom.

It was the chrome alarm on the bedside table—the expensive JAZ alarm from the 1925 Exposition des Arts Décoratifs, the show in Paris that had originated the art deco movement.

The hair on her arm stood up. She didn't believe in ghosts, but this was a little spooky. She released the velvet rope and stepped into the room. She turned slowly, looking for evidence that the room had been disturbed. Everything seemed to be in its usual place.

She walked to the bedside table, punched in the button to silence the clock, then peered at the thin red alarm hand. It was set on 8:50.

Sammi frowned. It had to have been set this morning, because otherwise, it would have gone off last night. It was two days before Ms. Arnette's regularly scheduled cleaning day, and the woman rigidly adhered to her schedule. It was odd that she'd been in here this morning.

Oh, well. She must have noticed some extra dust or something and accidentally set the alarm clock while cleaning it.

Sammi turned to leave the room, then stopped as something else caught her eye. The corner of the red wool bedspread on the side away from the door was rumpled. Sammi walked over to straighten it. As she smoothed the cover over the pillow, she found a four-inch-long white hair—the same color and length as Ms. Arnette's hair—on the pillowcase.

That was strange. Not inexplicable, since Ms. Arnette cleaned the room, but unusual. Sammi brushed it off, then left the room, flipping off the light and refastening the velvet rope behind her.

Chapter Five

Luke? It's Sammi."

"Well, hello."

The deep voice of her life coach resonated through the phone, sending a shiver of attraction down Sammi's spine. She nudged Joe's paws aside and plopped down beside him on her living room sofa. "How's your cold?"

He cleared his throat. "It's getting better."

She adjusted the phone to her ear. "I know I'm only supposed to call you on Saturdays and Thursdays, but you told me during our first conversation that I could call anytime I needed to, and, well, I've had a rough day." She paused and drew a breath. "Do you have time to talk?"

"Uh—yeah. I have fifteen minutes until my next client calls. What's up?"

She rubbed Joe's head. The dog gave her a slurpy kiss. "I injured another man."

A beat of silence pulsed through the phone. "Oh, yeah? What happened?"

"Well, I was following your instructions, and . . ." Sammi relayed the whole messy chain of events, ending with the spilled coffee. "Why do I always do this to men I'm attracted to?"

Another pause echoed through the line. "You were attracted to him?"

"Oh, yeah."

"What, exactly, did you find attractive?"

It was oddly disturbing, talking about Chase to Luke. She uncurled her legs and rose from the sofa. Joe jumped down beside her. "Well . . . for starters, he was tall and dark and handsome." She felt attracted all over again, just picturing him. "He was a total hunk."

"A, um, hunk."

"Uh-huh. But the thing that really got me were his eyes."

"His eyes?"

"Yeah." She crossed the room and smiled, remembering them. "They were brown and kind of shaped like George Clooney's, and he had this way of looking at me that made my stomach seize up."

The life coach cleared his throat. "In a good way, I hope."

"A very good way. And it wasn't just physical. I liked other things about him, too."

"Such as?"

She stopped by the window and gazed out at the night. "He was self-confident and intelligent, and he likes to run, just like I do. He has a sense of humor, and he was easy to talk to, and . . . well, I liked everything about him. Except for the fact he's an FBI agent."

"What's wrong with that?"

"They carry guns. And people who carry guns sooner or later end up using them, and someone gets shot." She turned away from the window. "Believe me, I know. My father was a police officer, and he was paralyzed by a bullet."

"Oh, wow. That had to be tough."

"It was awful. Beyond awful. But even before he was shot, his job was a problem. Mom worried every time he went to work. When he worked nights, she used to sit up, listening to a police scanner." Sammi strode into the kitchen. "And we all had to put up with his bad moods when he got home. Mom said he dealt with crummy people and depressing things all day, so he brought all that negativity and stress home with him."

"Lots of jobs involve stress."

"I know, I know, but it's not usually life-or-death stress. And most jobs don't make people cynical and distant and curt."

"Your dad was cynical and distant and curt?"

She felt guilty admitting it. She'd loved her dad, and talking this way felt somehow disloyal. "Yeah. He didn't mean to be, but sometimes—a lot of the time—he was." She sighed and opened the fridge. "And then there was the whole law-enforcement-officer-personality thing."

"What do you mean?"

"You know—the whole authority-figure thing. A lot of cops are bossy and controlling and rigid." Sammi stared at the place where the yogurt used to be. Chloe had apparently cleaned her out.

"Sounds to me like you're kind of rigid yourself, slapping labels on an entire career field of people."

"Ouch." Was she? Maybe so. "All I know is what I've seen." She found a mandarin orange fruit cup. Closing the fridge, she ripped off the lid, opened the silverware drawer, and extracted a spoon.

"Well, you're not going to see this guy again, so it doesn't really matter."

Sammi froze, the spoon in her hand. "Who said I wasn't going to see him again?"

A long pause echoed through the phone. "Well, from what you just said, I assumed you don't plan any further contact."

Sammi stuck the spoon in the fruit, strangely upset by the thought.

"Do you?" he prompted.

"I guess not," she said with considerable reluctance. "I didn't get his number. I tried to look him up, but he's not listed in the phone directory, and when I Googled him, I found nothing. Nothing at all. Which I thought was kind of weird, but then I figured it must be some kind of FBI thing."

"Yeah. Probably so." His voice was low and almost gruff. "Let's move on to the real issue here, which is you injuring another man. What were you thinking right before you spilled coffee on him?"

"Well, right before I sloshed it on his hand, I was thinking, 'Don't spill it! Don't spill it!'"

"That's your problem, right there. Negative thoughts get negative results. Worrying about something makes you choke, and that makes it more likely to happen."

"With my track record, I have good reason to worry."

"You've got to change the tape in your head. Athletes train themselves to visualize the results they want—catching the pass, making the touchdown, kicking the ball between the goalposts. See yourself winning and that's what you'll do."

"All of a sudden you sound like a real coach."

He cleared his throat. "Yeah, well, I have a sports background."

"I know. I looked you up on the Internet." She scooped out a spoonful of tiny oranges. "I was hoping to find a picture of you."

"You were? Why?"

Was it her imagination, or was some chemistry brewing over the phone line? She was tempted to try to elicit some kind of inappropriate response from him. She leaned against the counter. "I was curious. Don't you ever wonder what your clients look like?"

"Well—unless their appearance is an issue for them, it isn't an issue to me."

"So you're not at all curious what I look like?"

He paused. "I don't, uh, think that's any of my business, unless it's something you want to address."

I'd like to address what you look like. The thought took her by surprise. What was going on with her? She hadn't been attracted to a man for months, yet here she was, having simultaneous hots for a law-enforcement officer she'd just met and a life coach she'd never seen.

"When was the first time this man-bashing problem started?" he asked.

"After I broke up with my boyfriend." She carried the fruit cup to the breakfast nook and sat down at the table. "About a year and a half ago."

"So what happened?"

"I caught him with another woman." She stared down at the orange slices, her chest heavy at the memory.

"As you said earlier, ouch."

Sammi smiled. "Yeah."

"So then you started hurting men before they could hurt you?"

"Is that what you think, too?" Sammi frowned. "My sister says that's the reason, but I don't buy it."

"Why not?"

"Because it's too corny. I can't believe my subconscious is that hokey."

~

In his living room across town, Chase started to laugh. He put his hand across the phone and caught himself. He was deliberately speaking in a slower cadence and a higher pitch than normal so that she wouldn't recognize his voice, but laughs were harder to disguise. He had to watch himself on the phone, because she was too observant by half.

He cleared his throat. "So tell me about this boyfriend. What was his name?"

"Lance."

"Lance? As in lance a boil?"

It was Sammi's turn to laugh. "Exactly like that."

"Where did you meet him?"

"In New Orleans. I moved there to work on a historic-home-preservation project after Hurricane Katrina."

Chase strode across the room and gazed out onto his terrace. "And what does Sir Lance-a-boil do?"

"He's a real-estate developer. We met at a charity fund-raiser. He was very handsome and clever and charming."

A little zing of something sharp shot through Chase. It couldn't be jealousy. That would be ridiculous. He silently listed the reasons why. One: he hardly knew her. Two: she was off-limits for a relationship. Three: she was screwed up enough to hire a life coach, and he liked women who had their act together.

All the same, hearing her describe the assets of this jerk bothered him. He paced across his living room. "So it was largely a physical attraction."

"I guess. I met him under pretty emotional circumstances. The Katrina aftermath was just enormous, and I was working all hours, and everything was chaotic . . ." Her voice trailed off. "I think I was looking for someone or something to hold on to." She paused again. "The truth is, things were never all that great physically."

The confession irrationally pleased him. "Why was that?"

Silence beat through the phone. "Well, it's kind of personal."

"If a topic makes you uncomfortable, that's usually a clue that you need to talk about it." That was always the case with suspects, anyway. The things they shied away from discussing were usually the very things that would make or break the case. "A coach can't tape a player's leg if he doesn't know where it hurts."

He paced his living room and waited. No information was forthcoming. "So were there . . . technical difficulties?" he prodded.

He heard something that sounded like a scraping chair. "Yeah." She paused. When she spoke again, her voice was barely above a whisper. "He said I wasn't sexy enough to keep him turned on."

"You're kidding."

"No. He started having problems, and—"

"He let you think it was your fault?"

"Yeah."

Chase scowled at his wall. "And you bought this bull?"

"Well . . . yeah. At the time, anyway. I've done a lot of reading since then, and now I think he had other issues, like drinking too much, and maybe feeling guilty that he was cheating on me—"

"Whoa. How soon did he start cheating on you?"

"I think it was pretty early on. Maybe even the whole time."

Chase stifled an oath. Man, this guy was a first-class a-hole.

"He wasn't the only one with technical difficulties," she continued.

Chase pulled his brows together. "You had them, too?"

"Yeah. I never . . ." She broke off. "I mean, the whole time I was with him, I never could . . ."

He read between the lines. "Never?"

"No."

"How did he respond to that?"

"He . . . didn't. I don't think he noticed."

"He just never happened to notice that you didn't get off?"

"He seemed to think I did." Her voice was low and so soft it was hard to hear. "Afterward, he'd say something like 'That was amazing,' and I'd say something like 'Mmphff,' and he'd just assume I thought it was amazing, too."

Stupid cocky bastard. "Why didn't you speak up?"

"I didn't want to hurt his feelings." She gave a mirthless

laugh. "Which is pretty ironic, considering that I started physically hurting other guys after we broke up."

"When did that begin?"

"Eight or nine months later, when I finally started dating again. A friend set me up with her brother. I accidentally knocked over a chair, and he stumbled over it. He broke a rib."

Chase winced.

"A few months later, I was climbing the stadium stairs at a football game. A woman stepped into the aisle in front of me, and I abruptly stopped. My date plowed into me, then lost his footing and fell down the steps."

"Yikes."

"Yeah." There was a rueful pause. "The next time I went out, I dropped a fork at the restaurant. My date bent down to pick it up, and I accidentally elbowed him in the eye."

It sounded as if he'd gotten off easy with just a scalded crotch. He'd better get into serious coach mode, because this gal needed some serious help.

He sat down on his couch. "In the game of life, fumbles are usually caused by nervousness, and the cure for nerves is practice. You need to build your self-confidence. So we're going to work on your assertiveness skills."

"Um . . . okay."

"Just like a quarterback calls the plays in a game, you need to call the plays in your life. So here's an assignment: I want you to go to a flea market or garage sale and buy something for half of its marked price."

"Half price? Won't an offer that low be kind of insulting?"

"That's the wrong mind-set. Don't worry about someone else's reaction; keep your eye on your goal. Focus is the key." His phone beeped. He was oddly reluctant to hang up. "That's my next client, Sammi. I've gotta go. Remember . . . to win at the game of life, you've got to know how to score. Call me at your usual time on Saturday and give me a full report, okay?"

"Okay. But I'm not sure I can afford two sessions a week on a regular basis. We haven't really discussed your fees, anyway. How do you want me to pay you?"

He had no intention of taking any money from her.

"Should I go through PayPal," she asked, "or do you want me to mail you a check?"

"We'll talk about it later. Gotta go," he said abruptly. "Talk to you Saturday."

"But—"

He hung up the phone to cut off her protest. If only, he thought as he blew out a sigh, he could cut off his thoughts about her as easily.

Chapter Six

Saturday dawned clear and unseasonably warm. Chase rose early, drove to the storage unit where Paul's dad stored his auto parts, loaded them into his Ford Explorer, then headed to the auto-swap-meet site on the far outskirts of Tulsa. He found the ten-by-ten booth marked "Maloney's Vintage Auto Parts" among the string of booths at the old flea-market site, then got to work setting up shop. He propped three 8-by-8-foot white pegboards against the back and side boards of the booth, then used hooks to hang the hubcaps on the pegboard, arranging them in neat rows, according to their make, model, and year. When he was finished, he listed them on an inventory sheet.

The last time he'd helped Paul and his dad at a swap meet, Paul had teased him about his systematic approach. "What are you doing—putting them in Dewey Decimal order? No need to be so damned particular."

That was easy for Paul to say—he'd never lived in a trailer with dirty dishes piled in the sink, roaches crawling out of the walls at night, and splinters of broken beer bottle glass hidden in the filthy carpet. When you grew up in chaos, you learned the value of order.

The overalls-clad man in the next booth glanced over as he set a yellowed box of old spark plugs on a folding metal table. He wore a ball cap that said "John Deere" and gummed a wad of chewing tobacco. "You're a friend of Maloney's kid, ain'tcha?" he asked, scratching a belly that jutted out like a sideways photo of Breadloaf Mountain.

Chase nodded. "I'm Chase Jones."

The man stuck out his hand. "Bubba Dunlap. I seen you around before. Where's Sonny and Pop?"

"At the hospital. Mr. Maloney had knee-replacement surgery."

"Oh, yeah. I remember him talkin' about that at the meet last month." He stuffed a fresh wad of Skoal in his mouth. "I've worked a lot of swap meets with the Maloneys. If there's anything I can do to help, you just let me know."

"Thanks," Chase said.

The man resumed pulling car parts out of a greasy cardboard box, and Chase finished setting up his merchandise.

Within half an hour, customers started wandering in to browse, shoot the breeze, and look over the merchandise. As Chase had noted at previous swap meets, some of the best customers were other dealers. Since they constantly recycled their merchandise among each other, it was hard to see how any of them made any money.

The Maloneys bought most of their merchandise on eBay, however, so Chase's business was brisk. By ten in the morning, he'd made as much money as some booths did all day.

"Is this a copy?" asked a man who looked like Willie Nelson sans ponytail, pointing to a 1956 Cadillac hubcap mounted to the back of the booth.

"No, sir. We only carry original parts." Chase carefully took it down and handed it to him. "Feel how heavy it is."

The man turned it in his thickly veined hands. His head bobbed on his skinny neck. "They don't make chrome like this anymore. Whatcha askin' for it?"

"Five hundred."

The man blew out a low whistle. "No way. I'll give you three."

Chase rubbed his jaw. "I could let you have it for four-fifty."

"Four."

Chase shook his head regretfully.

"Four twenty-five."

"Man, you're killin' me," Chase said. He blew out a sigh, but inside, he was high-fiving himself. Mr. Maloney would have been happy with the first offer. "That the best you can do?"

"Yep. Got a lot of other stuff I gotta buy today."

"Well . . ." Chase feigned reluctance. "All right. But don't tell anyone I let it go so low."

The man shot him a grin. "Don't worry. I won't."

Which was a guarantee he would—which was just what Chase wanted.

The man pulled a wad of bills wrapped with a rubber band out of his pocket and peeled off four hundreds, a twenty, and five. "Here you go."

Chase carefully stashed it in an envelope. In the world of swap meets, it was pretty much cash and carry. He was writing down the amount of the sale on the inventory sheet when he heard a familiar silky voice.

"Hello, Chase."

Chase jerked up his head and saw Sammi standing in front of the booth. She wore a fitted pink T-shirt and a pair of jeans, and her hair tumbled loosely around her shoulders.

His pulse spiked. He shoved his hands in his pocket and tried to act nonchalant. "Hi, Sammi. What are you doing here?"

"Well, you mentioned that this swap meet was going on, and I thought it might be a good place for my sister to find some art supplies. Chloe, this is Chase. Chase, my sister, Chloe."

Chase pulled his eyes from Sammi to the shorter woman beside her. She had Sammi's hazel eyes, but that's where the family resemblance ended. Chloe's midnight black hair had bright blue stripes, her eyes were rimmed with heavy black liner, and she wore torn black jeans and a black skull T-shirt. She extended a hand clad in a fingerless black glove and grinned. "So you're Sammi's latest victim."

Chase shook her hand, his eyebrows quirked. "Victim?"

Two bright pink spots formed on Sammi's cheeks. "I told her about the, uh, accidents," Sammi said.

"My sister only injures men she thinks are hot," Chloe said. "You should be flattered."

To Chase's amusement, Sammi shot Chloe a homicidal look, cleared her throat, and pretended her sister hadn't spoken. "Chloe's looking for some items to incorporate into her art."

Yeah, right. He wasn't buying it for a moment. All the same, he looked at Chloe and pretended to. "What kind of things are you looking for?"

"I'm not sure. I never know what I want until I see it."

"What's your medium?"

"Bowling balls."

Chase inclined his head. "Come again?"

"Her hobby is welding things to bowling balls," Sammi explained.

"It's not a hobby." Chloe shot her sister an indignant look. "It's a passion." She looked at Chase. "Mind if I look around and see if I can find something interesting to work with?"

"Not at all. Help yourself."

What about you? Chase thought, glancing at Sammi. *See anything you'd like to work with?* The blood pumped harder in his veins, even as he reminded himself that Sammi was off-limits.

Chloe wandered out of earshot.

Sammi looked at him. "How's your . . ." She hesitated, clearly looking for an appropriate word.

"Crotch?" he supplied.

Her lips curved upward. "I was going to say 'burned area.' "

Still on fire. "No damage done. How's your dog?"

"Good. I'm using the dog-training manual my life coach mentioned in our first session, and we've mastered everything in the first chapter."

"Did the chapter address how to keep your dog from strip-searching people?"

"No, but it covered sit and stay. We're currently working on 'Down, boy.'"

It sounded like a chapter Chase needed to read himself.

Sammi's gaze raked over the hubcaps hanging on the lean-to pegboard. "So this booth belongs to your partner's dad?"

"Yeah. He's always loved old cars, so when he retired, he started doing this as a part-time business."

She rocked back on the heels of her sandals. "It's really nice of you to fill in for him."

Chase lifted his shoulders. "He's a cool guy. Kind of like the dad I never had."

Her eyes fixed on him. They were amazing eyes—light olive green, with a halo of gold around the pupil. She pulled her brows together in concern. "You didn't have a dad?"

"Not one I'd want to claim." Why the heck had he said that? Something about her made him speak without thinking.

To his relief, Chloe chose that moment to amble up, holding a spiked hubcap. "How much is this?"

It was vintage Cadillac. "Five-fifty."

"That's all?" Her face lit up. "I'll take all five."

Chase shoved his hand in his pocket. "That's, um, five hundred and fifty. Dollars. Apiece."

"You're kidding." Chloe's eyes widened. "What's it made of—platinum?"

"Chrome. But they're the original of a 1959 Coupe de Ville. Now, these over here"—Chase gestured to the hubcaps at the rear of the booth—"are just twenty dollars." They were actually thirty, but what the hell—he'd pony up for the difference. Sammi had said Chloe was a starving artist.

"That's more like it," Chloe said, stepping toward them.

Following her, Chase pulled one down and handed it to her.

Chloe flipped it over. "Cute."

Chase grinned. "Not a description I've ever heard applied to a hubcap, but I'll take your word for it."

"I can make a bowling ball hat out of it." She lifted it to eye level and studied it. "Or maybe I could pull out the spikes and solder them on like hair."

"Don't let any of these car buffs hear you," Chase warned. "That's desecration talk."

Chloe turned the hubcap right-side up again. "This is great. I'll take it."

Sammi stepped forward. "What she means is, what's the best price you can give us on it?"

Oh, jeez—Sammi was going to pull her negotiating assignment on *him*. He rubbed his jaw. "I already lowballed it when I told you twenty, but I guess I can let it go for eighteen."

Sammi shook her head. "Too much. How about five?"

"Five dollars?"

"Well, she's only going to use the spokes, and it has ten. Fifty cents a spoke seems reasonable."

"No, it doesn't."

"Okay, okay. Seventy-five cents a spoke."

"Hubcaps aren't priced by the spoke."

"I'll pay the twenty, already," Chloe chimed in.

"No, you won't." Sammi took the hubcap from her sister and eyed it critically. "It has a scratch on it. This isn't worth a penny over eight dollars."

He'd been wrong about Sammi needing assertiveness training. She was as assertive as her overgrown dog. He shook his head. "Sorry, but that's just too low."

"Well, then, I'm sure there are hubcaps for sale at other booths."

"Hey, y'all, I've got some right here," called Bubba from the next booth, who'd been watching the proceedings with great interest. "I'm willin' to negotiate."

Sammi turned and shot Bubba a dazzling smile. "Terrific." She gave Chase a little wave and headed out of his booth. "It was really nice seeing you again. Come on, Chloe."

She was going to just walk away? "I can let you have it for ten," he found himself calling, even as he wondered what he was doing.

She turned back around and eyed him challengingly. "Nine and you have a deal."

What the hell. He'd already been planning on putting in the difference from his own pocket; might as well kick in a little more. "Okay. Nine."

"Thanks." She flashed a brilliant smile. "That's terrific!"

Yeah, terrific. Why had he thought she needed assertiveness training? When she dug in those kitten heels, she was tough as a tiger.

"At that price, I'll take all five of them," Chloe said.

Chase silently groaned as Chloe pulled a beaded wallet out of her purse and handed him a fifty-dollar bill. He gave her five dollars in change.

"Thanks," Chloe said, drifting over to look at Bubba's wares.

Chase started to the back of his booth to take down the other four hubcaps.

A rangy man with a buzz cut wandered up to Chase's booth. "Got a hood ornament for a '62 Impala?"

"Just a moment and I'll check."

"Go ahead and help him," Sammi said. "I'll get the hubcaps down."

Sammi strode to the back of the booth, reached up on the pegboard, and pulled on one of the hubcaps. The wall wobbled precariously, but the hubcap remained affixed to its hook.

"Hold on a moment and I'll get it for you," Chase told her.

"It's okay. I have it." Sammi grabbed hold of the hubcap again.

Oh, hell. "You need to lift it up off the hook," Chase warned. But it was too late. The pegboard shook and tilted forward. Sammi tried to steady it, but her efforts only shifted the wall's weight more off-kilter.

Chase dashed to the back of the booth, grabbed Sammi, and pulled her out of harm's way just as two hubcaps clattered loudly to the ground. He put his hands on the pegboard, hoping to stabilize it, as another hubcap rolled across the dirt floor.

The wall careened forward. A hubcap flew past his face like a UFO. Another one hit his head, and then the world went black.

～

Sammi watched in horror as the pegboard wall crashed down, trapping Chase beneath it. Her hand flew to her mouth. "Chase!" She rushed toward him on quaking legs, stumbling over hubcaps as she went.

"What in tarnation . . ." the man in the next booth exclaimed.

Oh, dear Lord, she'd done it again. She'd hurt Chase—and this time it looked serious. "I need help!" she called, tugging at the pegboard that lay across his chest.

The customer with the buzz cut rushed forward, and Bubba lumbered over as fast as his fat legs would carry him. The two men pulled the pegboard wall off Chase. Sammi crouched down beside him, her heart thumping hard. He lay slumped on the ground in an unconscious heap, blood pooling on the ground from his head.

"Is he dead?" Bubba asked. He pronounced the word like "day-id," and it took Sammi a moment to comprehend the question. When she did, she felt faint.

"Do you know CPR?" Bubba asked.

"Y-yes," Sammi said. She'd taken a first-aid course a couple of years ago, but she'd never had cause to use it.

"Yes, he's day-id, or yes, you know CPR?"

"Yes CPR. Someone call 911!" she shouted. Struggling to tamp down her panic, she tried to recall her training.

Pulse and breathing first. She checked Chase's neck and was relieved to feel a pulse strongly beating under her finger. She wasn't sure about his breathing. Better to be safe than sorry. She tilted back his head, pinched his nose, and put her mouth on his.

"Ugh," he muttered, moving beneath her.

"Oh, thank God!" She pulled back and placed a hand

on each side of his face. "Chase! Chase, can you hear me?"

His eyelids fluttered. So did her heart in her chest. Chase reached for his head and groaned. His hand came away covered in blood. He stared at it as if it were an alien object. "Wh-what happened?"

"A hubcap hit you," Sammi said, sitting back on her heels. "Lie still."

A crowd was forming around them.

He raised his head and winced. "How long was I out?"

"A couple of minutes. An ambulance is on the way."

"I don't need an ambulance." Chase struggled to sit up.

Sammi pushed him back down. "Yes, you do. You've got a pretty big cut in your head and you probably need stitches." She looked around. "Anyone got a first-aid kit?"

"I do," Bubba said. He waddled over to his front table, scavenged around under it, then waddled back, red-and-white case in hand.

Sammi's fingers trembled as she opened it and pulled out a wad of gauze. She leaned down and placed it on his head.

Chase jerked away. "Ow!"

"Hold still. I need to apply pressure to stop the bleeding."

"I'll be fine. Let me stand up."

A siren keened through the air in the distance.

"Not until the medics get here," Sammi said in her firmest voice.

To her relief, he didn't argue. She held the gauze to

his forehead as the ambulance pulled into view, the siren shrieking. It stopped in the parking lot, and two attendants bounded out of the back double doors.

"Over here!" Bubba called, waving his arm like a NASCAR flagman.

The attendants hurried over. They looked at Chase's head, asked questions, and peered into his eyes. "We need to take you in," the shorter medic said.

"No," Chase said, struggling to sit up. "I'm all right."

"You need stitches."

"Well, then, I'll drive myself to one of those doc-in-the-box places."

"You're not driving anywhere," said the medic with the gray mustache. "Your pupils are uneven, which means you have a concussion. You're gonna need a CT scan."

"But I can't just go off and leave all of this stuff."

"I'll watch your booth for the rest of the day," Chloe offered.

"I'll help," Bubba chimed in. "An' I can pack it up and haul it off and store it with my stuff. Don'cha worry about all this. Just get yourself patched up."

"My-my car," Chase mumbled. "I don't want to leave it way out here."

"I can drive it to the hospital behind the ambulance," Sammi volunteered.

Chase shook his head, then winced. "No. That's okay. I'll come get it later."

He was afraid she'd wreck it, Sammi thought with dismay. Well, who could blame him? A boulder formed in her throat. "If you don't trust me to drive it, Chloe can and I'll stay here."

He looked at her—or rather beside her; his eyes didn't

seem to quite focus—and gave her a crooked smile. "I trust you." With an effort, he reached into his side pocket, withdrew his keys, and held them out. "It's the blue Ford Explorer parked on the left side of the lot."

The weight on her chest lightened a bit, but her throat felt strangely tight. She nodded. "I'll see you at the hospital."

❧

The emergency-room doctor opened the door to the treatment room an hour and a half later, his white coat flapping. Chase's vision was so blurred that it looked like there were two of him, merging together, separating, then converging again. The doctors—correction—doctor was a tall man in his midthirties with a thin face and a congenial smile. He aimed it at Sammi, who was sitting in a chair against the wall.

Chase pulled the ice pack off his throbbing head and tried to focus. Sammi had been with him since he'd first arrived, and the truth was, he was glad she was there.

Although only God knew why. The woman was worse than the seven plagues of Egypt.

"What's the verdict?" Chase asked.

The doctor settled onto the backless wheeled stool beside the examination table, and turned toward Chase, his two faces smiling. "No sign of a fracture, but you've definitely got a concussion."

Great. Just great. Chase put the ice pack back on his head.

"You'll need to take it easy for a few days. Do you have someone to stay with you for the next twenty-four hours?"

"I don't need anyone. I'll be fine," Chase said.

The doctor frowned. "You have to be observed overnight. If you don't have someone who can watch you at home, then I'll need to admit you to the hospital."

Hell. It was a good thing he'd kept the double-vision problem to himself.

"I'll stay with him," Sammi piped up.

"Excellent." The doctor nodded approvingly and turned toward her. "You'll need to wake him every three hours during the night to make sure he can wake normally, but other than that, it's pretty much a matter of just keeping an eye on him. You'll need to make sure he doesn't fall unconscious again, isn't nauseous, or doesn't start having vision problems."

"Okay. I can handle it."

He smiled at Chase. "Looks like you're in good hands."

Yeah, Chase thought morosely. *The hands of the grim reaper.*

The stool creaked as the doctor rose. "I'll have the nurse bring you the instructions and discharge papers. We'll forward your records to your personal physician, and you'll need to make an appointment to see him in a week to get your stitches removed."

The doctor exited the room, his coat flapping like stork wings.

Sammi rose and stepped toward him. As she drew nearer, he saw two of her. "Thanks for bailing me out," he said.

"No problem. I can stay with you the whole weekend, if you like."

Oh, God—that would be the end of him. "No. Just get me home, and I can take it from there."

"You heard the doctor. I intend to see to it that you follow his orders." Her two foreheads suddenly puckered. "Is there someone else you want me to call—your mom, maybe, or a girlfriend?"

"No."

Both Sammis stood still, their four hands clasped together. "Well, if you don't want me to stay, I'll hire a private nurse."

Oh, hell. She thought he didn't want her around because she was so accident-prone. This was not the way to help her over her phobia. "No. No private nurses."

"Okay, then. I'll take you home and stay with you as long as you need me."

His head hurt too much to argue, and he'd need a ride home, anyway. They could continue this discussion later.

A middle-aged nurse with a handful of papers came into the room, looking as if she were being shadowed by a blurry Siamese twin. She handed the papers to him. "I need your signature on the release form."

It took several attempts to figure out which line was real. He finally aimed between the two and scrawled his name. His signature magically reproduced itself.

The nurse turned to Sammi and handed her the other papers, addressing her as if she were his mother or—God help him!—his wife. "You can give him Tylenol every four hours. And during the night, you'll need to wake him every three hours to make sure he can become conscious normally."

"It's not normal for anyone to become conscious every three hours during the night," Chase grumbled.

Sammi shot him a look. "It would be abnormal to continue sleeping when I'm trying to wake you up."

That was certainly a fact. His gaze locked on her long, smooth, all-the-way-to-New-York-and-back legs. Even though she appeared to have four of them, he was sure she'd have no trouble keeping him awake all night.

"For the next few days, you shouldn't make any important decisions or sign any legally binding papers. Any questions?" The nurse looked briskly from Sammi to Chase.

"Does he have any physical restrictions?" Sammi asked.

You read my mind, babe.

"He's supposed to rest. That means staying in bed today and taking it easy tomorrow and the day after. He should probably give it about a week before he resumes strenuous physical activity." The nurse headed for the door. "I'll go get a wheelchair."

Chase pulled the ice pack from his head and started to ease himself off the table. "I can walk just fine."

"Maybe so, but you're doing as little of it as possible today. And you're taking a wheelchair to the exit, or else you're not going anywhere."

What the hell; he'd do whatever was necessary to get out of here. He'd play along until Sammi got him to his apartment, and then he'd figure out a way to send her home.

Chapter Seven

Chase pulled out the keys to his apartment as Sammi stood beside him, her arm looped around his waist. She'd insisted on helping him from the car to his apartment door, even though he protested that he could make it just fine on his own. She was probably more of a hazard than a help, but she felt great, pressed up against him, her breasts warm and soft against his ribs. That blow to his head had done nothing to dampen her appeal.

Which might be a problem, since it seemed to have double-dosed his libido. He straightened and pulled away at his door. "Thanks for the ride. I can make it on my own just fine from here."

"Oh, no. You're going to follow the doctor's orders."

"It's not necessary. Really. You've done more than enough. I can manage on my own."

"I thought we settled this at the hospital." Her two sets of eyes fixed him with a determined glare. His double vision was improving, but he still saw two of everything at really close range. "I'm not leaving you alone. If you don't want me here, I'll get someone else, but you're going to have someone with you for the next twenty-four hours."

Hell. She was like a bulldog. Or maybe a boxer with a wallet. He might as well suck it up and accept the inevitable. He sighed. "I hate to put you out."

"Yeah, well, I hate that I knocked you out."

He tried to insert the key, but he couldn't figure out which of the two keyholes was real.

"Here." Taking the key from him, she unlocked the door.

"Come on in," he said unnecessarily as Sammi turned the doorknob and helped him inside.

She paused inside the doorway and looked around. "Did you just move in?"

"No. Why do you ask?"

"Because it looks like no one lives here. There's nothing on your walls or your coffee table or even your kitchen counters."

Except for the brown expandable file folder. Oh, God—even with his blurred vision, Chase could read her name on the first folder. In fact, he could read it twice. It seemed to be flashing in neon lights.

Normal. Act normal. He needed to keep his cool, assess the situation, and figure out a plan of action. Which was pretty obvious, really; he needed to get over there and snatch it up before she saw it.

In the meantime, he needed to divert her, and that meant carrying on a normal conversation. "I, uh, like to keep things neat. And I don't spend a lot of time here. And if I want to look at something, there's a great view off my balcony. Want to go see?" He turned in that direction, making her turn, too.

"I'll take a look after I get you settled. Is the bedroom in the back?"

Turning toward the bedroom meant turning toward the folder. He squeezed his arm around her and grinned down, his face scant inches from hers. "Wow. I've never known a woman so eager to get me in bed."

She did that funny blush thing. It was almost cruel, how easily he could make her face color. "You wish."

"Yeah, I do." Now, why had he said that? Sexual tension was already snaking around them like a cobra, and admitting his attraction just made it coil tighter.

He edged backward toward the kitchen counter. Sammi tightened her grip on him, apparently thinking he was woozy and weaving off course.

What the hell. He might as well play it that way. He abruptly lurched to the left and smacked his hand down on the lid of the file folder.

She nearly toppled them both over in her efforts to steady him. "Are-are you okay?" she asked breathily.

"Yeah. Just not as steady on my feet as I thought."

"We need to get you to bed."

"Okay." He scooped up the folder and tucked it under his free arm.

"What's that?"

"Files for a case I'm working on," he said.

She frowned. "You're supposed to be resting, not working. Besides, you're not supposed to make any important decisions for the next twenty-four hours."

"So I won't decide anything. I'll just read over the files."

He readjusted his arm around her back, pulling her closer, and inhaled the scent of her hair. Candy apples—

that's what it reminded him of. A strand brushed against his cheek, snagging on his five-o'clock shadow. The sudden, unexpected intimacy sent a shockwave of arousal through him as she helped him through his bedroom door.

"Here you go." She stopped beside his king-sized bed and eased him down on the black-and-white-striped comforter. He felt a sudden, irrational urge to grab her and pull her onto the mattress with him.

Instead, he set the file facedown on the floor between the nightstand and the bed. She moved to the other side of the bed and fluffed the pillows, stacking two of them together against the plain wooden headboard.

"There." She watched him lean back against them. "Can I get you your pajamas?"

"I don't have any."

"So what do you sleep in?" Judging from the way her ears turned as pink as a rabbit's, she realized the answer as soon as she asked the question. She waved her hand as if to erase the question. "Never mind. Do you have any sweatpants, or anything more comfortable than jeans?"

He started to nod. The movement made his head throb. "Top drawer of my dresser."

Sammi walked across the room, opened the drawer, and pulled out a pair of neatly folded gray sweats. She handed them to him, then regarded him with a frown.

"Your T-shirt's covered with blood, but I'm afraid you'll damage your bandage if you pull it off over your head. Maybe I should cut it off you."

His mouth quirked in a grin. "Sounds kinky, but okay."

She lifted one eyebrow. "Don't get excited. You're on your own with the pants."

"Darn."

"I'll go get you some ice while you change. Do you have any scissors?"

"Yeah. In the kitchen drawer by the stove."

She pulled the door closed behind her. He scrambled out of his jeans, folded them, and pulled on his sweats as she knocked on the door.

"You decent?" she called.

"Yeah." Physically, at least. Mentally was another story.

She stepped into the room, somehow raising the temperature of it. Her gaze rested on the jeans and socks he'd just removed, and her left eyebrow rose. "You fold your dirty clothes?"

He lifted his shoulders. "I don't like things messy."

She moved toward him and knelt on the bed. "Wow. Your mom taught you well."

The thought of his mom made his jaw tighten. "Yeah."

"Where is she, anyway?"

"She's dead."

"Oh, I'm so sorry!"

Oh, sheez. Her face held a stricken look, as if she thought it had just happened. "She died of cancer when I was fourteen," he added to clarify.

"That must have been awful," she murmured.

Beyond awful. He'd not only lost a mother, but he'd had to become one for his nine-year-old brother, because their dad raised his alcohol consumption to a new high. But why was he blabbing about his personal life? He never talked about this stuff. It only made people feel sorry for him, and he hated sympathy as much as he hated people urging him to share his pain. That blow to his head must have done more damage than he'd realized.

"Yeah, well, everyone has to deal with something. Ready to do surgery on my shirt?"

"I am if you are." Sammi smiled, but her eyes looked worried. "I promise to be very, very careful."

Given her track record, he was probably taking his life in his hands, but she needed a chance to redeem herself if she was ever going to get over her hazard-to-all-mankind mentality. "I'm not worried. I'd like to make two requests, though."

"Yes?"

"Cut the shirt at the back of my neck instead of at the front, and aim the scissors down."

"So that if it slips, I won't cut your jugular?"

He grinned. "Nothing personal."

"I understand." She moved beside him, her breasts even with his face. A hint of cleavage peeked out the V neck of her T shirt. He breathed in the fresh green scent of her.

"You must think I'm the world's biggest klutz," she said.

Actually, I'm thinking that you're the world's best-smelling woman—and I'm fighting the urge not to stare at your breasts. "Nah. Accidents happen."

"But they happen around me more than around the average person." Her fingers were warm on his neck as she lifted the fabric of his shirt.

"Well, if you're worrying about it, that makes it more likely to happen. Your thoughts program your actions."

Sammi drew back and looked at him. "Someone else just told me almost the exact same thing."

Oh, hell. If he'd made a slipup like that on an undercover operation, his ass would be grass. He feigned a blank expression. "Oh, yeah? Who was that?"

"My life coach."

"Sounds like a smart guy. Is he helping you?"

"It's too early to be sure, but yeah, I think so." She turned her attention back to his shirt, putting her breasts in his face again. "Sit really still, okay?"

"Okay." He complied to the point of not breathing. The blade of the scissors slid icily against his skin. Just when he thought his lungs were going to burst, he heard a snip.

She must have been holding her breath, too, because her breasts relaxed against him as she exhaled. The scissors clunked when she put them on the nightstand. "I'm just going to rip the fabric the rest of the way with my hands, okay?"

"Can I videotape this? I've always wanted to have a woman literally rip the clothes off my body."

She grinned. "Very funny."

"You think? I would have rated it just nominally amusing."

He was rewarded with a laugh. "I'd better get behind you to do this." She kicked off her sandals and crawled behind him on the mattress, sitting on her knees, one on each side of him. "Now sit still." The shirt ripped loudly as she pulled it. Cool air hit his back.

She scrambled off the bed. "Raise your hands over your head." She reached for the bottom of his shirt and lifted it off. "There!" she said triumphantly.

He lowered his arms and saw her gaze rest on his naked

chest. It took her a moment to raise her eyes to his face, and when she did, her cheeks were pink. "Do you have any button-up shirts?"

"None that aren't starched."

"Well, you can't pull anything over your head."

"So I'll just go without."

Her throat worked as she swallowed. "Fine." She edged toward the door. "I'll let you rest, and I'll see what I can find in the kitchen to fix for dinner."

"Good luck with that."

"Surely there's something."

"Yeah," he said dryly. "The phone for calling in a pizza."

"Well, then, I'll call Chloe and have her bring over some groceries."

"Really, Sammi—pizza's fine."

"No man I injure is going to eat pizza for dinner."

How many men had she injured before she instituted that particular rule? And how many kitchens had she burned down as a result? Voicing the questions would probably serve no good purpose, so he kept them to himself.

"Chloe needs to bring me a toothbrush, a change of clothes, and few other things, anyway." She paused at the doorway. "Do you need anything?"

Yeah. *You. Naked. Here. Now.* He squirmed uneasily. He had no business entertaining thoughts like that, but he couldn't seem to help himself. "No."

"Okay. Call me if you do." She closed the door as she left the room, leaving him to the fantasies throbbing in his wounded head.

≈

An hour later, Sammi opened Chase's front door to find Chloe on the other side, juggling two paper grocery sacks, a duffel bag, Chase's swap meet lockbox, and Joe on a red leash.

Sammi reached for the duffel bag and the dog's leash. "Thanks so much for bringing all this stuff."

"No problem."

Joe jumped on Sammi, putting his front paws on her shoulder, and licked her forehead. She patted his warm shoulder. "Good to see you, too, boy. Now get down."

Joe obediently dropped to all fours.

"Sit."

The dog complied. His stubby tail thudded on the carpet.

Chloe stared. "He actually did it!"

Sammi proudly stroked Joe's head. "I've been using that dog-training book my life coach suggested."

"Wow. Maybe you should get a training book, too." Chloe headed for the kitchen. "Only instead of learning to sit, you could learn not to hurt the hotties."

"That's what my life coach is helping me with."

"His results aren't very impressive." Chloe set the lockbox and grocery bags on the counter. "Where's the hunk?"

"In his bedroom."

"And you're out here? What's wrong with you, girl? That man is smoking!"

Sammi had to agree—especially after seeing Chase without a shirt. She'd known the man was buff, but the sight of his bare chest had practically made steam come out of her ears. Just thinking about his ripped abs brought on a fresh wave of heat.

"I'll give you this—you really know how to pick 'em." Chloe plucked a grape off the clump that Sammi pulled out of the grocery bag. "So what's the deal, Sammi—the hotter they are, the more seriously you injure them?"

"Very funny."

"I wasn't trying to be funny. I was just trying to figure out your methodology." She ate another grape. "Actually, it's a very strategic move. Get him alone, stay at his place, cook for him, then nurse him back to health. It's the perfect setup to make him fall in love with you."

Sammi rolled her eyes as she pulled a box of lasagna noodles from the grocery bag. "Like I hurt him on purpose."

"Who knows? Maybe your subconscious is actually working in your favor this time."

"You think my subconscious is demented enough to deliberately conk him out?"

"Who knows what goes on in that mind of yours?"

"I just want a normal relationship without all the inadvertent S and M." She put a package of ground meat in the refrigerator. "But not necessarily with this guy. He's FBI, Chloe."

"So?"

"He's a cop. An über cop." And Chloe knew what that meant. There was no doubt their dad had loved them, but he'd been strict and inflexible.

"Not all cops are the same, Sammi. That's like saying you're like Ms. Arnette because you're both curators."

"That's not an apt comparison. She didn't set out to be a curator; she was Chandler Phelps's personal assistant, and she was given the museum job as a reward for years of loyal service."

"Did you ever wonder exactly what services she performed?"

Sammi had heard rumors, but she'd never taken them seriously. Ms. Arnette was too stiff and stodgy and straitlaced to be anyone's mistress. Besides, Chandler Phelps's wife had been an acclaimed beauty, which meant Mr. Phelps apparently went for the glamorous type. Nothing about Ms. Arnette fit the description. Sammi shook her head. "No way. I doubt the poor old thing has ever even been kissed. Which is really sad, when you think about it."

Chloe ate another grape. "Sad would be you ignoring this hunk because of some stupid anticop prejudice."

"I can't believe that you, of all people, are saying this to me. You don't like control freaks any more than I do."

"Yeah, but not all cops are control freaks. And besides, you have no room to talk."

"What do you mean?"

"You're pretty controlling yourself, always trying to fix everything for everyone."

Sammi gazed at her, wounded. "I just try to help."

Chloe raised an eyebrow. "Dad thought he was helping, too."

Unbidden, her father's voice echoed in Sammi's head.

You need to bring up your grade in math. Never mind that it was a B, the first one she'd gotten in three years.

In the real world, second place is the same as losing. You need to practice harder. Never mind that a sprained ankle had kept her out of training two weeks before the track race.

It's ten-oh-two, and I told you to be home by ten o'clock. You need to learn the importance of punctuality, so you're grounded for a month. Never mind that according to her watch, she was three minutes early.

Chloe plucked another grape and leaned against the counter. "I think you're worrying about nothing. From what I saw, this guy is nothing like Dad. And he seems a big step up from the wimps and losers you usually date."

"I don't just date wimps and losers!"

"Oh, come on. You find men who are projects, not partners."

There was no denying that she didn't have a great track record. She'd dated a guy in college who was in his ninth year of a four-year degree because he couldn't decide on a major. She'd gone out with a moody pharmaceutical sales rep who'd turned out to be addicted to his own samples, and a stockbroker who always forgot his wallet, so she ended up paying for all their dates.

And then there had been Lance. Just the thought of him made her feel small and somehow defective.

"Lance seemed normal," Sammi ventured.

"Yeah. Until you discovered he was a cheating dirtbag."

Which had hurt—really hurt. Truth be told, it had destroyed her self-confidence.

Chloe opened Chase's refrigerator and stared inside. "I don't think you should write this guy off just because he's in law enforcement."

"Yeah, well, there's more baggage that comes with the job than just the enforcer mentality." Sammi pulled a carton of ricotta cheese from the grocery sack. "Remember how Mom used to listen to the police scanner every time Dad was at work? She spent her life worrying that something would happen to him." It was not a lifestyle Sammi wanted for herself.

"Yeah. But then, Mom was always a nervous Nellie."

"As it turned out, with good cause."

The memory of the awful day their father had been shot hung in the air between them. She and Chloe had been at high school when their ashen-faced grandmother had arrived with the news and taken them to the hospital. In her mind's eye, Sammi could still see her mother's tear-streaked face in the fluorescent lights of the ICU waiting room, hear the beeps and swooshes of the medical equipment keeping him alive, picture her father's tube-riddled body, lying helpless and unmoving on a hospital bed.

Chloe closed the refrigerator door. "That was a freak accident."

"It's an occupational hazard, and you know it." Sammi folded the paper bag. "But I don't know why we're even talking about it, because it's a nonissue. Chase thinks I'm a bigger health hazard than Typhoid Mary."

Chloe's mouth curved in a knowing grin. "From the way he looked at you at the swap meet, I think he'd love to catch what you're carrying."

The thought made her heartrate kick up a notch. "You think?"

"Yeah, I do."

Sammi knew it was illogical, but as she bent to stash the sack under the sink, she couldn't help smiling.

～

"This is really good." Chase looked up from the plate of lasagna, sautéed green beans, and Caesar salad he was balancing on a lap tray. "Delicious, in fact."

Sammi smiled at him from her perch on the edge of the bed. "Don't sound so surprised."

"I'm not." Okay, well, he was. The scents wafting from the kitchen for the last hour had made his mouth water, but he hadn't really expected this. "Where'd you learn to cook like this?"

"From my grandmother."

"The one who lived in Tulsa?"

Sammi nodded. "Chloe and I stayed with her and Granddad every summer. They had the coolest little art deco home."

"So that's where you got your interest in all things art deco."

Sammi nodded. "My grandfather's dad was a stonemason, and he helped build some of Tulsa's landmark art deco buildings. He may have actually worked on my house, because he did some projects with the architect who designed it."

"Wow. That's cool." No wonder she was so attached to the place.

"Yeah. Anyway, after my grandparents died, their house was sold. Within a year, the whole neighborhood was torn down for a strip mall. And that's when I got interested in recent history, and the importance of preserving it." She took a sip of iced tea, then set down the glass. "What about you? Were you close to your grandparents?"

He shook his head, then winced as his wound throbbed. "I never knew either set of them." His father had been disowned by his parents before Chase was born, and his mother's parents had died when he was an infant.

"So what did you do in the summers?"

A picture of his family's rusted mobile home formed

in his mind—the hole in the front screen door, the rancid smell of his father's cigarettes and spilled beer, the windows lined with aluminum foil so his dad could sleep off hangovers in the dark. He and his brother had spent as little time there as possible. They'd played broomball on the pot-holed asphalt road, tossed a football back and forth in the pasture behind the trailer park, and built a fort in an old oak tree near the dump. "I mainly watched my little brother while my mom worked."

"What did she do?"

"She was a waitress." The next question was going to be about his dad, and he didn't want to go there. He was about to steer the conversation back to her cooking when Luke's cell phone rang.

"I'll get it," Sammi said, reaching forward.

Chase put out his hand, stopping her. "No!" It had to be Horace. If Sammi answered and Horace asked to speak to Luke, Sammi would put two and two together. The fact that Jones was such a common last name and she didn't know his brother's first name were the only things preventing her from figuring out that his brother was her life coach, as it was.

Except he wasn't. Chase was. But she thought Chase was Luke. Man, what a tangled mess this was!

Releasing her hand, he picked up the phone. "I'm expecting a call from my partner about a case. I'll need to talk to him privately." The phone rang again in his hand.

"Oh. Of course." Sammi picked up his dinner tray as she rose, then placed it on the opposite nightstand.

"Thanks," Chase said as she headed for the bedroom door.

"No problem."

Chase waited until she'd closed the door behind her, then swung his feet off the bed and opened the phone.

"Coach?" Horace's reedy voice sounded through the receiver.

"Hi, Horace. How are you?"

Horace proceeded to tell him. Chase walked to the far side of the room and sank onto the floor beside the bed to ensure that Sammi couldn't hear him through the wall, then spent twenty minutes listening to Horace go on and on about his mother's freakishly precise dishwashing ritual, which she insisted he follow.

"So, Horace," Chase said when he finally managed to get a word in edgewise. "How did your assignment go? Did you look for an apartment?"

"Yes, but that created a whole other problem. Mom found an extra newspaper in my car, and she went ballistic. She ranted and raved about waste and slovenliness and how she'd thought she'd raised me better."

"What did you do?" Chase asked.

"That thing you told me to do a few months ago."

Chase thumbed through the thick sheaf of papers in Horace's file. He no longer saw two of everything—it was more like one and a half—but his eyes still couldn't focus well enough to read Luke's hand-scrawled notes. "I've, uh, told you lots of things," he said warily. "Which one do you mean?"

"The thing where I pretend I have safety guards all around me, and Mom's words just bounce off them, and I mentally tell myself 'Eye on the goal, eye on the goal' over and over."

Man, his brother doled out some lame advice. "That works for you?"

"Well, I like to substitute the words 'Na na na na boo boo, Na na na na boo boo.' And yeah, it works for a few minutes, but then it wears off."

"When it wears off, that's when you need to walk."

"Walk? Walk where?"

"Away. To another room. Out of the house. Anywhere she's not."

"But-but I can't do that." Horace's voice rose an octave in alarm. "How would I do that?"

"You'd say, 'I've got to go' or 'Thanks for sharing' and then you'd get up and walk away."

"But—where would I go? I live there. I'd have to come back, and when I did, she'd start in all over again."

"Well, then, you could leave again."

"But . . ."

Chase squinted down at his brother's notes, then covered one eye. *Don't push him,* he managed to read. *Assure him he doesn't have to do anything he's not ready to do.* "Just think about it, Horace. Just start considering the possibility."

With one eye still closed, Chase glanced at his bedside clock. Just five more minutes—thank God. "So did you come up with another rap?"

"Yeah."

"Well, lay it on me."

Horace slipped into a Snoop Dogg voice and a cheerleader beat:

I went out looking for a crib of my own,
A place where I could hang and just be alone
I found a place that was really the bomb

But I couldn't rent it till I dealt with my mom.
Bazoom chock-a-lock-a-lock, bazoom chock-a-lock-a-
*   lock, bazoom, bazoom, bazoom!*

Horace paused and shifted back to his normal voice. "That's as far as I got."

"It's a great start, Horace. I can't wait until you finish it."

"Yeah, but there's a problem. I can only rap about things I can imagine, and I can't really imagine standing up to my mom."

"You're getting there," Chase reassured him. "Rap about what you want your life to be like, and it'll help you make it happen." He covered his eye and glanced back at his brother's notes. "This week, I want you to talk to the property managers at two of the apartments you picked out."

"Talk to them?" His already-high voice went up to a squeak. "You mean, on the phone?"

"Yeah."

"Oh, gee—I don't know if I can do that. What will I say?"

"You'll ask about the apartments. How much do the utilities run a month? Does the apartment complex have a workout room? That kind of stuff."

"Oh, golly. I don't want to bother anyone."

"You wouldn't be bothering them. They *want* people to call. That's why they run ads, Horace."

"But-but . . . They'll want me to come look at them, and I don't think I can."

"You don't have to right now. Just make a couple of phone calls."

"Well . . ."

A beep sounded in Chase's ear, indicating he had another incoming call. Oh, Christ—he hoped like hell it wasn't Sammi calling from the other room. Surely she'd skip her session since she wasn't home, wouldn't she? But in the pit of his stomach, he knew otherwise.

"Our time's up, Horace. This is my next client. I'll talk to you next week."

He drew a deep breath, clicked the receiver, and heard Sammi's soft voice pour over him.

"Luke? It's Sammi."

Damn. He could see her out his sliding glass door, stepping onto the balcony that ran from the living room to his bedroom, her cell phone to her ear. At any moment, she could turn and see him, and it wouldn't take much in the way of lip-reading skills to figure out he was talking to her.

He scrambled to his feet and strode to the bathroom, closing the door behind him and turning on the shower so she wouldn't hear him through the wall.

"Hi, Sammi." He deliberately raised his voice and slowed the cadence of his speech. "How are things going?"

She paused. "You sound like you're in a rainstorm."

Hell. She was hearing the shower. And since his area code was Tulsa, a rainstorm didn't make sense. He paced the small room. "I, uh, have a fountain in my backyard. So how are things going?"

"Not so great." A forlorn sigh echoed through the phone. "I hurt Chase again."

"Oh, yeah?" Even as he said it, his conscience prickled. "Tell me about it."

She filled him in on the events of the day. "And now I'm at his apartment, and I think he has a girlfriend."

What? He made a deliberate effort to keep his voice calm. "What gives you that impression?"

"Well, his phone rang while he was eating dinner, and I started to answer it, and he practically knocked it out of my hand to grab it himself. He told me he was expecting a call about a case and he needed to talk in private, but he looked funny when he said it. Now he's been in there for more than thirty minutes, talking in really low tones."

Chase sat on the bathroom floor, his back against the tub. "If he has a girlfriend, why isn't she there with him instead of you?"

"She must live out of town. The FBI's field office is in Oklahoma City, and Chase goes there all the time, so maybe she lives there." She sighed. "Now he's in the bathroom, and I think I hear the shower. He probably needed to cool down after talking to her."

Oh, jeez—did she think he was in here *wanking?* Chase dropped his forehead to his knees, then jumped as he hit his wound.

"I don't know why I care," she continued. "I don't want to get involved with someone as rigid and stodgy as he is, anyway."

She thought he was rigid? And *stodgy?* He raised his head. "What makes you think he's like that?"

"Well, his place is as sterile as the Skylab, I found three to-do lists in his Explorer, and the hubcaps at his swap-meet booth were alphabetized. Plus he folds his dirty clothes."

What's wrong with that? he started to ask, then realized it would sound defensive. He decided to backtrack the conversation. "I thought you told me he didn't have a girlfriend."

"He could have lied. That's what men do."

"Wow. Not too jaded, are you?"

"I guess I kind of am."

"Did you even consider the possibility that he was talking about work, like he said?"

"No. Not really."

"So your knee-jerk reaction is to assume he's lying?"

She seemed to ponder that. "My knee-jerk reaction is to be cautious and avoid rejection."

"What makes you think he'd reject you?"

"Because I keep hurting him, for starters. Why would he want to hang around someone abusive?"

She didn't have the first idea about abusive behavior. "You had some accidents. That's not the same as abuse."

"Well, it's made him wary of me. You should have seen the way he looked at his dinner plate—as if he suspected I'd poisoned his food. But it's more than that. He acts kind of standoffish." She paused. "He probably finds me as boring as my last boyfriend did."

"The cheating boyfriend?"

"Yeah."

"How did you find out he was cheating?"

She hesitated. The silence stretched out until he thought she wasn't going to answer. "I caught him with another woman," she finally said. "In *my* apartment." Another pause. "In *my* bed."

"Yikes."

"Yeah." She blew out a sigh. "I'd given him a key to my place so he could take care of my cats while I was on a business trip. I came home early and walked in, and there he was, in my bed, with a skinny blonde."

"Oh, wow. You must have felt like . . ." He hadn't used any sports terminology tonight; he'd better haul some out. "Like you'd been tackled by a three-hundred-pound linebacker."

"Yeah," she said glumly. "With a gorilla on his back."

"Why did he bring a woman to your place?"

"Because my apartment looked like a woman lived there, and he wanted her to think he was married."

Chase frowned. "Why would he want that?"

"So she wouldn't expect a real relationship."

"Wow. What a fine, upstanding guy."

"Yeah." Sarcasm dripped from the word. She was silent a long moment, then drew a shaky breath. When she spoke again, her voice sounded small and wounded. "He told me he needed to be with other women because I was boring in bed."

What an a-hole. Anger, hot as the steam wafting from the shower, boiled inside of Chase. "And you believed him?"

"Well, apparently it's true. I mean, I obviously wasn't enough for him." She paused again. "And ever since, I've been afraid of getting close to a man and being found . . . lacking."

"You're not lacking anything!"

"How do you know? You've never even seen me."

Oops. Big oops. "Because a woman can't be boring in bed unless she's with a man who can't excite her. And from what you told me previously, Sir Lance-a-boil was a dud in that department." Chase rose to his feet, too worked up to sit still. "I can't believe this jerk. He tried to shift the blame for his cheating onto you, and you let him get away with it. It ticks me off that you're letting him have so much power over you."

"It does?"

"Yeah. He got caught with his pants down—literally— and he tried to spin the situation so it's your fault."

"I never thought of it quite like that."

"This creepoid made you afraid that something's wrong with you, and now you keep running men off so you won't have to face your fear."

"Maybe so." A sniff sounded through the phone.

"No maybe about it." Hell—this had to stop. He had to help her get over this. He paced the small bathroom. "Sammi, you've got to rebuild your confidence. This whole thing has just become one big, bad, self-perpetuating cycle, and you've got to stop it."

"How do I do that?"

"You have to get back in the game. You have to spend some time with a guy and not hurt him."

"But I hurt every man I'm interested in."

"So maybe you need to find one you're not all that interested in, and practice."

"But I don't hurt men who are just friends."

Chase jammed a hand through his hair, then winced as he hit his bandage. "So find a man you just sort of like."

"Where am I going to find a guy like that?"

He should encourage her to go to a singles bar, or meet someone online, or ask a friend to fix her up. But that wasn't what he found himself saying. "You've already said you don't want to get involved with this FBI guy because he's a law-enforcement officer."

"Well, yeah. But he's not interested in me. After I leave here, he's not going to want to see me."

Was she nuts? "Why do you think that?"

"I've injured him to the point where he wants nothing to do with me."

"You don't know that for a fact. Act as if you think he's interested, and see what happens."

"You mean, tonight?" She sounded alarmed.

"Sure."

"But he's hurt, and . . ."

He broke in. "Sammi, do you want to break this pattern of behavior, or not?"

"Of course I do."

"So let's establish some objective criteria for measuring your progress. If you see him twice and don't hurt him, will you be convinced you've broken this streak?"

"I—I'm not sure."

"Well, what if you saw him three times?"

"I don't know. Maybe."

"We need to set a definite goal, Sammi. You have to give a concrete answer." He paced the tiny bathroom— three steps forward, then three steps back. "If you go out with Chase three times in a row and don't injure him, will you be convinced you're no longer a hazard to mankind? Yes or no?"

"Well . . . yes."

He blew out a relieved sigh. "Great. So now we have a goal."

"But . . . if I'm only seeing him to prove something, that isn't fair to him, is it? I don't want to just use him."

Use me, baby, use me. "You won't be," he assured her.

"This isn't going to be anything heavy. Think of it as dating light."

"Dating light?"

"Yeah. Nothing heavy or physical. You know—the preliminary stuff, when a couple is just kind of checking each other out. They go out a few times, they flirt, they don't really click, and they stop seeing each other. No harm, no foul."

"But what if he doesn't want to go out with me?"

I don't think that'll be a problem. "There you go again, jinxing yourself with negative thinking. Just hang out with him tonight and think positive thoughts. And stop worrying about hurting him."

"That's kind of like telling me not to think about a pink elephant."

He searched his mind for one of his brother's lame phrases. "The only way to score is to keep your head in the game."

"What?"

"Focus on the moment. Don't get all caught up worrying about what might happen later."

"Oh. When you said something about scoring, I thought you meant something else."

He grinned and shook his head, then flinched when it hurt. "You can do it. Call me tomorrow and let me know how our game plan worked."

"Wait! We never discussed your fee."

Chase clicked a button on the phone, simulating another incoming call. "There's my other line—I've got to go." He hung up fast, then leaned back against the sink and closed his eyes.

What the hell had he just done?

Chapter Eight

The evening wind ruffled Sammi's hair as she clicked off the phone. Wrapping her arms around herself, she walked the length of the terrace and peered through the window of Chase's bedroom. The bathroom door was still closed. Sammi pulled her brows together. What if he'd gotten dizzy and passed out in the shower?

She headed back inside, crossed the living room, and knocked on Chase's bedroom door. "Chase?" No answer. She turned the knob, walked into the bedroom, and rapped on the bathroom door. "Chase? Are you okay?"

"Yeah," he called. "I'll be out in a moment."

Relieved, Sammi wandered over to his bed, fluffed the pillows, and straightened the covers. As she started to pick up his dinner tray from his nightstand, her gaze fell on the brown expandable file folder on the floor beside it. What the heck was in it? He'd acted as if the file were top secret.

Maybe she could take a quick peek while he was in the shower. What could it hurt? It wasn't like she was going to sabotage an investigation or anything.

She started to reach for the folder, then jumped as the bathroom door creaked open. She whipped around. Chase strode into the bedroom, a cloud of steam behind him, wearing only a towel slung low around his hips.

Good gravy. He looked like an underwear model, minus the underwear. His legs were toned and dusted with dark hair. His stomach and chest were pure chiseled muscle. He stopped in his tracks and stared at her.

She rapidly picked up his dinner tray, nearly knocking over his glass of iced tea in the process. "Uh, hi." Good Lord, but he was hot. It wasn't just the steam wafting out the open bathroom door that was making her flush. "I-I was just straightening up," she stammered. "I'll just go in the other room and—and let you get dressed." Swallowing hard, she scurried from the room, closing the door behind her.

~

She was rinsing the last plate under the kitchen faucet and wishing she could rinse the sight of Chase's nearly naked body from her mind when he sauntered out of the bedroom a few moments later, wearing nothing but blue sweatpants.

She quickly turned to the dishwasher and jammed the plate between the racks, hoping to hide her heated face. "You're supposed to be in bed." She busied herself locating the dishwashing detergent under the sink, then poured it into the dishwasher.

"I'm supposed to rest." He draped his large frame on the sofa. "I can do that on the sofa just as well as in bed, can't I?"

"Well . . . I guess." She closed the dishwasher door and switched it on.

"I've got some movies from Netflix." He patted the sofa beside him. "Come help me pick one out."

His eyes were inviting, and the invitation seemed to extend to more than movies. Her mouth suddenly went dry. Her coach had told her to act as if he were interested. The funny thing was, it suddenly seemed like he really was. Oh, dear—the evening now felt like a date, which meant she was likely to do something disastrous.

Don't worry about hurting him, her coach had said. *Keep your head on the block.* Or was it on the field? Maybe on the game. She wasn't very good at sports terms, but it was something like that, and it meant focus on the moment. And she knew she wasn't supposed to worry about scoring.

She focused on walking from the kitchen to the living room and carefully sitting down, without tripping or falling or bopping him on the head. She sat on the opposite side of the sofa from him, but it still felt disconcertingly close.

"Scoot over so you can pick a movie," he said.

She inched nearer. His left hand touched hers as he passed her the stack of DVDs. She swore she felt a sizzle.

She sorted through the discs. "How about this one?" She held up *One Flew Over the Cuckoo's Nest.* It somehow seemed appropriate.

"Great. That's one of my all-time favorites."

He was fond of crazy people. That boded well.

He reached for the DVD and started to rise. She put her hand on his upper arm to stop him, then immediately pulled it back. There was that sizzle thing again—plus his biceps were hard and his skin was warm, and touching his naked arm seemed entirely too intimate. "I'll do it," she said. "You're supposed to be resting, remember?"

She crossed the room and inserted the disc and then turned around to see him gazing at her, as if the entertainment had already begun and he was enjoying the show. Instead of looking away when she caught him, he smiled unapologetically. As the movie started, her pulse raced like the lunatics making a break for it as she reseated herself at the far end of the couch.

He gave her a slow grin. "I have a concussion, not cooties." He patted the sofa. "Come on over."

Sammi edged closer. He stretched his right arm across the back of the couch, his fingers just inches from her head. He wasn't touching her, exactly, yet she swore she could feel his body heat. It kept her hyperaware of him throughout the movie.

When the credits rolled, Chase turned toward her. "What do you want to watch now?"

You. Sammi's heart thudded hard against her chest. *Easy, girl,* she told herself. He was for practice only. She made a show of checking her watch. "I don't think you're supposed to sit up all night watching movies. It's time for bed."

"Wow." His eyes held a teasing gleam. "Don't know that I've had a woman ever proposition me so bluntly."

To her chagrin, Sammi felt her face flame. "That was a medical suggestion, not a proposition," she said dryly.

"Pity."

"Off to bed." She waved her hand.

"By myself?"

The heat in her face went up a degree. "Yes, by yourself."

"What will you do?"

She placed her hand on the sofa. "I'll just stretch out here."

"I have a king-sized bed," he said with a suggestive grin. "We could share."

"I don't think so."

His lips curved up. "I'm wounded. I'm perfectly harmless."

He didn't look harmless—not with that cheeky grin, and his naked chest so close she could smell the soap on his skin. He looked virile and healthy and all too ready for something besides sleep.

"No chance."

"Well, you'll need to help me back to bed."

She started to remind him that he'd walked into the living room all by himself, then decided that would be uncharitable. He was hurt, after all, and it was her fault. "Are you sure you want to risk it? I haven't been exactly good for your health."

"I'll risk it if you will."

She put her arm around his naked back. He wrapped his arm around her waist in a way that felt all too intimate and not at all impaired. His skin was warm under her hand, his insanely buff chest hard against the side of her breast. His five-o'clock shadow grazed her forehead as she walked beside him into the bedroom.

"Here you go," she said, releasing him at the side of the bed and quickly stepping back. "I'll wake you in three hours to make sure you're okay." She turned to leave.

He caught her hand.

"Thanks for all your help."

"No problem. It's my fault you're hurt."

"It was an accident, nothing more."

Her mouth went dry and her mind went blank. "Well—good night." She started to extract her hand from his, but he squeezed her fingers.

"Hold on—you'll need a blanket." He leaned forward and handed her the soft red one folded at the foot of the bed. "And a pillow." He gave her the one next to his on the bed.

"Thanks." There was something unnervingly intimate about sharing his bed linens. The pillow smelled like him—clean and soapy and masculine.

"Do you need an alarm?" he asked.

"Nah. I'll use my cell phone."

He sat there and looked at her, his gaze holding her like a chain. Something more seemed to be required. If he'd been anyone else, she would have kissed him on the cheek, but she was afraid he'd misinterpret it. Heck—she was afraid *she'd* misinterpret it.

"Well, good night. Let me know if you need anything." She fled the bedroom, closing the door behind. She ducked into the half bath and changed into the red T-shirt and navy stretch shorts that Chloe had brought, then washed her face, brushed her teeth, and settled on the sofa. The leather was clammy against her skin. Sammi tossed and turned for more than an hour. She must have finally dozed off, because she awakened to her buzzing phone at 2:00 a.m.

She turned it off, peeled back the blanket, and padded into Chase's bedroom. The dim light through the sliding glass door lit the room in a pale glow. He lay on his side, facing away from her. "Chase," she said softly.

He didn't move. The mattress gave as she sat on it. "Chase."

Still nothing. Worried, she touched his arm. "Chase, you need to wake up. " He remained unresponsive.

Alarm shot through her. What if he weren't just asleep, but unconscious? She scooted closer and leaned over him. "Chase—are you okay?"

He shot up like a missile, knocking her off the bed. She stumbled backward, bumped into his dresser, richocheted off it, and fell against the open bathroom door. Starlight burst across her eyes.

"Holy cow—Sammi, are you all right?"

The back of her skull hurt like the dickens. She opened her eyes to find him out of bed and leaning over her, his brown eyes worried. She touched the back of her crown, and felt something wet.

"Let me see." He flipped on the light, then crouched down beside her. He placed a hand on either side of her face and gently tilted her head. "You're bleeding."

"I'm fine."

"Sit tight." He strode into the bathroom, then returned with a damp washcloth and a first-aid kit.

She sat up, holding her head, feeling like a moron, and struggled to her feet.

He put his arm around her and helped her to the bed. "Sit down."

She sank to the edge of the mattress. He angled the flexible metal arm of the bedside task light toward her. His eyes were somber as he dabbed at her head. "The cut's superficial, but you've got a big lump. You should probably get it looked at."

"No." Sammi tried to shake her head, but the movement made her head throb.

"You made me go to the emergency room."

"Yeah, but I didn't lose consciousness, and I don't need stitches." She'd be darned if she'd go to the emergency room for the second time in the same day.

His brows pulled together in a frown. "Well, hold this and put some pressure on it. I'll go get you some ice."

"I can get it." She started to stand. "You're the one who's supposed to be taking it easy."

"But you're the one who's currently bleeding." His stern look squelched any further protest. "Don't move."

He returned a moment later with a plastic bag full of ice, as well as a couple of packages of gauze. "Let's see how you're doing."

He took the washcloth off her head and examined the cut. "The bleeding's stopped. I'll bandage it up, and then you can put ice on it." He placed a square of gauze over the wound high on the back of her head, then looped gauze around her head twice, wrapping it across her forehead like a sweatband. He tied it, then leaned back and grinned. "You look like someone from an eighties workout video."

"Thanks a lot," she said dryly.

"You're welcome." He took the bag of ice and put it back on her head. "So how do you feel?"

"Like an idiot."

"Are you dizzy?"

Only when you look at me like that. "I'm fine." She started to rise. "Well, I'll go back to the sofa and let you get some sleep."

He stepped in front of her, blocking her path. "You're not going anywhere. Scoot over."

"What?"

He waved his hand, motioning her to the other side of the bed. "You need to be awakened every three hours to make sure you're okay, too. I'll set the alarm and we'll check on each other."

"This is ridiculous."

"No kidding. Scoot on over."

She slid to the far side of the bed.

"If it makes you feel better, we can put a pillow between us." He picked one up and plopped it beside her, then slanted her a grin. "Maybe we've stumbled onto a new medical protocol—the concussion buddy system. Hospitals everywhere will use it as a cost-cutting measure."

"I wouldn't want to do this in a hospital setting."

"Me, neither. I'd probably get buddied with a flatulent truck driver named Gus."

Sammi laughed.

He adjusted the covers. "I promise I didn't do this just to get you in bed with me."

She tried to keep her tone light, but her racing heart made it difficult. "Are you sure?"

"Well, I can honestly tell you I didn't do it consciously. I can't vouch for what shenanigans my subconscious might be up to."

Wow—that was odd. She turned her head and looked at him. "My sister and I were just talking about that. And my life coach and I talked about it the other day."

He grew very still. "Oh, yeah?"

"Yeah. About how the subconscious sometimes has an agenda that we don't consciously know about."

"Hmm." He carefully put one arm behind his head. His biceps formed a round mountain on the pillow. "What's your subconscious's agenda?"

She was afraid to even tell him her conscious one. She rolled over and lay on her side. "Right now it wants to get some sleep."

"Okay." He leaned over her to set the alarm. Her breath caught in her throat as he hovered over her, his naked chest close to hers. His body heat seemed to scorch her. She held her breath until he pulled back.

"Do you need anything before I turn off the light?" he asked. "Tylenol, a glass of water?"

A cold shower. "No. I'm fine."

"Okay. Good night."

He flipped off the light. The darkness was jarringly intimate. In a few moments her eyes adjusted enough to realize they weren't in total blackness. Soft yellow light still gleamed through the sliding glass door to the terrace.

She glanced over at Chase. He was turned away from her, his naked back exposed. She could see the muscles in his shoulders, the slope of his biceps. She closed her eyes, but the image of his body seemed imprinted on the inside of her eyelids.

She tried to divert her thoughts. She counted sheep. She went through the multiplication tables. She mentally named the seven wonders of the world, then tried to name the seven deadly sins. She could come up with only five—the last one being lust. She lay there, aroused and restless, listening to him breathe, burning with deadly sin number five.

∽

The sheets rustled and the mattress bounced again as Sammi once more flipped over. Chase opened his lids to find her gazing at him.

She started. "I didn't mean to wake you."

"You didn't." Because he'd never been asleep. The woman moved more than a nest of rattlers.

"I'm having a hard time going to sleep."

"I noticed." He rolled onto his back and folded his arms behind his head, careful not to jar his head wound. "What's on your mind?"

She moved onto her back, as well, carefully placing the pillow under her neck to protect the sore spot on her head. "I'm thinking how odd it is that we're lying here in bed together and I really don't know all that much about you."

It was even odder than she imagined. "What do you want to know?"

"Basic stuff—like about your family and why you're an FBI agent, and, well . . ." She paused, and her eyes cut toward him. "I don't even know if you have a girlfriend."

Sheez—did she still think he'd been wanking in the shower? The thought made him shift uneasily onto his side and prop his head on his elbow. "I thought we covered all that when we first met."

"We covered married. I'm not sure if we covered dating."

"I thought we covered both. Why the sudden concern?"

"Because I'm lying here in bed with you." She paused a moment. "And I wondered if there's anyone out there who might be upset by that fact."

Someone who might walk through the door and find them, like she'd found that jerkoff she'd been dating. But he wasn't supposed to know about that. "No. I'm not seeing anyone." He'd better ask her, too. "You?"

"No." She shifted onto her side and propped up on an elbow, facing him. "So why aren't you married?"

"I haven't met the right woman."

"Did you ever think you had?"

"I guess I came close a time or two."

"What happened?"

The same thing that always happened. "She wanted to move things to the next level, and when she pushed for that, I realized I couldn't see myself growing old with her."

"Why not?"

"Nobody has met the criteria."

Her eyes widened. "You have *criteria?*"

He creased the fold of the sheet. "Well, yeah."

"Is this all written out, like a job description?"

The amused tone in her voice made him defensive. "Hey, everyone has certain things they're looking for in a significant other."

"So it *is* written out!"

He failed to see what was so funny about it. "I happen to believe that choosing a life partner is serious business. It ought to be thought out logically and rationally."

"Love isn't always rational. Sometimes the heart knows things that the head doesn't."

"I don't believe that."

"Well, I do. My grandparents had the happiest marriage I've ever seen, but they came from totally different worlds and seemed like complete opposites."

He waited, hoping she'd continue.

She did. "My grandmother was from a well-to-do family in Philadelphia, and my grandfather was an oilfield roughneck in town to pick up some equipment. They met on the subway. Grams never rode it, but her car was in the shop that day. Anyway, in the span of four hours, Gramps convinced her to break her engagement to another man, marry him, and move to Oklahoma. Gramps said that the moment he set eyes on her, he just knew. And Grams said the same thing. It made no logical sense, but their hearts just knew."

"They got lucky. For every story like that, there are thousands of couples who fall into that 'opposites attract' trap and end up completely miserable."

"I don't think it was luck at all. I think it was meant to be. I think divine providence brought them together."

He should have known she'd believe in something illogical like that. "So you're going to leave everything up to divine providence? You don't have any idea what you're looking for in a guy?"

"Well, of course I have *ideas*."

"Well, let's have them."

She folded her hands on her stomach and gazed up at the ceiling. "I want someone honest and trustworthy. Someone who doesn't try to control me—who can accept me just as I am, without trying to fix me or improve me or make me feel like I can't live up to some impossible standard."

He glanced over at her. "Sounds like your ex was really hard on you."

"Yeah." She was silent for a moment. "And to some extent, so was my dad."

He hadn't seen that one coming. He turned his head and looked at her profile. "Oh, yeah?"

She picked at an invisible piece of lint on the blanket. "I know Dad meant well, but he was always pushing my sister and me to try harder and do better and be the best we could be. Sometimes I felt like no matter how well I did something, it wasn't good enough. And he was really overprotective."

"At least your father cared about you."

"Yours didn't?"

Chase blew out a snort. "He didn't care about anything except where his next beer was coming from." Chase shifted uneasily. Why was he running his mouth? "Back to your criteria."

"Would you please not call it that?"

"You didn't mention physical attraction," Chase pointed out. "Don't you think that's important?"

"Well, yeah. Of course. It goes without saying." She squirmed beneath the sheet, as if the question made her uncomfortable. "You're the one with the written list. What's on it?"

No way was he going to share his SCABHOG inventory. "Sorry. That's classified information."

"That's not fair!"

He lifted his shoulders. "Alas, unfairness is the tragic nature of life."

She playfully elbowed him. "So tell me about your family."

He drew a deep breath and searched his mind for something innocuous to share. "Mom was great. She worked all the time, so she wasn't around as much as she wanted to be, but she was terrific."

"And your dad?"

"My father . . ." The word tasted bitter on his tongue.

It conjured up ugly memories—the sour scent of the old man's BO and his boozy breath; the roar of his angry, slurred voice; the changing colors of his mother's black eye.

What the hell. Might as well tell her. "My father was an alcoholic. He was arrested when I was eighteen, and he died of cirrhosis in prison. That pretty well sums up his life."

She went silent for a moment. "Why was he in prison?"

"Well, in addition to his drinking problem and anger management issues, he had a serious gambling habit. He got in debt to some nasty loan sharks, so he took a gig running drugs to pay them off." If he closed his eyes, Chase could see the red and blue flashing lights of police cars circled around the trailer the night he'd been arrested. "Turns out the FBI had the drug operation under surveillance."

"That must have been awful." Her voice was a gentle breath in the night.

"Not really. My brother and I were a lot better off with him in jail."

"Is your dad's situation the reason you became an FBI agent?"

She could put two and two together awfully fast. He liked that about her. He liked it a lot. "Yeah. An agent interviewed me to see if I knew anything or could identify anyone, and I thought he was the coolest guy I'd ever met." He'd worn a suit, and when he sat down, his jacket had opened to reveal a shoulder holster over a crisply pressed shirt. "He talked to me like I was a real person. He asked me what I wanted to do with my life, and out of the blue,

I said an FBI agent. And I realized I meant it. And from that moment on, that was all I ever wanted to do."

"You wanted to be the opposite of your father." Sammi's gaze seemed to go right through him, between the cells of his skin, straight into his veins.

"I don't know why I'm telling you all this."

"Because I asked."

He watched a moth flutter outside the glass door. "Yeah, well, just because someone asks, I don't usually spill my guts."

"This is kind of an unusual situation. You don't usually find yourself having a getting-to-know-you conversation when you're already in bed with someone."

In Chase's experience, all too often he had. But the conversations had never been anywhere near this intimate.

He turned his head on the pillow and looked at her. "I'm not all that hard to get to know. I mean, I'm a pretty straightforward guy." *When I'm not pretending to be my brother, that is.* His conscience burned at the thought.

She smiled at him. "What you see is what you get, huh?"

No, not at all. But I wish I'd get what I'm seeing right now. Lying on her side like that, she was all dangerous curves—lush breasts, a nipped-in waist, and flared hips. Attraction surged through him. He trained his eyes back on the ceiling.

"You're a really nice guy," she said. "I'm glad I met you."

God, he felt like a heel.

She misinterpreted his silence. "I bet you wish you'd never met me, though." Her voice was soft, but Chase heard the forlorn undernote. "Then you wouldn't have a concussion, and your wallet wouldn't be all chewed up, and . . ."

Aw, hell. He couldn't let her think he was rejecting her because of a few klutzy moves. Convincing her she wasn't bad luck to men was the whole reason he was coaching her. He rolled onto his side and touched her hand. "If none of that had happened, you wouldn't be here."

Her palm turned up, and she took his fingers in hers. Since when had holding hands become so intensely erotic? Her fingers fired every nerve cell in his body.

He should have looked away, but his gaze seemed Super Glued to hers. Electricity hovered between them like thunderclouds, hot and heavy and highly charged. The moment stretched and lengthened, and the longer it lasted, the hotter the air grew between them. The distance between them was somehow shrinking. And then his mouth was on hers, and hers was on his, and lightning was striking all over the place.

Oh, God, her lips were soft—soft and plump and hot. He took her bottom lip between his and gently tugged. She moaned against his mouth.

That soft little sound made coherent thought go up in flames. Nothing mattered, nothing existed except her seeking, craving, exploring lips. She pulled him down, her mouth urgent and wet and hungry.

Her breasts pressed against his naked chest. A fresh firestorm of sensation scorched through him.

He reached beneath her and cupped her bottom. She moved her head, jarring his wound.

He inadvertently flinched.

She immediately pulled back, her forehead creased,

her eyes open and worried. Her hands cradled his face. "Oh, no—did I hurt you again?"

"No."

"Are you sure?"

"Absolutely." He was absolutely sure of something else—this was a terrible, terrible idea. What the hell was he doing? She wasn't the type of woman who took sex casually. He was her life coach, damn it. He was supposed to be helping her, not trying to get in her pants.

This wasn't dating light. This was petting heavy.

He forced himself to pull back and roll away. "I didn't mean for that to happen. I'm sorry."

She put her hand on his chest. "Don't be. I'm not."

He dragged in a ragged breath. "Look—this is a bad idea. I don't want to take advantage of you."

"You're not."

"You might think I'm not, but the only reason you're here is because you feel guilty about beaning me with a hubcap. And you've had a blow to *your* head, too, which makes this a doubly bad idea. I don't want to risk doing anything you'll regret in the morning." The mattress creaked as he climbed out of bed. "I'm going to sleep on the sofa. I'll be back to check on you in two hours."

He strode out the bedroom door and pulled it shut behind him. He didn't have an alarm clock, but he wouldn't need one. There was no way he was going to sleep a wink the rest of the night.

Chapter Nine

Let me get this straight." Chloe braked for a stoplight, then slanted a glance at Sammi the next morning as she drove her home from Chase's apartment. "You were in bed with Agent Hottie and nothing happened?"

"That's right." Sammi squinted against the morning light. She'd hardly slept all night, and the bump on her head hurt like blazes.

"How disappointing!"

No kidding. She decided to pretend otherwise for her own sake as well as Chloe's. "I barely know him. Not to mention that he had a concussion, and I'd hit my head, too."

Chloe shook her head. "Must have been a serious head injury to keep you from wanting to get close to a guy like that."

It wasn't a matter of not wanting to, Sammi thought as she watched the joggers and walkers along the paths in Riverside Park. And while she had no intention of telling her nosy little sister, it wasn't exactly as if nothing at all had happened.

She couldn't believe how that kiss had affected her—

how her mind had turned to mush, how time and place had fallen away, how she'd ached for more, more, *more*. No telling what would have happened if she hadn't bumped Chase's head.

She blew out a sigh. Who was she kidding? She knew exactly what would have happened, and it would have been a mistake. A disaster. She didn't want to get involved with a man who wore a gun as an accessory.

And yet, the chemistry had been like a force of nature.

It was a good thing he'd stopped things when he had, because she'd been beyond the point of rational thought. He'd said he didn't want to do anything that she'd regret in the morning, but she was pretty sure he would have regretted it more. After all, she was the reason he was laid up in bed in the first place.

He'd sure acted awkward this morning. He'd stayed on the other side of the kitchen while she made coffee, he'd refused to make eye contact, he'd kept the conversation brief and neutral. When Chloe arrived to drive her home, he'd extended his hand to her.

A handshake. He'd told her good-bye with a hand-shake!

"So when are you going to see him again?"

She blew out a sigh. "Probably never. He seemed pretty eager to get rid of me this morning." Sammi gazed glumly out the window at a little boy on a bike. "And who could blame him? I'm a walking health hazard."

"I think he's drawn to danger." Chloe gave a sly grin as she turned her rattletrap of a car into Sammi's driveway. "I saw the way he looked at you."

Yeah. Like I was about to sprout a second head.

Sammi unfastened her seat belt as Chloe killed the engine. "Thanks for the ride—and for taking care of Joe last night."

"Not to mention bringing you groceries and clothes, and manning the booth for Chase all afternoon," Chloe reminded her.

"Thanks for all of that, too. I really appreciate it."

"No problem. I only mention it because I wanted to point out that I'm not a total mooch. I do occasionally give back."

Sammi gave her a hug. "I know you do, sweetie."

Chloe hugged her back, then shot her a winsome grin. "Since that's the case, how about I come in and do a load of laundry?"

Some things never changed. Sammi laughed and opened the car door. "As if I could stop you."

~

Paul's eyes rounded with incredulity as he sat beside Chase on the bench at the back of the indoor firing range two days later. "This babe was in your bed all night, and nothing happened?"

"That's right." Chase pulled his eye shield, ear protection, and handgun out of his equipment bag and eyed the torso target at the end of the range.

Paul shook his graying head. "You're losing your touch, man. How am I supposed to live vicariously through you if you're not even gonna try?"

Chase rolled his eyes. Paul was forty-two, married to a terrific woman, and the father of a little boy he adored. There was no way he envied Chase's single lifestyle, but it was a running shtick between them. Chase started to put the sunglasses-style eye-gear on top of his head, then winced at he hit his bandaged wound. "We both had head injuries."

"Man, you must have been practically unconscious."

He wished to hell he had been. Then he never would have kissed her—or had she kissed him? He wasn't entirely clear how it had happened—and he wouldn't be obsessing about it now. Not that he was going to share that with Paul. "It wouldn't have been right."

"Because she's too much of a flake?"

"She's not really all that flaky." Even to his own ears, he sounded strangely defensive. He put the headphones around his neck and pulled out his Glock 22. "She made sure her sister inventoried everything in your booth against my list and brought by the money. She even called Bubba and made arrangements for you to pick up your dad's stuff later this week. And she drove a hard bargain negotiating for her sister's hubcaps." Although Paul would never know how hard a bargain, since Chase had put the difference in the lockbox before he'd handed it off to Paul earlier in the day.

Paul shoved his eye shield on his nose and glanced at Chase curiously. "So what's this girl like when she's not beating you up?"

"Smart. Funny. Passionate about all things art deco." He turned his handgun, checking to make sure the safety was on, then pulled out the extended magazine. "Beautiful. Energetic. And kindhearted." He thought about the way she'd empathized with her boss and landlord. "Too kindhearted, actually. She needs to stop letting people take advantage of her."

Paul shook his burly head. "She lets people take advantage of her, and you let her lie in your bed untouched? Man, you're losing your mojo."

Chase rolled his eyes. "I can't get involved with her while I'm coaching her."

"So resign and date her."

Chase shook his head. "I think I'm really helping her."

"Well, then, coach her and forget about dating her."

"That's complicated, too." Never mind that the complication was of his own making, since he'd given her the assignment of going out with him. What the hell had he been thinking? "I don't want her to think she's run me off by hurting me."

Paul pulled his gun out of his equipment bag. "So what are you going to do?"

"Date her therapeutically."

Paul roared.

"I'm serious. I'm going to prove to her that she can go out with a guy and not hurt him."

"How do you plan to do that?"

"I'll take her out three times, and when nothing happens, she'll realize it's all in her head."

"What if something happens?"

"It won't. I'll control the situation."

Paul blew out a snort. "You have a lot to learn about women if you really think you have any control where they're concerned."

"Hey, it's just three dates. I can handle it. I'll have her straightened out before my brother gets back."

"Any word on how he's doing?"

Chase dropped a forty-five into his magazine. "I talked to the regional commander Friday, and he says Luke's fine. Anxious to come home." And no doubt worried about whether or not Chase was taking good care of his clients.

"Any new developments on the Lambino trial while I was out with Dad?"

"Yeah." Chase loaded another bullet into the magazine chamber. "Forensics matched a rubber burn at the crime scene with the tires on Gianno Lambino's car, so with Luke's testimony, it should be a cut-and-dried case."

"They still think the only shooter out there is the dim-wit nephew?"

Chase nodded. "And the DA's certain one or both of his uncles will implicate him in exchange for a lighter sentence."

"That's good news for Luke." Paul wiped the barrel of his gun with a chamois cloth. "So after the trial, your brother will be a free man, ready to get back to coaching loonies."

"I'll be glad to turn them over to him, that's for sure."

"Except for Calamity Jane. Because you're going to have her cured by then." The sardonic note in Paul's voice wasn't lost on Chase. "So where're you taking her for these three dates?"

Chase loaded another bullet. "I figured I'd start with lunch. That ought to be a nice, safe activity."

"Maybe you should rethink that." Paul's mouth pulled in a dry smile. "Steaming trays of food, chairs that can topple, sharp knives—it doesn't sound too safe to me."

"I meant from a not-getting-too-involved standpoint."

Chase kept his eye on his gun, but he could feel Paul's gaze. "So that's an issue, is it?"

"Hey, I just want to keep things platonic," Chase said,

feeling inexplicably defensive. "I don't want to lead her on or anything."

"Because there's some serious sizzle between you two." Paul's eyes held an irritatingly amused glint.

"I didn't say that."

"You didn't need to."

"I just want to keep things light." Chase clicked another bullet into the magazine. "I don't want her to get hurt."

"From what I'm hearing, you're the one who'd better watch out. You've gotten more injuries from this gal in a week than you've gotten from ten years on the job."

Chase pulled on his ear protectors, mercifully ending the conversation. "Just shut up and shoot, why don't you?"

He hated to admit it, but Paul was right.

$\sim$

Streaks of pink and orange colored the sunset sky as Walter Landry rang the doorbell of his rental house. Through the door, he could hear that Marmaduke of a dog announcing his arrival.

A light clicked on in the living room, then Sammi's face appeared at the side window. Her brow furrowed when she saw him. Walter's fingers tightened on the legal papers in his hand. It had been a long while since anyone's face had lit up when he'd darkened their door, but Sammi looked like the grim reaper had come to call.

Hell, he shouldn't be surprised; she was overly attached to the house, and she knew he never came around with good news. Still, she was an awfully sweet girl—she'd even brought him soup a few months back when he'd had the flu—and it bothered him that her immediate response to him was dismay.

The locks clicked and clattered, then the door squeaked open. The dog's muzzle nudged out the door. Sammi grabbed his thick red collar. "Hello, Mr. Landry." She sounded cordial enough, but her eyes looked wary.

"Evenin', Sammi. Evenin', pup."

Walter started to pet the dog, but the moment he reached out his hand, the beast growled. The dog probably sensed that Sammi wasn't happy to see him. "Can I come in a moment?"

"Sure." She stepped to the other side of the dog, allowing him in. Her gaze locked on the papers in his hand. She bit her bottom lip. "Do you want to sit down?"

"No, this will just take a moment." He stood there awkwardly, trying to figure out a way to break the news to her.

Sammi spared him the effort. "You sold it, didn't you?"

His late wife, Helen, had always said he had a terrible poker face. Not that she really would have known, since he'd never played poker. Truth was, he never played much of anything. He'd always been too busy working.

Walter grimly nodded.

Sammi's eyes welled. "No one came by and asked to see inside."

Walter fastened his gaze on his old brown Bass Weejuns.

"Which means the buyer's going to tear it down." It was a statement, not a question.

"Now, Sammi . . ."

A tear streaked down her cheek. "I'm right, aren't I?

You've sold it to someone who's going to tear it down."
Her voice choked on the last word.

Oh, hell—he hated that he'd made her cry. Walter
shifted the papers to his other hand. "It's the way of the
world, Sammi. You can't stop progress."

"It's not progress to destroy a treasure." The dog beside
her growled. Still holding his collar with one hand, she
wiped her cheek with the other. "Can't you wait just a few
more months?" Her hazel eyes made a heart-wrenching
plea.

He shook his head. "The paperwork's already signed.
The sale's going to close in six weeks. I'm afraid you'll
have to be out by then." He handed her the papers.

She glanced down at them, then looked at him as if he'd
handed her a dead kitten. "Is this an eviction notice?"

"Well, it's a written notice to vacate the premises in
five weeks."

Another tear snaked down her face. With one hand on
the dog's collar and the other clutching the papers, she
couldn't even wipe it away. Walter felt a ridiculous urge to
do it for her, the way he used to wipe his daughter's tears
when she skinned her knee.

Damn it, it was business. Why did she have to make
him feel like an ogre? "It more than meets the terms of
a month-to-month lease, Sammi." He moved toward the
door and opened it.

She followed him onto the porch, her hand still on the
dog's collar. "Who's the buyer?"

If he told her, she'd just go pester him. He shook his
head. "I can't tell you that."

Her mouth tightened. "Can't, or won't?"

"Guess it's kind of the same thing." He lifted his shoulders in a helpless shrug, gave her an apologetic smile, and walked outside.

"I can't believe you're doing this!" Sammi called as he walked down the sidewalk. The dog barked loudly.

He felt like a heel, but what was he supposed to do? The property was a liability, and he needed to get rid of it. He paused under the whispering leaves of the sweetgum and turned around. "I'll tell you what, Sammi. You've been a really good tenant, so I'll waive your last month's rent, and I'll give you back your deposit."

"Money can't fix this!"

It couldn't fix most things, he thought sadly—leastwise, not the things that really mattered. Why hadn't he known that earlier? Why was he figuring it out only now, when it was too late to do anything about it?

It turned out that life was a series of choices, and he'd made a lot of bad ones. *I'll just work half an hour more; Anne won't care if I miss her band concert; Helen will understand if I don't go to the church potluck.* Funny how at the time he hadn't seen how important all those little choices were. Taken together, they'd added up to a life.

"I'm sorry," he whispered to Helen as the star-shaped leaves of her sweetgum waved overhead.

He turned to apologize to Sammi again, but when he looked at the house, she'd already closed the door.

Chapter Ten

Mother went through everything in my room while I was at work today," Horace moaned. "I know, because I placed a hair on a drawer so I could tell if it had been opened, and it was gone."

"How did that make you feel?" After three weeks, Chase had learned that the odious phrase covered just about anything any of his clients said. He stood up and paced his living room, leaving Horace's folder on the kitchen counter.

"Violated."

"Did you talk to her about it?"

"Oh, no! She'd want to know how I knew, and then she'd trick me into telling her, and then she'd be furious that I'd set her up."

Chase drew in a deep breath as he circled his sofa. The glacial pace of his brother's methods was growing more and more irritating. His other clients were progressing just as slowly, and Chase was losing patience. "Horace, does this situation make you happy?"

"Of course not!"

"Well, then, why don't you change it?"

"I-I am," Horace sputtered. "I mean, I'm trying, Coach. But Mother has done so much for me. I-I can't just walk out and abandon her. She needs me."

"Does she?" he pressed. "Or does she just want to control you?"

"She-she says it would kill her if I left."

Chase blew out a sigh. Regardless of his personal feelings on the matter, he'd promised Luke he'd follow his instructions. Chase strode back to the kitchen and flipped open the file. *Don't pressure him into doing anything he's not ready to do,* Chase read for the millionth time. Horace was obviously not ready to move out of his mother's house.

Chase closed his eyes and rubbed the bridge of his nose. "Let's talk about your assignment. Did you call about an apartment?"

"Yes." Horace spent the next five minutes explaining in excruciating detail how terrifying the experience was. "But the fourth place I called, I only hung up four times before I worked up the nerve to talk."

"That's great, Horace. What did you say?"

"I said, 'You have an apartment for rent?' and he said, 'Yes.' And I said, 'Great.' And I hung up."

Oh, brother. *Celebrate small steps of progress,* Luke had instructed. "That's good, Horace. That's a move in the right direction."

"The next call, I only hung up three times. And by the last one, I spoke the second time I dialed."

Man, this was pathetic. Beyond pathetic. "Good going. You're making real headway. Now, the next time you call about a place, I want you to ask some more questions."

"I have to call again?" Anxiety shot his voice into the soprano range.

"Yes, you do. And I want you to drive by and look at some complexes."

"Drive by?" Panic tinged his voice.

"Yes."

"I-I don't have to get out of the car and go in, do I?"

"Not if you don't think you can."

"But—but . . ." He sputtered in alarm. "When would I find time to do that?"

"I'm sure you can figure it out. On your lunch hour, or after work . . ."

"That would make me late getting home, and Mother wouldn't like that."

Of course she wouldn't. "You'll manage, Horace. I have confidence in you. And this time next week, you can tell me all about it."

"I-I'll try."

"Atta boy. Now—do you have a new rap for me?"

"Yeah, I do." Horace's voice cheered up. "It's a fantasy rap." He cleared his throat, made a few beat-box mouth noises, then lowered his voice to a hip-hop jive:

I was in the elevator at the end of the day
When the babe from Escrow looked my way.
I said, 'Hey, honey, want to boogie on down?
There's a hot dance club on the other side of town.'

More beat-box noises emanated through the phone, and then Horace continued.

She said, 'Why wait? I'm feelin' pretty loose—
Why don't we get down and do the wild watoose?'
She reached out and punched the elevator button,
Then got all over me like mint jelly on mutton.

More beat-box noises ensued.

Uh-huh, mint jelly, uh-huh, on your belly.

Uh-huh, I'll lick it off, then uh-huh, we'll boff.

Chase's stomach hurt from laughing. "Wow," he said when he could catch his breath. "Horace, that was amazing."

"You liked it?" he asked eagerly.

"I loved it. You're awesome, dude."

Chase hung up and shook his head. Horace became an entirely different person when he rapped. If he would channel that passion and energy into standing up to his mother, he'd be living the life of his dreams in no time.

Same with Sammi. Once she let a man see the passion and energy hiding behind her insecurity, she'd be in a hot-and-heavy, altar-bound relationship before she knew it.

The thought made Chase's stomach tighten with something that felt disturbingly like jealousy. He tried to reason away the emotion as he headed for the kitchen. She was a coaching client, not a potential girlfriend, for Pete's sake. Besides, he didn't want to get involved with a havoc-wreaking nut job.

Although she wasn't nearly as nutty as he'd first thought. He absently opened the fridge and pulled out a Coke. In fact, compared to her sister, she actually seemed almost sane. But then, she was a far cry from SCABHOG material.

Or was she?

Popping the top, he strode to the terrace window and thoughtfully gazed out at the city lights. She was smart— no doubt about that. And she was extremely capable, judging from the way she'd steamrolled him into going to the hospital and following doctor's orders. She was active—he'd met her while jogging, after all. And she was definitely beautiful; when he looked at her, he didn't just feel sparks—he felt a whole power plant download.

From the way she'd renovated the house, she was indisputably hardworking. And from the sounds of all the projects she was managing at work, she had to be organized and goal-oriented.

But she was still a walking disaster. A smart, capable, active, beautiful, hardworking, organized, goal-oriented disaster, but a disaster nonetheless. She wasn't logical. She wasn't rational. She followed her heart instead of her head and expected things to just magically work out. He needed a woman who was calm, orderly, predictable, and reasonable, and Sammi was a wrecking ball.

So why couldn't he get her out of his head?

The phone rang. Once again, there was that weird electric zap of anticipation at just the thought of talking to her. Scowling at himself, he crossed the room and answered it.

"I'm losing my mind," Sammi said promptly.

"Over what?"

"Well, for starters, over Chase." She proceeded to give him a play-by-play of the evening at his apartment, ending with, ". . . and then we looked at each other, and well . . . I kissed him."

"You kissed him, or he kissed you?" He still wasn't clear exactly how it had happened.

"A little of both." She paused. "A lot of both, actually."

He could picture her smiling on the other end of the phone. Chase swallowed and strode to the window. The situation called for the standard question, yet it seemed all wrong to ask it. He asked it anyway. "And how did that make you feel?"

"It's really hard to describe."

"Give it a try."

"Well . . . I'd have to say it was excruciating."

Chase's heart nose-dived. "You found it painful?"

"Painfully exciting. I've never felt so turned on in my life. I felt like I was on fire, burning up from the inside out."

He started to feel that way himself, just listening to her. "Really."

"Yeah. And then I did it again."

"You kissed him again?" Chase only remembered one long, continuous, moving-all-over-each-other's-faces kiss, not two separate ones, but she might have perceived things differently.

"No. I hurt him again. I accidentally bopped his wound."

"That wasn't enough to hurt him." As soon as he said it, he realized it was an inappropriate insight for a detached third party to have. "I mean, it couldn't have been very forceful if you were kissing at the time. It's a law of physics that proximity diminishes force."

"It was forceful enough to make him flinch, and then he got up and went to sleep on the couch." He heard the dog bark through the phone. He pictured her rubbing his giant head. "And the next morning, he acted like he couldn't wait for me to be gone. And he hasn't called." Her voice held a forlorn waver. "I guess I really blew it."

"Nah. I'm sure you'll hear from him." Although Chase was reluctant to phone her for a totally different reason than she thought. Even though he raised his voice and slowed his speech when he talked to her as Luke, he was afraid that she'd recognize his voice on the phone.

"I hope so," Sammi sighed. "I could sure use a bright spot in my life, because everything else is sliding south."

"What else is happening?"

"My landlord did it. He sold the home to someone who plans to tear it down, and I have to move out in five weeks."

"Where are you going to move?"

"I'm not sure. If worst comes to worst, I guess I'll store my stuff and move in with my sister for a while."

"Doesn't she live in a garret?" Oh, hell; had she told that to Chase or Luke?

Fortunately, it didn't become an issue. "Yeah. I didn't say it would be pleasant. Hopefully, though, I won't have to move that soon."

"Why not?"

"If a building has historical significance, the Historical Preservation Commission can keep it from being torn down while it's being appraised for the National Registry of Historic Sites. One of the museum board members is also on the Preservation Commission—they're both volunteer positions—and I called him. He's agreed to get a stay on the demolition permit."

Chase grinned. He liked the way her mind worked. "Very resourceful. That's terrific!"

"Not from my landlord's perspective. He's going to be furious. And I've probably created yet another problem with my boss."

"The woman who won't retire?"

"Yeah. She'll have a fit that I called a board member."

"Why?"

"She doesn't like me to have contact with the board. She thinks it undermines her authority."

He frowned as he paced his living room. Sammi was going to have a rough day tomorrow. He wished there were some way he could make it better.

Maybe there was, he thought, stopping in midstride. Maybe he could take her to lunch. A short workday lunch might kill two birds with one stone: it would pick up her spirits while getting date number one out of the way quickly and easily.

He grinned at the plan, trying to ignore the way the thought of lunch with Sammi picked up his spirits, as well.

~

"I'll relay the message to Sammi, Mr. Gordon," Arlene said into her office phone the next morning. "Good-bye."

As soon as the other line clicked off, Arlene banged her phone into the cradle, then pushed out of her chair. How dare Sammi call a board member without her permission! Arlene was the senior curator; she and she alone would talk to the board of directors.

It was a principle she'd learned from Chandler. He'd always insisted on restricting access to the major stockholders. He'd said the key to managing them was to limit their contact to opposing views, especially within the company. And Lord only knew that Sammi had opposing views.

Well, Arlene would put a stop to this. Anger churning in her chest, she stalked off in search of Sammi and followed her voice toward the library.

Arlene stopped at the threshold of the mahogany-walled room. Sammi stood before a group of elderly ladies, her back to the doorway, wearing a long brown 1930s-era dress.

Hellfire—she'd forgotten that Sammi was conducting one of her ridiculous historical luncheon tours, dressed up as Chandler's mother. Harriet and Chandler Sr. had built the mansion in the 1930s and lived here for three decades before retiring to Florida and leaving the place to Chandler Jr., and Sammi's tours always focused on the mansion's early days.

Lord, but she hated the whole historical-tour concept. Sammi had gotten the board to sign off on the half-cocked idea while Arlene was home recovering from the heart attack, and now Sammi conducted the tours regularly.

Today she was wearing a feathered cloche like Harriet Phelps always favored. It always irritated Arlene to see Sammi dressed up as Chandler's mother, but today, it really made her blood boil. Sammi was trying to undermine her, just like that old bag had done all those years ago.

The old woman had been wearing a feathered hat like Sammi's the day she'd marched into the executive offices of Phelps Oil, her thin lips taut, her double chin tilted up, her eyes cold as a trout's. It had been nearly forty years ago, but Arlene remembered it as if it were yesterday.

"Mrs. Phelps—how nice to see you." Arlene had looked up from her desk and smiled.

The older woman had stared, her eyes icy enough to sink the *Titanic*.

Arlene's mouth had gone dry, but she'd forced her lips to keep smiling. "I'm sorry, but Chandler is in Bartlesville at a meeting this afternoon."

"I know." Her voice had a chilled, clipped tone. "I came to talk to you."

Arlene had been wearing the pearls Chandler had given her for Christmas. She'd touched the neckline of her navy paisley dress, feeling the warm stones beneath her fingers. "To me?"

Harriet's frosty gaze had fixed on the pearls. "Yes. Let's go into Chandler's office."

"I—I don't think . . ."

Harriet had marched into the office, leaving Arlene with nothing to do but rise from her desk and follow her. The receptionist had eyed them curiously.

"Close the door," Harriet had ordered.

Arlene hesitantly had closed the heavy wooden door.

"Sit down." Harriet had pointed to a chair.

Arlene had crossed the room, her heels sinking into the plush Persian carpet, and stiffly lowered herself onto a cordovan leather chair opposite the desk. Harriet had stood in front of the desk, her arms folded, her expensive Chanel bag dangling from her right wrist. "I know what's going on with you and my son, and I want it to stop."

Arlene's mouth had opened. Air refused to go in or out.

"Immediately." The older woman had unsnapped the quilted leather bag, then pulled out an oversized black leather checkbook and a gold pen. "How much?"

"I beg your pardon?"

She'd poised the pen over the checkbook. "How much do you want to go away and never see my son again?"

"I—I . . ." Arlene's mind had frozen.

"I'm prepared to write you a check right now. What about five thousand dollars?"

Arlene had stared at her blankly.

"Ten?"

Nausea had risen in her throat.

"Oh, all right." The older woman had sniffed peevishly through her thin, patrician nose. "Fifteen." She'd turned her back to Sammi, placed the checkbook on the desk, and begun to write.

"I-I don't want your money," Arlene had stuttered.

"Don't be ridiculous." The pen scratched on the check. "Of course you do."

"No! I won't—I won't take it."

Harriet had ripped out the check, smacked it down on the desk, and straightened. "This situation can't continue. It's untenable, and I just won't have it. You will leave the employ of this company at once, and you will never see my son again. Do you understand?"

Arlene's heart had thumped hard in her chest. She'd lifted her head, looked the old woman in the eye, and spoken in a voice that had been as soft as it was firm. "I understand that I was hired by Mr. Phelps. I understand that he is my employer. As such, I understand that he, and he alone, can fire me." Arlene had stiffly risen to her feet. "I also understand that I have work to do, so if you'll excuse me, I'll get to it."

The woman's chins had quivered with rage, and the feather had wobbled on her hat as Arlene had turned and marched out.

The feather on Sammi's hat wobbled now. "If you'll move this way, I'll show you the kitchen," Sammi was saying. "It was designed by Sir Allan Frank, and it was way ahead of its time."

The gawking ladies shuffled after her. Arlene glanced at her watch, then turned on her heel. She couldn't yank

Sammi out of the tour without creating a scene. She'd have to talk to her later.

Seemed like she was always needing to talk to the young woman about something she'd done or said without Arlene's approval. The fact was, Arlene didn't approve of Sammi working there. She certainly didn't approve of the way the board had rushed out and hired her, assuming that Arlene wouldn't come back.

True, Arlene had planned to retire in six months, and true, she'd been out for three of those months, but nothing had been set in stone. It was her decision, when to retire—and after spending all that time home alone with nothing to do, she'd rethought the entire concept.

Especially if retiring meant that Sammi was going to take over. In the three months the girl had run the museum by herself, she'd turned things upside down. She'd converted the old carriage house into a photo exhibit hall, she'd launched these ridiculous living-history tours, she'd posted little historical notes all over the place, and now she wanted to put together an exhibit of Justine Chandler's clothes in the basement.

Which made Arlene furious. Justine didn't deserve to be immortalized. Chandler had loved *her.* His wife had been nothing but an obstacle standing between him and Arlene. For forty-seven years, Arlene had tried to ignore the woman's existence, but now, thanks to Sammi, she was going to have to paw through her trunks and handle all her things.

Arlene had complained bitterly to the board. "The clothing exhibit is a prime example of how Sammi's derailing the museum's mission. This place isn't a fashion museum. It's a waste of resources to have two curators, anyway."

"Now, Arlene, this is a big museum," the board president had said. "There's plenty of room for a new exhibit, and Sammi's bringing in some terrific new ideas. Besides, we need someone in place who can take over when you decide to retire."

Arlene had argued that she should be able to choose her own person to mentor, but the board wouldn't hear of it. So here they were, paying two executive directors' salaries—although hers was significantly higher; she'd made sure of that—while Sammi disrupted the peaceful routines she'd followed for years.

Adding insult to injury, all of the museum employees seemed positively enchanted with her. Arlene's own assistant, Gretchen, had eagerly jumped on Sammi's bandwagon, even giving up her lunch hour to help with the historical luncheons.

She'd never once offered to skip lunch to help Arlene with anything, Arlene thought as she stalked past Gretchen's empty desk on her way back to her office.

Which hurt. Arlene hated to admit it, but everyone's positive reaction to Sammi made her feel like second-best.

Again.

With a sigh, Arlene settled behind her desk and reached for the mail.

"Excuse me."

She looked up to see a man with thick gray hair standing in the doorway. He looked like a thinner, older version of the man who played "House" on TV.

"Can you tell me where I can find Samantha Matthews?" he asked in a deep baritone.

"She's conducting a tour right now. May I help you with something?"

"No. It's a, uh, personal matter."

Arlene's stomach tightened. Wasn't that always the way with men—going after the girls half their age. Her mouth flattened. "I see."

~

From her disapproving scowl, the woman apparently had the wrong impression. Walter put up both hands, alarmed. "Oh, no—it's not like that," he said quickly. "I'm her landlord." He stepped into the office and stuck out his hand over the neat desk. "Walter Landry."

"Oh." The woman's mouth softened. Her eyes did, too. The chair creaked as she rose to her feet. She had a slim figure, although it was hard to tell much about it under her boxy jacket. She reached out and took his hand. "I'm Arlene Arnette."

"Nice to meet you." Her hand was narrow and soft and warm. He found himself oddly reluctant to release it. It had been a long time since he'd held a woman's hand.

"I'm the museum curator." Arlene fingered her pearl necklace. "Can I help you with something?"

Walter pulled his brows together. "I thought Sammi was the curator."

Arlene's lips pinched together again. "Yes, well, she was hired as the interim curator when I was on a leave of absence and the board thought I wasn't coming back. But I'm the *head* curator." She smoothed her skirt. "So you're the man who's selling the Deshuilles-designed house?"

Oh, boy. Here came another dressing-down by another art deco buff. He straightened defensively. "Yes. The place is so tiny it's virtually unlivable, and it needs a fortune in repairs, and the neighborhood is being transitioned to new homes, and—"

The woman held up her hand. "You don't have to sell me."

"Really." He looked at her with renewed interest. Her white hair was brushed back rather severely, but she had great skin—as luminous and poreless as the inside of a shell. His wife would have said she'd probably never set foot in the sun. "I thought everyone who worked at an art deco museum would be pro-preservation no matter what."

"This is the *Phelps* museum." Arlene raised her chin. "Contrary to what Sammi might think, we are in the business of preserving the Phelps legacy, not every art deco building in the city."

Walter felt himself relax. "Well, I'm certainly glad to hear it."

"I assume you're here to see Sammi about calling the Preservation Commission?"

Walter raised his eyebrows. "You know about that?"

"One of our museum board members also serves on the commission." Her lips pressed into a tight, displeased line. "In my opinion, Sammi really overstepped her bounds."

"She sure has." Walter bobbed his head in agreement. "It's my property, not hers."

"And she had no business contacting a board member without my knowledge, either. The girl crossed a line."

"A couple of them, apparently." Walter shoved his hands in the pockets of his gray slacks. "I'm trying to unload that house so I can move to Tucson, and now she's got the sale snagged up."

"She's good at snagging things up," Arlene said. "When she gets something in her head, you can't stop her."

Walter nodded. "She's stubborn as a mule. A lot like my wife."

Arlene fingered her necklace again. "What does she think about this?"

"My wife? Oh, she's gone. I mean, she died. Three years ago."

"Oh, I'm sorry." Arlene got that awkward, stricken expression that people always got when he mentioned his wife's death. "I-I'm sure you miss her."

He nodded his head. Telling folks he was a widower was a real conversation stopper. He never knew what to say next. He decided to turn the topic back to her. "So—what about you? Are you married?"

"No."

"Guess you've lost a spouse, too."

"No. I never married."

"That's hard to believe." Good heavens, why had he blurted out that? He was getting deeper and deeper into conversational quicksand. "I mean, a lovely woman like yourself. It seems like a man . . ." His face heated. He pulled his hands out of his pockets, shoved them back in, then cleared his throat. "So, um, when will Sammi be done?"

"Not for at least an hour and a half. She's holding a historical lunch."

"What's that?"

"One of Sammi's big ideas. She throws a formal

luncheon in the dining room and dresses up in vintage clothes, just like it's the nineteen-thirties."

"Unusual concept."

Her lips pinched together. "Yes. You can count on Sammi to come up with the unusual."

Walter grinned at her sour expression. "I take it you don't much care for the idea."

She shook her head. "It's too much trouble, and it causes too much wear and tear on the place. Sammi sold the board on it while I was out. Once she sets her mind on something, she refuses to take no for an answer."

"Don't I know it."

Arlene smiled. It was amazing how the expression transformed her face. Walter smiled back. The moment stretched until he suddenly realized he'd been standing there too long. He awkwardly looked at his watch. "Well, it sounds like I've got some time to kill, and it's lunchtime. Are there any good restaurants around here?"

"There's Chiquita's Cantina, if you like Mexican food. It's just across the street."

"I love Mexican. Would you care to join me?"

Her eyes widened in surprise. "Well, I . . ."

"If you don't have plans." What the hell was he doing? Was he actually asking her for a date? He shifted his weight to his other foot.

"Well, I brought a sandwich, but . . ." She hesitated.

"To tell you the truth, I hate to eat alone," he blurted. "It's one of the hardest parts about being a widower." Oh, Christ—now he sounded pathetic.

But it seemed to work.

She treated him to another smile. "I'd be delighted to join you."

~

The air-conditioning inside the Phelps Museum was a welcome relief from the heat radiating off the asphalt parking lot outside. Chase closed the massive double door behind him and looked around. Wow. Black-and-white marble on the floor, an enormous chandelier, massive staircases that swirled up to the second story—it looked like Fred Astaire was going to dance out from behind one of the massive silk drapes at any moment.

The entry was deserted. A glassed-in ticket booth against the wall sported a sign that read, "Closed for lunch. Ticket sales resume at 1:30."

Voices echoed faintly from a back room. One of them sounded like Sammi's. Funny how just the sound of her voice made his pulse race.

He headed down the foyer toward the voices, then paused on the threshold of the dining room. He felt like he'd stumbled onto the set of a play. A dozen or more women, all wearing hats and old-fashioned clothing, sat around a long, lace-draped table set with formal china, stemware, candles, and fresh flowers. He backed away, ready to beat a silent retreat, when the slender woman at the head of the table looked straight at him.

"Chase!"

The elfin face under the feathered skullcap hat lit with a smile. The warmth of it shot straight to his head like a gulp of whiskey.

"Excuse me, ladies," Sammi said, placing her napkin on the white tablecloth. "I'll be right back."

She rose and hurried toward him, the brown silk of

her dowdy dress rustling as she moved. "Hello," she said, joining him in the hallway.

"Hi, yourself. I didn't mean to interrupt."

"It's okay." She peered at the Band-Aid at the juncture of his forehead and scalp. "How's your head?"

"Fine. How's yours?"

"Good as new."

"Glad to hear it. When I saw all those feathers on your head, I was afraid your goose egg was hatching."

She grinned and touched the silly skullcap. "This was all the rage in the 1930s."

"It probably wasn't very popular with the birds."

She laughed. "Probably not. Did you stop by just to give me a hard time?"

"That's just a side benefit. I actually stopped by to see if I could take you to lunch."

"Oh, how nice! But I'm in the middle of an event, and"—she looked down at her outfit—"I'm not really dressed for it."

During his first coaching conversation with Sammi, she'd bemoaned the fact she didn't have a twenty-first-century wardrobe. This must be what she meant. "Do you dress like Mamie Eisenhower every day?"

"Only on days when I'm hosting living-history luncheons or tours."

"How often is that?"

"I started out doing them just once a month, but they were so popular that we expanded to doing each once a week. We have a waiting list."

"Wow. Was this your idea?"

She nodded. "My boss hates it."

Chase craned his neck and looked into the room. "Looks like the ladies in there are having a good time."

"Oh, they love it. We serve one of the menus that the first Mrs. Phelps actually used for a luncheon in 1932 and try to make them feel like real guests."

"Great idea."

"There's a lot of interest in art deco. Unfortunately, I can't make my landlord understand that." Her face turned somber. "He told me last night that he's going to sell the house to someone who's going to tear it down."

Chase summoned an expression of surprised dismay. "That's a real shame."

"Yeah. I just can't let that happen, so I called the Historic Preservation Commission and got them to put a stay on the demolition permit."

"Great idea."

"It's just a stopgap measure. But I'm trying to drum up some public support."

"How are you doing that?"

"Well, after the luncheon, I always give a slide-show presentation about art deco in Tulsa." She leaned close and lowered her voice. "I've put some slides of my house in it, and I'm going to ask these ladies to contact the Preservation Commission and ask them to veto the demolition permit."

He grinned at her cleverness.

Sammi looked over her shoulder as a maid in a long black gown with a white apron began clearing the table. "I'd better get back in there."

Chase nodded. "We'll do lunch another day."

"Actually, lunch is kind of hard for me." She tilted her head and gazed up at him. "What about dinner?"

Her hazel eyes seemed to suck all reason right out of his brain. "Great," he found himself saying. "Are you free tonight?"

She nodded.

What was he doing? A dinner date was a real date—the kind with romantic implications. The very kind he needed to avoid. He was veering from his plan. Warning bells clanged in his head, but the pull of her gaze overrode practical considerations. "Terrific. I'll pick you up at seven."

"Okay."

She started to walk away, then turned and flashed a smile. "I promise I'll change clothes."

Just don't change into anything too sexy, Chase thought as he crossed the empty lobby, his footsteps echoing on the marble. If she had this kind of effect on him when she was dressed like Mary Poppins and looked like she had a bird perched on her head, he'd hate to see his reaction if she wore something low cut and clingy.

"Thank you so much, dearie." The heavily rouged gray-haired lady in the pink hat and petunia-printed dress stopped on her way out of the mansion's massive double doors forty minutes later and took Sammi's hand. "Everything was just wonderful."

"I'm so glad you enjoyed it," Sammi said warmly. "Thank you for coming."

The woman's crow's-feet crinkled. "I'm going to write the Preservation Commission about saving that little house, just like you suggested."

"I will, too," chimed in a lady in blue-and-white-dotted chiffon.

"Me, three," said a tiny woman who looked like Dr. Ruth.

"Thank you." Every letter the commission got would strengthen her case. "Good-bye." Sammi waved as the women shuffled out the door, then turned to see her landlord and Ms. Arnette standing side-by-side in the foyer.

"Mr. Landry." Her stomach tightened. There was only one reason he would be here, and it wasn't for a tour.

Ms. Arnette tilted up her chin. "We need to talk to you, Sammi."

We? Sammi's gaze darted from one to the other. Since when had the two of them even met, much less formed an alliance?

"I had a call from Mr. Gordon." Ms. Arnette's eyes were oddly glassy, but her mouth had that tight, I-just-sucked-a-lemon look that Sammi had come to dread.

"And my realtor received a call from the Historic Preservation Commission," Mr. Landry added.

Oh, boy. They were double-teaming her. Sammi pulled herself to her full height and braced for an assault.

"You called a board member behind my back," Ms. Arnette said accusingly.

"Actually," Sammi said, "I called Mr. Gordon in his capacity as a member of the Preservation Commission."

"You wouldn't have known him if it weren't for your job here. You misused your position."

Oh, jeez. Ms. Arnette had a lot of weird ideas about hierarchy and who should talk to whom—kind of like who got to talk to the wizard. "I'm sorry you feel that way, Ms.

Arnette, but I don't lose my rights as a private citizen just because I work here."

Mr. Landry took a step forward, his eyes narrow, his mouth tight. "And I don't lose my rights as a homeowner just because you're renting my property."

Holy mackerel. The old guy's eyes were practically spitting fire. "It's not just a piece of property, Mr. Landry. It's a rare example of a fine architect's work, and a priceless interpretation of art deco style on a modest scale."

"I don't care what you call it; that house belongs to me." His finger thumped against his plaid-shirt-covered chest. "Not to you, not to the city, and not to that danged commission. It's my property. Mine." He self-jabbed his chest again. "As the property owner, I have the right to dispose of it as I see fit."

Great. Just great. "Well, Mr. Landry, the Preservation Commission will make that determination."

His ruddy face reddened.

The sudden clink of breaking china made everyone jump. The catering service supplied the china for the weekly lun cheon, so Sammi wasn't too worried, but it gave her the out she needed. "Oh, dear—I need to go see what happened. If you'll excuse me . . ." She took a step back.

"That better not be one of the Phelpses' possessions that just broke," Ms. Arnette warned, as if it were in Sammi's power to retroactively fix things.

"We're not done here." Mr. Landry scowled.

"I'm afraid we are," Sammi said. She tried to soften the words with an apologetic smile. "It's in the commission's hands, and they'll make a ruling on it at their next meeting." She took another step back and lifted her hand in a little wave. "Nice seeing you, Mr. Landry." And with that, she made her escape.

〜

"She doesn't back down easily, that's for sure," Walter mumbled as he followed Arlene to her office.

"I told you," Arlene said, weaving slightly.

She never drank at lunch, but Walter had ordered one of the restaurant's two-for-one margarita specials while she was in the ladies' room. She'd intended to just take a sip, but the frozen concoction had been so delicious that she'd drained the entire glass. Walter had ordered another round, and before she knew it, she'd told Walter all of her problems with Sammi—how the girl wouldn't leave well enough alone, how determined she was to change things, how she just wouldn't take no for an answer. The only thing Arlene hadn't vented was the way Sammi's presence hurt her.

How could the board have replaced her so easily? The question gnawed at her like a rat with a wedge of cheddar. Between her time as Chandler's assistant and her tenure as museum curator, she'd worked for the Phelpses' interests for forty-seven years, yet they'd waited less than two weeks to bring in someone less than half her age. It was as if she were nothing more than a dirty oil filter: Disposable. Expendable. Worn-out and used up.

And every day, Sammi continued to make her feel that way. Oh, the girl didn't do it deliberately; she was annoyingly kind and respectful, which made it all the harder, because it would be easier on Arlene if she could just outright dislike the young woman.

But she didn't really dislike Sammi. She disliked the

way the girl's eager-beaver enthusiasm, irritating energy, and innovative ideas were destroying her legacy. Before too long, all of her work would be erased or so severely modified that it was no longer recognizable. After a while, it would be as if Arlene had never even been there.

As if she'd never existed.

And that was what Arlene feared most of all: that no one would know or care that she had ever lived. When she'd had her heart attack, that possibility had hurt more than the chest pain. Her last thought as she was wheeled into surgery wasn't "Will I die?" but "Will anyone care that I ever lived?"

Only two things had ever really mattered to her: her work, and Chandler. With those gone, what did she have? What had she done? Who the hell was she? She didn't have any children or family or any real friends. That had been brought glaringly home when she'd been released from the hospital and spent day after day alone, the phone calls and visits few and increasingly far apart.

Walter's words brought her back to the present. "My wife was just like Sammi. Nutty as a pecan over that little igloo of a house."

Arlene looked at him, trying to determine if he considered being like his wife a good thing or a bad thing. "Really."

He nodded. "One of our worst arguments ever was over that place. I bought a beautiful big home in Country Club Estates, and she refused to move out of that squalid little box."

Arlene sank into one of the armless chairs across from her desk. "Why?"

Walter sat down beside her. "At the time, I thought

she was just mad that I'd bought the place without consulting her."

Arlene raised her eyebrows. "You bought a house without consulting your wife?"

"Yeah."

"Why on earth did you do that?" Too late, Arlene realized the question was both rude and none of her business. Drinking tequila at lunch had a bad effect on her manners.

Walter ran a hand through his hair and answered it anyway. "The place was a real steal. It wasn't going to be on the market long, so I had to act fast."

"Still, it seems like you could have discussed it with her."

"Yeah, I probably could have." He slumped in the chair. "I guess I just didn't want to give her the chance to talk me out of it." He gazed out the window, but he didn't look like he was really seeing the mansion's rose garden. "It was the type of house I'd always wanted—a real showplace."

"And you didn't think she'd like it?"

He shook his head. "It wasn't her style. She liked simple stuff."

"And you bought it, knowing that?"

"Yeah." He blew out a sigh. "Looking back, I can see it was wrong. I guess I just did what I wanted to do."

Chandler had been the same way. He'd always done things his way, and to hell with anyone else's feelings. An unexpected surge of anger welled up in her. "Isn't that just like a man."

"Oh, I don't know that you can fault my whole gender. I was probably worse than most." He fell silent for a moment. "Helen said she didn't want to move because a bigger house meant she'd see less of me, because I'd be working all the harder to make the bigger mortgage. Of course, I wouldn't listen. And darned if she wasn't right."

"Did you and Helen argue often?"

"No. Hardly ever."

"Probably because you were never around."

"Maybe so. I'd prefer to think it's because we were happy together. At any rate, *I* was happy. I'm not so sure about her anymore." He looked down at his hands. "I probably could have been a better husband."

Anger flared in Arlene's chest again, pulsing its way up her neck, heating her face. Men were all the same—if a man was happy and the woman in his life wasn't making a fuss, then everything was just fine and dandy. She wondered how many times Walter had cheated on Helen.

He looked up at her. "How come you never married?"

"Because . . ." *I never met the right man.* She started to give him the standard lie, but the words stuck in her throat. She'd met the right man, all right—just under the wrong circumstances. This philandering husband needed to hear the other side of the story. He'd probably never given any thought to what happened to the other woman.

She lifted her chin and stared him defiantly in the eye. "The man I loved already had a wife."

Walter's brown eyes widened. "Oh. Oh, I see."

She narrowed her eyes. "Do you?"

"Yes." He straightened and leaned back in the chair, like a man edging away from a too-hot fire. "Yes, I think so."

She leaned forward. "And what, exactly, do you see? Do you see that when a married man has an affair, it's not just his wife he's hurting?"

"I—I never thought of that."

"I'm sure you didn't. Men only think about themselves. They don't stop to think what they're putting the other woman through."

His brow knit like a cabled sweater. "The truth is, I've never given it any thought at all. I-I never needed to." His brown eyes settled on her. "I never cheated on my wife."

"Oh." Arlene's mouth stayed stuck for a moment. "When you said you could have been a better husband . . . and that you always did what you wanted . . . I just thought . . . I thought . . ." Shame heated her face. "Oh, dear. I'm sorry."

He waved his hand. "No apology necessary."

She looked down at her hands and folded them tightly together. Dear God in heaven—she'd never have another drink at lunch as long as she lived. "I-I guess you think I'm a terrible person."

He lifted his shoulders. "Not up to me to judge. I'm sure you had your reasons."

A soft knock sounded on the door. The museum receptionist, a mousy girl with stringy brown hair named Jillian, opened it a crack and tentatively poked her head into the office. "Excuse me, Ms. Arnette—the contractor is here about that leak in the basement bathroom."

Thank God for a way out of this mortifying situation. "Tell him I'll be right with him."

Walter stood as Jillian retreated. Arlene rose, as well, and awkwardly stuck out her hand. "Well—thank you for lunch."

His large, slightly calloused hand enfolded hers. It was warm and dry, and a little skitter of heat danced up her arm. "Thanks for joining me. We'll have to do it again."

Arlene nodded and watched him leave her office. He

didn't mean it; he was just being polite. A faithfully married man mourning his wife was not going to keep company with a homewrecker.

What on earth had possessed her to tell him that? It had always been her carefully guarded secret. Why had she just spilled it like that? And what was with that rush of anger? This wasn't like her at all. It had to be the tequila.

It had certainly been an exercise in poor judgment. Maybe she was getting senile. Maybe the board was right; maybe she should consider permanent retirement.

But oh, dear lord—that was like considering death. During those three months at home after her heart attack, she'd felt like she was dead already—forgotten, invisible, useless. She'd had no purpose, no reason for getting up in the morning. She didn't have a life outside of work. Years of sitting home waiting for Chandler to call had become a habit, and after his death, she'd just stuck to it.

Of course, she thought with an unexpected surge of irritation, he'd called only when it suited him. And truth be told, it hadn't suited him all that often during the last years of his life.

"Enough," she muttered under her breath, smoothing her jacket. No good would come from thinking along these lines. She wouldn't tarnish Chandler's memory by dwelling on his faults. She'd known she was walking a lonely path when she'd first taken up with him. There was no point in wallowing in regrets about it now.

And yet, lately the regrets had been seeping in anyway, unwanted, cold, and destructive, like water in a basement bathroom.

Chapter Eleven

Joe's deep, someone's-at-the-door bark reverberated through the house. Sammi took a last glance at herself in the bathroom mirror and smoothed her hair. She'd straightened it, curled it, then straightened it again in an uncharacteristic fit of indecisiveness. At least she'd had no trouble settling on her clothes; she was wearing her default, goes-anywhere black skirt, paired with a drapey white jersey blouse and high-heeled mules.

Why was she so concerned about the way she looked, anyway? She was only seeing Chase because her life coach had instructed her to.

At least, that was what she was trying to tell herself. She didn't want to get involved with a law-enforcement officer, she reminded herself. She wanted a man with a safe, predictable job—not a man whose job could leave him shot and paralyzed, or worse. She was going out with Chase to get over her date-bashing disorder, not because she intended to pursue a romantic relationship.

All the same, a shiver of anticipation shot up her spine

as the doorbell rang. Drawing a deep breath, Sammi grabbed her purse and went to the door.

Chase stood on the other side, wearing a long-sleeved blue shirt and khakis. His gaze ran over her, turning her knees to Jell-O. "You look great."

Pleasure coursed through her. "Thanks."

Joe shoved his head out the door beside her. Chase scratched his ear, causing the dog's tail to wave like a stubby metronome. Sammi coaxed the animal back inside and ordered him to stay, then closed the door and walked beside Chase to his SUV. When he opened the passenger door, Sammi was surprised to see a burly man sitting in the backseat.

"This is my partner, Paul," Chase said. "I thought it would be fun to have him and his wife join us."

That shot the concept of a romantic dinner for two. Which was just as well, Sammi told herself sternly. Tamping down her disappointment, she stretched out her hand and smiled. "Great! It's nice to meet you."

"Likewise." He had a friendly smile and salt-and-pepper hair. "Chase has told me a lot about you."

She gave a rueful smile. "How my dog ate his wallet, how I spilled coffee on his lap, or how I gave him a concussion?"

"He left out the coffee part."

Sammi laughed.

"Paul's wife is a neonatal nurse," Chase said as he backed the car out of the drive. "She's going to meet us at the restaurant."

"Great," Sammi said again. She twisted around to talk to Paul. "How's your dad's knee?"

"It's healing nicely, thanks. He's in physical therapy

and he's not too thrilled that they're working him so hard, but he's doing well."

"Glad to hear it." She turned and glanced at Chase. "So how long have you two been partners?"

"Three years."

"Three very loo-o-ng years," Paul added. "But we were friends before that."

The two men regaled her with stories about their work until Chase parked the car across the street from Zapeta's, a tony restaurant near Utica Square. The restaurant's entrance was covered by a curved burgundy canopy and framed by sculpted shrubbery lit with tiny lights. Chase held the heavy beveled-glass door for Sammi, and she stepped into the dimly lit restaurant.

A petite blonde with stylish short hair and warm brown eyes rose from a seat in the foyer. She hugged Chase, then greeted Paul with a kiss full on the mouth. Paul put his arm around her waist and pulled her close, his eyes softening as he looked at her.

"Sammi, this is my wife, Melanie," Paul said.

Sammi shook the blonde's hand. "Nice to meet you."

"Nice to meet you, too." Melanie gave her a warm smile.

"I'll, uh, see about our table," Chase said. He stepped up and spoke to the host at the podium.

Melanie eyed her with frank curiosity. "I've known Chase for three years, and this is the first time he's ever voluntarily introduced us to a woman in his life."

Despite herself, Sammi's heart sped up. She grinned. "The implication being, you sometimes force him to?"

Paul laughed. "You've got her number. Mel is an incorrigible busybody."

Melanie playfully elbowed her husband. "Like you're

not." She turned back to Sammi. "You must have made quite an impression on him."

Delight galloped through her. She tried to rein it in. "Having your dog pull down his shorts will do that," she said dryly.

She related the tale of how they'd met, much to Melanie's amusement. Chase rejoined them, and the host picked up four leather-covered menus and led them to a table set with white tablecloths, yellow roses, and votive candles. Chase held out Sammi's chair and seated himself beside her.

"I understand you're a neonatal nurse," Sammi said after they'd given the waiter their orders.

Melanie nodded. "I primarily work with preemies."

"She's really good at dealing with infantile behavior," Chase said dryly. "That's why she married Paul."

Throughout the meals, the conversation was easy and fun and full of laughter. Chase was attentive and amusing, and more than once, Sammi surreptitiously glanced at him, only to find him looking at her, as well.

Melanie and Paul shared an easy, bantering rapport and an obvious affection for each other. A twinge of longing coursed through Sammi as she watched them. They had what she wanted: a relationship filled with warmth and humor and depth.

She cast a sideways glance at Chase and met his gaze. He smiled, and a distinct spark shot between them. Rattled, she turned her attention back to her pasta, but she was keenly aware of Chase's every move beside her.

As the waiter cleared their plates, Melanie put her napkin on the table and looked at Sammi. "Care to go with me to the powder room?"

"Absolutely."

The two women made their way to the back of the restaurant and stepped into a room with Venetian plaster walls, taupe-shaded chandeliers, and matching sconces. Melanie set her purse on the marble countertop and took out a lipstick, gazing at Sammi in one of the three gold-framed mirrors. "So what do you think about Chase?"

She'd known the question was coming, but she still felt oddly unprepared to answer it. "He's great." Sammi pulled her small black purse off her shoulder and unzipped it.

Melanie nodded. "We've been hoping he'd meet a girl and settle down."

"Why hasn't he?"

"He doesn't let people get close very easily." Melanie leaned toward her reflection to apply the lipstick. "He and his brother had a pretty rough childhood, and he doesn't often let down his guard."

"He told me a little about his dad," Sammi said, pulling a hairbrush out of her purse.

"Did he tell you he took care of his mom while she was dying, and pretty much raised his little brother?"

Sammi looked at her in the mirror and shook her head. "He just said he watched him a lot while their mother worked."

"Yeah, well, he did more than watch him. Chase was thirteen and his brother eight when his mom died. The dad was always either gone or drunk, so he was no help. He was finally arrested when Chase was barely eighteen and his brother was thirteen. Instead of letting Luke go to a foster home, Chase worked two jobs to support him."

"Wow."

"I don't know too many teenagers who would put their own lives on hold for five years to care for a sibling. He's a special guy."

Sammi was discovering how special by the moment. "He and Luke must be close."

Melanie nodded. "Although you wouldn't necessarily know it to see them together. They're always trying to prove each other wrong and one-up each other, and they argue about everything from the best way to barbecue ribs to whether OSU or OU is the better university. But they've got a really strong bond." She snapped the lid back on her lipstick. "And it's killing Chase that he's gotten the kid brother he's always watched out for into such a—" Melanie stopped abruptly.

"Such a what?" Sammi prompted. *Bind? Bad situation?*

Melanie shook her head and gave an apologetic smile. "I'm sorry. I'm speaking out of turn—as usual. Chase would be upset that I even brought up the subject."

"Since I don't even know what the subject is, no harm done." Sammi smiled reassuringly. "In any event, he'll never know you said a word."

"Thanks." Melanie gave her a quick grin, then dropped her lipstick into her purse and clicked it closed. "Ready to get back to the table?"

"Sure." Sammi followed Melanie out of the powder room, wondering what sort of situation Chase had inadvertently gotten his brother into, and why Melanie couldn't talk about it. The woman hadn't been shy about sharing information about Chase up to that point.

Maybe she could figure out a way to get Chase to tell her himself.

~

"I really liked your friends."

Chase glanced over at Sammi as he steered his car

down Peoria Avenue. "Yeah? They liked you, too." Too much, actually. He'd invited Paul and Melanie on the spur of the moment, wanting to make the evening feel more like a group outing than a date. He hadn't meant for it to turn into an I'm-serious-about-this-girl-and-want-her-to-meet-my-friends sort of date. He'd unwittingly stepped their relationship up a notch.

"Melanie invited me to a Pokeno party next month."

"Really." What the hell was Pokeno?

"Yeah. I really like her." She looked over at him. "I understand you're their son's godfather."

The thought of the impish four-year-old made him grin. "Yeah. Max is a great kid."

"Apparently you help coach his pee-wee baseball team and you taught him how to fish."

Man, Melanie really knew how to run her mouth. "Good to see she didn't leave anything out. Must have been some visit to the ladies' room."

"It was quite the fact-finding mission." Sammi grinned. "But then, I got in a little extra reconnaissance when you and Paul were talking to that person from the DA's office."

Oh, jeez—there was no telling what Melanie had told Sammi. Paul had reassured him that his wife had no idea Chase was filling in for Luke's life-coaching clients, but the instant bond between the two women made him uneasy. If she mentioned Luke's name or occupation, Sammi was likely to put two and two together.

"Did you find out anything of interest?"

"Lots of things."

"Should I be worried?"

"Actually, Melanie thinks very highly of you."

"Good to know I have her fooled."

Chase pulled into Sammi's drive. "Sit tight. I'll get your door." Chase got out and walked around to the passenger side. He took her hand to help her out of the SUV, then reluctantly relinquished it.

He'd been dying to touch her all night. The way her silky blouse slid against her skin had been taunting him ever since he'd first picked her up. It was a good thing the evening was nearly over.

The gaslight by the door danced on her hair as she dug in her purse for her key. "Want to come in for some coffee?" she asked.

He shifted his stance. "I'd, uh, probably better get going."

"You're afraid I'm going to burn you again, aren't you?"

"No. It's just . . . it's—it's a work night, and . . . and . . ." Oh, jeez—she was biting her bottom lip.

She tried to grin, but her lips wobbled. "I can understand if you're afraid of me." He was—but not for the reason she thought.

She shifted her gaze down to her feet, but not before he saw the insecurity in her eyes.

What the hell. One quick cup of coffee wouldn't hurt anything. "Actually, a cup of coffee sounds great."

Joe's deep bark sounded on the other side of the door as she inserted her key. Chase followed her into her time warp of a house as the giant dog did a happy dance around Sammi.

"If he bothers you, I can put him out," she said.

The whole purpose of being here was to prove that he was unfazed by any of the previous mishaps. Chase shook his head and patted his back pocket. "I swapped my wallet for a money clip, so I'm good."

Chase petted the dog's head, then followed Sammi into

the kitchen. She pulled a rawhide bone out of the pantry and gave it to Joe, then put on the coffee.

"Let's go sit down while it brews." Chase followed her back into the living room and sank beside her on the fan-backed sofa. She folded one leg over the other. Man, she had world-class legs—smooth and long and shapely. He fought to keep his gaze—and his thoughts—above the waist, and seized on the first topic that came to mind.

"Did you have any pets before Joe?"

She nodded. "I used to have cats, but I developed a bad allergy. After that, I had a Scottie mix." Her voice grew somber. "He died just before I moved to Tulsa."

"Oh." What kind of condolences were expected for a pet? "I'm sorry."

"Thanks." She unfolded her legs. His mouth went dry as her skirt fluttered up her thigh. "What about you?" she asked.

He'd lost track of the topic. He dragged his eyes away from her legs and back up to her face.

"Why don't you have a pet?" she prompted.

"I'm gone too much. It wouldn't be fair to the animal."

"Did you have a pet when you were a child?"

"Not officially. But I had a stealth cat."

She laughed. "A stray?"

He nodded. "My brother and I secretly fed it." It was one of the many secrets they'd kept as kids—wearing long-sleeved shirts in the summer to hide their bruises, making up stories to cover for their father's lack of a job, inventing reasons why they didn't have money for school field trips. He'd grown up in a tangled nest of lies, and he'd vowed that if he ever clawed his way out, he'd never lie again.

Yeah, right. He swallowed down a lump of guilt.

"Melanie told me a little about your brother," Sammi said.

Oh, hell. "Yeah?" He deliberately kept his voice nonchalant, even though his pulse was racing. "What did she say?"

"Just that you two are really close."

His shoulder muscles tensed, even as he put on his give-nothing-away neutral expression. How much did she know? Hell. If Melanie had said that his brother was a life coach or even mentioned his name, Sammi would figure it out—not to mention that the whole Witness Protection thing was supposed to be secret. Sammi wasn't a security risk, and Luke wasn't in danger as long as his whereabouts were unknown, but still, it would be a breach of protocol.

Sammi shifted her torso. The silky fabric of her blouse moved over her breasts, exposing a glimpse of deeper cleavage. "She said that you took care of him when you were kids."

Chase lifted his shoulders. "He's family. It was no big deal."

"Yeah, it was." The way she looked at him made his heart beat faster. "And I really admire you for it. It says a lot about your character."

Yeah, right. And if she ever found out how he was deceiving her now, it would say a whole lot more.

"You haven't told me a lot about your brother," she continued. "You said he was a consultant, but you didn't say what kind. I don't even know his name."

Oh, hell. She was looking straight at him, with those eyes that seemed to see right through him. He couldn't pull off a lie; his gut was knotted with guilt, and she was sure to read it. She was already reading something into his hesitation. Her head tilted to one side, and her brows scrunched together. "Chase? Are you okay?"

Diversion—that was his only recourse. He grabbed the first thing that came to mind. "The truth is, I'm having a hard time following this conversation, because I can't think about anything except how beautiful you are, and how much I like you, and how much I want to kiss you."

Her eyes widened as he leaned forward and placed his hand on her upper arm. Her mouth formed a very kissable little "oh" of surprise as he moved in to lightly, softly drop a mere whisper of a kiss on her mouth. She sat perfectly still for a second. Her eyelids fluttered closed—and then her arms wound around his neck, and she was kissing him back.

Dear God in heaven. A lightning bolt of desire shot through him, so hard and hot he barely knew what hit him. All he knew was he couldn't get enough. She tasted both sweet and salty, and she smelled like flowers and herbal shampoo and, most compellingly, an undernote of warm, willing woman that was Sammi's scent alone.

She strained toward him, pulling him close, pulling him down, until he was lying on top of her on the sofa. Her breasts pressed against his chest, warm, soft, tempting mounds that he ached to touch. He moved his hand down her outer ribs and caressed the sides of her breasts, his mouth mating with hers in a hot slide of need.

She moaned and wrapped one of those long, lush legs around his. Every thought fled his mind as his mouth moved over her skin.

He kissed her neck, kissed the soft shell of her ear, then returned to her wet, succulent mouth. He couldn't get enough of her, couldn't get close enough. Her leg tightened around his. She clutched his back, tugging erotically on the back of his belt.

He deepened the kiss. Her mouth opened and flowered, and her grip on the back of his belt tightened. He felt her hands slide down his butt. She tugged on the back of his belt again, this time with such force that the buckle dug into his belly.

Holy mackerel. He was content to take things slow, but from the insistent way she was groping him, apparently she wanted to pick up the pace. It felt as if she were trying to pull off his pants without unfastening his belt.

Well, whatever she wanted, he was up for the job. "Unbuckle it," he whispered against her ear.

"What?" The word was a hot breath.

"My belt. Unbuckle it." He pulled back to give her access. The buckle bit harder into his skin. The tugging was getting seriously uncomfortable now.

She opened her eyes and fixed him with a passion-glazed stare. *"What?"*

"If you don't want to, I'll do it myself." He reached for the buckle.

She drew back, her eyes wide and alarmed. "This is all moving too fast."

"I thought so, too, but . . ." Jesus Christ! It felt like she was shoving her entire hand straight up his inseam. "Sweetheart, you really need to let go. You're killing me."

"I—think we just need to call a halt to things." She put her hands against his chest.

Wait a minute. If her hands are on my chest, who the hell is pushing up my butt?

Chase twisted around to see Joe standing on his hind

legs, his front paws braced on Chase's crotch, his mouth yanking earnestly at his belt.

"Hey!" Chase swatted at the dog with his leg. At the same time, Sammi sat up, which sent Chase rolling to the floor. The dog gave a startled yelp and dashed to the far side of the room.

Chase scrambled to right himself. Sammi jumped to her feet, her expression alarmed.

"Your dog was chewing my belt," Chase hurried to explain, "and I thought it was you."

Sammi's brow scrunched together. "You thought *I* was chewing your belt?"

"No! I thought you were tugging on my belt, and poking at my . . ." He stopped, cleared his throat and started again. "I thought you were trying to pull my pants down without unfastening my belt."

"What?" She stared at him as if he were insane.

He swallowed hard. "While I was kissing you," he tried to explain. "Your dog was trying to pull down my pants, and I thought it was you."

She stared at him another moment, and then she snickered. Her snicker became a laugh.

It was contagious. The next thing he knew, they were both gasping for air. Chase laughed as he hadn't laughed in years, until his stomach hurt and his face was sore. Every time he'd nearly get a grip, she'd start in again, which would set him off on another round. The dog joined in with a plaintive howl, which made them both double over.

When they finally caught their breath, Sammi wiped the tears running down her cheeks. "I thought you'd suddenly turned awfully demanding."

"I thought the same thing about you."

She burst into a fresh peal of laughter. "I did it again, didn't I?" She wiped her wet lashes. "I hurt you."

Oh, hell. He was supposed to be helping her get over that stupid neurosis, not making it worse. "No." He adamantly shook his head. "No. It wasn't you; it was your dog. And I wasn't hurt. I was just slightly molested."

"That sounds wrong on so many levels."

So was kissing her. He grinned and rose to his feet. "I'd better get going."

"But you haven't had your coffee."

"It's late. I need to go."

She stood and walked him to the door. He dropped a kiss on her lips. The urge to pull her back into his arms and pick up right where they'd left off threatened to overtake him.

"I'm sorry," she said, holding Joe by the collar as she opened the door.

"Don't be. I'm not."

But he was. What the hell was he doing? Chase believed in planning his work and working his plan, and he'd just made a huge deviation from his charted course of action. He was supposed to date her casually, restore her confidence, then ease out of the picture. He wasn't supposed to get physically involved with her. He damned sure wasn't supposed to develop feelings for her. What was going on here? He had a better time with Sammi when things went wrong than he'd ever had with anyone else when things went right.

He'd have to do a better job at keeping things under control, he thought as he headed to his car. Next time he saw her, he had to make sure things stayed light. Light and easy and platonic.

Problem was, when it came to Sammi, his feelings weren't platonic at all.

Chapter Twelve

So how are things going?" her coach asked Thursday evening.

"Not great." Sammi twirled the cord of her bedroom phone, a reproduction of a 1930s boudoir model. "I haven't heard from Chase since we went out to dinner last week."

"Tell me what happened."

As she paced her bedroom, Sammi relayed all the details, including the kiss, Joe's attack, and the laughter. "And then he left, and I haven't heard from him since." She stretched out on her bed. "I guess he's not all that interested."

"If he weren't interested, he wouldn't have kissed you."

"Maybe it was a pity kiss."

"Did it feel like a pity kiss?"

Just thinking about it made her warm and tingly. She smiled up at the ceiling. "No."

"So—how did it feel?"

"Hot. Really, really hot." So hot it was a wonder there

weren't scorch marks on the sofa. She rolled over on her belly. "But that's just my perspective."

"If you thought it was hot, I'm sure he thought so, too."

"Maybe my hot is someone else's tepid."

"You sound pretty hot."

So do you. Sexual tension burned through the phone line, throwing her off guard. What was going on? She'd always been a one-man woman. How could she be drawn to her life coach at the same time she was so attracted to Chase?

"I don't think you can tell that over the phone." She sat up and swung her legs to the floor. "Anyway, apparently I scared him off."

"Maybe his job took him out of town."

"Phones work out of town."

"Well, some guys just don't like to talk on the phone."

She stood up and straightened a print of Jackson Pollock's *Moon-Woman* on her bedroom wall. "He talked on the phone for more than half an hour the night he got that concussion," she reminded him.

"I thought you said he was talking to his partner."

"Yeah, that's what he said."

"Maybe he hates to talk on the phone, but he has to do it for work, so he avoids it during his spare time."

Sammi frowned. Luke seemed to be going out of his way to excuse Chase's lack of communication. "I don't think so. And even if that were the case—which I sincerely doubt—if he really liked me, he'd suck it up and call." She walked to her vanity table and sat down on the satin stool. "I think I must not measure up to his criteria for sore pig surgery."

"His *what?*"

"He has this whole list of stuff he's looking for in a woman, and when I talked to his partner's wife yesterday, she told me he calls it his sore pig surgery. It's some sort of code or something."

On the other end of the phone, Chase was seized by a sudden, violent cough attack. She was about to ask if he was okay when he finally cleared his throat. "Sorry," he said, his voice ragged.

"You really need to see someone about that cold of yours," she told him. "It's gone on way too long."

"Yeah. I might do that." He cleared his throat again. "Why, um, were you talking with his partner's wife yesterday?"

"Because she'd invited me to a Pokeno party at her place, and she called to give me the time and address."

"What's Pokeno?"

"It's sort of like bingo with cards. It's a women's party thing."

"Oh. So . . . what else did she tell you about him?"

"That he has a life plan all mapped out with timelines and everything, and he thinks he can follow it. Isn't that the dumbest thing you've ever heard?"

A brief pause echoed over the line. "Actually, I think it's pretty smart. You have to know what you want before you can get it."

"But if you have too narrow of a concept of what you want, you might miss out on something even better. Chase is completely ignoring the divine plan."

"Divine plan?"

"Yeah. The thread he's supposed to pull through the tapestry of the universe."

Silence pulsed over the line. "You think he has one?"

"Sure. Everyone does. But if we think we already know what's best and close our minds to the clues the universe is giving us, we end up getting all off course and tangled up." She aligned the perfume bottles on her vanity table. "That's sort of why I hired you. To give me spiritual promptings and help me get on the right path. Or at least off the wrong one."

"Whoa. Time out, Sammi." His voice rose in what sounded like alarm. "I'm not a guru or prophet or psychic or anything. Don't look to me for spiritual advice."

"I don't look to *you*. But God often talks through other people."

"What makes you think he's talking through me?"

She rose and crossed the room again. "Well, I'd prayed for guidance, and then your newspaper ad caught my eye, and I felt an urge to call your number. So I think that was a spiritual prompting."

"I'm just a regular guy, Sammi. I'm not doling out heavenly advice here."

"If you were, you wouldn't know it."

"Yeah, well, trust me, I'm not." His voice was low and gruff. "And I don't want you thinking I'm some sort of celestial messenger or something."

Sammi pulled her brows together. "You sound upset."

"I'm fine. How the heck did we get off on this, anyway? You were telling me about Chase and his criteria."

"Right. He thinks he knows exactly what he wants, and apparently it's not a woman who constantly inflicts bodily harm." Sammi sank back on her bed. "Which means I'm batting a thousand in the injuring-and-running-off-guys department."

"But you said he didn't get hurt."

"He didn't leave with any cuts or burns. But it had to hurt to fall off the couch after my dog molested him."

"Couch rolling and dog molestation don't count. You didn't injure the guy yourself."

"Still, here's the thing: Chase is looking for a woman with a neat, orderly, totally together life, and everything about mine is messy and chaotic." She sighed. "And I really hate it, because I'm crazy about him."

The phone was silent for a long moment. "But you don't want to get involved with him. You're only seeing him to get over your man-mangling habit, remember?"

"Yeah. But I really, really like him."

"You're not supposed to."

"I can't help it."

"Yes, you can." He spoke in an authoritative, no-nonsense tone. "You need to stick to the original plan. Go out with this guy two more times and prove to yourself that you can date a man without injuring him. That's the whole goal of this exercise."

"I'm not sure I see it as just an exercise anymore."

"Well, it is. It's a practice session."

"What if it's not?"

"It is." His voice had a hard edge she'd never heard before. "And I want you to keep in mind that the point of practice is to sharpen your skills so you play your best in the real game. This is not the game."

"But—"

"No buts about it." His tone was steely. "You can't change the rules in the middle of a game, and the rules are, you're not supposed to get attached to this guy."

The tone of his voice said there was no point in discussing it further. But in the back of her mind, she couldn't help wondering: *What if I can't help it?*

~

The next day, Sammi stood in front of twelve graphic-arts students from Tulsa University who were clustered around a display of black-and-white photos in the museum carriage house.

"As you probably know, the art deco movement started in Paris in 1925 at the Exposition Internationale des Arts Décoratifs et Industriels," Sammi said, pointing to a daguerreotype of what looked like an old World's Fair site. "The style incorporated lots of influences. One of the biggest ones was the opening of Tutankhamen's tomb."

Sammi's cell phone rang. She pulled it from her pocket, glanced at the number, and briefly closed her eyes. Ms. Arnette—calling from the main house, yet again. The woman had been constantly on her case for the past two weeks.

"Excuse me," Sammi said apologetically to the group. "I have to take this. Go ahead and browse through the photos, and I'll be back to answer any questions in a moment." Sammi hurried out to the rose garden and opened her phone.

"Sammi, please come to my office," Ms. Arnette said, using that imperious tone that set Sammi's teeth on edge. The woman never bothered to ask if she was busy or in the middle of something; she just expected Sammi to drop everything at her slightest whim.

When Ms. Arnette had first returned to work, Sammi had tactfully suggested that they set a time each week to go over their calendars.

Ms. Arnette's eyes had widened, as if she were appalled. "Whenever Mr. Phelps needed me for something, he didn't make an appointment or ask if I was busy. I worked for him, and you work for me."

Actually, I work for the board, Sammi had wanted to say but thought it wise to keep her mouth shut.

"I have a college class touring the art exhibit," Sammi told Ms. Arnette now. "I'll be free in about twenty minutes."

Stony silence reigned for a full ten seconds. "If that's the best you can do, well, I suppose I'll see you then."

Sammi hung up the phone and blew out an exasperated breath. The woman had always been difficult, but she'd gotten worse in the last few weeks. She badgered Sammi about little things, interrupted her constantly, and questioned her every move. Sammi suspected she was trying to get her to inappropriately explode or resign.

Well, Sammi had no intention of doing either. She'd simply grin and bear it and wait the woman out.

Her life coach had advised her differently last night. Sammi watched a bee hover above a white rose as the conversation replayed in her mind.

"Sounds to me like you need to talk to the museum's board of directors," he'd said. "After all, they hired you."

Sammi had gazed out her living room window and watched the wind blow the star-shaped leaves of the large tree in her front lawn. In the last week, the tips of the leaves had started to turn gold. "I don't want to cause Ms. Arnette unnecessary trouble."

"That's very nice, Sammi, but nice is not always the way to go."

"I know, but this is a special case."

"I have a feeling that you think everyone is a special case."

"Yeah, well, everyone is."

"That's what makes *you* special, Sammi." Maybe it was just his lingering cold, but his voice had come out low and husky, and the tone had seemed fond and familiar and almost, well, intimate. It had made her heart quicken.

The bee floated to another rose, and a gust of wind blew Sammi's hair across her face. She pulled it back, pulling her thoughts back to the present.

She needed to get back to the tour, then go see what Ms. Arnette wanted this time. Jamming her phone in her jacket pocket, she turned and headed back into the carriage house.

~

Arlene glanced up as Sammi entered her office twenty minutes later. Usually she rose whenever someone came in, but it was important to keep Sammi in her place.

It was becoming more and more difficult to be around the young woman. Arlene found it almost physically painful to look at her now. Young, eager, and educated, Sammi was everything she was not.

"Have a seat, Sammi."

Sammi perched on the edge of an armless chair, her back erect, her hands folded in her lap. She wore a navy pantsuit today, and her blondish-brown hair was pulled back in a low ponytail. It was hard to find fault with her appearance, although Arlene wished she could.

She tapped her fingers on the paper in front of her. "It's time for your job performance review."

Sammi's eyebrows rose. "I thought they were done annually. And . . ."

"Yes?"

She hesitated. "Actually, I thought the board would do mine."

Arlene stiffened. "Well, you thought wrong. I'm the senior curator, and I do the reviews of everyone on the museum staff. And I've decided to start doing them semi-annually." She pulled out a sheet of paper and passed it across her desk.

Sammi's forehead creased as she looked at it. "These are awfully low marks."

"Yes, well, your performance has been less than stellar."

Sammi's frown deepened. She looked up at Arlene, her hazel eyes troubled. "But I handle all of my responsibilities."

"You handle the responsibilities that interest you. You don't satisfactorily do the things I request."

"Give me an example."

Arlene bristled. "When I asked you to come in here just now, you told me you were busy and would have to come later."

"I was conducting a scheduled tour."

"You ignored my direction."

"What did you want me to do? Just bail on them?"

"There is no need to talk to me in that tone." Arlene tapped her desk with her finger. "This right here is an example of your bad attitude."

"I don't have a bad attitude!"

"Now you're being argumentative."

Sammi drew in a deep breath and closed her eyes for

a moment. She looked like she might be counting to ten. "Ms. Arnette, I'm doing my best. Could you please tell me how I could improve?"

You could quit. But she couldn't say that. No, in this day and age, you had to have a paper trail documenting everything before you could fire someone.

Sammi leaned forward. "I understand that you're not a fan of some of the new programs, but the board approved them and supports them."

That's because you pushed them through while I was out. And now I'm having to go through Justine's things, and I hate it so much that just the thought makes me nauseous. Arlene lifted her chin. "I don't appreciate your insolent attitude."

"With all due respect, this isn't about attitude. This is about you not making a place for me here."

That's because there isn't a place. Arlene hunched forward on her desk. "The board hired you because they thought I wasn't coming back, and now that I am, you need to accept that you're in a subordinate role."

"I don't have a problem with that. But if I'm to be a subordinate, you have to be a leader, and that means you need to embrace the new programs."

Arlene's jaw clenched. "I don't have to do any such thing."

Sammi closed her eyes again. When she opened them, they were disarmingly filled with sympathy. "It must have been awfully hard on you, coming back and discovering I'd been hired to replace you."

Arlene jerked her gaze away, oddly rattled by the warmth in Sammi's eyes. "You will never replace me. You may have the job, but you will not replace me."

"No. I'm sure that's true." Sammi's voice was calm and soft. She leaned forward. "Ms. Arnette, may I ask you a frank question?"

As if I could stop you. "Of course."

"You seem to dislike me. Have I done something to offend you?"

Yes. You exist. You're eager and bright, and you make me feel old and useless. Arlene twisted her fingers together. "You're being ridiculous. This is a matter of performance, not likes and dislikes." She waved her hand dismissively. "Take your review and look it over. If you have any comments, write them on the form."

"I'll do that."

"Good. I'll expect it signed and on my desk before I leave for the day."

Sammi's eyes rounded. "But it's twenty minutes before closing time."

"Well, if you'd come in here when I requested it, you'd have had plenty of time."

Sammi unfolded from the chair, stiff as an ironing board. Her footsteps clicked angrily on the granite floor as she headed out of the office.

As the door swung closed behind her, Arlene turned toward the window and caught a glimpse of her reflection. Her forehead was pulled in a frown, and her lips were puckered in displeasure. She looked like a bitter old shrew.

She sank her head in her hands.

Oh, God—when had she become such an awful person? This wasn't the woman she'd dreamed of becoming when she'd so eagerly left her parents' farm as a young girl.

With a heavy sigh, she tried to turn her attention to the papers on her desk, but she couldn't concentrate on anything. Guilt burned in her stomach like an ulcer.

She was only doing what she had to do, she told herself. Hadn't Chandler taught her that it was a dog-eat-dog world, and you had to protect your turf? She'd certainly seen him do it enough times. That time the receptionist with the blond beehive hair had started gossiping about them and he'd let her go with no notice. The time the company vice president disagreed with Chandler and ended up transferred to Alaska. The time Chandler's accountant had questioned some of his expenditures and found himself terminated.

Why, Chandler had been defending his turf against a rival oil company the very day Arlene had met him. She'd been all of twenty-one years old, but it seemed like just yesterday.

He'd been seated behind his desk, the phone to his ear, his tie loosened, his sleeves rolled up. He'd looked like a movie star, and for the first time, Arlene knew what it meant to go weak at the knees. Broad-shouldered as John Wayne, handsome as Cary Grant, and tough-talking as Lee Marvin, he'd been in his early forties—all-powerful, sophisticated, and worldly.

"That oil lease is ours, Harry," he'd barked into the phone as the personnel manager had steered Arlene to the door of his office, "and Extech is not going to get it away from us. Get them on the other line and double the offer. Do it now. I'll wait." He'd looked up, the phone still to his ear, and motioned them in.

"Mr. Phelps, this is Arlene Arnette," said the personnel manager, a stumpy woman with helmet hair and cat-eye glasses on a chain around her neck. "She's applying for the secretarial position."

Chandler's gaze had raked over her, starting with her borrowed navy pumps, moving to the stockings she'd bought for graduation from stenography school the week before, up to the blue serge suit she'd sewn herself on her mother's old Singer. When his eyes met hers, she'd felt like she was plunging down the hill on the state fair roller coaster—thrilled, excited, and afraid she was about to be sick.

"Do you take shorthand?" he'd asked.

"Yes, sir."

"Type?"

"Yes, sir. Sixty-five words a minute."

He'd held up his hand and turned his attention back to the phone, apparently listening to the party on the other end. "What? Hell. Didn't you tell him you're my authorized agent?" He paused a moment, then blew out a hard breath. "All right, then. Tell him I'm on my way."

He'd pressed the lever on his phone, then punched the interoffice button. "Helga—who's the pilot on call today? Well, find the hell out, and have him meet me at the airport. I need to go to Houston. When? Now, dammit!"

He'd slammed down the phone, risen from his chair, grabbed his jacket, and fixed Arlene with his brown eyes. "Ready to go?"

"Go where?"

"To some godforsaken hellhole of a town outside of Houston. I can dictate some letters to you on the way."

"You-you mean I'm hired?"

"If you're ready to start right now."

"How-how long will we be gone?"

"Well, if we can track down this jackass and get him to sign the papers, we might be back by evening. Otherwise, we'll have to stay overnight. "

"Overnight? I-I don't have anything packed."

"You can get anything you need once we get there." His eyes held a challenging glitter. "You coming, or not?"

He didn't think she'd do it. She didn't think so, either. Her parents were expecting her back at their Okfuskee farm by evening. How could she just up and go to Houston with a strange man?

On the other hand, how could she not? She longed for a life beyond picking bush beans, attending covered dish dinners at First Baptist, and marrying one of the pimply-faced local boys from her rural high school.

Here was her chance. Another opportunity like this wasn't likely to come along. She'd lifted her chin and met Chandler's gaze dead-on. "I'll need a steno pad."

His lip had curled into a grin that made heat pool low in her belly, and from that moment on, she'd lived her life on Chandler time. Whatever he wanted, whenever he wanted it, she'd been up for the challenge. She'd been ready for anything.

Anything, that was, except the plane crash that had killed him and Justine twenty-seven years ago. She hadn't been ready for that.

And she wasn't ready for retirement now. She leaned back in her office chair and sighed. The museum board president had called again yesterday to ask about her plans.

"I really don't know," she'd replied. "I haven't given it any thought."

"I suggest you do, Arlene," he'd said, his voice gentle. "None of us is getting any younger."

She hated the thought of leaving the museum in Sammi's hands, but she didn't have the stomach for any more nasty scenes like the one she'd just pulled. She didn't have Chandler's ruthless streak or killer instinct. The whole incident had left her feeling drained and disgusted with herself.

She leaned back in her chair and toyed with her pearls. She couldn't remember the last time she'd really felt good about herself—except for that lunch with Walter.

It was funny how that kept replaying in her mind. For that one hour, she'd felt interesting and interested. She and Walter didn't really have anything in common except Sammi, but they'd had no trouble finding other things to talk about. He'd asked her lots of questions, and he'd seemed really interested in the answers. He'd even told her she was fascinating.

Just the thought made her smile. Had anyone ever found her fascinating before? Maybe Chandler had, at first—but as time went on his attention had shifted away from her and back to himself. Their relationship had become purely one-sided.

She gazed out the window as if she were seeing the rose garden for the first time and stroked the largest pearl in the center of the necklace. She'd never thought of Chandler in critical terms before, but lately, she was doing a lot of it.

It was going through Justine's belongings, she thought darkly. Handling that woman's things was corroding her memories of Chandler. She hated to admit it, but she couldn't really picture his face now, unless she was looking at his photograph or painting, and even then, it didn't seem to depict the man she knew.

Or the man she'd thought she'd known. As she dug through Justine's things, buried memories kept surfacing like moldy potatoes.

The times he'd been cold and distant. The times he'd ignored Arlene or found fault with her work. The awful, gripping fear that things were over, and he just hadn't bothered to tell her.

No matter how long he stayed away, though, he always came back. "You're the only person who sees good in me," he'd told her. "The only person who can make me feel better about myself."

But who, Arlene wondered, had ever done that for her?

∼

Chase's pulse skipped a beat as Sammi came out the back door of the museum half an hour later. The afternoon sun danced on her hair, making it gleam like polished gold.

He scowled at the thought. Since when did he think in terms of shampoo commercials? And if he was suddenly going to do so, why was it about a woman who was clearly off-limits?

He watched her walk across the parking lot and felt his chest constrict. Something was wrong; her gaze was fixed on the ground, her gait lacked its usual bounce, and her expression was uncharacteristically glum. Even her shoulders looked rounded and sad.

Chase rolled down his car window. "Hey, little girl— want some candy?" he called.

Sammi looked up and smiled. "Depends," she said, adjusting her purse on her shoulder and squinting against the sun. "Got any chocolate?"

"Come closer and find out."

She shook her head. "I only get within grabbing range of suspicious men if they have serious chocolate, and I'm having the kind of day that requires massive amounts."

"Well, get in and we'll go find some."

Grinning, she walked to the car as he climbed out. "You've really got to work on your pickup lines."

"Hey, it got you over here." He leaned over and kissed her on the cheek. The scent of her perfume and shampoo gave him a buzz.

She tucked a strand of hair behind her ears. "What brings you here?"

"You do."

"Don't you know how to use a phone?"

He'd wanted to call a couple dozen times, but he hadn't dared risk it. "I thought it would be harder for you to say no in person."

"Say no to what?"

"To the offer of a wildly romantic evening at the Funtastic Pizza Palace." He leaned against his vehicle. "It's Paul's bowling night, and Melanie was invited to a baby shower, so I volunteered to watch Max. I wondered if you'd join me."

She beamed as if he'd offered an evening in Paris. "That sounds terrific."

"It does?"

"Sure. When does all this start?"

"Pretty much right now. You can either come with me now to pick him up, or you can meet us at the restaurant in about an hour." Either way, they'd end the evening in a public place. He didn't trust himself to take her home.

She looked down at her pantsuit. "I'm good to go."

"Great." He opened the door to his Ford. "Hop in. I'll bring you back for your car at the end of the evening."

She climbed in and fastened her seat belt. "What have you been up to all week?"

He started the engine. "Testifying in federal court in Oklahoma City."

"Do you have to do that often?"

He put the vehicle in gear and steered out of the parking lot. "Whenever a perp I arrest is brought to trial."

"That must give you a sense of satisfaction."

"Yeah." He was going to get the most satisfaction ever in a couple of weeks when he testified against the elder Lambinos—and even more when the idiot nephew was arrested and tried. The local police had picked up Johnny on a minor infraction and pumped him for information, but he'd lawyered up and they'd had to let him go. Until the uncles implicated him, there simply wasn't enough evidence to charge him.

The local police had him under surveillance, though, and he was living up to his reputation as being none too bright. For two weeks, he'd watched Luke's empty house. Apparently he'd bought the story that Luke was out of town on an extended vacation and had yet to learn that Luke and Chase were brothers.

Chase glanced over at Sammi. "You looked kind of down when you came out of the museum. Bad day?"

She pushed back her hair and blew out a sigh. "Ms. Arnette was trying to make it one, but I'm not going to let her."

"Want to talk about it?"

"No." She flashed him a big smile. "I want to hear about your court cases."

Chase told her, and before he knew it, he was pulling into the driveway of Paul and Melanie's brick-and-stucco home in a south Tulsa subdivision.

Melanie greeted them at the door, but before she could even say hello, a little towheaded boy bounded around the corner. "Chase!"

"Hi, sport." Chase caught the boy as he flew into his arms and gave him a big hug.

The boy grabbed his hand when Chase set him down. "You gotta come see! I got a fire truck, and it sprays real water!"

"Real water, huh?" He shot Sammi and Melanie a wink. "Glad it's not that phony stuff."

"It shoots it *everywhere*." The boy stuck his arms straight out and made a whooshing sound as he spun around.

"It's a bath toy," Melanie explained. "We got it yesterday to encourage him to take a bath. He's only supposed to fill it with water when he's in the tub."

"Come see!" The little boy tugged at Chase's hand.

"Just a moment. First I want you to meet a friend of mine. Max, this is Miss Sammi."

Sammi squatted down so she was face-to-face with Max and smiled. "Nice to meet you."

The boy regarded her with curious blue eyes. "You've got a boy's name!"

She grinned. "It's short for Samantha."

"Oh. Want to see my fire engine?"

"I'd love to, if it's okay with your mom."

"It's fine by me," Melanie said. "But Max—you have to wait until bathtime before you put any water in it."

"Okay." The boy grabbed Sammi by one hand, Chase by the other. "Come on!"

~

An hour later, Chase watched as Max pulled a long string of tickets out of the arcade machine at the noisy pizzeria. "Look at all my tickets!" the boy shouted above all the whirring, clanging, and ringing. "I must have a jillion!"

"You've got a lot, all right," Sammi said.

"Yeah!" The boy handed them to her. "How many do I have now?"

Sammi counted them. "Added to the ones you already have, that's three hundred and twenty-four."

"Let's go see what stuff it'll buy." He tugged her hand, pulling her toward the counter.

"Whoa, there, champ," Chase said. "Don't you want to eat some pizza first?"

"Nah. I want to check out the toys."

"Why don't you place our order and then we'll join you in a minute," Sammi suggested.

"Okay." Chase watched Max tug Sammi to the counter that held the redeemable toys and grinned. The boy had taken a real shine to her.

But then, so had Chase. He liked her upbeat nature, liked the way she laughed, liked her up-for-anything enthusiasm—not to mention how much he liked her kissable mouth, mile-long legs, and every other part of her wonderland.

He just liked Sammi, period. And the more time he

spent with her, the more things he found to admire. She'd jumped into the sea of balls to help Max find some lost tickets, and she'd crawled into the ladder tube to help a pregnant mother extract her crying three-year-old. How many people would so wholeheartedly go out of their way to be helpful and kind?

He was crazy about her. He hated the idea of going out with her one more time, then never seeing her again—but he hated the idea of hurting her even more. He couldn't continue to see her without telling her the truth, and if he told her, it was likely to destroy any progress he'd helped her make.

He blew out a hard sigh. For Sammi's sake, he needed to stick with his original plan. But it was going to be hard as hell.

She slipped into the booth across from him. "Max ran into a classmate from preschool." She inclined her head toward a driving game, where Max stood beside a dark-haired boy about his size making va-room va-room motor noises. A dark-haired woman stood nearby. "His friend's mother is going to watch them while they play a few more games. Max needs twenty more tickets to get a fireman's hat."

Chase glanced from the boys back to Sammi and grinned. "Max really likes you, even though you've got girl cooties."

"I hope you can overlook them, as well." The corners of Sammi's eyes creased as she smiled. "He's a great kid."

"Yeah, he is."

She took a sip of her iced tea and eyed him over the rim. "Does your life plan include having kids of your own someday?"

"As a matter of fact, it does. I plan to have exactly two point five."

She gave him a wry grin. "That'll be a neat trick. Of course, first you have to do your sore pig surgery."

Chase burst into laughter. He'd nearly choked when she'd called it that on the phone the other night. "Do my *what?*"

She took a sip of tea and eyed him over the rim. "Melanie told me that your criteria for a woman are called sore pig surgery."

Chase laughed again."It's Operation SCABHOG."

"Oh, pardon me." She gave him a wry grin. "That sounds *so* much nicer."

"It's an acronym."

"Thank goodness." She propped her head on her hands and grinned at him. "What does it stand for?"

What the hell—might as well tell her. He was only going to see her one more time. "Smart, capable, active, beautiful, honorable, organized, and goal-oriented."

"Sounds like you're describing yourself."

"Aw, gee." Chase gave her a teasing grin. "Do you really think I'm beautiful?"

She laughed. "You're impossible."

"Actually, I'm possible. Very possible." *Too possible, as far as you're concerned.*

The air between them grew charged and hot. He forced his eyes away. He was supposed to flirt with her, dammit, but every time he did, things got too heated. He took a sip of iced tea to cool himself down and looked around.

His gaze landed on a lanky man near the emergency exit. Chase's muscles tensed; something about the guy bothered him. He eyed him more intently. The man was crouched beside a curly-haired four- or five-year-old girl in a pink Dora the Explorer T-shirt. As Chase watched, the man lifted his ferret-like face and scanned the room as if he were sizing up the situation. He looked disturbingly familiar.

Wanted poster familiar.

Chase slid out of the booth. "Keep an eye on Max," he said tersely.

"Why? What's wrong?"

But Chase didn't have time to answer, because at that moment, the man clamped a hand over the girl's mouth, snatched her up, and pushed out the emergency exit.

Adrenaline dumped into Chase's veins. He ran across the room, weaving around a waitress carrying a tray of drinks. She jumped back and spilled them onto a heavyset man standing by a video machine.

"Hey!" he shouted.

Chase charged past and pushed out the emergency door, into the night air.

The man was already in the parking lot, shoving the wailing child into the driver's side of a black Silverado. Dammit, Chase didn't have his gun. "Freeze!" he shouted anyway, hoping to buy some time. Sure enough, the man hesitated and looked up, then pushed the child onto the floor of the passenger seat.

Chase had to get there, *now*. If the man slammed and locked the door, it would be too late.

The man straightened in the driver's seat. Chase's lungs burned as he raced to close the distance. He was almost there—almost.

He watched the man's wiry arm reach for the truck door. His heart crashing in his chest, Chase lunged forward and hurled himself into the truck, landing on top of the man.

The man struggled, trying to force Chase out of the vehicle, but Chase grabbed him around the neck, hauled him out of the truck, and slammed him onto the pavement.

The man grunted as Chase rolled him over, held him down by the back of the neck, and sat on his back.

"Dear God in heaven!" Chase heard a woman gasp.

Chase grabbed the man's hands and held them behind his back, then looked up to see a grandmotherly woman in a floral dress holding a bouquet of birthday balloons.

"What's going on?" asked an elderly gentleman beside her.

"FBI," Chase said. "You got a phone?"

The elderly man nodded, bobbing the white tufts of hair around the bald circle on his head.

"Then do me a favor and call 911." Holding the perpetrator's wrists with one hand, Chase reached in his back pocket and extracted his handcuffs, then expertly snapped them onto the man's wrists.

A childlike scream shrieked from the pickup. Chase looked at the elderly woman, who was clutching her purse in front of her like a shield. "Ma'am, would you mind seeing to the little girl in the truck?" he asked. "This man was trying to abduct her."

"Oh, my heavens!" the woman breathed.

"You got it all wrong," protested the man on the pavement. "I'm her father."

"No! He's not my daddy!" the little girl sobbed.

The woman scurried to the passenger side of the truck, opened the door, and pulled out the weeping child.

Chase searched the man's pants pockets. In the left

front one, he found a handgun. In the right, he found a hunting knife. Sticking the weapons under his belt, he found the man's wallet in his back pocket. He yanked it out, just as a stream of people poured out of the restaurant's emergency exit.

"Hannah?" called a frantic blond woman. "Hannah?"

"Mommy!" The little girl broke away from the elderly woman's embrace and ran toward the blonde.

"What happened?" the woman cried, kneeling down to cradle the child.

"This man tried to abduct your daughter," Chase said.

"Oh, my God!" The woman picked up the girl and hugged her to her chest.

Chase spotted Sammi in the crowd, her arm around Max. He motioned to her with a jerk of his head. She said something to the mother of Max's friend, and the woman put her hand on Max's shoulder. Sammi stepped through the crowd toward him.

"Do me a favor and read his ID to me," Chase called, tossing her the man's wallet.

Sammi caught it, then stepped into the light of the streetlamp and opened it. "It says he's James Dale Raymond."

A pedophile wanted by the FBI for kidnapping, rape, and child pornography. "You sorry sonuvabitch," Chase muttered. He tightened his grip on the man and struggled to get a grip on his emotions, as well. As far as he was concerned, no lowlife was lower than a child sex offender.

"The police are on the way," the elderly man said, closing his cell phone.

"That's lucky for you," Chase muttered to the man. Lucky for him, as well; he was fighting the urge to slam his fist through the fugitive's face, and that was just for warmup.

～

Sammi took Max back inside the restaurant while Chase dealt with the police. She challenged him to a game of arcade basketball and tried to act calm, but her insides were twisted into knots.

She'd known Chase was a law-enforcement officer, but she'd begun to mentally gloss over the fact. After all, he didn't wear a uniform, and she'd never seen him with a gun.

Until today. Watching him pull a gun out of that man's pocket had yanked a primitive chain in her brain, leaving her completely unnerved.

"Your turn." Max handed her the tennis-ball-sized basketball. She tossed it toward the basket and watched it bounce off the rim.

"Looks like you need to work on your free shot, Sammi."

She turned to see Chase strolling up as if nothing had happened. He winked at Max.

"I beat her three times in a row," the boy gleefully exclaimed.

"Wow." Chase grinned and ruffled his hair. "You're almost ready for the pros."

"Nah. I gotta get real tall first."

Chase looked at Sammi and laughed.

Max looked up earnestly. "Is the bad guy going to jail?"

"Yep. For a long, long time."

"What did he do, anyway?"

"He broke some laws."

"Like stealing?"

"Yeah."

"He had a gun, didn't he?"

"Yep."

"My daddy has a gun," Max said solemnly.

"I know. That's because your dad is an FBI agent."

"Like you."

"That's right."

Max cocked his head to the side. "Are you ever scared of gettin' shot?"

Chase cast Sammi a sideways look, and she had the eerie sensation that he could read her mind. "Sometimes. But I've had a lot of training, and so has your dad. We've learned how to take guns away from bad people so that nobody gets hurt."

Max nodded. "I'm gonna learn how to do that when I grow up."

"I thought you were going to be a basketball player."

"I'm gonna be both. An' I'm going to be a fireman, too."

Chase looked at Sammi and grinned. "Well, in that case, you're going to need a lot of energy. What do you say we order that pizza?"

"Yeah!"

Sammi didn't have much of an appetite, but Max and Chase ate like hungry savages. While Max played one last game, Chase filled her in on the details of exactly what happened. Later they stopped at Baskin-Robbins for ice cream, then drove back to the boy's home.

Sammi drew a bath, and Max gleefully climbed into the tub, wearing his new plastic fireman's hat. He took it off long enough to allow Sammi to shampoo his hair, then promptly plopped it on again and played rowdily with his fire engine until the water grew cold.

He dried off, pulled on a pair of fire-truck-printed PJs, then snuggled, all pink and soap-scented, between them on the sofa. Chase read him the same story three times. The party then moved into his race-car-themed bedroom, where Chase and Sammi knelt on either side of him at his bedside as he bowed his white-blond head and said his prayers. Sammi tucked him in, and when Chase smiled at her as the boy's chubby arms stretched around her neck to give her a baby-shampoo-scented hug, a lump formed in her throat. It grew into a solid mass as she watched Chase bend down and drop a kiss on the top of the child's head.

Oh, dear Lord, she realized with alarm. She was falling for Chase.

She wrapped her arms around herself protectively and headed for the hallway.

Chase closed the door to Max's bedroom, then followed Sammi to the living room. "He's a great kid, isn't he?" Chase said.

"Yeah." *And you're a great guy.* She watched him settle on the sofa beside her and struggled to act normal, as if she hadn't just realized that her heart was in free fall. "You were amazing with that kidnapper."

He lifted his shoulders. "Just doing my job."

"What made you notice the man?"

"He looked like he was about to pull something."

"How did you pick up on that all the way across a room?"

He lifted his shoulders. "When you grow up like I did, you get pretty good at picking up signals."

She looked at Chase's tightly clenched jaw and picked up a few signals of her own. "Your dad was really rough on you, wasn't he?" she asked gently.

He shrugged again. "Let's just say he was a good role model of what not to be."

Which made Chase all the more amazing. Her heart tumbled harder. How could she not fall for this man?

A key rattled in the front door, and then it swung open. Melanie stepped into the room, her purse and a pink party-favor bag in her hand. "Hello!" she said merrily. "How was your evening?"

"Completely uneventful," Chase said with a sly grin at Sammi.

"If that was uneventful, I don't want to see your idea of exciting," Sammi retorted.

Melanie looked from one to the other. "What happened?"

"Well . . ." Chase rubbed his chin.

Melanie's brow creased in concern.

"Don't worry—Max is just fine," Sammi said quickly. "But there was a little incident at the Pizza Palace."

After filling Melanie in on the evening's events, Chase and Sammi said their good-byes. The last of the summer's cicadas croaked in the trees as they walked to his car.

"Thanks for joining Max and me tonight," Chase said as he clicked on his seat belt.

"It was a blast. Except for that little attempted-kidnapping incident." She looked at him as he started the engine. "I've gotta say, you sure know how to show a girl a thrilling time."

He shot her a crooked grin. "It was all a setup to impress you."

"Well, it worked." She gazed at his profile in the dark as

he backed his Explorer out of the driveway. "If it weren't for you, who knows what would be happening to that little girl right now?"

His jaw tightened. "I'm afraid I know all too well."

And it bothered the hell out of him; she could tell. Sympathy swelled in her chest. "It's got to be hard, seeing some of the things you see."

"Yeah. Especially if a kid's involved."

She thought of the way her dad used to come home moody and distant, unable to shake the things he'd seen that day. "How do you cope with it?"

He steered the car down the street. "By knowing I'm trying to do something about it."

"Are you ever afraid of getting shot?"

"Nah. I never think about it."

Sammi sighed. "I don't guess officers ever do."

He looked over at her, his brown eyes warm. "It must have been hard on your family when your dad was injured."

That was putting it mildly. The day her father had come home from the hospital was burned into her memory like a brand.

He'd insisted on wheeling himself up the new ramp to the front door, even though it was a steep incline and he was still weak from surgery. His face had been as bloodless and pale as an onion, his mouth twisted into a grimace. When he'd run out of steam halfway up, their mother had rushed to help. Sammi and Chloe had done the same, dropping the "welcome home" banner they'd been holding at the door. Her father had practically bared his teeth at them. "Let me do it myself!" he barked.

He'd struggled for an excruciating twenty more minutes, backing up, going forward, getting stuck. It became the pattern of their lives. He needed help; he didn't want it; he was forced to accept it; he resented the people who provided it.

Chase braked at a stoplight. "After what happened to your dad, I'm surprised you'd want to date a law-enforcement officer."

"I don't." Sammi grinned at him. "But I can't seem to help myself."

                         ~

Her hazel eyes held Chase in a headlock. He couldn't look away, even though he knew he needed to. The air grew steamy enough to fog up the windshield, and sexual tension stretched between them like a rubber band.

Hell. This was supposed to be dating light. He jerked his gaze to the window, looked out, and grabbed the first diversion he saw. "Hey, what's going on at the Java Hut?"

Sammi glanced at the riverfront coffee shop, where a group of people were seated on a brightly lit patio, watching a woman at the microphone. "It's poetry and music night," she said. "Customers can get up and perform."

Chase stepped on the accelerator as the light changed. "I don't understand why people are willing to get up and make fools of themselves. I wouldn't be caught dead emoting in public like that."

From the corner of his eye, he saw her grin. "Sounds like you have some issues."

"Yeah, I guess I do."

"Care to tell me why?"

"Not really."

"Come on," she coaxed.

He blew out a sigh. "My father used to get drunk and think he could sing. He embarrassed me more times than I can count."

"And you don't want to be like him." Her voice was soft.

"Yeah." How the hell had he gotten onto this subject? He'd been looking for a way to lighten things up, and instead he was baring his soul. "Believe me, I'm doing the world a favor. I have a voice like a frog in a bucket." He was relieved to see the museum loom into view. "Do you sing?"

"Only in the shower."

He turned into the parking lot and braked beside her car. "I'd like to hear that sometime. See it, too."

She playfully slapped his arm.

He put the car into gear. "Hey, you just assaulted an officer."

She grinned. "Is there a penalty for that?"

"You bet."

She slanted him a sly grin through lowered lashes. "Maybe we can work out a deal."

"Are you offering me a bribe?"

"Maybe. But since I don't know if you're wired, I'd better just give it to you instead of offering it aloud." She leaned forward, put her hands on his face, and gave him a light kiss.

She started to pull back. He should have let her, but God help him, the touch of her lips drove him crazy. He grabbed her head, wove his fingers into her hair, and kissed her back.

Conscious thought unspooled, then unraveled. Her mouth was sweet and hot and intoxicating. She moaned against his mouth, and the sound drove him crazy. He was about to pull her over the console onto his lap when a bright light beamed in the window, shining directly in his eyes.

Alarm shot through him. His first reaction was to put out his arm and shield Sammi.

The light moved around. "You okay in there?" called a man's voice.

"It's just Ernie, the night guard," Sammi whispered. She smoothed her jacket, ran a hand through her hair, then opened the car door. "Good evening, Ernie," she said, climbing out.

"Oh, it's you, Ms. Matthews. Sorry to disturb you."

"That's quite all right. I went to dinner with a friend, and he's just bringing me back to my car."

Chase waved through the open door. Ernie smiled and nodded. "I was wondering what it was still doing here."

"How's your wife?" Sammi asked.

"Oh, she's much better, thanks. I want to thank you again for that casserole."

"My pleasure. I'm glad she's better."

Chase climbed out of the car. "Ernie, this is Chase Jones," Sammi said. "Chase is in law enforcement, just like you are."

Sammi's overinflated description of Ernie's job seemed to please him. "Oh, yeah? Nice to meet you. What branch are you with?"

"The FBI."

"Oh, wow. A G-man, huh? I wanted to join the FBI, but I didn't have a college degree. But I served with the Tulsa Police for thirty years."

"Good for you. That's real frontline work."

Ernie's head bobbed proudly. "Yeah. Retired from the force five years ago, and been working here ever since."

"Ernie keeps this place safe at night," Sammi explained.

Ernie tipped his hat. "Sorry to bother you folks. Have a nice evening."

"I need to go," Sammi said to Chase as Ernie ambled back to his patrol car.

Yes, she did—before he did anything foolish like pull her back into his arms. Chase walked her to her car, opened the door for her, then dropped a kiss on her forehead.

"Good night. Drive safe."

"You, too." She shot him a winsome smile. "Thanks for an unforgettable evening."

Even without the arrest, it would have been unforgettable, Chase thought as he watched her drive off. Sammi had a way of getting him to tell her things that normally couldn't be pried out of him with a crowbar. The bureau should hire her as an interrogation specialist, he thought wryly.

But extracting information wasn't her only talent. She made him feel things—deep, warm, moving things.

He opened the door of his Explorer and climbed in, scowling at his thoughts. He wasn't supposed to be feeling things for her, dammit.

But how could he help it? She was the kind of woman who knew the night watchman's family and took them food. A casserole, for Pete's sake! How many thirty-year-old single women even knew how to make casseroles?

She was the kind who'd climb into a sea of balls with a bunch of four-year-olds, who'd adopt an overgrown dog with a leather fetish, who'd unself-consciously dress up in ugly old clothes to thrill groups of museumgoers, who'd offer to bring homemade soup to a man she'd only talked to on the phone.

She saw everyone as special—which was the thing that made *her* special.

More than special. One in a million. Make that a billion. And she deserved a guy who would treat her right, right from the get-go. A guy who was honest and trustworthy, a guy who hadn't tricked her or lied to her.

A nerve twitched in Chase's jaw as he started his engine. As soon as he took her on one more date and cured her of her man-harming ways, she was sure to find such a guy.

And Chase already hated his guts.

Chapter Thirteen

Looks like I need to make more margaritas," Melanie said as she emptied the green contents of the glass pitcher into a salt-rimmed glass held by a smiling brunette.

"And more salsa!" called an outgoing blonde named Hailey above the chatter of female voices in Melanie's living room.

Sammi picked up the empty salsa bowl and followed Melanie through the perfume-scented throng into the kitchen. Most of the women Melanie had invited to her party were married to law-enforcement officers, and they were a warm and inclusive group. "Your friends are really nice. Thanks for inviting me."

"I'm glad you could come." Melanie opened the freezer, pulled out some ice, and plopped it in the pitcher. "It's hard to get a word in edgewise with this group, though. I've barely had a chance to talk to you all evening. How are things going with Chase?"

"I have no idea." Sammi leaned against the kitchen counter and sighed. "What's the deal with Chase and telephones?"

Melanie opened the refrigerator and pulled out a bottle of margarita mixer and a jar of salsa. She handed the jar to Sammi. "What do you mean?"

"Well, he hardly ever calls."

"Hmm." Melanie picked up a bottle of tequila from the counter. "Maybe he's afraid his phone is bugged."

Sammi's eyebrows flew up. "You're kidding."

She shook her head. "These guys are overly cautious when it comes to people they care about."

People they care about. A little thrill shot through her that she might be in that category where Chase was concerned.

"Maybe he's taking special precautions because of the Lambino case."

Sammi unscrewed the lid. "Wouldn't Paul be taking the same precautions?"

"Well, Chase is more involved in the case, because—" Melanie abruptly stopped and gave an apologetic smile. "I'm sorry. I'm not allowed to talk about it."

What was the deal? Sammi wanted to press her further, but a petite blonde named Kaitlyn wandered into the kitchen, along with a tall brunette wearing a ponytail. Both carried empty margarita glasses. "What are you two talking about?" Kaitlyn asked.

"About dating a guy in the bureau," Melanie said.

"I'm an expert." Kaitlyn opened a fresh bag of tortilla chips. "I dated two of them before I married Michael. What do you want to know?"

"How do you handle a guy with a dangerous job?" Sammi said, setting the lid on the counter.

"That's easy. You don't." Kaitlyn crunched the chip.

"But doesn't the worry drive you crazy?" Sammi

poured the sauce into the bowl. "My dad was a police officer in Dallas, and he was shot in the line of duty."

"Oh, I'm so sorry," the brunette said.

"Yeah." Kaitlyn's brow creased.

"Even before it happened, my mother was a basket case every time he left the house." Sammi wiped the rim of the jar with a paper towel.

"I relate to your mom," said the brunette.

"Well, I handle it by reminding myself that life is risky," Melanie said. "The hospitals are full of people, and so are the obituaries."

Sammi cleaned a dab of salsa off the countertop. "That hardly seems comforting."

"Yeah, but here's the thing: very few of those people were injured in the line of duty. Most of them got sick or old or were in accidents—things that can happen to any of us, regardless of what job we have or how careful we are." Melanie screwed the lid back on the tequila bottle. "If we worried about every little thing that could ever happen, we'd never leave the house."

"If we really thought about it, we wouldn't stay in the house, either, because that's where most accidents happen," Kaitlyn added. "We'd all just huddle outside under a tree."

"And get hit by lightning," the brunette said. "Or a meteor."

Everyone laughed.

Sammi wasn't ready to concede the point. "But there's an increased risk with a law-enforcement officer."

"Sure." Melanie poured the greenish-yellow mixer into the pitcher. "And a willingness to accept that risk is part of what makes our guys who they are. So we have to accept it, too. To wish Paul had a different job would be to wish he were a different man, and I can't do that. I love the man he is." She picked up a long-handled spoon and stirred the pitcher. "Besides, without people like Paul and Chase, the hospitals and obituaries would be a lot fuller than they are. They make this world a safer place for all the rest of us."

"She's right, but it's still not always easy," the brunette said, reaching for another chip.

Kaitlyn nodded. "Loving a law-enforcement officer isn't for everyone."

"Are you in love with Chase?" the brunette asked.

Sammi's heart hammered. She'd deliberately avoided even thinking the word.

"Of course she is," Kaitlyn said. "How could she resist?"

The brunette sighed. "Chase is pretty dreamy, all right."

Sammi screwed the lid on the salsa jar and handed it back to Melanie, hoping no one noticed that her hand was shaking. "We've only been out a few times."

"It doesn't take long when you meet the right guy," Kaitlyn said. "I knew Michael was the one by the end of our first date."

"I was head-over-heels right from the start, too," said the brunette.

"Attraction isn't the same as love," Sammi said.

"No, but it's a great place to start."

To her relief, Melanie held up a full pitcher of margaritas. "Hey, who wants a refill?"

~

Arlene lifted a black wool dress from the wooden trunk, her mood just as dark and heavy as the fabric. For twenty years she'd left Justine's clothes alone, ignoring them and pretending they didn't exist. Pretty much the way she'd always dealt with Justine.

She smoothed the dress. Despite the astronomical price tags, Justine's clothes had mostly struck Arlene as dowdy. But then, Arlene had thought Justine was ancient, because she'd been fifteen years her senior. Chandler had been twenty-one years older than she was, but on him, the years had seemed like an asset.

Arlene inspected the embroidered label hand-sewn in the back of the dress. It was an Oleg Cassini—a designer favored by Jacqueline Kennedy—and it smelled faintly of old perfume. The scent was hauntingly familiar. Arlene's stomach dipped as she recognized it. The perfume from their anniversary trip.

Oh, that trip had been a spike through Arlene's heart. Arlene sank onto the folding chair she'd positioned next to the trunks. The dress fell across her lap as her thoughts flew back to 1965.

She and Chandler had been three years into their affair. She'd been taking notes during a staff meeting when Chandler had dropped the bomb. "I'm going abroad for two weeks next month. Mike will be in charge while I'm out."

Arlene had frozen. He couldn't be going. He had meetings booked throughout the month. She knew, because she made all of his appointments.

He'd avoided looking at her, and he'd been uncharacteristically unavailable the rest of the afternoon.

At the end of the day, Arlene could stand it no longer.

She'd sauntered into his office, stood before his enormous ebony-inlaid desk with a hand on her hip, and put on her most flirtatious smile. "I didn't know you were going to Europe. Should I start packing?"

Chandler had toyed with his tie, a sure sign he was uneasy. "I'm, uh, taking Justine."

"Oh?"

He'd cleared his throat. "It's our anniversary."

"I see." He was married, and married people celebrated anniversaries. That shouldn't have come as a surprise. Still, her gut had cinched tighter than the Windsor knot in Chandler's tie.

"It was Justine's idea," he said, as if that made it all right. "She made all the arrangements."

Her mouth had gone cotton-ball dry. Arlene always handled Chandler's travel plans.

"She, uh, went through a travel agent," Chandler explained.

Had she done it on her own, or had Chandler told her to call an agent to avoid a scene like this one? For the first time since their relationship began, she allowed herself to examine a disquieting thought, one that nibbled at the edge of her mind: What if Chandler were lying to her just like he lied to Justine?

"So—are you and Justine staying in separate rooms?"

"Of course."

On an anniversary trip? A seed of doubt was planted. Arlene knew they had separate bedrooms at home, and Chandler said he no longer slept with his wife—that he was trapped in a loveless marriage, that he stayed with Justine only out of a sense of obligation, that she was emotionally fragile because their only child had died, that his religion prohibited divorce, and that she would never give him one, anyway. It was Arlene he loved, Arlene who was his soul mate, but when it came to Justine, his hands were tied.

And yet, in the back of her mind—way back, because that was where she'd shoved the thought and where she tried to keep it—she'd always wondered if that were really the truth.

When Chandler had come to see her the night before he left for Europe, she'd cried and peppered him with questions. He'd angrily snatched up his jacket and headed for the door.

"Dammit, Arlene—if I want this kind of crap, I can get it at home." He'd stormed out, leaving her bereft.

She'd broken their unspoken agreement. She was supposed to be his refuge from problems, not a source of new ones. He came to her for pleasure and comfort, with no obligation to reciprocate.

And for all this, she got . . . what? Not money; she refused to be a kept woman and worked hard for her salary.

Not status; their relationship was a total secret.

Not even time; Chandler could give her only two or three stolen hours a week.

But she loved him, and she thought he loved her, and at the time, that had seemed like enough.

Arlene had thought she would die of loneliness while he was in Europe. When he returned, he was all love and kisses. He'd handed her two presents. The first one was a gorgeous gossamer negligee. She'd put it on, and he'd promptly peeled it off. Afterward, she'd risen from the bed, padded naked across the room, and opened the second present.

It was a bottle of expensive French perfume. She'd dabbed a drop on the inside of her wrists and inhaled. "Oh, it smells divine," she'd said. "I'll wear it every day."

"Better not wear it to the office," he'd warned. "People might put two and two together."

It was only after he'd left that it occurred to her that both gifts were things she could wear only for him.

Later, an even more painful realization hit. Justine stopped by the office to get Chandler's opinion on a guest list, and as she'd unwrapped a bead-eyed dead mink from around her neck, a familiar fragrance had shimmered from her skin. "What wonderful perfume!" gushed the receptionist.

"Thank you," Justine had said. "Chandler had it blended especially for me in Paris."

"You gave me a perfume you had made for Justine?" Arlene had raged at Chandler later that night when he'd come to her house.

"I had you in mind when I described the woman it was for," Chandler had said. "And I was thinking of us. This way, if I come home smelling of your perfume, Justine won't know that I've seen you."

There were several major flaws with that reasoning, but one cut her to the quick: Justine could wear her perfume anywhere, anytime, and no one would think it was the scent of adultery.

Well, Arlene didn't have to smell it anymore. She crammed the dress into a trash can.

The basement phone buzzed. Arlene strode to the credenza in the foyer and picked it up. "You have a phone call from Walter Landry on line five," her assistant said.

Arlene's pulse quickened. "Thank you." She drew a steadying breath and punched the button. "Hello, Walter."

"Hello, yourself." His deep voice flowed over her like warm water. "I was in the neighborhood and wondered if I could take you to lunch."

She smiled, and her hand fluttered to her chest. Why, oh, why had she worn this plain brown sweater set today? "Well, I—"

"I really enjoyed your company the other day. Please say yes."

She started to refuse from force of habit, then stopped herself. There was no reason to say no. And it would be a welcome break in this awful trunk sorting. "Well, then—yes."

"Great! I'll be there in about twenty minutes."

~

Walter took her to the Piccadilly Cafeteria.

"I've never been here," Arlene said as he handed her a tray.

"It's not very fancy, but the food's good. They serve a lot of vegetables." He picked up a set of napkin-wrapped flatware and set it on her tray. "I'm afraid I'm not very good about fixing them on my own."

"Did you and Helen come here?"

"All the time. It was probably our favorite restaurant. Except for special occasions, of course. For birthdays and such, we liked to go to the Brasserie." He picked up a tray and pack of flatware for himself, then placed his tray beside hers on the metal railing. "What's your favorite restaurant?"

"I don't really have one."

He gave her a roguish grin. "Oh. You're one of those girls who likes to eat around, huh?"

Her eyebrows rose. "What?"

"It was a joke." Oh, gee, he hoped she didn't take offense. "Not a very funny one, I'm afraid."

"It certainly wasn't." Her eyes flashed heat, but her tone was icy.

He'd insulted her. Chagrin filled Walter's chest as she stiffly filed past the food, ordering vegetable soup and cornbread.

"Will these be together?" the cashier at the end of the cafeteria line asked.

"No," Arlene said quickly. "Separate checks, please."

Oh, jeez. He followed her to a table and slid into the booth across from her. "I'm sorry for that crack back there. I didn't mean anything."

She leaned across the table, her eyes furious. "Just because I had a gentleman friend doesn't mean I was promiscuous."

Walter drew back against the red plaid booth. "I—I never thought that."

"You certainly seemed to be implying it."

"No! No." He ran a hand down his face and leaned forward, his forearms on the table. "That just popped out because it was something I would have said to Helen. She and I always made these stupid little jokes to each other, a lot of them off-color. I'm sorry. That wasn't any sort of comment about you or your—your lifestyle." He blew out a sigh. "I'm afraid I just don't know how to act around a woman."

Arlene gazed at him a long moment, as if she were taking his measure. In silence, she lifted her bowl of soup off the tray and set it on the table, then looked back up and gave him an apologetic grin. "I'm sorry. I guess I'm a little sensitive on the topic." She moved her cornbread from the tray to the table. "Correction; I *know* I'm sensitive." Her iced tea sloshed a little as she lifted it. "I never talk about my personal life. Quite frankly, I'm embarrassed that I told you about it."

"Don't be."

"Well, I am. And I don't want you to think that I'm— that I'm . . ." Her face colored.

She was pretty when she blushed. It made her seem somehow more accessible. "I think nothing of the sort." Walter took her tray and fitted it under his, then carried them both to a stack of trays against the wall. "Let's start over," he said when he slid back into the booth across from her. "We were talking about restaurants, and you said you didn't have a favorite. I guess that means you like a lot of different ones."

"Well . . . yes. But mainly it means I don't go out much."

"No?"

She shook her head. "I never have."

"Even when you were seeing your . . ." Oh, dear heavens. He probably shouldn't have said that.

Her mouth took on a tight look. "Especially then."

"Why not?"

"My . . . gentleman friend was very well known, so we couldn't be seen together."

"Oh." There were a lot of repercussions to this illicit affair thing that he hadn't considered.

"We did go out of town together occasionally. We went to Dallas twice, and to Vegas once, and one time we went to New York."

"That had to be nice. How long were you two together?"

"Twenty years."

His eyes widened. "Wow. That's longer than some—" He cut himself off abruptly.

"Marriages. I know." She broke off a piece of cornbread. "You must think I'm awful, carrying on with a married man."

He lifted his shoulders. "If Helen had been married when I met her, who knows what I would have done?"

She gave him a grateful smile. "What do you miss most about her?"

"Everything." From waking up to see her face on the pillow beside him to falling asleep curled around her, and all the stuff in between.

"What kind of things did you do together?"

"All the little, normal stuff. We ate breakfast and dinner together every day. We talked and read the paper and worked on the lawn. We ran errands and watched TV and sometimes went out with other couples." He sighed. "I'm afraid I wasn't very good company."

"I bet Helen didn't think that." Arlene's face looked wistful. "What other sorts of things did you do?"

He searched his mind. "Well, when we were younger, we played in a bowling league."

"Really? I've only been bowling one time, and that was back in high school. What else did you do?"

"Not nearly enough stuff. I always had my nose to the grindstone." He sighed and let his mind wander back. "When our daughter was young, we were involved in Scouting and school activities. And there were two summers in a row when we rented a cabin at the lake and went boating and waterskiing. And sometimes we went to concerts and movies."

"I would have loved to have done those things."

"Why didn't you?"

"Well, my gentleman friend couldn't go with me, and I wanted to be at home in case he called."

This woman had spent her whole life sitting by a phone? "What about after you split?"

"Oh, we didn't split. He died."

"Oh. Sorry." Although he wasn't. Not a bit. "When was that?"

"Twenty years ago." She looked down at her bowl of soup. "Back then, I thought I was too old to take up any kind of sport. Funny, isn't it?" She looked up, her eyes sad, her mouth twisted in an ironic smile. "Now I really am."

"You're never too old to have fun. Why don't I take you bowling?"

Her eyebrows flew up, as if the concept were alarming.

"You'll love it. We'll have a blast."

"Oh, I can't. I'd look like a fool."

"So? I haven't bowled in dozens of years, either. We'll look foolish together. What do we care what a bunch of strangers think of us?"

She stared at him.

Walter's heart sank. He probably should have told her she wouldn't look foolish or have just let the subject drop.

He just couldn't seem to get things right with this woman. "Aw, gee. I've gone and offended you again."

"No! No. It's just—well, I've spent so much time worrying about what other people thought or didn't think or knew or guessed that my mind didn't even work that way. I would never think of just going out and not caring about people's opinions."

"Well, want to give it a try?"

Her lips twitched into a smile, and the beauty of it made Walter's mouth go dry.

"Okay."

Okay? She'd agreed to it! "How about the Saturday after next?"

He didn't realize he was holding his breath until she nodded.

"All right. It sounds like fun."

It did, indeed. For the first time in a long time, Walter actually had something to look forward to.

Chapter Fourteen

". . . And the first apartment had this big, high ceiling that went up two stories, and then slanted down."

"Did you like it?" Chase held the phone against his shoulder and rubbed black polish on the toe of a dress shoe as he listened to Horace's tinny voice.

"Oh, no. That slanted ceiling would make me dizzy. But I felt so pumped up from looking at it that I went and looked at two more apartments."

"Way to go, Horace!"

"And you know what, Coach? It was kind of fun!"

"That's great. I'm proud of you, man." Chase turned the shoe and spread the polish down the side. "Did you like one of them?"

"Yeah. I found a place that's just perfect. And they'll let me paint the walls red and everything!"

"That's terrific. So did you sign a lease?"

"Oh, no!" His voice rose an octave. "I've told you—I can't do that. Mother would go ballistic."

"So? If you move out, you won't have to deal with her."

"But—but I can't just abandon her! She went through so much to give me life."

"Let's think this through logically, Horace. You do realize that every human being is born, right?"

"Well, yes."

"So every human being has a mother. Do you think that all the people who live on their own are doing something wrong?"

"Well, no."

Chase rubbed his shoe. "See the disconnect here?"

"Well, yes, but Mother is very sensitive."

"Lots of people are sensitive. That doesn't give them the right to control other people's lives."

"I just can't do it yet."

"But you'd like to?"

"Oh, yeah!"

"Well, then, that's half the ballgame. You have to keep your eye on the goal if you want to score." Chase put the rag back in his shoe-shine kit and pulled out a brush. "Here's your assignment for next time: I want you to go furniture shopping for that apartment."

"But—but . . ."

"You don't have to buy anything; just pick out what you *would* buy if you were moving into it, according to your budget and tastes."

"It's just a fantasy, right?"

"That's right."

"Well, okay. I can do that." He paused a moment. "It's kind of fun, living out these fantasies."

"Good. That's the whole idea." Chase buffed his shoe. "Now . . . do you have another rap for me?"

"Yeah, I do." He cleared his throat, then made some beatbox noises.

I got a new crib and it looks real fine.

It makes the Playboy Mansion look like Toddler Time.

Hot chicks in bikinis like to tan by the pool

So I sidled up to one and I acted real cool.

I said, 'Hey honey, don't think I'm leching,

But you wanna come up and see my etchings?'

Chase exploded in laughter.

"I'm not done yet," Horace whined.

"Sorry. Please continue."

Horace cleared his throat, then resumed his rapper voice.

She said, 'Why, sure; you're a stone-cold hunk.

'A fine man like you shouldn't live like a monk.'

Bazoom, chocca-locca-locca. Zoom, chocca-locca-

    locca.

Zoom! Chocca-locca-locca. Zoom!

He paused dramatically. "So what do you think?"

"I think you're awesome, dude. The only thing that could make it better is hearing you play the accordion with it."

"Really? Okay. Next time I'm gonna do that. It might be hard to sneak the accordion out of the house past Mother, but I'll figure out a way."

Anything that got Horace to defy Mommy Dearest was a step in the right direction. "Great. I'll be looking forward to that."

Chase hung up and grinned. Horace was really making strides. Now if he could just make some, as well.

Drawing a deep breath, he worked the brush back and

forth across the insteps of his shoes until they gleamed. Sammi would be calling next, and the thought of talking to her tangled his stomach into a knot of anticipation and guilt. He carefully packed up his shoe-polishing kit, threw away the newspaper covering his dining table, and put his shoes and the kit back in his closet.

The situation really sucked, he thought as he strode back into the kitchen. On the one hand, he was helping her. On the other, he felt like a dishonest heel. And he was afraid that both he and Sammi were in over their heads, attraction-wise.

He knew he was. He opened the fridge and pulled out a beer. The idea of seeing her one more time, then never again, made him miserable. Popping the top on the can, he picked up his notepad and stared at the list of options he'd written out last night.

Option one: Continue as her coach. He'd see her one more time, and never again. He'd need to talk to her a few times afterward to help her sort out her job and living situation, and probably guide her to the beginning of another relationship. The thought twisted his gut into a pretzel.

Option two: Resign as her coach. That was the simplest, cleanest way out of the situation. But it meant he couldn't date her, because he refused to start off a relationship based on lies.

Which led to *Option three: Tell her the truth and hope that she'd forgive him.* But this option came with an inherent danger: What if it made her trust men less than ever? What if, instead of helping her, he set her back?

Chase raked both hands through his hair. That was unthinkable. He couldn't leave her in worse shape than she'd been in when she first came to him.

The options weren't workable. He'd have to combine all three. He'd date her one more time, prove to her she was over her fear, and resign as her coach. Then, after some time had passed, he'd tell her the truth.

Right on cue, the phone rang. Chase took a fortifying swig of beer and answered it.

"You'll never guess what happened," Sammi said in a rush.

"What?"

"Well, Chase asked me to help babysit his partner's little boy, and we took him out for pizza, and . . ." She went through the whole chain of events.

"Chase was amazing," she said. "And at the end of the evening, he kissed me, and . . ." Her voice trailed off.

"And?" he prompted.

She gave a dreamy sigh. "It was incredible. And I think he thought so, too."

"I'm, uh, sure he did."

"I'm actually beginning to believe that maybe you're right."

"Of course I'm right." He paused a moment. "About what?"

She laughed. "That my ex was the one with the problem. That maybe I'm not so boring, after all."

"I can't imagine a man ever getting bored with you."

Too late, Chase realized that it was an odd thing for a man who'd never met her to say. The whole tone of this conversation was too intimate for Sammi to be having with another man, anyway.

Hell. Was he jealous—of *himself?* This was all too

weird and complicated. He rose and paced his living room. "Did you hurt him?"

"No! I didn't hurt him at all. I didn't even hurt myself."

"Wow, that's two in a row."

"Actually, just one."

"Two," Chase said firmly. "Your dog's actions don't count. So one time more makes three, and after three dates without inflicting injuries, you'll officially be over this whole thing. And then you'll be ready to move on."

"Oh, I don't intend to move on. I'm crazy about this guy."

A totally inappropriate rush of pleasure pulsed through Chase.

"But—what about him being FBI?"

"Well, I've changed my mind about that. You should have seen him in action. It's like he has a sixth sense or something—like he has a gift, like it's what he's meant to do. I think being an agent isn't just his job; it's his calling."

Chase swallowed, his throat suddenly tight.

"That whole incident made me realize that there are risks everywhere. I mean, that little girl and her mom just went out for a pizza, and look what happened. Talking to Melanie and her friends helped me put things in perspective, too. Sure, officers and agents are in more danger than most people, but you have to weigh the risk against the reward."

"The reward being . . ."

"Being with the right man." She hesitated. "And . . . Chase might just be him."

Chase's heart pounded hard and fast in his chest. "You still don't know him very well."

"I know him well enough to know I don't want to date anyone else."

"What if you don't know him as well as you think?"

"What do you mean?" He could hear the frown in her voice.

"Well, what if you discovered that he's lied to you?"

She was silent for a moment. "You think there's a possibility he's seeing someone else?"

"No! I don't think anything of the kind. This is strictly an exercise in 'what if.' "

"Well, Chase wouldn't lie." Her voice was firm, her tone certain. "He's a stand-up guy, and I trust him."

Chase looked up at his ceiling and closed his eyes. He was in big trouble here. Big, big trouble.

"In fact, I'm ready to take it to the next level," she said.

"That level being . . . ?"

"Physical."

Chase swallowed hard. He was in a heap o' hurt, all right—because until he leveled with Sammi, physical involvement was off the table.

"You're veering from your original purpose here," he told her. "In order to score in the game of life, you have to play by the rules. And the rules here are, you're supposed to go out with this guy three times and prove to yourself that you can date a man without wounding him. You need to complete your third date before you even think about ratcheting up the romance."

"Why?"

"Because those are the rules of the game," he said firmly.

"I thought the point of the game was to score."

"Not like that."

Sammi laughed. "Okay. I'll finish the third date. But after that, all bets are off."

∾

Sammi walked through the beaded curtain that led to the back room of the Dragon Ink Tattoo Parlor three nights later and found Chloe leaning over a pale, shirtless man stretched out on a sheet-draped table. His long gray hair spilled out from under a red do-rag, and his stomach rose like a giant uncooked dinner roll. His chest was covered with a thicket of gray hair, except for a shaved three-by-three-inch square above his pierced left nipple, where Chloe was tattooing what looked like the head of a Lhasa apso.

The man waved a tattooed hand. "Hey."

Chloe looked up, a contraption in her hand that looked like a dental drill with a blue plastic bag over it. "Hi, Sammi. What's up?"

Sammi took a step back out the door. "I, uh, didn't know you were with a customer. The manager told me it was okay to come back here."

"Oh, sure, it's fine," Chloe said blithely. "Judd doesn't mind. Do you, Judd?"

"Nah. The more, the merrier."

Sammi had been in the tattoo parlor before, but she'd never actually watched her sister at work. The sight was somewhat unnerving. "I was, uh, dropping off the supplies for the signs."

"Oh, good. Tuesdays are usually pretty slow, so I should have time to work on them tonight."

Judd's leathery face turned toward her. "What kind of signs are you makin'?"

"Sammi's organizing a protest." Chloe held the electric needle against his skin and stepped on the pedal on the floor. Judd closed his eyes and grimaced as the machine buzzed.

"It's more of a rally, actually," Sammi corrected.

Chloe lifted her foot. "She's trying to convince the Preservation Commission to keep her landlord from tearing down a historic house."

"Cool," Judd said. "When's it going down?"

"Thursday morning at ten," Chloe informed him, stepping on the pedal and making the needle whine. "Sammi's calling the media and hopes to turn it into a big event."

"Awesome," Judd said through gritted teeth. He looked at Sammi over Chloe's head. "Need some help?"

"She needs all the help she can get," Chloe cut in before Sammi could even open her mouth "The more people, the bigger the story."

"I can get a group together," Judd offered. "Just tell me when and where, and we'll be there on our hogs."

Sammi frowned. "Hogs?"

"Motorcycles," Chloe translated. She grinned up at Sammi. "He doesn't mean women."

Judd lifted his head from the table. "Why would she think I meant women?"

Chloe dismissively waved the hand not holding the electric needle. "Oh, she knows this guy who calls them hogs."

"What a jerk." Judd gave his head a disgusted shake. "That's downright disrespectful."

There was probably no point in explaining the context. She winced as Chloe fired up the needle again.

Chloe raised her voice to be heard over the machine's buzz. "Speaking of Chase, have you heard from him?"

Sammi nodded. "He called this evening."

"He actually picked up a phone? Praise be and glory hallelujah."

It had been a brief call, and the connection had been awful, but at least he'd phoned. It was ridiculous how happy that call had made her.

"He's in Washington for a weeklong seminar," Sammi volunteered.

"So he'll miss the rally?"

"Afraid so. But he'll be back for the weekend. He's taking me on a mystery date on Saturday."

"A mystery date?"

"Yeah. He won't tell me where we're going; he just said to dress super casual, and he'd pick me up at four."

"I took my girlfriend on a surprise date once," Judd offered.

"Oh, yeah?" Chloe moved the needle to another spot.

"Yeah. I blindfolded her and put her on the back of my Harley, then took her to the rattlesnake hunt in Okemah. Afterward, we got matching snake tattoos on our butts."

"Wow." Sammi grinned at Chloe. "I bet that's a memory that will live forever."

"Yeah. Want to see? The snake looks like it's crawling into . . ." He started to unbuckle his studded belt.

Sammi raised her hand. "No, no. That's quite okay."

Chloe shot her a teasing grin. "Maybe that's what Chase has in mind."

Sammi shook her head. "I don't think he's planned anything quite that exciting."

"Well, ya never know," Judd said. "You might get lucky."

Chloe's eyes glittered with amusement.

Sammi placed the poster board and paints on the counter, then headed for the beaded entryway. "I'll try to hold a good thought."

~

Arlene placed the signed letter in the outbox on her desk on Thursday morning, then fished it out to review it a second time. It was unlike her to deliberately dawdle, but it was Thursday morning, and she hated the thought of going to the basement and sorting through Justine's trunks.

Well, there was no help for it. The hated task wouldn't do itself. With a heavy sigh, she placed the letter back in the wire box and started to rise from her chair.

The intercom buzzed. "Mr. Landry is on line one," the receptionist said.

A burst of pleasure flushed through Arlene. Settling back in her chair, she punched the blinking phone button and lifted the receiver to her ear. "Hello, Walter. How are you?"

"Terrible." He sounded it. His tone was terse, his voice as rough and hard as gravel. "Sammi's ruining my life."

Arlene frowned. "What has she done now?"

"My lawyer and I had a meeting with the Preservation Commission this morning to try to get the ban on the demolition permit lifted. Guess who was staging a protest rally outside the building?"

"Oh, dear!"

"You can say that again. She was marching around with a bunch of old ladies and biker types, and they were all carrying signs."

"Good heavens."

"You don't know anything about it?"

"Mercy, no! All I know is she's taking a personal-leave day."

"Well, she's spending it running a media circus. All the stations were there." His words were clipped and short. "Do you have a TV there?"

"No."

Arlene could hear a tapping sound, as if he were irritably drumming his fingers or rapping a pencil. "It's going to be on the noon news. What do you say we could go someplace that has a TV and watch it together over lunch?"

Arlene's heart unexpectedly lurched. "All—all right."

"Are there any restaurants with TVs near the museum?"

"The only one I can think of always has the TV turned to the sports channel."

"Yeah. That's the case with most of them." He blew out a sigh.

"I live nearby," Arlene ventured.

"Great! I'll pick up something for lunch and meet you there at, say, eleven-forty-five?"

She hadn't really meant to invite him; she'd simply been thinking out loud. But it *did* make sense; she wanted to see the news story—and she wanted to see Walter again. "All right. That sounds fine."

"What's your address?"

She gave it to him, then hung up the phone. Her hand fluttered to her pearls, then dropped to her plain white cotton blouse. It wasn't her most attractive shirt; why was she always wearing something dowdy when Walter called? Maybe she could go home and change before he arrived.

The thought jarred her. Why was she worried about what she was going to wear? Walter wasn't a romantic interest. He was a . . .

What? A friend? She didn't know him well enough to even call him that, although they certainly were on friendly terms. He was more like an acquaintance. Yes, that's what he was. An acquaintance. That was all.

Wasn't it?

She pushed out of her chair, irritated at her thoughts. Of course that was all. Why was she in such a dither about what to call him, anyway? She didn't need to label their relationship.

Not that it was a relationship.

Arlene resolutely marched to the basement, opened a trunk, and set to the task of sorting through Justine's belongings. When she reached bottom, she realized she didn't have that cloying, breathing-through-a-straw tightness in her chest that the sorting work usually gave her. Knowing that she'd see Walter at noon had lightened the task considerably.

At 11:15, she went upstairs and grabbed her purse from her office. "I've got a doctor's appointment," she told the receptionist and then wondered why she'd felt the need to lie. Force of habit, most likely. That was what she'd always done when she'd sneaked out of the office to meet Chandler for a nooner.

Not that this was anything like that. It was lunch, that was all.

Her shoes squished on the hot asphalt as she headed to her car. Maybe she should change into her pumps before Walter arrived. They made her look taller, which made her look thinner. And she'd change into her burgundy blouse, then change back into the white one before she returned to work so she wouldn't stir up any gossip.

There was nothing wrong with wanting to look her best for lunch with an acquaintance, she told herself as she settled behind the steering wheel. Nothing wrong with it at all.

$\sim$

Anger had boiled in Walter's chest all morning, but the sight of Arlene opening her front door immediately iced it down. She was wearing a wine-colored blouse that made her skin glow, and her lips gleamed with a lighter shade of the same hue. Funny; he didn't recall her wearing lipstick before. Her cheeks were rosy, too. She looked lovely.

All of a sudden, he didn't know what to do with his hands. He awkwardly clutched the bag holding their lunch with one and shoved the other in his pocket, then pulled it out. "Hi, there, Arlene." To his own ears, his voice sounded funny. He cleared his throat. "You look real nice today."

Her hand moved to her neck. He'd noticed that she touched her pearls a lot. He suspected that her gentleman friend had given them to her. "Thank you." The color heightened in her cheeks.

He held up a large white bag. "I wasn't sure what kind

of food you liked, so I went by Chiquita's Cantina and got you the same thing you ordered the other day."

Little smile lines fanned out from her eyes. "How thoughtful." She pulled the door wider. "Come on in."

He stepped into a small living room. It was neat and tidy and almost entirely beige—the walls, the carpet, the sofa, and the chairs. A large tapestry on the wall over the sofa provided the only color. It looked out-of-place and expensive. It was the kind of thing one might expect to find hanging in a mansion rather than in a modest home like this one. Unless he missed his guess, it, too, was a gift from her gentleman friend. An odd bite of displeasure nibbled at his gut.

"Do you mind eating in the kitchen?" Arlene asked. "I have a TV in there."

"No, no, I don't mind at all. Helen and I always ate in the kitchen."

Probably not the best idea, talking about Helen. He wasn't sure why, exactly; he just had the feeling that maybe he shouldn't rub his marriage in Arlene's face. She'd gotten awfully prickly about her single status the last time they were together.

He trailed after her into the kitchen, noting the way her black skirt curved in at the waist and flared at the knee. She'd worn a boxy jacket both times he'd seen her, and he'd wondered what she looked like beneath it. Turned out she had a shapely figure—very shapely, indeed.

"What can I get you to drink?" Arlene asked. "Iced tea, coffee, water, cola?"

"Iced tea would be great." He leaned against the white Formica countertop and looked around the spotless kitchen as she pulled two glasses down from the cupboard. The walls were covered with blue-and-white wallpaper, and the cabinets were painted a glossy white. Two blue-and-yellow-striped place mats sat side by side on the small table in the dining area, facing a small television on the counter. "This is a nice place. Lived here long?"

"Thirty years." She opened her freezer. Ice plinked against the glass as she dropped it in.

"Lived by yourself all that time?"

She paused and looked at him, frost curling around her from the open freezer door.

Oh, dear. He hadn't meant to imply anything. "I-I was wondering if a sister or friend or someone lived here with you."

She shook her head and dropped another cube of ice into the glass. "No. I've always lived alone."

He wondered if she found it lonely. He sure did. Maybe it was the contrast from having been married thirty-four years, but coming home to an empty house was the loneliest feeling in the world.

She closed the freezer and looked at him, her gaze a little wary. "I wasn't a kept woman, if that's what you're asking. I bought this place all on my own."

He swallowed hard. "I-I wasn't asking anything, really. Just making conversation."

She bustled over to the counter and set down the glasses beside a pitcher of tea and a little plate of sliced lemon, then glanced at him as she pulled an iced tea spoon out of a drawer. "So Sammi organized some kind of protest?" she asked, obviously wanting to change the subject.

Walter nodded. "When I walked up to the commission headquarters, there were protesters and TV cameras and reporters all over the place."

"Were you interviewed?"

"I'm afraid so."

"Well, that's good." She splashed tea into the glasses. "They gave you a chance to tell your side of the story."

"I'm afraid I didn't do a very good job of it."

Funny, he thought; he never use the word "afraid" conversationally—he'd always feared it would make him look soft-bellied—and he'd just used it twice in a row.

Arlene carried the iced tea glasses to the table and put them on the place mats. Walter picked up the little plate of lemon and carried it to the table, as well. She headed back to the counter, opened the white bag, and pulled out two Styrofoam cartons. "I think I'll plate these and microwave them."

"Good idea." He watched her pull two blue-rimmed plates out of the cabinet, then arrange the black beans, rice, and chicken enchiladas on them. "Would you mind putting the chips in the bowl on the counter?" she asked as she placed one of the plates in the microwave.

"Not at all." Truth be told, he missed the little niceties of meal preparation. Most of the time he ate fast food straight out of the bag because setting the table for one was just too darned lonely.

The microwave beeped. Arlene pulled out the plate and put in the second one. "Looks like we're almost ready. Why don't you turn on the TV and have a seat?"

∽

Arlene carried the heated plates to the table as Walter picked up the remote control. She put a plate in front of him, then set her own plate on the next place mat and slid into the chair beside him.

"This looks lovely," he said. "Nicer than in the restaurant. We've even got cloth napkins!"

Arlene unfolded hers in her lap, pleased that he'd noticed. The pompous swells of news music filled the room.

"We timed things just right," she said.

The music crescendoed as the camera zoomed in on a blonde seated at the anchor desk. After a lead story about an overnight burglary, the anchor shifted the papers in her hand and looked at the camera. "The Historic Preservation Commission was the scene of a demonstration this morning. Marie Mareno has the story."

The screen filled with the image of a brunette with a microphone. Behind her, a tattooed man wearing a black studded collar, a do-rag, and a leather vest held a sign that said "Save our heritage."

"I'm standing in front of the Tulsa Preservation Commission," the reporter said, "where a large group gathered to show their support for saving a tiny art deco home built in 1933." The camera panned to show a dozen or so protesters. It was an unlikely bunch: little old ladies in vintage pastel dresses, men in biker gear, and women in tight leather pants. All of them held hand-painted signs in brilliant Day-Glo colors.

"The owner of the home, Walter Landry, has applied for a demolition permit."

Walter's face appeared on the screen. Beside her, he cringed. "Good heavens, when did I get so old and awful-looking?" he muttered.

Arlene didn't think he looked awful. She thought he looked distinguished. She was about to tell him so, but he started talking onscreen.

"The house is small, outdated, and practically unlivable," Walter told the reporter. "More than half of the other old homes in the neighborhood have already been torn down to make way for bigger, more modern homes, and I have the right to sell mine to someone who wants to do the same."

The camera went back to the reporter. "And that is exactly the problem, according to Art Deco Museum curator Sammi Matthews."

They should be calling her the junior curator, or a least a co-curator, Arlene thought indignantly. They made it sound as if Sammi had completely replaced her.

Sammi's heart-shaped face popped on the screen, her hair rioting in the wind. "The house was designed by Raymond Deshuilles, the architect who built the Aston mansion and many other Tulsa landmarks. He believed that style transcended money. To prove it, he built five modest homes in the Green Lawn area, and this is the only one that remains."

An image of a small stucco house flashed on the screen. Beside her, Walter shook his head in annoyance. "She's gussied up the flower beds with begonias and periwinkles."

The reporter's face filled the screen. "A rather unusual mix of people showed up this morning to support the house's preservation."

Unusual? They were outright weirdos, Arlene thought as the camera panned the motley group. The camera tightened on a heavyset man wearing a pirate-style headscarf and black clothes with multiple zippers. His arms were covered in tattoos, and his face sported more jewelry than a Zales showcase.

The reporter thrust the microphone in his face. "What brought you out this morning?"

He squinted at the camera with glazed eyes. "Mr. Art Deco is a righteous dude, and we can't let him be put down by the man, man." A stud gleamed in his tongue as he spoke. "Hey, do you know where the doughnuts are?"

The reporter turned to a woman next to him, who had hair dark as a black hole, a spiked collar, and black lipstick. "And you?" the reporter asked.

"That little house is an endangered species. It's the dodo bird of architecture, and we need to protect it."

The reporter turned to a tiny elderly woman with a face as wrinkled as a shar-pei's. She wore a violet sweat suit, a straw hat, and white gloves, and she carried a sign that read "Beauty has no expiration date."

"Why are you supporting the house?"

"Because it's a lot like us. It might be old and out of date, but it's one of a kind and it was made by a master."

The reporter went back to Sammi. "Obviously, you have a lot of support. What do you think should be done with the house?"

"There are a couple of options. It could be sold to a private owner who would preserve its historical integrity."

"Yeah. Like you," Walter muttered.

"Or, better yet," Sammi continued, "the state historical society or a private museum could take it over so the public could tour and appreciate it."

"A private museum such as the Phelps Museum?" the reporter asked.

Sammi nodded. "That would be ideal."

Ideal, indeed! What on earth was the girl thinking?

"Wow. That would be great!" Walter muttered.

"The protest seems to have worked," the reporter said. "The commission voted to uphold the demolition ban while the issue is studied. For the next three months at least, the little house is safe from the wrecking ball."

Walter clicked off the TV and turned to Arlene, his eyes hopeful. "Do you think your museum might really be interested in buying the house?"

Arlene pulled her gaze from the blank screen. "Of course not."

His face fell. "Why not?"

"Because my museum is dedicated to preserving the Phelps legacy, not saving ramshackle little houses all over the town."

"Maybe it could do both."

"No." Arlene vigorously shook her head. "Absolutely not. Chandler shouldn't have to share the limelight with some architect who designed tract houses."

"Well, then, maybe the state historical society will be interested in buying it."

Arlene blew out a derisive huff of air. "That'll never happen. They're in the middle of a budget cutback. And even if they did have the money, acquiring a new property would be a long, drawn-out political process that could take years."

Disappointment registered again on Walter's face.

"She's trying to get you to sell it to her, Walter." It was the sort of ploy oil-lease owners used to play—rousing public sentiment against Phelps Oil, stalling to see if they could get better terms. Chandler had encountered it dozens of times. "She's trying to pull the wool over your eyes so she can get what she wants."

"I don't think Sammi's like that," Walter said. "She

makes me mad as hell and she has no business interfering, but she's basically a real nice girl." He put his napkin in his lap and picked up his fork. "She's always prompt with her rent, and she takes real good care of the property. She even brought me homemade soup when I had the flu a few months ago."

"She does nice things in order to get what she wants," Arlene said, spearing a bite of enchilada. "I know the type."

Walter looked at her. "Sounds like you've had personal experience along these lines."

"Oh, yes, indeed."

"Who did that to you, Arlene?"

Chandler. The thought shocked and alarmed her. No. She didn't mean that. She couldn't mean that! She meant his associates and rivals. She shook her head, trying to straighten her thoughts. "I saw it time and time again. People would schmooze and flatter and pretend to care about you, and all the time, they were simply serving their own purposes."

"Anyone in particular?" Walter's gaze seemed to go right through her. She had the unsettling feeling that she was being x-rayed, that he was seeing things inside of her that she couldn't see herself.

"Everyone in general." She picked up her fork and forced a smile, not wanting to linger on the topic, not wanting to delve any deeper into murky waters. "We'd better eat before our food gets cold."

But something inside her felt cold already—cold and numb and frozen.

Chapter Fifteen

The chime of the doorbell, followed by Joe's deep, frantic barks, jarred Sammi from a deep sleep. Alarmed, she pushed her hair out of her eyes, sat up in bed, and glanced at her bedside clock: 3:55. Who on earth would be ringing the doorbell at this hour?

Climbing out of bed, she headed to the living room and peered out the window. In the dim glow of the porch light, she recognized a tall male figure. *Chase.* Her already racing heart rate amped up its speed.

The three locks on the door clicked noisily as she unfastened them. She grabbed Joe's collar and pulled the door open. "What's going on?"

"I'm ready for our date." His gaze wandered over the Hello Kitty short-shorts and tank she wore to bed, and he grinned. "You, apparently, are not."

Joe wriggled in a happy dance. Releasing his collar, Sammi pushed a tangled mass of hair out of her eyes. "You said you'd be here at four."

Chase petted the ridiculously gleeful dog. "Oh, gee, don't tell me I'm too early."

"By about twelve hours."

He glanced at his watch. "Nah, just a couple of minutes. It's three fifty-eight."

She squinted at him. "You meant four *in the morning?*"

"Sure. Did I neglect to tell you that?"

She wasn't buying his expression of wide-eyed innocence. "Yes." She crossed her arms. "You somehow forgot that little detail."

"Oh. Well, go get ready." He made a shooing gesture with his hand. "We don't want to be late."

"For what?"

"It's a surprise." He handed her a warm Styrofoam cup of coffee. "Here. I had a feeling you'd be needing this."

Taking the coffee, she hurried to her bathroom, washed her face, brushed her teeth, and pulled her hair into a ponytail. She pulled out her makeup bag, gazed at her sleep-swollen eyes, then decided against makeup. It was four o'clock in the freaking morning; he'd just have to take her au naturel.

Five minutes later, she was in his car, dressed in jeans, a short-sleeved white sweater, and a scarlet fleece hoodie. She took a sip of coffee, savoring the rich flavor. "Where the heck are we going?"

"If I tell you, it'll ruin the surprise."

"Just promise me you're not taking me to hunt rattlesnakes and get a tattoo."

He raised a quizzical eyebrow, and she told him about Chloe's client. He asked about the rally, and she gave him a full report.

"How was your trip to D.C.?" she asked.

He regaled her with tales about the seminar, then asked

about her week at work. The conversation drifted to other things, and time flew by. The next time she paid attention to their surroundings, Chase had turned off the highway onto a side road.

He drove down a long, winding stretch of pitch-black asphalt, then pulled into a gravel parking area under a lamppost. "Here we are."

She strained to see beyond the light from the lamppost. The headlights seemed to be reflecting off water. "Which is where?"

"Lake Eufaula." Chase killed the engine. "And there's Fred."

Oh, great. Chase had invited a third party to join them again. She swallowed down her disappointment as a burly, gray-haired man in an orange hunting vest stepped into the lamppost's ring of light. "And Fred is . . . ?"

"Our striper guide."

"Are we also going to have a polka-dot guide?"

Chase grinned. "No. And the plaid guide couldn't join us, either."

Laughing, she scrambled out of the car.

"Fred is the best fishing guide in the business," Chase told her as he introduced them.

"You're gonna jinx me, tellin' her that," the older man said in a deep southern accent. "You two ready to go?"

They headed down a dock toward a craft that looked like a wide speedboat. Chase helped her aboard, then sat beside her on a long padded bench. Fred lumbered onto the boat, flipped up a seat cushion, and pulled out a life vest.

He handed it to Sammi. "Better put this on. If you happen to fall overboard, I don't want you to drown."

Sammi looked at Chase as she pulled on the life vest. "Where's yours?"

"Fred doesn't care if I drown."

She struggled to adjust the life-vest straps. "With me in the boat, you're more likely to end up in the water than I am," she warned.

"I'm not afraid to take my chances." His tone was teasing, but his gaze was warm. He helped her tighten the top tie of her life vest.

"Maybe you should be," Sammi said somberly.

"Nah." He tightened the second strap for her. "I trust you."

Something about the simple statement made her breath catch. "That might not be wise."

He snapped her life vest closed and gazed into her eyes. "The thing that's not wise, Sammi, is not trusting yourself."

Fred started the engine, and the boat roared across the water. Chilly air slapped Sammi in the face. She shivered, and Chase put his arm around her shoulder. "Cold?" he asked, speaking close to her ear to be heard over the engine.

"A little."

He rubbed her arm, which made her shiver for an entirely different reason.

Fred sat in the front, steering the craft with one hand while watching his underwater radar. At length, he pulled back the throttle, slowing the boat's roar to a purr. "We're coming up on a school of striper," he called. He killed the engine. The sudden silence was jarring. The waves from the boat's wake slapped against the sides. "Let's get the lines in."

Rising from his seat, Fred pulled two rods and reels from a rack at the front of the boat.

Chase helped Sammi to her feet as Fred handed her one.

"Are you familiar with a rod and reel?" Fred asked.

"We're vaguely acquainted." She'd used a rod and reel a couple of times as a kid when her grandfather had taken her fishing. "I wouldn't say we're familiar."

Fred grinned. "Hold the button on the reel, and throw it like this." He hoisted the reel to the side, gave a quick flick of his wrist, and sent the line soaring. "Then wind it in, nice and steady, and do it again." The reel clicked as he wound it.

On her first try, the lure didn't make it out of the boat, but her second cast was surprisingly powerful.

"You're a natural," Fred said as she reeled in her line. He looked over at Chase. "Watch out, or she's gonna fish circles around you."

"Is this a competitive sport?" Sammi asked.

"Oh, yeah. People fish in tournaments for big money." A gap in Fred's tooth gleamed in the dawn light as he grinned. "Of course, everything's a tournament where Chase's concerned. He's competitive about everything."

"I guess you'll really hate it when I catch more fish than you, huh?" She threw him a challenging look.

"Not gonna happen."

"Wanna bet?"

"Sure. But I have to warn you: fish find me irresistible."

Fish weren't alone. When he looked at her like that, she found him pretty irresistible, as well. "What are we betting?"

"Winner's choice."

Before she could reply, the water around the boat started bubbling.

"What's going on?" Sammi asked, alarmed.

"We're in a school of striper, and they're feeding," Fred explained.

Sammi's line went taut, and her rod bent. Adrenaline rushed through her. "Hey—I've got one!" she shouted.

"Keep the line tense and reel it in, nice and steady," Chase advised. He stepped closer, ready to assist, but Sammi had it under control.

A thrill of excitement rushed through her as she lifted the fish from the water. "I've caught one!"

"Good going!" Fred bent down and scooped the fish into a net. "And it's a keeper."

He just might be, Sammi thought, glancing at Chase. *He just might be.*

~

By the time they docked at the pier two hours later, the sun was up and the ice chest was loaded with striper. Chase jumped onto the pier and reached out a hand to Sammi.

She took it and climbed out of the boat, then waved to Fred. "Thanks a million! I had a fantastic time."

"My pleasure," Fred said. "Any time you want to go again, just give me a call. Chase has my number."

She gave Chase a teasing smile. "Maybe next time I can give you some fishing lessons."

Chase rolled his eyes and climbed back in the boat to haul out the cooler. Sammi had caught five more fish than he had, and he'd heard about it all the way back to the dock.

"Need some help cleaning the fish?" Fred asked as he helped Chase move the cooler to the dock.

"Nah." Chase picked up the handle of the wheeled cooler. "Sammi and I will take care of it."

"All right, then. See y'all later." With a jaunty salute, Fred climbed back in the boat, unlooped the rope from the mooring, and cast off.

Sammi stared at Chase as the boat puttered away. "*We're* going to clean the fish?"

"Sure." It was a key part of his plan to make it through another date with Sammi without getting physical. After all, what could be less romantic than gutting fish? "It's the law of the lake. You catch 'em, you clean 'em."

"Aren't you worried about being near me if I'm wielding a knife?"

"No, because we'll be wearing steel mesh gloves. They've got them at the cleaning station on the next pier."

"Sounds like you thought of everything."

Except for the fact that I'd find you irresistible even covered in fish gore, Chase thought twenty minutes later as they joked and teased their way through the odious task. Even cleaning fish with Sammi was fun.

She dropped the last fillet back in the ice chest, closed the lid, and pulled off the bulky gloves. "What are we going to do with them now?"

"Take them home and freeze them."

"No way." She turned on the faucet in the giant sink at the cleaning station, then pumped liquid soap into her palm from the grubby bottle at the counter. "The whole point of fishing is to have fresh fish."

"Yeah, well, it probably is, except I don't really cook." Chase closed the cooler lid, then peeled off his gloves and joined her at the sink. "So I always end up freezing them and giving them to Paul and Melanie."

"There's more than enough here for Paul, Melanie, you, and several small nations."

"We *did* make quite a haul."

"*I* made quite a haul."

He leaned forward from the waist. "I bow to your superior striper skills."

"You'll have to do more than bow. I won the bet, remember?"

"As if you'd let me forget."

"And you said the winner gets to determine the prize."

Uh-oh. This could be trouble. "Which is?"

"You have to come over and grill some striper for me this evening."

Chase squirted some soap in his hands and rubbed them together. After he dropped her off at her house, it would be the end of their third date. He would have proved to her that she was over her spate of date battering. And he would have fulfilled his official duties as her coach.

Which meant it would be time to level with her. Tonight was as good a time as any.

He swallowed hard and nodded as the water sluiced over his fingers. "Okay. You're on."

∼

"You can't seduce a man with your house smelling like fish," said Chloe a little after 5:00 that afternoon as she petted Joe's head. Sammi had called and asked her to keep Joe at her apartment for the night to minimize the chance of any more mishaps.

"Who said I plan to seduce him?"

"Well, if you don't, you're crazy."

Grinning, Sammi tilted the mixing bowl and poured chocolate mousse into two stemmed glasses. "I'm having him to dinner, that's all." And for all she knew, that really might be all. Despite the chemistry between them and the fun they'd had that morning, Chase had seemed oddly distant on the drive home. It was almost as if he'd erected a wall. He'd been quiet almost to the point of terseness, and when he'd dropped her off at her house, he'd held her at arm's length and kissed her forehead.

Her forehead!

Well, she intended to loosen him up tonight.

She put the empty bowl on the counter. "The house isn't going to smell like fish, anyway, because he's going to grill them outside."

Chloe ran her finger along the side of the bowl, skimming off some leftover mousse. "Ah. Good idea." She licked the foamy chocolate off her finger. "So let's run through the checklist."

"Checklist for what?"

"Romance 101. Do you have candles?"

Sammi decided to humor her. "Check."

"Wine?"

"Check."

"Decadent dessert?"

Sammi plucked two strawberries from a bowl of fruit

on her counter and placed one atop each glass of mousse, then carefully carried them to the refrigerator. "Check."

"Sexy outfit?"

"Well, sort of check."

"What are you planning to wear?" Chloe demanded.

"I don't know. Probably just jeans and a sleeveless turtleneck."

"No, no, no!" Chloe wagged a finger. "That's a kindergarten-teacher outfit. You'd wear that if you wanted to wipe his nose, not ravish his body. Wear your denim skirt."

"It's kind of short."

"That's the idea. And how about that low-cut black wrap top—the one you always safety-pin at the neckline?"

"Maybe."

"Wear it. But don't pin it." Chloe reached for a strawberry. "If you pin it, you're holding back, and nothing should hold you back this evening."

Sammi's pulse sped up as she rinsed the bowl. "You're making too big a deal of this."

Chloe waved her protests aside with a flick of her wrist. "You need to wear high heels," she continued. "Your black sandals are perfect. And you have to wear really hot underwear so you'll feel sexy."

Sammi took the bowl away from Chloe and put it in the sink. "I've got that part covered."

"Well, don't cover that part too much."

Sammi rolled her eyes. "Very funny."

"And Sammi . . ."

"Yes?"

"Relax. I think you should open a bottle of wine and have a drink before he gets here. In fact, I'll open one now and have a drink with you." Chloe opened Sammi's fridge, reached in, and pulled out a bottle of pinot grigio.

"Make yourself at home, why don't you," Sammi said sardonically.

"Thanks. Don't mind if I do." Chloe nudged Sammi aside to reach into the drawer that held the corkscrew. Extracting it, she glanced over at Sammi. "Are you still afraid you're going to hurt him? Because you've been on three dates, and if you don't count Joe giving him a massive wedgie, you haven't hurt him once."

Maybe it was odd, but injuring Chase tonight hadn't crossed her mind. "You know, I'm not afraid of hurting him." Sammi squirted some dishwashing soap into the bowl. "I'm afraid of him hurting me."

Chloe peeled the seal off the cork. "What do you mean?"

Sammi turned on the faucet. "What if things get romantic and he doesn't find me exciting enough?"

Chloe met her gaze, her eyes warm. "You still believe that crap Lance told you?"

She didn't want to. And part of her didn't. But another part—a wounded, insecure, quaking part—still feared he was right. She lifted her shoulders. "Sort of."

Chloe put her hands on her hips. "He was a cheat and a liar, and he told you that stuff to justify his own bad behavior."

Sammi couldn't vouch for Lance's reasoning, but she could vouch for his bad behavior. She scrubbed the bowl, wishing she could scrub away the scene that seemed permanently etched on the insides of her eyelids.

She'd returned a day early from her business meeting in D.C. She'd greeted her cats at her apartment door, then dragged her suitcase down the carpeted hallway, looking forward to a warm bath. Her bedroom door had been closed. That was odd, she'd thought—but maybe Lance had closed it to keep the cats out of the room. She'd turned the doorknob, picked up the handle of her suitcase, and rolled it into the room.

And then she stopped. Because there, in the middle of her bed, gleamed Lance's white butt. It took her a moment to process what she was seeing. It looked like his legs were misshapen. And then a blond head lifted from the pink pillowcase and peered around Lance's shoulder, and Sammi realized that the woman's legs were wound around Lance's thighs.

"He's a total jerk," Chloe declared.

"I know." Sammi rinsed the bowl, then picked up a dish towel and rubbed it dry. "But how do I know there's not anything to the stuff he said? What if I'm somehow . . . insufficient?"

"Sammi, there's nothing wrong with you, aside from your decision to ever get involved with that creepoid. But I brought you some things to help shore up your confidence in that department." Chloe worked the tip of the corkscrew into the wine bottle. "Look in my purse."

Sammi headed to the table and opened Chloe's enormous vintage macramé tote. She pulled out a large plastic bag. "The Adult Toybox?" she read.

"Yeah. It's owned by the same lady who owns the tattoo parlor, and she gives me free samples." Chloe tugged on the wine cork. It came out with a resounding pop. "If you feel like things need spicing up, these ought to do the trick."

Sammi arched her brow as she pulled out a bottle labeled "Love Juice."

"That's tingling massage oil." Chloe reached into the cabinet and pulled down two wineglasses.

Sammi lifted out what looked like two Zorro masks without the eyeholes.

"Those are blindfolds," Chloe said helpfully. "You've also got two sets of handcuffs."

"Handcuffs?"

"Well, I know Chase owns some, but I didn't know whether or not he'd bring them."

Sammi pulled out an enormous lime green dildo and read the sticker attached to the side. "Glow in the dark?"

"So you won't lose it," Chloe said helpfully. "The batteries are already installed. I also brought a sexy board game, some body paint, an assortment of other his-and-her electronic items, and some other stuff."

Sammi dropped the dildo back in the bag. "You are seriously deranged. You know that, don't you?"

"Yeah. But so are you, buying into Lance's bull." Chloe tipped the wine bottle and carefully filled the glasses. "I thought that having some instant excitement at hand might make you feel more confident."

Sammi couldn't envision any romantic circumstances where it would be helpful to whip out a dildo and suggest, "Here, try this!" but Chloe meant well, and it was the thought that counted. "Thanks, Chloe."

"No problem." Chloe handed her a wineglass. "Now drink up and go draw a bubble bath. I'll put the goodies in your bedside drawer, then take Joe and leave."

"You forgot a few items," Sammi said, setting down her glass to look through the rest of the bag's contents. "I don't see any whips or chains, and you left out the Mistress of Pain costume."

Chloe gave her a roguish grin. "You want to save something for next time."

Sammi laughed and picked up her glass. "You know, you're really jumping the gun here. Who says anything is going to happen tonight?"

"You don't have to say a thing. I can tell that you're in love."

Sammi froze, the wineglass in her hand. "I'm in like," she told Chloe forcefully. "In heavy, heavy like."

"Right." Chloe shot her a maddeningly knowing grin.

Sammi took a sip of wine, her thoughts swarming like a hive of bees. She couldn't be in love—not unless Chase was, as well. She couldn't stand the thought of feeling this way—*that* way, she mentally corrected—alone. And she had no idea if Chase thought she was SCABHOG material or not. At times, he couldn't seem to get close enough; at other times, he acted as if he were deliberately trying to keep his distance.

Well, tonight, she hoped to break down his barriers. But that didn't mean she was getting in over her head.

Did it?

She took a deep gulp of wine, topped off her glass, then headed to the bathtub. She refused to ruin the evening by overanalyzing it before it began.

Chapter Sixteen

That was delicious," Sammi said, taking a last bite of fish. "You grill striper almost as well as I catch them."

"Remind me to never lose another bet to you." Chase grinned and took a sip of wine. "You're a really obnoxious winner."

"You should see me when I lose. That's when I'm really hard to take."

She was hard to take right now. In fact, the way her silky blouse played peek-a-boo with her cleavage across the table was pure torture. All evening he'd fought to keep his mind on the fact he needed to level with her, and off her curves, but it was a losing a battle. From the moment she'd opened the door wearing that short skirt and sash-tied blouse, he'd had trouble thinking straight.

It didn't help that she'd set the dining room table with candles and put some slow, smoky jazz on her CD player. How was a guy supposed to keep his head with all this going on? A couple of glasses of wine thrown into the mix didn't help any.

She set down her fork, took a sip of wine, and licked

her lips. The memory of kissing her flashed through his mind in excruciating detail. He was dying to kiss her again, to feel her soft curves against his body, to smell the scent of her skin.

But before he did anything of the kind, he had to tell her the truth. He couldn't let things go any further without confessing that he was her coach.

He'd decided to tell her after dinner. Well, here it was. After dinner.

He set down his napkin and drew a deep breath.

"Would you care for dessert?" Sammi asked.

He had no appetite, but he was grateful for a temporary reprieve. Maybe in the interim he could come up with a way to break it to her. "Sure."

She leaned forward, revealing a distracting depth of cleavage, and gave him a teasing smile. "First you have to fulfill the other terms of the bet."

He quirked up an eyebrow. "There are other terms?"

"Since you lost, you have to clear the table."

"That wasn't a condition of the bet."

"We didn't set any conditions. It was winner's choice, remember?"

"A terrible oversight on my part. Any other conditions I should know about?"

"Well, there is one other little thing." Mischief gleamed in her eyes. "But I'm saving it for later."

Chase shook his head. "I insist on paying my debt in full, right here, right now."

Her eyes heated to pure trouble, and he realized he'd stepped onto dangerous ground. "You have to kiss me," she said, her voice barely above a whisper.

His pulse beat harder. Hell. He couldn't very well refuse. Besides, one kiss would soften the impact of what he had to tell her. He'd keep the table between them to prevent things from escalating out of control. Taking her hands, he rose and leaned forward, pulling her toward him.

The minute her mouth touched his, he knew he'd miscalculated. Her lips were a portal to every nerve in his body.

She tasted like wine—sweet and tart and intoxicating. She smelled like fruity shampoo and soft perfume and that singular, distinctive Sammi scent that made him dizzy with desire. He angled his mouth over hers, deepening the kiss. Her lips were soft and wet and eager, parting for him, urging him on. Her hands moved to the side of his face, then into his hair.

He wished he'd already cleared the table so he could pull her right onto it. Desire curled around them like smoke. He could almost smell it.

Oh, dear God—he *did* smell it! Alarmed, he opened his eyes to see that the sash of her blouse was in flames. He jerked back, grabbed his water glass, and threw the contents on her.

"What—why . . . ?" She opened her eyes and stared at him.

"Your shirt." He snatched the glass from her place setting and hurled its contents on her, as well. The flame was extinguished, but the ends of the sash still smoldered.

"Yikes!" She jumped back. He grabbed the other end of the tie and pulled, undoing the bow. She yanked off the blouse as if it were a snake about to bite her. Chase picked the smoldering shirt off the floor and dashed to the kitchen, where he threw it in the sink.

He turned on the faucet. Her blouse hissed as water doused the final embers. "I can't believe that just happened," Sammi said beside him.

Chase turned toward her and noticed she was shivering. "Are you burned?"

"No. I-I'm fine. In shock, but fine."

She was wearing a sheer black bra. He could see the dusky pink of her nipples through the fabric, and the sight set off another type of fire deep inside him. She folded her arms across her chest, suddenly self-conscious.

He rapidly unbuttoned his shirt, pulled it off, and handed it to her. "Here."

"Th-thanks." She turned her back to him to slip it on.

Sexual tension coiled around him. He cleared his throat. "While you're regrouping, I'll clean up."

He headed back to the dining room, mopped up the water, and gathered up the dishes. He returned to the kitchen to find her clutching his shirt around her, her expression morose.

"I did it again, didn't I?" She lifted sad hazel eyes to his. "I ruined the evening."

The dishes clattered as he set them in the sink. "You didn't ruin it." He leaned against the counter and smiled. "You just . . . enlivened it."

She gave him a shaky grin. The sight of it made his heart turn over. *Tell her,* his conscience demanded. *Tell her now.*

He dragged his hand through his hair and swallowed. "Actually, it's probably good we were interrupted. Instead of just getting carried away, we need to sit down and talk."

She turned away, her hand to her mouth. Tears sprang to her eyes.

Concerned, he took a step toward her. He lifted her hair from her face and saw tears streaking down her cheeks. "Hey—what's the matter?"

"I-I *wanted* to get carried away." Her voice was small and broken. She wiped her cheeks with both hands. "I wanted everything to be romantic."

"It was."

A tear dripped off her chin. "*Was*. Past tense. Before I threw cold water on everything."

Chase tried to lighten the moment. "Actually, I was the one who threw the cold water."

"I do this every time." She threw out her hands, which made the unbuttoned shirt gape open. She yanked it closed. "I always sabotage things, because I'm afraid of—of . . ." Fresh tears filled her eyes.

He moved closer. "Of what?"

"Of being . . ." Her voice trailed off to a whisper.

He needed her to tell him, face-to-face. If she willingly told him her secrets when she knew she was talking to Chase, it would make it less awful that he'd been privy to them without her knowledge. "You're afraid of being what?" he urged.

"Known." The word was a broken whisper. She turned away.

He put his hands on her shoulders and turned her back around. "What don't you want me to know about you, Sammi?"

She looked down. A tear dripped down her cheek. "That I'm inadequate."

Aw, hell. Chase moved closer, rubbing his hands down

her upper arms. "Sammi, sweetie, you are the most completely adequate woman I've ever known."

It had the desired effect. Her lips curved in a tremulous grin even as another tear dropped off her chin.

"I mean it." His hands moved to the sides of her face. "You're so adequate you're actually tolerable. You meet all of the minimum requirements. I'm sure you're even satisfactory."

Her wobbly grin widened. It shifted a tectonic plate in his heart. He ran the pads of his thumbs across her cheeks, wiping away the tears, and cradled her face. "Sammi, honey—do you have any idea what you do to me?"

"Yeah. Apparently I make you want to *talk*."

He gazed at her, his chest tight. "That's not what you make me want to do."

"No?" Her eyes were hazel syringes of truth serum, searching for an injection site.

Oh, God—how was he supposed to handle this? He needed to level with her, but if he told her the truth now, he'd only perpetuate her cycle of self-doubt and self-sabotage. He desperately wanted to do the right thing—but what, exactly, was it? The apparent right thing seemed all wrong at the moment.

The last thing she needed right now was rejection. Right now, she needed to be shown that she was desired and desirable, that she hadn't scared him off with her klutz attacks, that she was worth all risk to life and limb.

He was out of his depth. He solved problems with logic, but logic didn't apply here. This was a matter of the heart. He drew a deep breath and let his heart do the talking.

"Sammi," he murmured. "It's going to take a lot more than setting yourself on fire to keep me away from you."

He pulled her close and kissed her. Her arms wound around his neck, her body melting into his.

He bent down, hooked his arms under her knees, and picked her up. She gasped with surprise as he lifted her and carried her down the hall.

~

It was a good thing he was holding her, because she just might have swooned. The warmth of his naked chest, the soapy sandalwood scent of his neck, the glitter of intent in his dark eyes were enough to make her pull a Scarlett O'Hara.

The mattress squeaked as he gently set her on the taupe satin bedspread. She reached for the lamp switch.

"Keep it on," he said, sitting on the mattress beside her. "I want to see you."

Her muscles tensed. What if he didn't like what he saw? But the look in his eyes as he stretched out beside her told her he liked it plenty so far.

She was certainly enjoying the view, as well. She leaned back against the pillows, drinking in the sight of his broad chest, his ripped abs, his sculpted arms.

He reached out and unfastened the front hook of her bra. She held her breath as he pulled it apart, then lost her nerve and crossed her arms to cover herself.

"What's the matter?" Chase asked.

"I-I'm too small," she murmured.

"Says who?"

Sammi felt her face burn. "Lance. He wanted me to get breast implants."

"Lance needed a brain implant." He leaned down and reclaimed her lips.

The kiss swept away all coherent thought. Before she knew it, she'd wound her arms around his neck, letting the shirt fall open.

He gazed down at her. "Oh, man," he murmured, his voice soft and gravelly. "You're so damned beautiful it almost hurts."

He touched her breasts, slowly and reverently. There was no mistaking the heat in his eyes. It burned away her self-consciousness like the sun on fog, allowing her to focus on the here and now, on the moment, on *him*.

She reached for him and pulled him down, aching to feel the length and weight and warmth of him, to feel his chest against hers. His mouth once again met hers, and she ventured her tongue between his lips. He tasted salty and sweet and vaguely of wine. He pulled her lower lip into his mouth, and she groaned at the heady, intoxicating sensation.

He eased her shirt and bra off her arms, then leaned over her, his hands skimming down her sides. "Beautiful," he murmured as he trailed kisses across her face, down her throat, and across her chest. "So beautiful." He softly stroked her breasts, then lowered his mouth to kiss first one, then the other. Her nerve endings danced with pleasure.

"Perfect. You're just perfect," Chase murmured, taking a pebbled tip in his mouth.

It was as if a live wire linked the tips of her breasts to her intimate core. His hands slid downward. He found the edge of her denim skirt and eased it up, stroking the outside of her thigh, moving to the inside, sliding, gliding higher. She moved beneath him, silently urging him to touch her where she ached to be touched. His mouth trailed down her belly. He drew back and unbuttoned her skirt, then unfastened the zipper and slowly, slowly pulled it down.

He sucked in his breath as he saw her black lace thong. "Wow."

Sammi grinned, loving the look on his face, loving the fact that she'd put it there. "You're overdressed for the occasion," she said, sitting up and reaching for his belt buckle.

He groaned as she unfastened it. His erection, hot and large and rigid, pressed against the zipper as she struggled to pull it down. He stood and peeled off his jeans and boxer briefs in record time, pausing to pull a foil packet out of his pocket and place it on the nightstand.

The sight of him in the lamplight, hard-muscled and massively aroused, sent a shiver up her spine. The bed dipped as he climbed back on it. She reached for him, but he moved lower on the bed.

"I want to touch you," she murmured.

"Not yet." He grazed a trail of kisses across her chest, her breasts, her belly, her hips. He shifted down on the bed and kissed her inner thigh, his fingers toying with the elastic of her panties.

He took his time, fingering the edges of her panties, stroking her through the barrier of thin fabric until her breath came in gasps. By the time he finally pulled her panties down and off, she was throbbing with need. And then his lips and fingers were on her and in her, and she was speeding down a hill in a runaway train, a train that was shaking and exploding as it flew right off a cliff.

She must have cried out, because she heard a cry.

When she finally landed, he was hovering over her, his eyes warm. "Thank you," she breathed.

His mouth curved in a grin. "The pleasure was all mine."

She touched his cheek and smiled back. His five-o'clock shadow rasped against her fingers. "Not yet. But we can fix that."

She reached for the condom on the bedside table and ripped it open, then carefully rolled it down his throbbing shaft.

"Sammi . . ." he murmured, reaching for her.

She pulled him down on top her as she stretched out on the bed. She wrapped her legs around him and lifted her hips, then gasped as he started to enter her.

He instantly stilled. "Am I hurting you?"

"No," she whispered. "But you'll kill me if you make me wait any longer."

She was grateful that he didn't. Slowly, slowly he filled her, filling her heart as well as her body. She moved against him and they found their rhythm, and the next thing she knew, she was on that train again, rushing downhill with no brakes, picking up speed, flying past the point of no return with wild abandon.

And this time, she took him with her.

～

Around midnight, Sammi rose from the bed, grabbed Chase's shirt off the floor, and pulled it on. "I need a glass of water. How about you?"

He rolled over and watched her fasten the middle two buttons, leaving a tempting shadow of cleavage. The shirt came to the top of her long legs and barely covered the essentials. It looked far better on her than it ever had on him. "The only thing I need is more of you." He flashed a grin. "And maybe a couple more condoms."

She grinned. "Check the nightstand table."

He enjoyed the view as she left the room, then rolled over, sat up, and pulled open the drawer. His brows shot up. Holy Moses—it looked like she'd cleaned out Sex Toys 'R' Us.

He was holding a lime green dildo as she walked back in, a glass in her hand. She froze in the doorway.

He wagged the faux johnson. "Your battery bill must be pretty high."

Her face flamed with color.

He pulled a blindfold and French tickler from the drawer. "Play around with this stuff often?"

She sank to the edge of the bed, her face flaming. "I, uh, just got it all this afternoon."

"I don't know if I should be insulted or not."

"Actually, Chloe gave them to me." Sammi set the glass on the nightstand. "Her boss owns the Adult Toy Box and she gives Chloe free samples, and Chloe gave them to me, because . . ." She fell silent.

The handcuffs jangled as he lifted them. "Because you told her you wanted to chain me up and have your way with me?"

"No."

He lifted a blue plastic circular item labeled "Vibrating Cock Ring." "Because you have a thing for intimate torture devices?"

"No!"

He picked up a deck of cards and riffled through them. Each one pictured a couple in an impossibly contorted sexual position. "Because you're trying out to be an Olympic gymnast?"

The red on Sammi's face deepened.

He rummaged in the drawer. "Hmm. Love juice, nipple pinchers, edible panties—this is quite the collection."

Sammi buried her face in her hands.

He was immediately contrite. "Hey—are you upset?" He moved to the edge of the bed, swung his legs to the floor, and put his arm around her. "I was just teasing. If you want to play around with this stuff, count me in."

"No!" She looked embarrassed and upset and like she might burst into tears. "It's for . . . backup. In case you got, you know—bored, and things started to go south."

"If I got *bored?*" His eyebrows rose. "Did you really think that if I ended up in your bedroom, I could possibly be *bored?*"

"Well, that's what used to happen." She stared down at her hands.

"That's what that SOB told you?" Chase had never known that such tenderness toward one person could co-exist with such rage toward another.

She nodded and twisted her fingers together.

A nerve ticked in Chase's jaw. Man, he hoped he never ran into this jerk, because he wasn't sure he could resist the urge to rearrange his dental work. He gently tilted Sammi's downturned face toward him.

"Sammi, sweetheart, boredom was never Lance's problem. His problem was the butt growing out of his neck."

She gave a crooked grin.

"Seriously." He gently tucked her hair behind her ear. "You are exciting as hell. I get a woody just thinking about you."

He was gratified to see her lips curve up.

"Think I'm kidding?"

She glanced down at the sheet, which was tenting in his lap, then laughed.

"In fact, the only thing that's keeping me from ravishing you right now is the lack of a condom. That's the one item your collection is missing."

"They're in the drawer on the other side of the bed."

"Well, then, come here, vixen." He hauled her onto the mattress and kissed her thoroughly, then began to slowly make love to her all over again. She was sexy and soft and giving and warm, and she excited him beyond endurance. When he felt her shudder and contract around him, he followed her off the launch pad, only to discover that she'd rocketed him to a height he'd never reached before, a height where he apparently needed oxygen, because he found it hard to breathe.

He was falling for her—falling hard.

She looked up at him, her eyes misty and tender, and he knew he wasn't falling alone.

Oh, God. He'd rather break his own neck than break her heart, and yet when he told her the truth, she was going to be hurt. She was going to be angry. She might even storm off and refuse to ever see him again, and he couldn't really blame her if she did.

But he couldn't let that happen. He had to make her hear him out, had to make her understand, had to make her forgive him.

Because he'd finally found the woman he wasn't sure even existed. Sammi was his romantic Yeti, the Loch Ness Monster of his heart.

He'd finally found the SCABHOG of his dreams.

Chapter Seventeen

Sammi sat at her kitchen table a little after noon the next day, cruising the real-estate rental listings on her laptop, when Chloe's vintage VW rattled into her driveway. A moment later, she heard Chloe's key in the door, the creak of the hinges, and the familiar tip-tap of Joe's claws on the hardwood.

"In here!" Sammi called.

Joe yanked the leash out of Chloe's hand as she rounded the corner and bounded for Sammi. The giant dog put his paws on her shoulders and slurped her face with kisses.

Sammi put up her hands to ward off the dog-spit facial. "Hello to you, too, boy." She unfastened the leash and rubbed his ears. Joe longingly sniffed her leather clogs. "What's the matter, boy—wouldn't Chloe play footsie with you last night?"

"Bet *you* didn't have a problem finding a footsie partner." Chloe grinned slyly.

Sammi stroked the dog's head. "For your information, no footsie transpired."

"So what did?"

"As if I'm going to tell you."

"You don't have to. That glow on your face says it all."
Chloe smiled in an annoyingly know-it-all fashion as she
headed for the refrigerator. "I take it you didn't inflict any
mortal wounds."

"No. But I did set my shirt on fire."

Chloe wryly shook her head. "The lengths you'll go to
get attention."

"It was an accident."

Chloe helped herself to a Coke and slammed the refrigerator door. "More than likely it was a subconscious
desire to shed your clothes."

Sammi rolled her eyes. "Why do I put up with you?"

"Because I'm your sister, and you love me."

"Uh-huh."

Chloe pulled the tab on the can. "Not that my opinion
counts for much, but I wholeheartedly approve." Chloe
seated herself at the table. "Chase is gorgeous, he's a gen-
uinely nice guy, and he's looking to find 'the one.' "

"Yeah. But I don't know that he sees me as his 'one.' "

"Why not?"

Sammi gazed at her computer as it went into hiberna-
tion. "Because afterward he got kind of funny."

"Funny, how?"

"It's hard to say, exactly. He just seemed to withdraw
and get all quiet."

"He's a guy, that's all." She took a sip of her cola.
"They're all like that."

"Since when did you become an expert on men? As I
recall, you haven't had a steady boyfriend since college."

"That doesn't mean that I'm not a keen observer of
human nature."

"Yeah? Well, what does it mean that he cleared out of here at the crack of dawn, telling me he has a lot of work to tackle?"

Chloe lifted her shoulders. "Probably that he has a lot of work to tackle."

"On a Sunday?"

"You told me the FBI is twenty-four seven."

Sammi shook her head. "Something just seemed off."

"Did you make plans to see each other again?"

She nodded. "We're going camping next weekend."

"Camping as in going to a lodge, or camping outside?"

"Outside."

"In an RV?"

"No. In a tent."

"Whoa." Chloe's eyes bugged out. "You? In a tent? You're the poster child for bug and reptile phobias."

"I'm only afraid of the dangerous ones," Sammi said defensively.

"Since you don't know which are dangerous and which are harmless, that means you're afraid of all of them."

"If I'm with someone who's knowledgeable, well, then, I'll be okay."

Chloe took a long swig of cola and regarded Sammi over the top of the can. "No doubt about it. You're in deep."

It was true. She only prayed he felt the same way about her.

Joe nudged her hand. Sammi reached out and stroked his flank. "Speaking of scary animals, can you watch Joe again next weekend?"

"Sure. But you'd better loan me those sandals of yours, 'cause I didn't like the way he was eyeing my Doc Martens."

~

Ten trunks remaining. Arlene stood in front of them and drew a deep breath. The janitor had hauled off the twenty-seven she'd already emptied. That made thirty-seven steamer trunks in all, full of years and years of Justine's clothing.

Why had Justine kept them? It wasn't like she was going to wear them again; she bought new clothes every season. The amount of money Justine Phelps spent on clothing would have financed several small nations.

The trunks had been stacked in the back of the basement like coffins in a mausoleum, the most recent ones first, which meant Arlene was working her way back through time. Each trunk might contain pieces from several seasons, but Arlene was now, apparently, in the early 1960s—around the time she'd started working for Phelps Oil.

The hinges squeaked as Arlene opened the lid of the next trunk. The fragile tissue crinkled as she parted it to reveal the top garment. Arlene's breath caught in her throat as she lifted out a scarlet evening gown, as dazzling as a Christmas ornament. The silk slipped between her fingers, smooth as water. It was a sleek, fitted column of a dress, with a bodice that sparkled with ruby-colored beads. It was exquisite, dramatic—and familiar.

Arlene knew exactly when she'd seen it. She sank onto the lid of an adjacent trunk and closed her eyes as the memories washed over her.

It had been the weekend before Christmas in 1962—the night of the annual Christmas party, the first year she'd worked at Phelps Oil. Every December, the staff from the executive offices was invited to the Phelps mansion for a glamorous evening of live music, champagne, and exotic hors d'oeuvres. Arlene had heard about the much-anticipated event on her very first day of work.

No one anticipated it more that year than Arlene. If she could get into the inner sanctum of Chandler's home, she'd thought, maybe she could find the key that would unlock the inner sanctum of his heart. She was dying to see the inside of his house, to get a glimpse of his private life, to see his wife in person.

Arlene had seen Justine's wedding photo on Chandler's desk, of course. She'd looked lovely in it, but didn't every woman look beautiful on her wedding day? Besides, that photo was fifteen years old. Surely she was an old hag by now. Maybe if Chandler saw them side by side, he'd realize that it was Arlene he loved, Arlene that he wanted to share his life with.

God, how foolish she'd been. Arlene sank onto the lid of the next still-closed trunk and shut her eyes.

She'd sewn a special dress for the party—bright red velvet, with a full skirt and a satin sash—and worn rollers in her hair all day so it would stay curled. She'd taken pains with her makeup. She'd looked, she was sure, better than she'd ever looked in her life.

She'd driven her old Chevy to the mansion, parked it on the street, and walked up the long drive, past the trees draped with Christmas lights. She'd practically been shaking with excitement when the butler had opened the door and she'd stepped into the stunning black-and-white foyer.

It looked like a grand hotel rather than a home. Dazzled, Arlene stared up at the brilliant chandelier. A black-and-white-clad maid had materialized at her elbow. "May I take your coat?"

Arlene had shrugged out of it, accepted a glass of champagne from a passing waiter, and eagerly scanned the room for Chandler.

She'd seen him, all right—standing beside Justine, his hand on the small of her back, directly beneath the immense chandelier in the center of the black marble starburst on the floor. That gesture—his hand on her back, so natural, so proprietary—had twisted Justine's gut like twine. They'd looked perfect together.

Justine had looked perfect, period. She'd been wearing the jewel of a crimson gown that Arlene held now, as if she were the centerpiece of the room.

And, of course, she was. This was her home. Her life.

And Chandler was her husband.

Arlene's confidence had shriveled like a grape at the Sunsweet plant. What, oh, what had she been thinking? Justine belonged in Chandler's world. She'd been a debutante, she'd studied abroad, she knew about fine dining and wine and art and a million other things that a farm girl like Arlene would never know. Beside her, Arlene must look like a country bumpkin in her homemade dress, with her Dippity-Dooed hair and her Thom McAn shoes.

Chandler had said that he and his wife led separate lives, that it wasn't really a marriage, that they didn't even share a bedroom. Up until now, Arlene had thought of Justine as nothing but an obstacle, a roadblock standing between her and Chandler. Now, however, she saw Justine as part of the road.

Arlene had taken a long swig of champagne.

"Miss Arnette?"

Numbly, Arlene had turned to see a man in a tuxedo beside her.

"Come with me, please."

She'd drained her glass, then accompanied the man to the side of the foyer and down a narrow hallway. Thinking that he was taking her to a private rendezvous with Chandler, Arlene's heart had thudded furiously. Chandler did love her, after all.

The man led her into the kitchen. A maid looked up from the platter she was arranging. The chef eyed her curiously over a pan of sautéing mushrooms. The tuxedoed man had leaned close and spoken softly. "I'm sorry, but you'll have to leave."

"I beg your pardon?"

"I've been instructed to tell you to leave." The man's eyes were kind, but his tone was firm.

The champagne hit Arlene's empty stomach, making the room spin. "Instructed? By whom?"

"That really doesn't matter."

"It's Mrs. Phelps, isn't it?"

"You are not welcome here, Miss Arnette. You need to leave."

"But—but the other guests are my coworkers! How will I explain . . ."

The maid from the foyer reappeared with her coat and held it open. Numbly, Arlene put her arms through the sleeves.

"I suggest a sudden headache." The man took her arm and escorted her out the back door.

"Ms. Arnette?"

Arlene opened her eyes, the old humiliation still burning in her chest, to see Sammi in the doorway. Arlene rose to her feet, still clutching the dress.

"Are you all right?" Sammi's forehead creased with concern.

"I'm fine."

"You look a little pale. Can I get you some water?"

"I'm perfectly fine." Arlene turned toward the clothes rack.

Sammi's gaze lit on the red silk. "Oh, what a beautiful gown!" she exclaimed.

Delightful. Now she was going to praise Justine's taste in clothes. "It's one of Justine's older ones."

"She must have looked gorgeous in it. From her photos and portraits, she was a beautiful woman."

A fresh stab of pain pierced Arlene. It was ridiculous, feeling inferior to a dead woman, but Justine still managed to make her feel that way. Arlene's hand shook as she slid the dress onto a clothes hanger. "Did you need something?"

"Yes. I've come up with a way that we can expand our exhibit space."

Arlene smoothed the dress and tried to gather the tattered remnants of her patience. "It doesn't need to be expanded. And we don't have any more space, anyway."

"Well, you know the house I'm renting—"

Walter's house. Arlene held up both her hands. "I told you I don't want to hear another word about that house, and I meant it."

"But there's something you should know. It's going to be—"

Good lord—the girl just didn't know when to quit. Arlene put her hands on her hips. "The subject is closed."

"But—"

Frustration and anger curled in Arlene's stomach like a crouching tiger. "I mean it. Not one more word."

Sammi twisted her fingers together. "I really think you should hear me out."

The tiger in Arlene's belly switched its tail. "What part of 'not one word' don't you understand?"

Sammi drew in a breath and jerked her head in a stiff nod. "All right. I'll put it in an e-mail."

Arlene felt her left eye twitch. "When I say I don't want to hear about it, I mean in writing, in person, on the phone, or on the computer. Have I made myself clear?"

Sammi's back went rigid. Her eyes flashed with heat and two bright pink spots flamed on her cheeks. She was obviously struggling to retain her composure. "Very clear," she said curtly. She turned on her heel and ascended the stairs.

Dadblast that girl! Arlene's forehead throbbed. She rubbed it with her thumb and middle finger as she sat back down in the chair beside the trunk, then closed her eyes. When she opened them, a wispy bit of familiar pink chiffon chased all thoughts of Sammi from her mind. Leaning forward, she moved aside a wool dress and lifted out a filmy peignoir.

Oh, dear Lord—it wasn't just any peignoir; it was the same one Chandler had brought her from Paris! The same draped bodice edged with the same lace, the Valentino label in the back, the same high slit up the side.

Her hands tightened on the delicate fabric. A man didn't buy a negligee for a woman he wasn't sleeping with. No matter how much she might want to think otherwise, Arlene wasn't simple-minded enough to believe that for a minute.

She'd been suspicious about that anniversary trip. Apparently her suspicions had been justified.

Pain shot through her, sharp and hot. Her hands shook, making the nightgown flutter. Had Chandler had sex with Justine only on the trip, or did he make love to her at home, too? Had he been making love to both of them all along?

She'd known it was possible, of course. After all, Chandler and Justine were married, and married people slept together. He'd denied it when she'd asked him, but then, what could she expect from a married man who was cheating on his wife?

Another knife of pain stabbed her, but this time it was accompanied by a dagger of anger. Out of all the shops in Paris, Chandler hadn't bothered to find her a nightgown of her own? Good Lord, she'd thought the man had had more originality than that.

Another stab, deeper than before. Who had he been thinking about when he'd bought them—Justine, or her? When he'd made love to one woman, was he thinking about the other? Did he compare them? How different were they in bed? She'd always thought Justine must be a cold fish, but if she'd whisked her husband off on a romantic trip and inspired him to buy sexy lingerie, how cold could she have been?

A sick feeling gripped Arlene's chest. Breathing hard, she wadded up the gown, stalked across the room, and threw it into the trash can.

Her chest hurt. She put her hand on her racing heart, wondering if she were about to have another heart attack.

What the hell difference did it make? No one would care. The board would probably be relieved if she just dropped dead.

She might be relieved, as well.

Chapter Eighteen

I just can't do it, Coach," Horace whined through Luke's cell phone, his voice reverberating loudly in the close confines of the SUV on the darkened street. "I just can't tell Mother I'm going to move out."

Chase didn't need to look over at Paul to know he was smirking. Man, he hated coaching clients in front of his partner, but he and Paul were on stakeout and he had no choice. It didn't help that Horace's whiny voice carried loudly through the phone so that Paul could hear every word he was saying.

Chase draped his arm on the steering wheel, directed his gaze out the window, and tried to recall Luke's methodology. "Don't you want to?"

"Oh, yeah!"

"And from what you've told me the last time we talked, you've found the perfect apartment."

"Yeah," Horace said wistfully. "And I've found this big black leather sofa that would fit in there perfectly. But I just don't have the nerve to tell Mother."

"Let's think about a time when you felt afraid to do something, but you went ahead and did it anyway."

"There isn't any."

"Come on, Horace. Help me out here. How about when you went to interview for your job? Weren't you nervous then?"

Paul put on a faux-terrified expression and started shaking. Chase ignored him.

"Well, yes," Horace admitted.

"And you went anyway, and apparently you got the job."

"Yes. But that's because I was the only candidate. My company only pays about half what accountants at other companies get paid."

Yet another area to work on. Horace could keep his brother in business for years to come. Chase turned away from Paul, who was playing air violin, and decided to try another tack. "What about the first time you asked a girl for a date?"

"I've, uh, never actually done that."

Not to be believed, Paul was clutching his chest, feigning a heart attack. Chase shot him a warning look. "Well, what about as a kid? Surely you were afraid of something as you were growing up."

"Oh, I was afraid of everything. Especially the bullies, but I still went to school every day."

"Good. That's a great example. And how did you handle that?"

"I didn't. I got beat up every day."

Chase closed his eyes, not wanting to see Paul's reaction to that piece of news. "Well, how do you wish you'd handled it?"

"I wish I'd had some sort of superpower."

"Like what?"

"Like Superman. Only with an accordion."

Paul let out a snort. Chase shot him a warning glance and shook his head. He was out of his league here, and Paul wasn't helping. "Uh-huh. Well, how would you have handled it if you had superpowers?"

"Well, first I'd play 'Charge,' and then I'd kick in their faces until they looked like hamburger." Horace's voice took on more enthusiasm than Chase had ever heard him express. "Then I'd boot them into outer space, where they'd circle the earth attached to a visually amplified satellite that tracked me, so they'd be forced to spend the rest of eternity watching me with their girlfriends."

Paul's shoulders shook with the effort not to laugh.

"Wow. I can see you've put some thought into that."

"Yeah. A lot."

"Well, that's good." Or was it? Chase had no clue. He rubbed his forehead. "For the purposes of our exercise here, I want you to picture yourself doing something that's actually within the realm of your, um, abilities. If you could deal with those bullies again as just a normal human being, how would you handle it?"

"I dunno." There was a long pause, then Horace sighed. "Probably just get beat up again."

"Wrong answer, Horace. You need to start thinking of yourself as confident and capable and able to handle conflict."

"But I'm not."

"But you're in the process of becoming that way." *Or at least you're supposed to be*. Jeez, this guy was pathetic.

"Besides your mother, what are some of the things that make you anxious?"

"Everything."

"You need to be more specific. This week I want you to find a situation where you're anxious, Horace, and do the thing you fear."

"Maybe you could set something up for me."

"What?"

"Well, maybe you could pretend to mug me, and I could fight back."

Paul was on the floorboard, his face buried in the seat to muffle his laughter.

"Interesting concept." And stupid as hell. Chase could see the headlines now: *FBI Agent Attacks Man to Boost Loser's Self-Image.*

"That would be so cool!" Horace continued, sounding totally pumped. "Mom always says I'm a coward, so that's how I think about myself. If I could prove I wasn't, well, then, maybe she'd believe it, which means *I'd* believe it, and then maybe I wouldn't be. A coward, that is."

Was the guy coming unhinged? Horace couldn't seriously believe Chase was going to attack him.

Still, the idea seemed to have caught the man's imagination. *When you find something that works, build on it,* Luke had written. Maybe Chase could use this to spur Horace in the right direction. "You know what, Horace— I think you should spend some time this week imagining yourself fighting off a mugger. Better yet, picture yourself saving someone else from one."

"Oh, yeah!" Horace sounded excited. "That's good. That would be really heroic, wouldn't it?"

"Very heroic."

"So maybe you'll come by my office or home and pretend to attack a girl, and I'll get to save her?"

Paul's shoulders heaved as he pressed his face into the upholstery.

Chase closed his eyes and silently counted to three. "Well, Horace, you could mentally picture that. Or you could envision yourself acting brave and feeling confident in more normal situations."

"Okay."

"As the week goes on, I want you to keep an eye out for situations where you can step up to the plate and face down one of your fears. It doesn't have to be a big fear; it can be something simple, like talking to that girl in Escrow that you rapped about."

"Oh, no! She's scarier than Mother!"

Was there any hope for this man? Chase drew a deep breath. "Well, then, start smaller. Tell a waiter that you don't want mayonnaise on your hamburger, and ask him to get you another one."

"But I *like* mayonnaise."

"Whatever. That was just an example. The point is, you have to do something that makes you anxious."

"And sometime during the week, you'll surprise me with a situation, right?"

The concept seemed to have stirred Horace like nothing else had. "I never said that, Horace."

"You never said you wouldn't, either. And since it's supposed to be a surprise, it wouldn't be a surprise if you actually told me. I *get* it."

No, you don't. You don't get anything. "Horace—this isn't about me tricking you. This is about you being the quarterback of your own life. If you score a touchdown, that feeling of victory will give you courage to carry the ball again, and you can just keep on scoring."

"Yeah. Okay. "

"So—do you have a rap for me?"

"Yes. And I've got my accordion this time."

"Terrific!"

"Want to hear 'Lady of Spain' as a warmup?"

Paul snorted into the upholstery.

"We're running out of time," Chase said. "Better go straight to the rap."

"Okay."

An awful squawk made Chase close his eyes and hold the phone away from his ear. Horace played a few chords and slipped into his hip-hop voice with a cheerleader beat:

> *I went to a movie to see some action*
> *'Cause my social life didn't have any traction.*
> *I saw a seat beside hot blond twins,*
> *So I winked and waved, and they gave me grins.*
> *I said, 'Hey, ladies, is this seat taken?*
> *You both look hotter than sizzling bacon.'*
> *They giggled and said, 'Ooh, you look like trouble.*
> *How do you feel about seeing double?'*
> *Oomachucka, oomachucka, oomachucka, OOM!*
> *Double trouble all the way, boom boom BOOM!*

The final chord of the accordion squalled loudly through the receiver.

Beside Chase, Paul was facedown, gasping into the passenger seat.

"So what do you think?" Horace asked meekly.

"I think you're the man." Chase whacked Paul as he let out a snort. "You're a halftime show and a half."

"Really?"

"Absolutely. Have you ever thought about performing publicly?"

"Well, sure, I've *thought* about it. But I wouldn't dare. Besides, where would I perform?"

"There's a coffee shop near the river that has open-mike night for poets and musicians every Friday. It would be perfect for you."

"Really?" His voice quavered with eagerness, then dropped to despair. "But I couldn't. I'd be terrified! And Mother would have a fit."

"Your mother wouldn't need to know. Just think about it. Try picturing yourself jamming at a microphone, and imagine how it might feel."

"Wow, that could be so cool!"

"It sure could. I want you to think about it and visualize it. That's what extra point kickers do—they run the scene through in their minds, imagining it so thoroughly that they smell the sweat of the other team, hear the thud of their foot hitting the ball, see the ball sailing over the goalpost. They feel like they've already done it. So imagine it like that, and see how it would make you feel."

"Okay. Hey, I've got an idea! Maybe I'll picture myself rapping in public, and then saving a girl in the audience from a mugger."

"All right, buddy. Talk to you next week."

"Unless you mug me sooner."

Don't hold your breath. With a sigh, Chase hung up the phone.

Paul lifted his head. His face was red and creased from being pressed to the car seat, and tears ran down his face. It took him several moments to stop laughing and catch his breath. "Wow," he gasped. "That dude is seriously wacked!"

"He's getting better."

"That's better?"

"Yeah, believe it or not, it is."

Paul wiped his eyes. "I don't know how you kept it together."

Chase scowled at him. "You didn't help."

"I know, I know. Sorry." Laughter rumbled in his chest as the mere thought set him off again. "I gotta say, I'm impressed with how you handled it."

"Thanks."

Paul ran his big hand down his face. "So how are you handling Sammi? Have you told her the truth yet?"

Chase's stomach knotted. "No. I tried to, but . . ." *But I slept with her instead.* Man, how could he have been so stupid? How could he have thought that was a good idea? Yet it had seemed like his only recourse at the time. She'd been so anxious and insecure and vulnerable.

Right, bucko. So you thought you'd fix things by boffing her?

Chase muttered a low oath and raked a hand through his hair. Some life coach he'd turned out to be. And now she was going to call, and he'd have to lie to her again.

"I'm planning to tell her this weekend."

"Better do it." Paul's expression grew serious. "I gotta tell you, Melanie really likes her, and she'll never forgive you if you break that girl's heart."

Melanie's not alone. I'll never forgive myself. "I want to make sure she hears me out, so I'm taking her camping up at my property. I figure that if I get her alone out in the wilderness, she'll be stuck with me long enough to calm down and listen. If nothing else, we'll have a long drive back together."

"That's either brilliant, or the stupidest plan I've ever heard."

Chase lifted the nearly empty Starbucks cup from his drink holder and held it aloft. "Here's hoping for brilliant." He swallowed the last swig of cold coffee and grimaced.

"Guess you won't be coaching anyone for much longer," Paul said. "Isn't your brother due back next week?"

Chase nodded. "He'll be in Oklahoma City for the start of the trial on Monday, but he'll be in protective custody. I won't get to see him until after it's all over and the nephew is arrested."

Only problem was, the nephew had eluded surveillance, and no one had seen hide nor hair of him for the last week. It was only a matter of time until he was found again, but in the meantime, Chase was nervous.

He crumpled the empty coffee cup. "Luke's not safe until Johnny's locked up, because he thinks his uncles are as loyal to him as he is to them."

Paul shook his head. "Blind trust is a sad and pathetic thing."

Yeah. Like the way Sammi trusted him. Chase's stomach churned as the phone rang. "That's Sammi now."

Paul reached for the door handle. "Know what—I think we should watch for this guy from two different angles. I'll be across the street."

"Good. 'Cause it's kinda hard to do surveillance with your head in the car seat."

Paul grinned and shot him the finger. Chase waited

until the door slammed, then drew in a deep breath and answered the phone.

"Hi, Luke. It's Sammi." Her voice slipped around him, as warm and sensuous as tropical water.

"Great to hear from you. How are you?"

"Wonderful. I want to thank you so much for all of your advice."

Guilt vise-gripped his chest. "You sound like you're in a good mood."

"I am. Chase came over this weekend, and . . ." She managed to make the word "and" sound suggestive.

"And what?" Chase prompted.

"It was amazing."

Chase grinned at the dashboard. How could he feel so good and yet so awful at the same time? "So you had a good time."

"Fantastic. Beyond my wildest dreams."

"So all of your issues—"

"Aren't issues any longer. But I have a new one."

Uh-oh. "What's that?"

"I've fallen in love."

Chase felt as if he'd been thrown out of an airplane without a parachute. He dropped his head onto the rim of the steering wheel, then forced himself to straighten back up. "Isn't it awfully soon for that? You haven't known him all that long."

"I've known him long enough to know he's everything I'm looking for in a man."

His upper lip broke a sweat. "But . . . what if he's not?"

"He is. And it's not just my opinion; I've gotten to know his partner's wife really well, and she says what you see is what you get. According to her, Chase is just as terrific as he seems."

Oh, hell. He couldn't let her go on thinking he was a frickin' saint. "Hey—no one's perfect. I mean, everyone has flaws."

"Oh, I don't think he's perfect—not by any means. He has a lot of flaws."

Hearing that didn't please him as much as it should have. "Like what?"

"Well, he's something of a self-control freak. He's kind of obsessive about planning everything out and keeping things neat. He grew up in chaos, so he likes to know what to expect."

"Well, as faults go, that's not too bad."

"He has other ones."

"Yeah?" he asked warily. "What else?"

"Well, he's a little paranoid. He's always looking around and watching people and kind of evaluating them. He's hyperaware of his surroundings. But I think that's part of what makes him really terrific at his job, too. He noticed that pedophile acting odd all the way across the restaurant."

"Doesn't sound like too bad a trait."

"That's not all."

Holy cow, just how many faults did she think he had?

"He's terrible about staying in touch," she continued. "He hardly ever calls. And he's really reluctant to talk about emotions. After we've been close, he immediately tries to distance himself." She paused. "At the same time, though, I'm pretty sure he has feelings for me."

Oh, he had feelings, all right. If he didn't, he wouldn't

have a problem. His stomach twisted like a trailer in a tornado.

"The bottom line is, I trust him. And I was afraid I'd never trust another man."

Chase ran a hand down his face, feeling like the lowest of the low. "You've learned to trust yourself, Sammi. This is about you, not him."

"No. It's about the two of us together, and how he's changed my life." She paused. "Not that you haven't, too. You've been a big part of that. A huge part."

Oh, man—this was just getting worse and worse. He mopped his suddenly perspiring forehead.

"Look, Sammi—you've done all the work. And if you were to find out tomorrow that Chase and I were both pond-scum bottom-feeders, it wouldn't change the fact that you've made terrific progress."

"It's so funny that you'd use that term." She sounded surprised. "Chase has called people that, too."

Tell her, his conscience urged. "There's, um, actually a reason for that."

A scuffling noise sounded through the phone. "No, Joe!" Sammi said, apparently speaking away from the mouthpiece. "Drop it!" More scuffling sounds. Her voice came back clearly. "Hang on a moment. My dog just dragged my leather jacket out of the closet, and he's trying to make love to it."

The phone rattled. "Give it to me, Joe," he heard her say from a distance. "No, Joe. Down! Stop it, Joe. Joe, sit. Joe! Come back here, Joe!" The ruckus grew fainter. After several moments, she came back on the line. "I'm sorry about that."

"That's okay."

"You were about to tell me something about bottom-feeders."

Chase jammed a hand through his hair. He couldn't just dump this on her over the phone. She deserved to hear it in person, as he'd planned.

"It's a, uh, local term." Time to shift the topic—fast. "How is work going?"

"Well, you'll be glad to know I've been very assertive. I've invited the Preservation Commission, the museum board members, and the media to tour my home on Thursday. I'm turning the house into a museum. I'm labeling everything and putting up little signs explaining the significance of all the art deco features. I hope it'll help them see the historic value of the place."

"That's a terrific idea."

"Thanks." She sounded pleased.

Hell, she should be. The idea was brilliant. She'd texted him—as Chase, of course—with the idea the day before, and he'd encouraged her to go for it. "What does your boss think about it?"

"She doesn't know."

"You didn't tell her?"

"I tried, but she refused to listen. She said she didn't want to hear another word about the house and she kept cutting me off."

"So it's her own fault."

"Yes." Sammi sighed. "I feel really bad about it, but I have to stand up for what I believe in, and I believe in saving this house."

"Good for you."

"Chase said that, too. You and he have a lot in common. I think you'd really like him."

I'm not so sure about that. He shifted uneasily on the seat of his SUV.

"Anyway," she continued, "the fact that he believes in me has given me a lot of confidence. I can't tell you how much it means to have his support. And your support, too, of course."

"I don't think you need both of us anymore," Chase said. "You've really upped your game and learned how to score, so I think you've outgrown the need for a life coach."

"You think?"

"Yeah, I do."

"But I really like talking to you!"

"And I like talking to you. But my schedule is overbooked, and you've worked through your main issue. You're on a winning streak, and I think now you can just talk to Chase."

She paused a moment. "You know, I think you're right."

Chase hit a button on his phone. "My next client is calling. Remember to keep your head in the game."

"Wait! I need to pay you. Tell me where to send a check. Or do you want me to use PayPal? I can—"

He clicked again. "Bye, Sammi. It's been great working with you!"

He hung up and blew out a sigh.

There—he'd done it. He'd officially severed the coach/client relationship. Nothing stood between them having a romantic relationship now.

Nothing, that was, except for the truth—and the fact that she was likely to never want to speak to him again once she heard it.

Chapter Nineteen

Arlene walked into her kitchen three mornings later, her white-and-blue flannel bathrobe cinched tight, and put on a pot of coffee. While it brewed, she unlocked the three locks on her front door, bent down, and picked up her newspaper from the porch.

As she straightened, Walter's car pulled into her driveway. Her pulse quickened. What was he doing here? She hadn't seen him since he'd come to her house for lunch, but he'd called her several times just to chat. Just last night they'd talked for over an hour, and they had plans to go bowling tomorrow night.

Oh, dear—she must look a fright! She ran a hand through her hair, tugged the sash of her robe, and gave a tentative wave.

He waved back as he climbed out of his sedan, a newspaper in his hand. "Good morning," he called.

Her stomach fluttered as he walked toward her. Something in the way he moved reminded her of Clint Eastwood. "Good morning, Walter. What brings you here at this hour?"

He grinned. "Thought I might come by and get a cup of coffee."

It was an awfully familiar kind of thing to do. If the neighbors saw a strange man's car in her driveway first thing in the morning, they'd think he'd spent the night.

So? The devil's advocate in her mind responded. *He's not married—and Lord knows we're both of age.* It didn't have to be a big secret, like when Chandler came to call.

She smiled. "I just put some on. Come on in." She held the door, and he followed her through the living room to the kitchen. She self-consciously ran a hand through her hair. "If you'd given me some notice, I would have at least brushed my hair."

"I think you look lovely." He leaned against the counter as she pulled two mugs off little hooks under the counter. A thrill chased up her spine.

She fussed around, getting out milk and sugar. The coffeepot gurgled. "I must say, this is quite a surprise. A welcome one, of course, but quite unexpected."

He shuffled his feet. "The truth is, Arlene, there's something in the paper that's likely to upset you."

Arlene went very still. "What is it?"

"It's probably best if you just read it for yourself."

"Oh, dear. I don't like the sound of that."

"It's not all that bad. But I figure it'll be a surprise to you, since you didn't mention it on the phone last night." He pulled out a chair.

She lowered herself into it. He placed the Metro section on the table, and her eye flew to a photo below the fold. Sammi. Standing in front of the little house she rented from Walter, with the entire museum board on either side of her.

Arlene's breath caught. "What in blazes—"

"Better just read the story," Walter said gently.

"PHELPS MUSEUM BOARD CONSIDERS PURCHASE OF ART DECO HOME."

Outrage burned in Arlene's veins. She picked up the paper, then set it down, her fingers shaking too hard to hold it. How dare she! How dare Sammi call the board behind her back!

Arlene stared at the article. The words blurred through a red haze of fury:

The Executive Board of the Phelps Museum toured a small home in Tulsa's Rivertree Subdivision that has recently received a reprieve from the wrecking ball. Built in 1933, the property was designed by Raymond Deshuilles, a world-renowned art deco architect.

'Art deco architecture is an endangered species,' Phelps Museum Curator Sammi Matthews told the group. 'It's being destroyed in the name of progress, and in the process, we're losing a beautiful part of Tulsa's heritage.'

The architectural style, which began in Paris in 1925 and grew to international prominence between the World Wars, is usually found in public buildings and opulent mansions.

'Deshuilles is one of the few architects who translated the design into smaller homes,' Matthews said. 'He's famous for saying, "Economy need not preclude style." '

Deshuilles worked in Tulsa during the city's oil boom in the late 1920s and early 1930s. The Landry home is believed to be the last Deshuilles structure of its kind in the world.

The home first came to the attention of the board when

Matthews, who is renting the home, learned that a demo-lition permit had been issued for the property. Matthews took the matter to the Preservation Commission, which placed a hold on the permit for 90 days while the issue is studied.

'I would love to see the Phelps Mansion and Art Deco Museum buy and preserve the property,' Matthews said. 'It's a natural fit with the museum's mission.'

'We're investigating the possibility of expanding the museum's role in exhibiting and interpreting Tulsa's rich art deco history,' said Edward Harrison, president of the museum's board of directors.

Arlene tossed the paper on the table, anger bubbling in her chest. "Over my dead body."

"Now, Arlene—" Walter said gently, "it might not be a bad thing. I mean, I've been thinking about it, and as much as I hate someone telling me what to do or not to do, the fact remains, Sammi is probably right. It's a special little house."

He was taking Sammi's side? "No. It's unthinkable. The Phelps Museum is about Chandler Phelps. What does she know about the museum's mission? Besides, she's gone behind my back."

"Maybe you should just consider it," Walter suggested gently. "If you open your mind to the possibility, it might be good for everyone concerned."

"By everybody, you mean you." Arlene's pulse pounded in her temple. "So you can get top dollar for your house without a demolition permit."

Walter's face grew stony. "Is that what you think? That I came over here out of self-interest?"

"It's certainly sounding like it, the way you're taking her side."

"I came over because I thought you might be upset, not to further my own interests, Arlene. I'm not like that."

Arlene glared at him. "You're a man, aren't you?"

Walter's lips pulled into a hard line. "I don't know who your gentleman friend was, Arlene, but I know this: he was no gentleman. And you're sadly mistaken if you think every man is as self-serving as he was." He tossed the rest of the paper on the table. "I'll see myself out."

She stared at him as he stiffly walked out. She heard the front door close solidly behind him.

He was wrong. The board was wrong. Sammi was wrong.

They were wrong, wrong, *wrong*.

A horrible thought formed in her mind. It had been creeping in for some time, imperceptible as dust under a bed, but it had gathered into a dust bunny, large enough now to have a shape and form, too defined to ignore.

Maybe, just maybe, *she* was wrong. Maybe Chandler wasn't the man she'd lionized and canonized all these years. Maybe she'd been deluding herself about him, seeing only what she wanted to see, spinning their relationship into something it wasn't. Maybe she'd been lying to herself all these years, because all of her self-worth was tied up in him.

Maybe, just maybe, her whole life had been a waste.

~

Sammi's thoughts were on the weekend as she strode from the museum parking lot to her office in the carriage house later that morning. She was leaving work at noon, and Chase was picking her up an hour later to head to the mountains. She couldn't wait.

But first, she'd have to deal with Ms. Arnette. The woman was going to be furious about the article in this morning's paper. Sammi drew a deep, bracing breath and stepped into her office. Three things immediately struck her as wrong. Thing one: the lights were already on. Thing two: Ms. Arnette was sitting on Sammi's chair behind her desk. Thing three: a large cardboard box sat on the desk in front of her. Sammi froze in the doorway.

Ms. Arnette rose from Sammi's chair and leaned forward, her hands on Sammi's desk. "How dare you," she hissed. "How *dare* you call the board and invite them to that house behind my back!"

Sammi clutched her purse strap as if it could somehow protect her. "I tried to tell you, but you wouldn't listen."

Ms. Arnette straightened. "You obviously didn't try very hard."

Sammi fought to keep her voice calm. "Actually, I did, but you insisted you didn't want to hear anything further about the house."

Ms. Arnette shoved the box toward her. "You're fired. I've packed up all of your personal effects. I want you to take them and leave."

"You're firing me?" Sammi stared at her. "On what grounds?"

"Insubordination."

"I wasn't insubordinate!"

"Oh, indeed you were. I have documented evidence of your previous transgressions, and this is the final straw."

"With all due respect, Ms. Arnette, the board hired me. I don't think you can fire me."

The woman's face turned splotchy with rage. "The board hired *you* to replace *me* when they thought *I* was retiring." Her finger stabbed the air. "As you can see, I am *not* retired. I have tolerated your presence, your insolence, your refusal to listen, and your insistence on subverting the purpose of this institution for long enough. I will tolerate it no longer."

"But—"

Arlene held up both hands like a traffic cop. "As a long-term employee, I have the right to work for the Phelpses' interests as long as I want. And as long as I work here, you will not." She gave the box another jab. "Now take your things and go home."

Ms. Arnette's face was red with fury. Her eyes gleamed like angry coals. There was no point in arguing with her. Sammi picked up the box and headed out the door.

She'd go home, all right. And when she got there, she'd pick up the phone and call the board president.

Chapter Twenty

Chase could tell something was wrong the moment Sammi opened her front door. Her shoulders sagged, and even though she gave him a hug and a welcoming smile, her eyes lacked their usual brightness.

"What's wrong?" he asked.

She mustered a smile. "Nothing that will spoil our weekend." She picked up a duffel bag. "I'll tell you all about it on the way."

As he drove toward the Ouachita Mountains on the Oklahoma Arkansas border, she told him about Ms. Arnette's confrontation.

"What did the board president say when you called him?" Chase asked.

"He's out of town and won't return until Sunday evening," Sammi said glumly.

"I'm sure he'll back you up. The old bat can't just up and fire you."

Sammi brushed a strand of hair out of her eyes and gazed out the windshield. "I don't think she can, either. But it's obvious we can't work together. I can't go back to the mansion until she's gone. And who knows how long that will take?"

"The board will stand by you."

"I hope so. But if I'm not there, the historical tours will have to be canceled and the program will fall apart." She gazed out the side window. "On top of my problems at work, I have to move in two weeks, and I still haven't found a place to live, so I'll have to stay with Chloe for a while. I'm not looking forward to it."

He reached out and took her hand. "It's going to all work out. You're just having a run of bad luck."

And it was about to get even worse, he thought morosely. Man, he hated adding to her troubles; telling her how he'd deceived her seemed like kicking her when she was down. But he couldn't wait any longer. He'd already waited too long as it was.

She leaned against the headrest and sighed. "In addition to losing my job and my home, my life coach just bailed on me."

Chase's stomach knotted. "Oh, yeah?"

"Yeah. He said I'd conquered my issues and his schedule was overbooked, so congratulations on the progress, nice working with you, and sayonara." She gave him a teasing grin. "Please don't tell me you're going to give me the boot, too."

"Not a chance." *But that's not to say you won't want to give it to me, when you learn the truth.* Man, the guilt was killing him.

He'd given a lot of thought to the best way to break it to her, and he'd formulated a three-step plan:

1. Explain that he offered to take over his brother's

clients to persuade his brother to go into protective services.

2. Mention that his brother is a life coach, and his name is Luke.

3. Hold his breath during the 2.2 seconds it would take for Sammi to connect the dots.

His damage-containment plan was a little more complicated:

1. Tell her that he only meant to help.

2. Explain how things snowballed.

3. Reemphasize that he only wanted to help.

4. Apologize.

5. Apologize again.

6. Repeat steps as necessary.

She drew a deep breath, straightened, and smiled. "I refuse to let all this spoil the weekend. Tell me about our plans."

"When we get to my property, we're going to hike a couple of miles, then pitch a tent."

Chase had gone by his brother's condo to retrieve the tent. In the process, he'd noted a fresh footprint in the dirt, as well as four freshly burned Gitano cigarette butts under the bushes. Johnny Lambino smoked Gitanos; given the rarity of the cigarette, the odds were that he was once again watching Luke's place. Luke wouldn't be returning to his home until Johnny was locked up and the trial was over, so it didn't pose any immediate danger—but it *did* mean that Luke's would-be assassin was in town and looking for him. Chase had called headquarters and reported it, and the condo was now back under surveillance. Hopefully, the bureau would reestablish a tail on Johnny and keep an eye on him until his uncles gave him up for a plea bargain.

"A tent sounds romantic," Sammi said with a grin.

A nerve worked in Chase's jaw. The tent could be something straight out of _Arabian Nights,_ but once Sammi learned the truth, romance would be the last thing on her mind.

Judging from the sexy way she was smiling at him, apparently it was at the forefront now. "But then, who needs a tent?" she said.

Not him, that was for sure. He'd be fine with pulling off the road, dragging her across the console, and making love to her right there on the highway. But he couldn't touch her until he'd told her the truth.

He squeezed her fingers. "Hold that thought."

"I've been holding it all week."

"Me, too." He needed to switch to a less sexually charged topic before he did something he'd regret. He opened the armrest and pulled out a CD case.

"Want to hear some tunes?"

"Sure."

The conversation shifted to music and movies and other things, and before he knew it, Chase was turning off the interstate onto scenic Highway 271. The trees grew denser, the leaves more brightly colored.

"Oh, this is gorgeous!" Sammi murmured.

Chase nodded. "It's the peak of the fall foliage season. Thousands of tourists come up here every year just to drive through and look at the scenery."

"It's beautiful enough to make me completely forget my troubles." Sammi turned to him and smiled. "And that's just what I intend to do. I'm going to relax and enjoy the weekend and not think about anything unpleasant until Monday."

Chase tried to muster a smile, but it probably looked more like he had a case of indigestion. Which wasn't far from the truth; thinking about confessing that he'd been her coach was making his stomach turn like a rototiller.

He slowed to turn onto a dirt road.

"Paradise Valley Pass," Sammi read on the faded street sign. "What a romantic name."

They bounced along for about six miles, then turned left at a boulder onto an even narrower dirt path. A turn at the end of the path and three miles of bumpy trail later, he braked in front of a weathered cabin on the side of the mountain. The terrain rose sharply behind it. "Here it is," he said, killing the engine.

"I didn't know you had a cabin!"

"It's more of a shack. I'm fixing it up little by little, but it's a long ways from being inhabitable."

Sammi eyed the weathered clapboard building, which was no bigger than a large storage shed. "It's got potential."

The woman saw something good in everything. Why did that fact make him feel so damn bad? "Yeah. Potential to be a slightly nicer shack." He opened the car door. The wind was whipping up, and a nip was in the air. "What do you say we get our stuff together and head out? We've got a pretty long hike to our campsite, and I want to get there before dark."

"Sounds good."

They made their way up the path, joking and laughing, which had the odd effect of making Chase feel awful.

The mountains were ablaze with color. Sammi exclaimed at the vivid orange, gold, and scarlet leaves, stopping often to gaze out at the scenery. She scurried up a steep slope ahead of him. "Oh, the view up here is awesome!"

It sure is, Chase thought as he watched her. The sun rode low on the horizon behind her, setting her hair aglow. She was so damned beautiful he could hardly breathe.

She turned and looked at him, then pulled her brow into a worried frown. "Is something wrong?"

"From what I see, everything is perfect." Too perfect. She was everything he'd ever wanted in a woman, and a lot of things he never known to look for.

And there was a very good chance he was about to lose her.

She smiled at him, then moved close and looped her arms around his neck. His arms found their way around her, and the next thing he knew, he was kissing her as if there were no tomorrow, as if he could make time stand still, as if he could kiss her hard enough to prevent the pain he knew he was about to inflict on her.

Her hand moved up his neck. "I'm so happy to be here with you," she murmured against his ear.

You won't be happy much longer. He pulled back, cradled her face in his hands, and brushed a lock of hair off her cheek with his thumb. "Likewise." Drawing a deep breath, he reluctantly stepped back and dropped his hands. "We'd better get moving if we want to make it to the campsite before dark."

"Is it much farther?"

"Up that hill, then about another mile."

Less than thirty minutes later, they reached the clearing. The sun had dipped below the mountains, painting the clouds tangerine and azalea pink. Sammi drew in her breath as she gazed at the sky. "Wow."

That was the word for it, all right—along with *awe-inspiring, soul-stirring,* and *magnificent.*

He felt the same way about Sammi. Swallowing around the lump that seemed permanently lodged in his throat, he threw himself into setting up camp and building a fire.

The sky's colors had melted into dusk by the time they finally sat on a blanket and leaned against a log in front of the crackling fire. Chase pulled out a bottle of wine and opened it. He poured it into two tin cups, then handed her one and lifted the other. "To you."

She smiled back. "To us."

Every word, every smile, every gesture just made this harder. He drained his cup. She took a little sip.

"Drink up," he urged.

Her lips curved in a soft smile. "Are you trying to get me drunk so you can take advantage of me?"

He grinned. "Maybe."

She leaned toward him. "I'll let you in on a secret. You don't have to get me drunk."

Chase kissed her nose, then refilled her glass.

"Have you ever brought anyone else here?" she asked.

"My brother. But trust me, it wasn't the same."

She took another sip. "Speaking of your brother, you've never told me much about him. Where does he live?"

Here it was—the moment of truth. He swallowed hard and began. "In Tulsa, but right now he's in protective custody."

Her eyebrows rose in surprise. "Why?"

"He saw a mob hit. And the nephew of the men he's going to testify against is trying to kill him."

"Oh, that's awful!"

"Yeah. And I feel responsible, because I sent him to pick up a pizza at the restaurant where it happened."

She reached out a consoling hand. "You couldn't have known that was going to happen."

"No, but I should have." He took a sip of wine, but his mouth still felt dry. "Speaking of my brother, there's something I've been meaning to tell you about him."

"Yeah?"

He shifted on the log. "Well, it's about me, too."

"What is it?"

Damn, this was hard. "In order to get him to agree to go into Witness Protection, I offered to help with his consulting business."

"That was nice of you. How are you helping?"

"I'm, uh, working with some of his clients."

She took a sip of wine and smiled at him. "Wow, you're really multitalented."

She didn't suspect a thing. She still thought he was a totally stand-up guy. Well, that was about to change. "What kind of consultant is he?" she asked.

Chase swallowed. "Luke is a life coach."

Her lips parted and her brow furrowed. "A life coach? But you acted like you'd never heard of life coaches when I told you I had one." A beat of silence passed, and then her eyes widened. "His name is Luke?"

"Yeah." Chase steeled himself. It wouldn't take her long to put two and two together.

She sat up straighter. "Luke Jones?"

Here it came. "Yes."

"And . . . you've been working with his clients? Are you saying . . ." She jumped to her feet and shoved his shoulder, nearly knocking him backward over the log. *"You've been coaching me?"*

Chase scrambled to his feet. "I've been meaning to tell you."

"I can't believe this." She turned away, and then turned back. "I told you all my secrets!"

"I'm sorry. I wanted to tell you, but I could never find the right time."

"You coached me twice a week and saw me nearly every weekend, and you *couldn't find the time* to tell me?" She advanced toward him, fury etched in her face. "How long have you been my coach?"

"From your, uh, second call. I had dropped Luke's files, and I thought you were one of his regular clients, and . . ."

He could see the wheels spinning in her head. "So you told me to jog with Joe so you could *spy* on me?"

"I wasn't spying. I was . . ." He ducked as she hit him again. "Curious."

"Curious?" She managed to imbue the word with both incredulity and scalding scorn. "You let me talk *to* you *about* you. And—oh, my God." She put her hand to her head, as if it hurt. "You pretended you didn't know things I'd told you in our coaching sessions, and then you gave me advice about how to handle my relationship with you . . ." She turned her back to him, then whirled back around. Her eyes snapped like a whip. "You let me tell you all about how I felt about you! You *dog!*" She shoved him again.

A loud boom echoed off the mountain. A branch fell off an elm tree ten feet away.

Chase snatched her around the waist and pulled her behind a giant oak.

She struggled against him. "Get your hands off me, you two-faced liar!"

He tightened his grip. "Sammi—that was a gunshot."

"Oh, right." Her brow wrinkled in a scathing fashion. "Nice try, but you're not going to change the subject that easily."

"Stay still."

"I will *not* stay still. If it was a shot, it was probably a hunter."

"At night?"

She jerked away from him. "You *deserve* to be shot." She punched his right shoulder with her right hand. "And hamstrung." She punched his left shoulder with her left hand. She picked up speed, pummeling him with right–left girlie jabs. "And scalped." *Jab.* "And hanged." *Jab.* "And bitten by snakes." *Jab.* "And thrown in a lake of fire." *Jab.*

Another shot zinged by. This one richocheted off a rock above them, breaking off a piece, sending it flying through the air in splinters.

Chase threw her to the ground. She stared up at him, her mouth open.

"Oh, my God," she breathed. "Someone's really shooting at us!"

"Yeah."

"Who would do that?"

"My guess is it's the same guy who tried to shoot my brother."

"Why would he be after us?"

Because he'd been watching Luke's condo when Chase

went to get the tent, and he hadn't known that Luke had a brother. The realization hit with sickening certainty. "He thinks I'm Luke," Chase whispered tersely.

"Why would he think that?" Sammi asked hotly. "Have you been coaching him, too?"

Something rustled in the brush about a hundred yards away. Sammi heard it, too, because she suddenly lay perfectly still, her eyes enormous and scared.

"Stay here," Chase whispered in her ear, slowly easing himself off her. "I'm going to create a diversion, and then we'll run."

The hill sloped sharply behind them. He crept forward, grabbed a tree branch, and hurled it down the slope. Another shot sounded. Footsteps crunched down the hill.

"Come on." Chase yanked Sammi to her feet and ran.

The brush scraped at their legs, but Sammi followed Chase like a trouper, clambering beside him around the mountain, then down a slope into a deep gully. He tried to boost her up a twelve-foot cliff off the other side, but she couldn't get a grip.

"I'll go first," he said. "Grab hold of my belt and follow my foot placement."

He grabbed the edge of a jutting boulder, found a toe-hold in the rocky wall, and pulled himself up. The belt dug into his gut as Sammi grasped it and followed. Another finger pocket, another step. Another, and yet another, pulling Sammi with him as he climbed. He was nearing the top when he heard something clatter to the ground.

"Oh, no," she urgently whispered. "I knocked your cell phone off your belt!"

Hell—there went all hope of calling for backup. Not that there was much hope to start with, because the phone reception out here was spotty at best. It was Luke's cell phone, anyway. He'd left his own charging in the Explorer. "Don't worry about it. Let's just get the hell out of here."

A scrub oak jutted out of the rocky soil, its trunk almost horizontal to the ground, its branches growing straight up. Chase grabbed hold of it and hoisted himself to the top of the ravine, pulling Sammi with him. He helped her to her feet as the footsteps drew closer.

"Come on." He tightened his grip on her hand and started through the woods.

She tripped over a tree root and sprawled to the ground.

He stopped and helped her to her feet. "Can you walk?"

"Yeah."

"Then come on." Tugging her hand, he half pulled, half dragged her up a hill through the forest. He stopped in front of a giant rock.

"Get on your knees," he whispered.

"What?"

"There's an opening to a cave under the rock. Get on your knees and crawl in it."

She looked at him as if she were going to challenge him.

"*Now,* dammit."

She dropped to her knees. With an angry huff, she crawled forward. She was halfway inside when she turned around. For the first time since this whole thing started, he saw fear in her eyes. "Are you coming, too?"

"Yeah. As soon as I cover the entrance."

He grabbed some branches, placed them near the

opening, then crawled in, pulling the branches after him. Inside, the cave was nearly pitch-black.

"Scoot on back," he whispered to Sammi. "There's more space about five feet from the entrance."

"I—"

He put his hand over her mouth. "Shh. He's coming."

Outside the cave, twigs crackled. Branches snapped. Footsteps crunched on the dead leaves. The noise stopped just outside the cave.

"Sonuvabitch," they heard someone mutter.

After what seemed like forever, the footsteps sounded again.

He was walking away.

Thank God. Chase didn't realize he'd been holding his breath until he let it out. "We'll stay here for the night," he whispered. "It's going to be impossible to do anything until daylight."

He looked at Sammi, but it was so dark he could barely make out her outline. "Are you okay?" he whispered.

Was she okay? He had to be kidding.

"Oh, yeah, I'm just great," she whispered heatedly. "Thanks to you and your helpful advice, I've lost my job and my home. I've gotten involved with a lying, sneaky, conniving bastard, I've been shot at, and now I'm spending the night in a freakin' *cave*." Which, at the moment, struck her as the worst offense of all. "Some life coach you turned out to be!"

"I'm sorry."

"Yeah. You darn sure are."

Something rustled in the back of the cave. The hair stood up on the back of her neck.

"Chase." Her voice was raw, her throat tense. "There's something in here."

"Maybe a raccoon, or an opossum. Or a snake."

"A snake?" The thought made her shudder.

"Maybe. More than likely, though, it's just bats."

"Bats?" She reached out and grabbed his arm. "There are *bats* in here?" Panic rose in her throat.

"Shhh. They're more scared of you than you are of them."

A shiver shimmied through her. "That's impossible."

He put his arm around her. "Hey. It'll be okay."

"Oh, right." She slapped away his arm. It was one thing for her to touch him, and quite another for him to touch her. "Like I'm going to believe anything you tell me."

He blew out a long sigh. "Sammi—"

"Don't talk to me. I don't want to hear any more of your lies." Sammi pulled away and hugged her knees. She'd skinned them when she'd tripped on the tree root, and they were probably bleeding inside her jeans, but it was impossible to tell, because the denim was wet from crawling on the damp ground. A rock bit into her back-side, and another one poked her spine.

But her physical misery was nothing compared to the despair churning inside her. Chase had been her *life coach?* What a lying, sneaky bastard! She'd trusted him, both as her coach and lover, and he'd violated that trust on both ends. Humiliation and anger swirled inside her like steam. She'd told him all the intimate details of her life—all of her insecurities, all of her feelings about men, all of her feelings about *him*. He'd deceived her and given her *advice,* damn it—advice about things he'd had no business even knowing about, much less trying to help her with. He'd known she was trying to get over her lack of trust, and he'd given her all the more reason to never trust a man again.

The thing in the back of the cave rustled again. She shivered.

Chase moved closer. "It's probably just a raccoon."

"I hate caves."

"I'm no fan, either. But I hate getting shot even worse."

"I also hate men who lie to me," she whispered hotly, edging way from him. "Especially men I'm supposed to trust."

"Sammi—I never meant to hurt you."

Anger flared like a blowtorch. "I confided all my secrets to my life coach, and it was you all along. The more I think about it, the madder I get."

"I kept meaning to tell you. But I couldn't find a way to tell you that wouldn't end with you furious at me."

"Well, of course I'm furious at you!"

"It started out with the best of intentions."

"Oh, having me go to the park so you could get a look at me was based on a good intention?"

"Well, I was curious—I admit that. But I also thought it might be helpful. And I never meant to actually meet you. I wouldn't have, if your dog hadn't attacked me."

That was true, but it didn't let him off the hook.

"After that first time, I wasn't going to see you again," he continued. "And if you hadn't come to the swap meet, I never would have."

A fresh burst of indignation flared within her. "Oh, so it was my fault?"

"No. It was all mine. I'm not trying to pass the buck here. I'm just explaining how it got started."

"So why didn't you stop it? Why did you keep coaching me?"

"Because I thought I was helping."

Oh, God. How humiliating! Hot tears rolled down her cheeks. "Tell me one thing." A lump formed in her throat. She hated to ask, but she needed to know the answer. "When you made love to me—was that a form of therapy?"

"Hell, no!" Chase blew out a harsh sigh. "Damn it, Sammi! Why are you trying to turn this into something it's not?"

"Well, what, exactly, is it?"

"It's a case of me misjudging the situation." He blew out another hard breath. "Of me liking you and caring for you and wanting you so badly that I wasn't thinking straight." He shifted beside her. "Not that that's any excuse."

"You're damned right it isn't. And now you've screwed up my entire life."

"Sammi—come here." His hand touched her leg in the dark.

She scooted away. "Keep your distance."

"It's cold and getting colder, and we don't have a sleeping bag, and you're not wearing much of a jacket."

It was true. She was wearing only a red fleece hoodie over a long-sleeved T-shirt. She was shivering, but she wasn't sure if it was because of the chilly temperature or the icy ball inside of her that now sat where her heart had been.

She heard the rustle of fabric in the dark, then felt

something warm wrap around her. He'd pulled off his jacket and put it over her.

"You're going to freeze," she said.

"It's no more than I deserve."

"That's true." Still, she yanked off the jacket and thrust it at him. "Put your damn jacket back on."

"No. You keep it. But we should probably huddle together for warmth."

"Oh, right. Like that's gonna happen."

Outside the cave, a twig snapped.

She felt him tense beside her. "Shh," he whispered.

She went rigid. He crept to the entrance, quiet as a cat, and crouched behind the branches, ready to spring if the shooter entered. Long minutes ticked by. After what seemed like forever, he crept back toward her.

"Was it him?" she whispered.

"I'm not sure." His voice was little more than breath in her ear. "But the entrance is hidden, so if we're completely silent, we'll be okay."

He put his arm around her. She stiffened. Damn it, she didn't want to need him. She didn't want to find his arm reassuring, didn't want to crave his warmth, didn't want to feel his heart beat through his shirt when her own heart was breaking.

"Try to go to sleep," he whispered against her hair. He picked up his jacket and arranged it over her like a blanket.

Fat chance of that. All the same, she didn't pull away. She leaned against him and listened to his breathing, her own breath synchronizing with his.

She must have dozed off, because when she opened

her eyes, light filtered through the leaves in the cave opening.

Chase disentangled his arm from around her. "I'm going after him," he whispered. "Stay here and wait for me."

"But—"

"I can't go if you insist on accompanying me." His gaze was unwavering, his tone final. "That could mean we're stuck here for days."

She blew out a frustrated sigh. "Okay."

"I'll be back. Just wait here." He crept to the entrance and pulled aside a branch. He waited a moment, then pulled aside the others and eased himself out. He replaced the branches in front of the cave, and then he was gone.

Long moments ticked by. She ran her hands up and down her arms, trying to warm herself, but the absence of Chase's body heat made it seem impossible. She shivered against the cold rock, shifting her bottom and stretching out her legs, unable to find a comfortable position. She was chilled and cramped, and she needed to go to the bathroom. She glanced at her wristwatch: 6:00.

By the time her watch read 7:00, it seemed like days had passed and her bladder was ready to explode. She scrambled to her feet and shuffled, hunched over, to the back of the cave to relieve herself. As she edged her way back toward the light, black clusters of something that looked like bananas caught her eye. She twisted her head and squinted at them, then stepped closer. In the dim light, they looked like giant black cocoons, except . . . *Oh, dear God—they have big ears and monkey faces!* She let out a yelp, then put her hands over her mouth to squelch it.

Bats. Chase hadn't been kidding. The cave was infested with bats!

She'd rather take her chances with the gunman. Her heart pounding, she staggered, Quasimodo-style, toward the opening, then barreled through the branches. Twigs caught in her hair, scraped her face, and stung her hands, but she pushed through them and ran several yards away from the cave. She stopped and looked around, squinting in the sunlight. The leaves wore a white glaze of frost, and her breath looked like chimney puffs. Now what? She didn't know where Chase or the gunman had gone, didn't know which direction to go, and had no idea where the hell she was.

Her mind raced along the precipice of panic. A sudden thought halted it: *the phone*. She would try to retrace their steps and find Chase's dropped phone.

She usually had a really good sense of direction, but she'd been terrified last night, so her memory of their trek wasn't all that sharp. She seemed to recall that they'd approached the cave from the left, so she set out in that direction. The brown gnarl of a tree root nearly tripped her. Was this the one she'd stumbled over? Yes, she was pretty sure it was; the leaves were scrunched to one side, and the dirt looked all scuffed up. The ravine they'd climbed should be right ahead.

It was. She breathed a sigh of relief, then looked down. Oh, dear; it was a long way down—higher than a second-story window. She walked along the side of it, looking for an easier place to climb down. At length, she found a spot that had a ledge jutting out, with a sapling oak growing on the ledge. Taking a deep breath, she eased herself off the side of the ravine, then dropped four feet to the ledge.

So far, so good. She'd hang on to the oak and drop to the bottom. She grabbed the small tree, turned around, and eased herself off the ledge, only to have the roots pull out under her weight.

A sickening sensation of falling later, she opened her eyes. Thank God—a bush at the bottom had broken her fall. She pulled herself out of the branches, dusted herself off, and walked along the bottom of the ravine, back toward the spot they'd climbed the night before.

Where, exactly, was it? Leaves crunched under her sneakers as she roamed the ravine bottom, her heart sinking. The leaves were at least a foot thick. Even if she found the exact spot where the phone had fallen, chances were it was covered by leaves.

A branch snapped above her. Her heart stopped. Was it the gunman? A bear? A coyote? A snake?

No, the snakes would be more likely to be down here. Her pulse fluttered madly in her chest.

Stay calm, she ordered herself. *Stay calm, and look for the phone. Just look for something shiny.*

She slowly strode the length of the gulley, doing just that. She saw the glint of something resting against a tiny redbud tree. She bent down, hope rising in her chest like the sun at dawn.

A broken beer bottle. She sat back on her heels, disappointment bitter in her mouth. This was useless. The ravine was huge, the leaves were thick, and the chances of finding the phone were slim to none.

Tears sprang to her eyes. She wiped them away and resolutely rose to her feet. She had to keep going. A branch crackled under her heel, and then she heard something that sounded like a soft, single beep. Her pulse quickened. She stood still and listened, wondering if she'd imagined it.

There it was again! It sounded like the low-on-power warning of a cell phone. She took a few steps toward the sound, then waited. It sounded once more. She moved in, scanning the leaves, then knelt down when something gleamed in the sunlight.

A silver phone lay nestled in the brown leaves like an egg in a nest.

"Thank God!" she breathed, snatching it up and opening it.

The plate over the numbers was dented, the face was covered in grit, and the message window read "Low battery." Her stomach knotted. She tried to punch in 911. The button stuck on nine. The display window showed nothing but low battery.

No signal—just the warning beep that the battery was about to go out. She turned off the phone, her heart sinking. She'd climb out of the gully and try again.

It took her fifteen minutes to find a place where she could scramble out, and then another fifteen minutes to do so. When she turned on the phone, the display window was blank. Her heart dropped. The phone still beeped a low-battery warning. Saying a prayer, she punched in 911 again. The number didn't show on the display window, but the phone was ringing. "Come on," she muttered after the second ring. "Pick up!"

"Hello?" said what sounded like woman's voice.

"This is an emergency," Sammi whispered.

"What kind of emergency?"

"Someone is shooting at us."

"Really?" The voice grew oddly excited. "Where are you?"

"Near Talihina, off Highway 271. Can you get my location from my cell signal?"

"Oh, no. You'll have to give me directions. Let me get a pencil."

A long moment of battery-burning silence later, the voice was back. "Okay. Highway 271. Then what?"

She searched her memory for the landmarks they'd passed. "Turn left onto a dirt road called Paradise Valley Pass. Go down the road until you see a big boulder. Turn left, go until the road ends, then right to the cabin at the end."

The phone beeped another warning.

"Did you get that?"

"I-I think so." The wavering in the voice did nothing to inspire confidence.

"Hurry. Our lives are in . . ." The phone went dead. ". . . danger," she whispered to the silence.

Sammi closed the phone, drew a jagged breath, and prayed she'd given the right directions. She needed to believe she had, needed to believe that help was on the way.

What should she do in the interim? She couldn't go sit in a cave full of bats. Besides, she hated the idea of just sitting around and waiting to be rescued.

Especially by Chase. How could she trust him to even come back? He'd lied to her, misrepresented himself, and used false means to extract the most personal kinds of information, all in the name of helping her. Her fingers curled together in her palms, and her breath huffed out in angry frost clouds. No, she was through following

Chase's advice. From now on, she'd make her own decisions. She'd find her way back to the cabin, locate a hiding place, and wait for help to arrive.

A gunshot cracked the silence. It sounded a long distance away, but fear, thick and nauseating, singed her throat. *Please, dear God, let Chase be okay. Please, please, please be with him and protect him.*

Okay. She took it back about not trusting Chase to come back for her. He would. He'd risk his own life to save hers, but not because he loved her. He'd do it for anybody, because that was his job. He'd do it because that was the kind of man he was and that was what he believed in. She could trust him with her life.

Just not, apparently, with her heart.

~

It took more than two and a half hours to make the one-hour trek back to the cabin—partially because she stopped every time she heard branches break, partially because she was trying to be quiet, and partially because of a sudden downpour. The rain hadn't lasted long, but she'd lost her footing three times on the slippery leaves and fallen flat on her backside. Her hair was plastered to her head, her jeans were soaked all the way through, and she was uncontrollably shivering. She'd picked up her backpack at the campsite, though, so she had a towel and dry clothes to change into if she ever made it to the cabin.

She blew out a relieved breath when she saw the cabin roofline. What now? Did she dare go in, or should she just wait here?

A lightning bolt danced across the sky, followed by a deafening clap of thunder. Ooh-kay. Decision made.

Drawing a deep breath, she started for the clearing. As she walked past an enormous oak, an arm grabbed her around the neck.

Panic flooded her veins. The arm yanked her backward, snatching her breath away. She turned her head enough to see a swarthy face inside a black parka hood, and then her air supply was choked off. She lost her footing and fell. Her accoster hauled her to her feet, nearly breaking her neck in the process.

She tried to scream, but her efforts were immediately stifled by more pressure on her windpipe. "Make a sound and I'll kill you," the man grunted. "Understand?"

Her heart pounded like a jackhammer. He loosened the pressure on her neck, and she nodded.

"That's more like it. Now turn around."

He loosened his grip around her neck and yanked her around by the arm. He was a bulky man in his midthirties, with a big honker of a nose, shrubbery-like eyebrows, and a mean little mouth. His breath could have killed a snake at fifty paces. In his hand, he held an enormous gun.

Aiming it at her, he rummaged in her pockets. He pulled out the broken cell phone.

"Who'd you call?"

If he thought the law was on the way, maybe he'd leave her alone and run. "The-the FBI," she said. "And the sheriff and the police and the—the . . ." she thought, fast. They were out in the middle of nowhere. What kind of law enforcement would likely be nearby? ". . . and the Fish and Wildlife Commission."

"Hell." He pursed his lips and frowned. "Those Fish

and Wildlife guys are all over the place. They probably heard the gunshot."

"That—that's right." Her teeth chattered with cold and fear. *Stay calm,* she told herself. *Keep your head in the game.* "Th-they s-said they'll be here any moment. So you-you better go."

"No way. Call Luke."

"What?"

"Your boyfriend. Call Jones."

"I-I can't. The phone's dead."

"I don't mean on the phone. I mean call out his name. I know he's out here."

"No."

The man shoved the gun in her side. "Do it!"

He had a wild look in his eye that made her think she'd better comply. "Chase!" she yelled weakly.

He poked her harder with the gun. "What the hell are you doing? I told you to call his name."

"I am. He-he's Chase. Luke is his brother."

"What?" The man's eyebrows inched upward like caterpillars.

"L-Luke isn't here." She was shivering so hard it was difficult to speak. "I came with Chase, but he's n-not here, either, because he w-w-went for help." She wanted this cretin to turn and run. "He'll be back any moment. With the—the . . ." She grasped at the name that had seemed to worry him the most. ". . . the Fish and Wildlife people."

"Why's his car still here?"

"He-he was taking a shortcut."

He pulled those wild eyebrows together. "You're lying. Call his name again, or I'll kill you."

～

The fact that Johnny Lambino had his gun trained on Sammi made Chase's blood run cold. He'd been in lots of life-or-death situations, but he'd never felt this sense of urgency, this gut-twisting sense of terror. If Lambino hurt Sammi . . .

No. He couldn't let his head go there. He needed to focus on getting in position behind Lambino so he could take him out.

Chase ducked behind a boulder. "Drop the gun and I'll come out," he called.

Lambino swiveled around, pulling Sammi with him, and scanned the ledge above him, looking for Chase. "You think I'm stupid? I'm not dropping anything."

The moment he showed himself, Lambino would shoot, and then he'd no doubt kill Sammi, as well, in order to not leave any witnesses. "Let the lady go, and I'll come out."

"No way." Lambino poked the gun at Sammi and eyed her with a nasty leer. "I got a way to make your boyfriend come out of hiding, little lady. Take off your clothes."

Chase bit the inside of his lip, trying to bite back the red tide of rage surging inside him.

"Do it!" Lambino ordered.

Sammi toyed with the zipper of her hoodie. "The, uh, zipper's stuck."

Good, Chase thought grimly, as he crept through the trees. She still had her wits about her.

"Yeah, right." Lambino reached over and roughly yanked it down, pushing her to the ground in the same movement.

It was all Chase could do not to charge at the man. But he couldn't; not yet. Lambino had his gun trained on

Sammi. Chase crept through the trees, trying to get into position.

"Listen. I hear a car," Sammi said.

"Yeah, right," Lambino retorted.

Sure enough, Chase heard the rumble of a car engine. Lambino heard it, too, because he straightened and looked around. Hope rose in Chase's chest as he crept closer to Lambino. He'd thought Sammi was bluffing about calling the police—cell-phone coverage was practically nonexistent out here—but maybe she'd actually done it.

Lambino grew wild-eyed. "Get up." He roughly grabbed Sammi's arm and jerked her to her feet. "Let's go."

Sammi staged a deliberate stumble as a black Chevy Impala rattled up the road and stopped in front of the cabin. A humpty-dumpty of a man with a receding red hairline, high-waisted pants, and a tucked-in yellow polo shirt lumbered out of the vehicle. He opened the back door of the car, lifted out something boxy and large, and put a strap around his neck.

An accordion. Good God in heaven—this had to be Horace. What the *hell* was he doing *here?*

"Help!" Sammi called.

Horace wheeled around. His mouth fell open when he spotted Sammi.

"Help!" Sammi called again. "This man has a gun!"

Horace squared his shoulders, pressed his lips together in resolve, and strode toward them. "Unhand that woman!"

Lambino stared, his eyes as large as pine knotholes. "Who the hell are you?"

Chase took advantage of the diversion to creep forward on the ledge, five feet above Lambino and Sammi.

"I'm your worst nightmare." Horace squeezed the accordion. The "Charge" melody echoed surreally through the forest. "Drop that gun, or I'll drop it for you."

Lambino's eyebrows shot skyward. "What are you—nuts?"

"Oh, you want to play it that way, do you?" Horace's accordion squeaked out a few ominous chords of "Taps."

Chase heard the click of Lambino's gun cocking. It was now or never.

Throwing his full weight forward, he pounced onto Lambino. A gunshot exploded as Lambino hit the ground. The gun flew through the air.

It took less than five seconds for Chase to twist the man's hands behind his back. Lambino bucked beneath him. Chase put a knee in his kidney.

"Oomph!"

Chase looked at Sammi. "You okay?"

"Yeah."

He glanced over at Horace. The man was lying on the ground like a beached whale, the accordion on his chest. Chase's heart nose-dived.

"Sammi—run to my car and look under the front seat. I have a pair of handcuffs, a spare cell phone, and a first-aid kit. Toss me the cuffs, then call 911. Tell them we need the sheriff and an ambulance, stat."

Chapter Twenty-one

Twenty minutes later, three sheriff vehicles poured up the dirt road, sirens shrieking, an ambulance right behind. The deputies piled out and headed toward Lambino, who lay sprawled face-first on the ground, his hands cuffed behind his back.

Sammi sat on the ground beside Horace, holding a piece of gauze from Chase's first-aid kit over a wound in his hip. "Over here!" She waved as a blue-uniformed medic jumped out of the ambulance.

He raced toward them.

"What happened?" the medic asked as the ambulance driver joined them.

"He was shot," Sammi said. "He passed out for a moment, and he's bleeding."

"My accordion saved my life," Horace volunteered.

The ambulance driver joined the paramedic, and the two men quickly examined him. "Looks like the bullet just nicked you," the medic with graying temples told Horace, "but we need to take you in and get you checked out. You might have injured yourself when you fainted."

"I didn't faint," Horace protested. "I passed out from the pain."

Horace had regained consciousness almost immediately, then talked nonstop in a falsetto voice as they'd waited for the authorities. No wonder she'd mistaken him for a woman on the phone, Sammi thought; Horace's voice was higher than hers. Sammi learned that Horace, too, was a life-coaching client, who thought Chase was Luke.

"I asked Coach to set up an exercise to make me brave," Horace had told Sammi as she held the gauze over his wound. "When you called, I recognized the phone number, so I thought that's what was going on."

The phone's numbers had stuck, Sammi recalled. Maybe nine was Luke's programmed number for Horace—or perhaps she'd accidentally hit redial. Either way, it was a good thing the call had gone through.

"Horace saved the day," she told the medics now, hoping to boost Horace's spirits. "He was very brave. If it weren't for him, we'd probably be dead."

Horace smiled proudly, showing small, widely spaced teeth. "My accordion saved all of us. I think it was the C-note."

The paramedics looked at each other. "That's a first," the older one muttered.

"He's a real hero," Sammi said.

"What were you doing with an accordion out here?" the younger paramedic asked.

"I was pretending to be a superhero. Accordion Man. He wades into danger and stares death in the teeth, armed only with the power of the squeeze box."

"Make a note that this guy needs a psych evaluation,"

the older paramedic told the younger one as they headed to the ambulance to retrieve the gurney.

"Do I get to ride in the ambulance?" Horace asked eagerly.

"Yep. That's the idea."

"Oh, wow! This is so exciting!" His smile gave way to a worried frown. "But—but what about my car?"

"I'll drive it behind the ambulance and meet you at the hospital," Sammi offered.

"Really? Oh, golly—that would be great!" He reached in his pocket and handed her a keychain with a Playboy bunny on the key ring.

The medic retuned with the gurney. The two men attempted to hoist Horace onto it and failed. "Lift on the count of three," one said to the other. They counted off and tried again.

"No use," said the taller one, putting a hand to the small of his back.

"I'll give you a hand." Chase strode over and helped load Horace on the gurney. He turned toward Sammi as the medics wheeled Horace to the ambulance. Her stomach tensed as he worriedly searched her face.

"Are you okay?"

She stiffly nodded. "You?"

"Fine." He raked his hand through his hair and gazed at her, his eyes dark and troubled, their brown depths speaking a million words. "Sammi, I'm so sorry you had to go through that."

Something that felt dangerously like tenderness unfurled inside her. She fought to batten it down.

No. She no longer had any feelings for him. She refused to allow herself to. He'd lied to her—or at least grossly misrepresented the truth. While she'd been baring her heart and soul, he'd been thinking of her as . . . what? A pitiful wreck? A challenge? A project?

"I'm sorry about everything," he said.

You should be. Hurt and betrayal balled up in her throat. She didn't trust herself to speak.

He put his hands on her arms. His touch was both unbearably sweet and unendurably painful. "We'll talk on the way home. It'll take me a little while to finish up here, but—"

"Take your time." Sammi pulled away. "I'm driving Horace's car to the hospital behind the ambulance. After he's treated, I'll catch a ride home with him."

Chase started to protest, then blew out a hard breath and nodded. "That'll be good for Horace." His mouth curved in a wry grin. "You seem to make a habit of following ambulances."

She would have grinned if her heart hadn't been breaking. "Horace thinks you're a secret agent as well as a life coach. I covered for you. I told him you go by two names—Chase and Luke—to keep the two compartments of your life separate."

He nodded. "Thanks."

"I didn't do it for you. I did it for Horace. Now is not the time for him to learn that his life coach is a fake."

Chase winced. "Thanks." His Adam's apple worked as he swallowed. "You and I can talk once we get back to Tulsa." He pulled her to him and gave her a quick kiss on the forehead.

Emotion knotted in her throat. The kiss would have been comforting if he weren't the reason she needed to be comforted.

She pulled away. "You and I have nothing further to talk about."

"Sammi—"

The ambulance driver slammed the door. "Ready to go, miss?"

Sammi nodded, then turned back toward him. "Good-bye, Chase." Her eyes were somber, her tone final. And with that, she turned and headed for Horace's car.

Chapter Twenty-two

Arlene lifted a lime-green-and-turquoise shift out of one of Justine's trunks. It was 9:00 on Saturday morning, and Arlene didn't usually work on Saturdays, but she'd hated the idea of spending the day at home alone.

She had a bad feeling about firing Sammi. It had been a rash decision, and she was afraid it was going to backfire. It probably had been unwise, but something inside Arlene had snapped. She was sick to death of sharing Chandler with another woman. All those years, she'd played second fiddle to Justine, and now she was being forced to play second fiddle to Sammi.

Arlene picked up her notebook, wrote down the description and designer of the dress, then hung the garment on a wooden hanger and placed it on the portable dress rack. She'd just never had the right credentials, she thought bitterly. She didn't have a blueblood birth certificate, she'd never had a marriage license, and she'd never had a college diploma. She'd never had anything but a burning, passionate love for Chandler. And even that was slipping away. Ever since she'd found that nightgown in Justine's trunk, thinking about him made her sick inside.

She'd gone to Chandler's bedroom this morning, hoping to reclaim the tenderness that had driven her all these years. She'd lifted the velvet rope to his austere bedroom and let herself inside. As always, she'd breathed in deeply, hoping for some trace of a scent that reminded her of the man she'd loved.

Nothing. Just the faint smell of lemon oil radiating from the furniture. She'd crossed to the bed, taken off her shoes, and lifted the covers. Her fingers had frozen on the red wool bedspread.

Had Chandler and Justine made love in here, or in Justine's fancy floral bedroom? The fact was, they'd probably made love in both places. And knowing Chandler's predilection for variety, probably in every other room of the mansion, as well. The thought wrapped around her lungs and squeezed the breath out of her.

How often had Chandler and Justine done it? Had Chandler ever made love to both women on the same day?

Her ribs had felt as if they were biting into her skin. She'd flipped the covers up as if they were hot pancakes, then smoothed the bedspread and stepped back into her shoes. She refused to lie in a bed where another woman had slept with Chandler.

She hadn't found any comfort in her own bed last night, either. She used to take solace in the fact that she'd once shared the mattress with Chandler, but now the fact made her toss and turn. As she'd driven to the museum this morning, it occurred to her that it might be time she got a new bed.

She pulled a white cashmere coat out of Justine's trunk and shook it out. It was the color of cream and soft as a kitten, and it looked like it had never been worn. What a waste. What a terrible, terrible waste. Of course, the coat was completely impractical. One brush against anything dusty or dirty, and it would be ruined. Arlene had always worn black winter coats because they didn't show dirt.

Arlene chronicled the coat on her inventory list, carefully hung it on a heavy wooden hanger, then turned back to the trunk. There, on a black satin shawl, lay a white leather diary. A tiny key dangling from a yellowed ribbon was attached to the spine.

Arlene shook her head. Wasn't that just like Justine, to keep the key attached. Why did she even bother to lock it if the key were accessible to anyone who came along?

But then, Justine had never been known for her smarts. Chandler had once complained about his wife's ignorance of the business world. "I can never talk to her like I can talk to you," he'd told her. Arlene had reveled in her role as his business confidante. She'd encouraged him to pour out all of his problems and plans, to give her all the inside scoop on his associates and competitors, to tell her all his thoughts and feelings.

Sometimes, though, Arlene secretly wished that Chandler would show just a tiny bit of interest in her life. Just once in a while, it would be nice if he'd ask about her hopes and dreams.

But he never did. Maybe because he knew that they were all pinned on him. Or maybe, Arlene thought with a pang, he just hadn't cared. He'd seemed to take it as his due that he was the focus of her entire life without any thought of reciprocation.

She turned the diary in her hand, strangely reluctant to open it. She didn't know why; it was probably full of a lot of silly rubbish about teas and clothes and whatever other frivolous concerns occupied Justine's days. Arlene lifted the key and tried to insert it in the tiny lock, but for some reason, her hand shook, and she missed the keyhole. A feeling of dread filled her chest.

The murmur of voices reverberated off the marble floor on the first floor. The weekend tour guides had arrived; she was no longer alone in the museum.

A sense of relief flushed through her, as if she'd gotten a temporary reprieve. She'd read the diary later, she decided—at home, where she wouldn't be disturbed.

~

At 4:00 that afternoon, Arlene carried a cup of tea and the diary out to the wicker table on her screened-in porch. A cool autumn breeze carried the musty scent of falling leaves. Her garden was even brighter this time of year than when it was in full flower; the leaves of the maple glowed bright orange, the red-oak leaves flamed scarlet, and a sweetgum in the corner blazed sunshine yellow. She often came out to her porch to pay her bills and do mending, because the lovely setting made unpleasant tasks more palatable.

This task threatened to be unpleasant, indeed. Drawing a deep breath, she picked up the little key and fit it into the tiny lock. It clicked open. She pulled back the leather strap and parted the cover. Justine's round, girlish lettering filled the pages.

September 29, 1965
Dear diary,

    I don't know how much more humiliation I can take. I went to the Art Appreciation Club's luncheon today. While I was in a stall in the powder room, I heard two women (I think they were Laura Meyers and Susan Statton) come in and start talking. One of them—I think it was Laura—said she and her husband had seen Chandler out with that opera singer last night. "Poor Justine!" the other one said. "Do you think she has any idea?"

    Oh, I wanted to die! If I could have escaped through the sewer, I would have jumped in the toilet. It's bad enough that Chandler carries on with his secretary. At least he has the decency to keep that low-key, although I can't imagine that he's really fooling anyone. But must he flaunt his infidelity with other women, as well? I can't take it anymore. I won't take it anymore.

September 30th

    I did it! I left Chandler. Packed four suitcases and caught a flight to Chicago, with instructions to the staff to pack up the rest of my things and forward them.

    Apparently he was in quite the tizzy when he came home from Houston and found me gone. Wish I could have been a fly on the wall and seen that! He called and demanded I stop this foolishness and come home. I told him to go to hell.

October 1st

He showed up at the hotel at four in the morning, carrying flowers and candy and champagne, with the most remorseful long face you've ever seen. Broke my heart, it really did. He said he couldn't live without me, and he cried. Tears rolled down his cheeks. Well, I couldn't stand it. I took him in my arms.

He sobbed and begged me for another chance. Begged me to try for another child with him.

I told him I would no longer stand for being made a fool. He has to stop with the other women. He said he already has, that he loves me and me alone. He begged me to take him back and go on a second honeymoon to Europe.

Of course I said yes. I love him. I always have, and always will. He's never cried before. This time I think he means it. I pray he means it.

Arlene let the diary fall to the table. With a sob, she buried her face in her hands.

∽

At 5:00 sharp, Walter walked up to Arlene's door, shifted the bouquet of roses to his left hand, and rang the doorbell. He smoothed his blue bowling shirt and straightened the collar, hoping Arlene wouldn't think it was too hokey. He'd gone out and bought it, then taken it to the cleaners to be starched and pressed. He couldn't recall ever doing that before. But then, he hadn't courted a woman in forty-some–odd years.

He rang the bell again. No answer. He waited a long

interval, then rang again. Still no response. That was odd. Arlene's car was in the driveway.

He knocked, and then waited. He hoped she wasn't angry at him for the things he'd said yesterday morning. Or . . . anxiety crawled through his chest. Oh, dear, he thought with a frown—he hoped nothing had happened to Arlene, the way it had happened to Helen. When she'd had her stroke, he'd found her on the floor in the living room, unconscious, the television remote near her hand, the television blaring out an episode of *Maury*.

Arlene had already had one heart attack. What if she'd had another?

His hands tightened on the bouquet. Maybe she was in the backyard. He strode around to the side and let himself in the wooden gate. She had a lovely backyard; she liked to garden, just like Helen, and just like Helen, she had a sweetgum.

He looked around and saw her, sitting at a table in the screened-in porch. She had her head on her hands, and a little book beside her. It looked like she was crying.

He rapped on the door. "Arlene?"

She looked up and wiped her eyes. At least she wasn't unconscious. But, oh, dear—she looked like she'd gotten some bad news. The screen door squeaked as he pushed it open.

"Arlene—what's the matter?"

"I-I found Justine's diary." She shoved the little book toward him.

Who the hell was Justine?

"She—she left him," Arlene continued before Walter could ask. A sob rose in her throat. "She left Chandler! He said he could never leave her, that it would kill her if he walked out—but *she* left *him*. Apparently more than once! And each time, he chased after her, and begged and *cried* to get her back. He *cried!*"

She looked up, her face flushed. "The whole time he was telling me she would never grant him a divorce, that he couldn't abandon her, that she was emotionally fragile because their only child had died . . . the whole time, he was lying!"

So Chandler Phelps had been her gentleman friend. Walter had suspected as much, but Arlene had never said, and he'd never asked.

She rose from the chair, knocking it over, sending it clattering to the brick floor. Walter picked it up.

Arlene stared out at her garden, her arms wrapped around her waist. "That's not all, either. He was cheating on both of us."

Walter's brow furrowed. "What?"

"He was seeing other women. Besides Justine and me, I mean." Fresh tears coursed down her face. "There were always rumors, but I just wouldn't let myself believe them. Just like I wouldn't let myself believe that he and Justine ever . . ." Her voice broke off in a sob.

Walter started toward her, then stopped. He wanted to comfort her, but he didn't know what to say or what to do. He stood beside her and waited. One thing he'd learned from Helen was that sometimes a woman just needed to be heard.

She buried her face in her hands, then wiped at her cheeks and sniffed. "I turned a blind eye," she finally said. "I didn't want to see it. I've lived my entire life in denial." She stared out at the garden, twisting her fingers together. "I always thought I was the only one who loved Chandler, but Justine did, too. And Chandler loved her back! He didn't leave her because he didn't *want* to leave her."

Her head drooped forward. "I tried to take another woman's husband." She drew in a ragged breath. "I thought loving him made it right."

"You made a mistake."

"Worse than a mistake! When I think about the things I must have put that woman through . . ." She held her hand to her mouth. Her fingers shook. "It's just unforgivable."

"Nothing's unforgivable, Arlene."

She lifted her tear-streaked face. "I made that poor woman's life miserable."

"Justine made her own life miserable." Walter stepped closer. "I'm not saying what you did was right, but if it hadn't been you, it would have been someone else. Chandler was what he was. Justine chose to stay with him, knowing he was unfaithful."

"I hurt her."

"You were hurt, too."

"Yes. And now I have to face the fact that my entire life was a waste."

"It wasn't, Arlene. You had a successful career."

Her face twisted with bitterness. "And what good did that do anyone?"

He took a step toward her. "It did lots of good—good you can't even see. You helped make Phelps Oil a success. And because it succeeded, hundreds, maybe even thousands, of people were able to earn a livelihood and support their families. That's important—really important."

She looked up at him. "Do you think so?"

"Yes, I do. I think you've done more good than you'll ever know." And maybe he had, too, in spite of himself.

He and Helen had created a wonderful daughter, for starters. And his rental properties had provided homes, and his work at the plant had helped provide electricity. Maybe his life had counted for something, too.

"I was such an idiot." She wrapped her arms around herself and sank down in her chair, rocking back and forth, even though it wasn't a rocker. "I was a total cliché—a little country girl, all starry-eyed and full of big dreams, dazzled by the dashing older man. I thought life was a Doris Day movie."

"He took advantage of you."

"No. I knew right from wrong." She wiped her nose with a tissue. "I guess I got what I deserved."

"You deserved much, much more than Chandler Phelps."

"Oh, no," Arlene said quickly. "Chandler was way out of my league."

Anger flashed through him. "In what way? Was he better at putting someone else first? Did he have more of an ability to love? Did he dedicate his life to making someone else happy?"

She tilted her head and looked at him.

"You did all those things for him. So it seems to me that *you* were way out of *his* league." He hesitated, then decided to plunge ahead. "Just like Helen was out of mine. She treated me like I was the center of the universe, and I just assumed that's what I was supposed to be."

Arlene looked at him. "She was happy with you. I'm sure of it. I'm sure she knew she was loved."

"I didn't always show it. I wanted everything my way, on my terms. I could be pretty demanding, and sometimes I was short with her." He blew out a sigh. "She's probably up in heaven regretting that she didn't stand up to me more."

"No. I think you're the one with all the regrets."

The cicadas began an evening song. It was funny; before he'd met Arlene, he'd thought that his life was over, that his good years were used up, that he'd blindly blown the gifts of love that God had given him. He thought he had no reason to live. But Arlene felt that way, too—and even though she'd made some awfully poor choices, he could see beyond them, could see the love-hungry soul beneath. He could easily forgive her.

Forgiving himself was another matter.

He looked at her profile. Even from the side, he could see the dark circles of sadness under her eyes. "What I'm coming to realize, Arlene, is that we've all done and didn't do things we regret. The key is to learn from our mistakes and get on the right path."

She shook her head. "It's too late."

He gazed out at the leaves, gold and red and orange, blazing against the setting sun. The clouds were orange and pink and purple—heartbreakingly beautiful, as if God had saved the best part of the day for last.

"Who says?" he found himself asking.

She turned toward him and fixed him with her gray gaze. "What?"

"Well, we can't change the roads we've taken, but we can choose the road ahead."

Arlene gave him a get-real look. "I'm sixty-eight years old—two years away from seventy. There's not that much road left ahead."

"Who are you to say? You might have another thirty years."

"Old-age years," she said bitterly. "Winter-of-life years."

"Nah. You've still got a good long stretch of autumn left."

She gave a slight smile.

He waved his hand at the garden. "Look how beautiful autumn can be. And heck—winter can be fun. It's a time to snuggle by the fire, drink hot cocoa, and read some good books. It's a great time for good conversations and meals and companionship. And it's a terrific time to travel."

She gazed at him. Behind the tears, he thought he saw a hint of hope.

"There's still life ahead of us, Arlene." He swallowed hard. "And I think we should make the most of it."

She looked at him. "What—what are you saying?"

What the hell *was* he saying? The words bubbled up, and he just let them come out. "That maybe you and I-that we . . . that, well, maybe we could travel down the road a bit together. And see how it goes."

Her eyes rounded. Her lips parted.

"Look—I know you're all rattled and raw, and probably the last thing you want to do right now is think about getting involved. And to tell you the truth, the last thing I thought I wanted was to hook up with another woman. But maybe . . . when you're ready . . ." He grinned and lifted his shoulders. "Well, here I am. And I think you're awfully special." He cleared his throat, suddenly awkward. "I imagine you don't feel much like going out tonight." He started to rise from his chair. "I should probably go and leave you alone."

"No." She reached out for his hand. Her fingers were soft and pliant. "No. I've spent way too much time alone."

Chapter Twenty-three

Good-bye—that was all Sammi had said. Not "See you later" or "We'll talk soon." Just good-bye, cold and final.

The word drummed relentlessly in Chase's mind over the next week, drowning out everything else. When the older Lambinos were convicted and turned in their nephew, Chase couldn't really enjoy the victory. Even tonight, as he sat with his brother and Paul at the Wild Horse Saloon to celebrate Luke's release from Witness Protection, he didn't feel any joy. It was as if his capacity for happiness had been rolled in a thick, wet carpet labeled "good-bye."

Luke raised his mug of beer. He had a deep tan and sun-lightened hair, the result of spending the last six weeks fishing and hiking in the wilds of Montana. "Here's to having my life back," Luke said.

Chase raised his glass, as well. "And here's to no more life coaching."

Luke took a swig, then set down his mug. "I've gotta say, you carried the ball a whole hell of a lot better than I thought you would."

"Your confidence is inspiring."

"I mean it. I've talked to all the clients you handled in my absence, and you were A-team all the way. I can't believe Horace has finally moved out on his own."

Chase was having a hard time believing it himself. "Saving the day with his accordion gave him the shot of courage he needed to face down Mommy Dearest." Chase took a large swallow of beer.

"That, and Sammi," Luke said. "Horace said she helped him move in and get settled."

The mention of her name made Chase's heart tighten.

"I really like the sound of this girl," Luke said. "When am I going to get to meet her?"

"I don't know. She won't talk to me." Chase had repeatedly phoned her, but she refused to take his calls.

"Well, go over and see her," Paul said.

"I did. She wouldn't open the door."

"Can't say that I blame her." Luke took another sip of brew. "Coaching her and dating her at the same time was a really bad call."

Chase stared into his beer. "Don't I know it."

"Your only chance of patching things up is let her know how you feel," Luke said.

"Kind of hard to do when she won't talk to me."

"So send her an e-mail."

"She won't read it," Paul volunteered. "She told my wife she deletes everything from Chase without opening it."

"So try snail mail. Or a telegram."

"Yeah. Right," Chase said glumly. "Do they even have telegrams anymore?"

"Look, here's the bottom line: if you care about this

woman, you'll find a way to reach her. And if she cares about you, she'll find it in her heart to forgive you."

"Kind of hard to reach her when she refuses to hear from me."

"So get creative."

Sammi didn't want to hear from him—but maybe he could reach her through someone else. Chase set down his beer and gazed thoughtfully at the mug, an idea forming in his mind.

~

"I think you should forgive him," Chloe said the following Sunday as she wrapped one of Sammi's plates in newspaper.

"Why? So he can lie to me again?" Sammi folded down the flap on a moving box, then reached for the packing tape.

"He didn't really lie to you." Chloe placed the newspaper-wrapped plate inside the box on the counter. "He just left you to your own misconceptions."

"It's the same thing."

"No, it's not. Besides, he wouldn't have gotten involved with you if you hadn't pursued him."

"I did *not* pursue him!"

"Oh, please." Chloe pulled another plate out the cabinet. "We practically stalked him at the swap meet—and then you bopped him on the head, and insisted on playing Florence Nightingale, and ended up in bed with him."

Sammi indignantly ripped off a piece of tape. "You make it sound like it was all my fault."

"Well, it kinda was. You started it all."

Had she? In a way, maybe she had. "Well, it doesn't matter how it started. He still should have told me."

"Of course he should have. But when would have been a good time to do that?"

"Right off the bat!"

"Think it through, Sammi. When, exactly, would that have been? When you were gushing about him on the phone? That would have mortified you. When you were in the middle of a date? You would have had the same reaction you're having now."

"So?"

"So he didn't tell you because he didn't want to screw up a good thing. Seems to me that you, of all people— you who hired a life coach because you kept messing up dates—ought to understand not wanting to mess up a great relationship."

Sammi glared at her. "Whose side are you on, anyway?"

"Yours. And his. Because I think you two belong together. If you could just put your anger aside for a moment and think rationally, you'd see that, too."

"You think I'm being irrational?" She tried to put the tape on the seam of the box flaps, but it stuck to itself and balled up. She ripped it off. "I've lost my home and my job."

"You've got a job," Chloe interrupted. "You're on a paid leave of absence."

It was true, but Sammi was on a roll, and she was not going to let the facts slow her down. "I've spent the night in a bat cave, I've been shot at and physically accosted, I've fallen in love with a man who pretended to be someone else while I poured out my heart to him, and now my own sister is against me."

"I'm not against you. I'm for you. And did you hear what you just said?"

"What?"

"You said you'd fallen in love with Chase."

Alarm shot through her. "I did not."

"You did, too. You said you'd fallen. Past tense. No maybes or I-think-I-might-be-about-tos. You can deny it all you want, but you said it and you feel it."

Hell. There was no denying that she loved Chase. She was up to her eyeballs, over her head, heart and soul in love with Chase.

But he'd deliberately deceived her. How could she love a man she couldn't trust? She sank into a chair, her shoulders slumped. "My life could not get any worse."

The doorbell rang. Chloe peered out the window. "Don't look now, but it could."

Sammi closed her eyes. Someday she'd learn to quit throwing out that challenge to the universe. "If it's Chase again, I'm not here."

"It's not Chase. It's your boss and your landlord."

"Together?"

"Looks like they're *very* together. They're holding hands."

Had the universe completely spun off its axis? Drawing a tight breath, Sammi smoothed her blue T-shirt, headed for the entryway, and opened the door.

Sure enough, Mr. Landry and Ms. Arnette stood on the stoop. And sure enough, their hands were linked. Maybe it was just the light, but something about Ms. Arnette's face looked different. She looked softer. Friendlier. Prettier.

Mr. Landry looked surprisingly dapper in a corduroy jacket with leather-patched elbows. He smiled apologetically. "Sorry to drop by like this, Sammi, but we really need to talk to you."

About what? Pending lawsuits? Might as well find out. With a sigh of resignation, Sammi gestured to the living room. "Come on in."

"Oh, my—this is lovely," Ms. Arnette said, looking around as she stepped through the door. "I can see why you want to preserve this place."

Okay, now Sammi *knew* the universe had become unhinged. Mr. Landry waited until Ms. Arnette sat on the couch, then sank down beside her. They looked at each other, then Walter cleared his throat.

"I want . . ." they said simultaneously. They looked at each other again and grinned.

"After you," Ms. Arnette said.

"No, no." Mr. Landry swept his hand in front of him. "Ladies first."

Arlene fingered her necklace. Sammi realized she wasn't wearing her customary pearls, but a narrow gold chain with a something on it that looked like a star-shaped leaf. Sammi looked at her quizzically. She'd never seen the woman look anything less than completely self-composed, but right now she looked unsure of herself. Nervous, even.

～

Arlene stroked the leaf pendant that Walter had given her, drew a deep breath, and looked at Sammi. "I want to apologize. I know I've been resistant to the changes you want to make at the museum, and I know I've made things difficult for you. And I'm sorry."

Sammi stared at her, her hazel eyes wide and surprised.

"I haven't been fair to you." Walter gave her hand an encouraging little squeeze. Arlene drew a steadying breath. "The truth is, ever since you arrived, Sammi, I've felt, well . . . threatened. I thought that if you changed things at the museum, your changes would cancel out all my work. And my work had been my life."

She glanced over at the man beside her. He winked, and she smiled. "And then I met Walter, and, well, he's helped me see things differently."

Walter's arm settled around her, warm and reassuring. His arm made her feel different than Chandler's arm used to make her feel. When Chandler had put his arm around her, she'd felt as though she belonged to him. When Walter put his arm around her, she felt like she belonged to herself.

And she did. She knew that now. She was whole and complete, all on her own. She wasn't second-best or less than anyone else. It was high time she learned to love and accept herself just as she was. Maybe even time to let someone else love and accept her, too.

Arlene smiled at Sammi. "You're going to be a wonderful head curator, Sammi. First thing Monday morning, I'm telling the board that I'm retiring, effective immediately, and that they should look to you for leadership."

Sammi's mouth fell open.

Arlene grinned. That hadn't hurt a bit. In fact, she felt lighter and freer than she had in decades.

~

Walter rubbed his hand up and down Arlene's arm and smiled down at her, his chest filled with pride. She'd handled that like a champ. Now it was his turn.

He turned to Sammi. "I owe you an apology, as well," he told her. "You were right about this house being special. Truth is, my late wife thought so, too, and I—well, I just didn't want to listen. That's always been my Achilles' heel, not being willing to listen to anyone who has ideas that run contrary to mine."

Arlene pressed his hand. He pressed hers back.

"I can think of no better person to have this house than you, Sammi—so if you still want to buy it, why, I'd be more than happy to sell it to you for a price you can afford."

Sammi blinked. "I—I don't know what to say."

"It's simple. Say yes. And there's no hurry; I've decided to indefinitely postpone my move to Arizona."

Sammi scooted to the edge of her chair. "That's very kind, Mr. Landry—not to mention generous—but the truth is, this house should be shared with the public. I would love to see the museum buy it and move it."

"Move it?"

"Yes." Sammi leaned forward. "I checked into the possibility of having it relocated, and I found a company that specializes in that. They came out and looked at it, and they said this place is small enough and sturdy enough to be moved."

"Where would you put it?" Walter asked.

Sammi shot an anxious glance at Arlene. "I was thinking that the grounds behind the carriage house at the Phelps Mansion would be perfect."

Walter tensed as he looked down at Arlene. It was one

thing for her to turn over the reins to Sammi; it was quite another to be hit with a drastic change right off the bat.

But Arlene rose to the occasion. "What an interesting idea."

Sammi's face grew animated. "It could be a whole separate exhibit, showcasing the different interpretations of art deco."

Arlene turned to Walter. "And you could still sell the lot."

"That's true." He didn't really need the money, but he was sure he could think of ways to spend it on Arlene.

Maybe he would take her to Paris.

Arlene smiled at Sammi. "That's an absolutely, positively marvelous idea."

Sammi jumped from her chair, dashed across the room, and threw her arms around them both. "You two are wonderful!"

They were wonderful together, Walter thought as he smiled at Arlene. And if things worked out as he hoped, the house wasn't the only thing that would soon be relocated.

∾

"Sammi? This is Horace."

"Oh, Horace!" Sammi grinned as she held the phone to her ear with one hand and filled Joe's enormous bowl with dog food with the other. The dog's entire backside wiggled as he wagged his stump of a tail. "How are you? How's your hip?"

"Oh, it's fine. Nearly all healed. It's made me something of a celebrity at work."

"I imagine so! Are things going better there?" On the

trip back to Tulsa from the hospital, Horace had spilled out the story of his life.

"Much better. I've started eating lunch with some people from Escrow."

"That's wonderful. How's the apartment?"

"Oh, it's great! And I owe it all to you and Luke."

"I didn't do anything but help you move some boxes. You and Luke did all the real work."

"Yeah. Without his coaching, I never would have found the courage."

That wasn't Luke; that had been Chase. And as much as she wanted to fault him for impersonating his brother, she couldn't deny that he'd been a big help to Horace. "How is your mother taking it?"

"Oh, she says I'm giving her a stroke. But I keep my head in the game and my eye on the goal, just like Luke says."

"Good for you!"

"I bought her one of those necklaces people wear that will call 911 in case of an emergency. And I call her every day, but I don't let her run my life anymore."

"I'm so proud of you, Horace!"

"Thanks." He sounded proud of himself. "Listen—I called to tell you that I'm performing at the outdoor coffee shop on Riverside Drive on Saturday."

"That's wonderful!"

"Yeah. And I wanted to ask if you'd come. I figured that if Luke can be a secret agent as well as a life coach, well, I can be an accordion rapper as well as an accountant."

"That's terrific, Horace." Sammi hesitated. "Is he going to be there?"

"Luke? No. He'll be out of town, doing his secret-agent

stuff. That's why I'm calling you. I've never performed in public before, and I'm terrified. It would help a whole lot to see a friendly face in the crowd."

How could she refuse? "I wouldn't miss it for the world, Horace."

~

The scent of coffee wafted across Java Hut's outdoor courtyard as a long-faced man leaned toward the microphone, intoning each word like Lincoln delivering the Gettysburg Address.

Dropping like mouse turds,
Your harsh words,
Soiled my soul.
The wretched retchings of your rant
Left me feeling like an unwatered plant—
Shriveled, dry, and ready to crack.

"His poetry's doing that to me," Chloe muttered.

Sammi elbowed her. "Behave. It was your idea to come with me, remember?"

Beneath the table, Joe twitched his tail. It had also been Chloe's idea to bring the dog along on the outing.

The craggy-faced poet leaned toward the mike again.

Your anger dripped like blood from vampire's fangs
Or Vitalis from Elvis's bangs.

"Wow. He's really deep," Horace whispered, his eyes wide with awe.

"Yeah. Makes me wish I'd worn hip boots," Chloe said.

"Maybe I should try to put more angst into my rap," Horace worried.

Sammi patted his arm. "The world has enough angst, Horace. It needs more people who'll lighten the load."

"You think?"

"Yeah, I do."

The poet continued:

You ground my dreams
Like coffee beans,
And cracked the eggs of my tomorrows
Into a rancid omelette of sorrows.

The man gazed dramatically at the back wall like a basset hound in mourning, then bent in a deep bow.

The few scattered patrons offered up limp applause—except for Horace, who jumped to his feet, clapping loudly. He looked around and then promptly sat back down.

A jeans-clad brunette with long hair whose name tag identified her as the coffee shop manager stepped up to the microphone. "Thank you, Mark, for that insightful and thought-provoking piece." She looked at a list in her hand. "Next up is Horace Mann, who's going to treat us to his unique blend of accordion rap."

Horace's moon-pie face creased anxiously. "Oh, dear — that's me!"

Sammi patted his arm. "You're going to be great," she reassured him.

Horace opened the case on the table, pulled out his accordion and put it around his neck, then awkwardly lumbered from his chair. He shot Sammi a pleading glance. "Would you do me a favor and come sit closer?"

Sympathy surged through her. "Sure."

She and Chloe picked up their lattes and Joe's leash and moved to the wrought-iron table closest to the stage. Horace sat on the barstool and adjusted the microphone.

He played a reedy caterwaul of accordion chords, then leaned tentatively toward the mike. "Hi there." He tapped the mike. "I'm, uh, really nervous, so I have a friend who's going to help me out on the first song."

Sammi looked at Chloe, her eyebrows drawn in confusion. What was going on? Chloe refused to meet her gaze.

She was wondering if Horace was going to call her up to join him, when a tall man emerged from the shadows. Her heart stopped, then beat double time as the light hit his face. *Chase*. And he was headed toward Horace. Sammi's mouth fell open as he picked the microphone off the stand. Horace played several rhythmic accordion chords. As Sammi watched in shock, Chase held the mike close to his mouth.

> *My brother's life was threatened and he wouldn't leave*
>   *town*
> *'Cause his life-coach clients needed him around.*
> *So I offered to coach them while he was away*
> *And a woman called up on the very first day.*
> *I wanted to see her, so I went to watch her jog*
> *And wound up getting strip-searched by her dog.*

Horace leaned close to the microphone and rapped in a hip-hop rhythm.

> *She had a strip-searching dog,*
> *She was a SCABHOG.*
> *She's really, really hot,*
> *And he likes her a lot.*

Sammi was vaguely aware that people were laughing, but she was in too much shock to register much of anything beyond the fact that Chase was standing in the exact spot he'd sworn he'd never stand, doing exactly what he'd sworn he'd never do—performing in public. And he was looking straight at her while he did it.

He leaned toward the microphone again.

She knocked me off my feet, and it took me by surprise
How hard I fell when I looked into her eyes.
I wanted to level, but I didn't want to lose her
If I told her the truth, I knew it would bruise her.

Horace leaned forward and chimed in.

He knew she'd be hurt
If he dished the dirt,
So he kept his mouth shut,
And he acted like a butt.

Chase walked forward and dropped to one knee in front of Sammi.

So I wrote this rhyme, Sam, to tell you how I feel—
How I'm sorry that I tricked you and I acted like a heel.
The situation was deceptive, but my heart was true.
And the truth is, Sammi, I'm in love with you.

'*He loves you, girl,*' Horace sang. '*You're his whole world. Bop-a-doodle, bop-a-doodle, bing bang bong!*'

The audience burst into raucous cheers and applause, but it barely registered over the thud of Sammi's heart. Chase's eyes, melting and brown, poured into hers like hot chocolate. "Come on," he murmured. "Let's go someplace private to talk."

Chase pulled her to her feet, handed the microphone back to Horace, and tugged her around the building to the jogging trail. A sweetgum branch rustled overhead. He turned to face her, his dark eyes glowing somberly in the faint light of the streetlamp. Fall leaves swirled at their feet.

"Sammi, I used to think logic could fix any problem. I even tried to use it to fix you. But instead, you fixed me." He lifted her hands and gazed into her eyes. "You showed me that some things go beyond logic. Some things are matters of the heart. Some things are just meant to be."

Sammi's heart battered hard against her ribs.

"Like you and that big old mutt of yours," he continued. "Like you and your job." He moved closer, close enough that she could smell the soapy scent of his shaving cream, and moved his hands up her arms. His voice dropped to a husky rumble. "Like you and me."

She searched his face and saw his soul in his eyes—a soul she could trust with her life, with her heart, with her tomorrows.

"I love you, Sammi. Is there any way you can forgive me?"

She placed her palm against his freshly shaved cheek and gave him a tremulous smile. "I already have."

"Ah, Sammi." The corners of his eyes crinkled as he grinned. "You're the SCABHOG of my dreams." He pulled her close and kissed her until her head was woozy and her body on fire.

"I resigned as your coach," he murmured, his lips grazing her ear, "but I'd like to sign up as your teammate."

Her heart ran into the end zone and did a touchdown dance. She twined her arms around his neck and pulled him down for another kiss. "I think," she whispered against his lips, "that you've made the cut."

THE DISH

Where authors give you the inside scoop!

♥ ♥ ♥ ♥ ♥ ♥ ♥ ♥ ♥ ♥ ♥ ♥ ♥ ♥ ♥ ♥

From the desk of Jennifer Haymore

Dear Reader,

When Sophie, the heroine of A HINT OF WICKED (on sale now), first came to me describing her problem—that she happened to be married to two men at once, both of whom she loved unconditionally—I rubbed my hands together in glee. What a juicy, wicked dilemma! Yes, of course, I told her, I would be thrilled beyond measure to pen this tale.

"But how on earth will you resolve my problem?" she asked me.

"Easy," said I, proud of my fantabulous solution, and doubly proud of how quickly it had come to me. "You love them both, right?"

"Tremendously!" she declared, nodding vigorously.

"Then you'll live happily ever after with *both* your husbands," I decreed, leaning back in my chair and awaiting her exuberant and everlasting thanks.

Thus ensued a long, uncomfortable silence. Finally, Sophie looked up at me with somber, golden-brown eyes. "Forgive me, but that won't work. Neither of my husbands will accept such a solution."

"Huh. Are you saying they're the possessive caveman type?"

"Exactly." She leaned forward a bit and lowered her voice so that no one outside my office could hear her. "In fact, I'm certain if either one saw me so much as touch the other, murder might ensue. It's already come close to that. Thank heavens nobody has been shot." She gave me a significant look. "Yet."

"Hmmm," I said. "I could work on them . . ."

Sophie broke me off in mid-thought. "You could 'work on them' for eternity, but you see, there is another problem. One that might negate any possibility of future happiness for all three of us: I am a duchess. In England. In 1823."

"Ah. I see," I said. But alas, I didn't, not really. I figured, okay, if Sophie doesn't want both her husbands, I'll pick one, and we'll go with that. Cocky writer that I am, I thought maybe I could flip a coin. *Ha!*

Soon afterward, Sophie took me on her journey, and . . . *oh my!* It wasn't easy. Given two powerful, honorable, drop-dead gorgeous men, Sophie had to choose the one she wanted to stand beside for the rest of her days. Moreover, in doing so, she had to break the heart of the other man—a man she also still loved.

And I won't even begin to get into the quagmire of 1823 marriage laws! To work everything out without turning Sophie into a criminal, making her child illegitimate, or having her become a pariah or the laughingstock of society? Just about impossible!

Eventually, though, Sophie found her way. By the time I finished writing, I was so glad she let me be the one to share her tale with the world.

I truly hope you enjoy reading Sophie's story. Please feel free to stop by my Web site, www.jennifer haymore.com, where you can share your thoughts about the book, learn some bizarre and fascinating historical facts, and read more about the person who has most recently barged into my office demanding I write *his* story . . .

Sincerely,

Jennifer Haymore

♥ ♥ ♥ ♥ ♥ ♥ ♥ ♥ ♥ ♥ ♥ ♥ ♥ ♥

From the desk of Carolyn Jewel

Dear Reader,

People. Really. I tried to warn you with my first book, MY WICKED ENEMY, but I don't think you were paying attention. I'll try again with MY FORBIDDEN DESIRE, my second book (on sale now!). Will you all finally listen up? I certainly hope so. The world is a dangerous place, and not just in the obvious ways. True statement: Things around you aren't always what they seem. Same for people, too. Yeah, I know what you're thinking. How obvious can you get, Carolyn? But really, take a long, hard look at your boss. Is she (or he) really human? How do you know for sure?

Our capacity to deceive others is far exceeded by our capacity to deceive ourselves. Keep that in mind (but not before bed, wouldn't want to keep you up!).

Suppose, for the sake of argument, there really are monsters among us.

Not the human kind—I think, without further discussion, we can all agree *they* exist. I'm talking about something else. What if there really are creatures like demons or, oh, say, fiends? And "people" who can do magic. Why the quotes, you ask? Well, they wouldn't be regular folks like you and me, now would they?

Who would they be? Mages and witches, of course. They rose to prominence in the Dark Ages when they were busy protecting us from demons and the like. Demons, including fiends, were looking for a bigger place in the world then. But thanks to the mages, that didn't work so well. (Thank you, mages!) Over the years, though, some mages went from being the good guys to the not-so-good guys, and now the demons are fighting for their lives. They're sick and tired of being murdered and enslaved.

That's the backdrop of my books: an all-out war

between demons and fiends and mages and witches. But what if we take that one step further? What if a demon or a fiend fell in love with a witch or a mage? And now we've got my latest book, MY FORBIDDEN DESIRE.

Xia is a fiend. Alexandrine Marit is a witch. He hates witches for some very, very good reasons. Alexandrine isn't sure demons exist and, well, as witches go, she's not much of one . . . until she gets her hands on a talisman. Now Xia has to protect her from some very nasty people. And Alexandrine's view of the world pretty much explodes. What happens after that? You'll have to read it to find out.

Enjoy!

Carolyn Jewel

♥ ♥ ♥ ♥ ♥ ♥ ♥ ♥ ♥ ♥ ♥ ♥ ♥ ♥ ♥

From the desk of Robin Wells

Dear Reader,

Have you ever been in one of those slumps when everything in your life is going wrong? Well, the heroine of my latest romantic comedy, HOW TO

SCORE (on sale now), is in just such a situation, and she decides to hire a telephone life coach to help her straighten things out. Only problem is, the man Sammi is baring her soul to isn't a life coach at all; he's an FBI agent filling in for his brother—and the man Sammi is falling for.

The idea for this book came to me while writing BETWEEN THE SHEETS. The heroine of that story, Emma, needed to change her image after being involved in a terrible scandal, and I originally intended to have her hire a life coach to help her. Emma had other ideas, however, and the story went in another direction.

The concept of writing a book about a life coach continued to simmer in my subconscious. The topic intrigued me, probably because I'm a sucker for self-improvement plans. I devour magazine articles with titles such as "Organize Your House, Look like Angelina Jolie, Behave like Mother Teresa, Become the Perfect Parent, Stay Serene as a Monk, Clear Up Your Skin, and Scorch Your Sheets in Seven Easy Steps." (The advice never works, but hope springs eternal.)

What kind of woman, I wondered, would go beyond self-help books and actually hire a life coach? Probably a woman with problems on all fronts—problems with her job, problems with her living arrangements, problems with her family, and, most important, problems with her love life. Or lack there of. The wheels started spinning in my mind. Maybe my heroine's romantic problem could be of her own making. Maybe she had a painful secret that made her inadvertently drive away potential partners. The wheels started spinning faster. Yes! I was onto something!

I then turned my attention to the hero. What kind of man would make the most interesting life coach? Hmmm. He had to be tall, dark, and sexy as sin—that was a given. What if he wasn't a life coach at all? What if he was a highly structured pragmatist who thought everything could and should be solved through logic, careful planning, hard work, and self-discipline—the kind of man who thinks he has all the answers, who believes that if people would just follow his advice, their problems would all be solved? (My husband wants me to point out here that I, personally, have never known, much less married, a man like that.)

What if the hero also had a painful past that made him crave order, organization, and control? (Anyone who has seen my husband's sock drawer will know beyond a doubt that I really, truly did not base this hero on him.)

Once the characters came to life, the story took off. I set the book in Tulsa because I used to live in Oklahoma and know that the city is renowned for its art deco architecture. The museum, neighborhood, and restaurants in my book are fictional, but the issues facing "recent history" preservationists in Tulsa and other cities are all too real.

The secondary romance between the two older characters in the book came as a surprise to me; I originally planned for Sammi's blue-haired artist sister, Chloe, to have a love interest. Instead, Sammi's landlord and boss fell in love as they helped each other deal with past regrets, find self-forgiveness, and learn that it's never too late for new beginnings.

I hope you enjoy reading HOW TO SCORE as much as I enjoyed writing it. I invite you to drop by my Web site, www.robinwells.com, to share your thoughts, read an excerpt from my next novel, or just say hi!

All my best,

Robin Wells